PENANCE

"*Penance* is a rare novel, at once staggering in scope and achingly human. A brutal, white-knuckled tale of betrayal and redemption in which the sins of the fathers are laid upon their children tenfold, O'Shea's astonishing debut delivers pulse-pounding thrills and the beating heart to match. Fans of Le Carré and Lehane had best take note."

    Chris F. Holm, author of Dead Harvest *and* The Wrong Goodbye

"*Penance* is a rich, gritty, terrific novel. O'Shea can throw a punch and turn a phrase with the very best of them. Even better, he knows the human heart inside out."

    Lou Berney, author of Gutshot Straight *and* Whiplash River

"*Penance* has one foot in Bourne and the other in *The Untouchables*, but tells a very human story of loss and atonement. A great thriller that ranges from the streets of Seventies Chicago to the highest levels of modern power, with tight dialogue and righteous violence. One for fans of crime, espionage and mayhem."

    Jay Stringer, author of Old Gold

"Wonder how Harry Bosch would read walking the streets of Michael Mann's Chicago? Look no further than Detective John Lynch. Smart, sophisticated and as serious as a .45 in full battery, *Penance* makes the bulk of cliché-riddled crime fiction sound flat-footed by comparison."

    Peter Farris, author of Last Call for the Living

Also by Dan O'Shea

Old School

DAN O'SHEA

PENANCE

EXHIBIT A
An Angry Robot imprint
and a member of the Osprey Group

Lace Market House   43-01 24th St, Suite 220B
54-56 High Pavement   Long Island City,
Nottingham NG1 1HW   NY 11101
UK   USA

www.exhibitabooks.com
A is for attitude

An Exhibit A paperback original 2013

Cover photo Getty Images; design by Argh! Oxford
Set in Meridien and Franklin Gothic by EpubServices

Distributed in the United States by Random House, Inc., New York.

ISBN: 978 1 90922 313 4
Ebook ISBN: 978 1 90922 314 1

Printed in the United States of America

9 8 7 6 5 4 3 2 1

For my father, Dr Thomas A O'Shea,
who raised me in a house lousy with books.
I wish you'd been around to see this one, Dad.

CAST OF CHARACTERS

THE COPS (AND FRIENDS)

1971
Declan Lynch – Chicago police detective
Robert Riordan – Head of the Red Squad

Present Day
John Lynch – Chicago police detective, son of Declan Lynch, nephew of Rusty Lynch
Shlomo Bernstein – Chicago police detective
Harold Starshak – Chicago police captain, Lynch and Bernstein's CO
Darius Cunningham – Chicago police SWAT sharpshooter
Brian McCord – Medical examiner
Liz Johnson – Chicago *Tribune* reporter

THE SPOOKS

1971
Zeke Fisher – US intelligence operative

Present Day
Ishmael Fisher – InterGov operative
Colonel Tech Weaver – Head of InterGov, a US black ops group
Ferguson – InterGov operative
Chen – InterGov operative

THE POLITICIANS

1971

David Hurley, Sr – Mayor of Chicago
David Hurley, Jr– Hurley's son, Cook County DA, candidate for US Senate
Brendan Riley – Hurley's right hand man
Hastings Clarke – David Hurley's chief of staff and campaign manager
Rusty Lynch – Chicago city councilman, Declan Lynch's brother

Present Day

David Hurley III – Mayor of Chicago
Hastings Clarke – Politician
Rusty Lynch – Retired politician, John Lynch's uncle
Paddy Wang – Power broker
Tommy Riordan – Chicago political hack, son of Robert Riordan

CHAPTER 1 – CHICAGO

The pain was bad. Helen Marslovak had not taken her painkillers at lunch, not with confession today. If she took her pills, she'd be groggy. Confession was important now. She needed her head clear for that. But now the pain was bad.

She shivered inside her coat as she stepped out the side door of Sacred Heart and stopped to evaluate the stairs. They were dry, at least, but it was cold. (She was always cold now, the cold maybe the worst thing about the cancer, worse sometimes than even the pain.) The cold seemed to make the railing slippery – or maybe it was just her hands, she wasn't sure.

And then there was a hole in time. She had just picked up her right foot to take the first step and had a firm grasp on the railing and now she was on her back, head facing down, her legs pointing up the stairs. She felt the bite of the wind as her coat and her skirt rode up her legs. Not ladylike, she thought. And she must have wet herself because something warm and wet was running up her back. Something was wrong, her legs wouldn't move. But she was tired, and even colder, and she thought she would just lie here for a moment before she tried to pull herself up. Maybe someone would come along to...

Nearly half a mile away, Ishmael Leviticus Fisher slid a long green duffle into the back of a rusted Ford 150 and closed the lid on the truck cap. As he pulled away, heading for the expressway, his strong, slender fingers ran over the worn wooden beads of his rosary with practiced precision. The Sorrowful Mysteries.

Detective John Lynch tried to remember the last time he'd been to Sacred Heart. The church was just west of Narragansett, a mile or so south of Belmont. Not quite in Coptown proper – that northwest corner of the city near Niles and Park Ridge that was full of cop families, fireman families. Close enough, though. Streets and Sanitation guys probably. CTA guys.

He'd been down to Sacred Heart during his marriage for sure. He remembered fighting in the car with Katie heading to one of the weddings on the Slavic side of her family. There was a mess of them in Sacred Heart. Summertime, back in 86. Neither of them bothering with being civil anymore, both of them knowing the marital jig was pretty well up, just trying to get their licks in before the bell. It was August that year when the drunk kid in the Trans Am made the whole divorce thing moot, picking off Katie's Civic on the Kennedy at 2.00am one Saturday morning. Lynch was working third shift, Wentworth. Never did find out where she'd been, what she was coming home from.

Sacred Heart was long with a steep slate roof, brown brick, running east to west. Main door faced west, a glassed-in vestibule with a side door faced south. Rose window over the vestibule, four tall stained glass windows down the side.

Lynch had been to his share of cop funerals, starting with his father's when he was ten. The cluster of uniforms on the steps at the side door of the church brought that back as he nosed the brown Crown Victoria into a handicapped spot at the end of the walk. Same weather as then; low March sky with all the gray charm of a wet basement floor. He remembered arriving at the church the morning of his father's funeral, awkward in the new suit, his mom and sister in black, all the uniforms milling around. And then the honor guard forming up, the

Emerald Society in front with the bagpipes, six guys in their dress blues taking the coffin from the hearse, Lynch still not quite believing that it was his dad in there, that he was never coming back. Sitting through the service, watching his mom stiffen as the mayor got up to give the eulogy, turning Declan Lynch into an icon Lynch had never known, feeling something new in the air, like watching a religion being born.

No funeral today, but there was still a body. Lynch shrugged into his leather car coat and climbed out of the Crown Vic. Twinge in the knee, the one that had turned him from a third-round draft choice in Green Bay into a cop. Still six feet one inch, one hundred and ninety-five pounds. Hell, ten pounds under his playing weight.

Sergeant Kowalski was shooing the uniforms away from the steps. Lynch liked to get a fresh read on the stiff before everybody started downloading the whats and whens on him. Liked a minute alone to form his own impressions. Kowalski knew to give him his space. Lynch squatted down next to the body.

The woman was sprawled face-up on the stairs, her head on the bottom stair. Flat, moon-shaped face – Polish, Lynch bet. She looked surprised. Not the first time Lynch had seen that. Lynch had heard a lot about stiffs looking peaceful, but most of them he'd seen looked like they were in pain. The lucky ones looked surprised.

A lot of blood had run down under her head, some catching in the white-gray hair, some pooling on the walk. Entrance wound was center chest, right next to one of the buttons on the coat. No blood there. Lynch knew that the human body was a big, tough, blood-filled balloon. More blood in there than most people think. Five or six quarts – ten pounds or better. When you blow a hole in somebody, the blood comes out and keeps coming out until it clots or the heart stops. No blood on the chest meant the heart had stopped right off, nothing pumped out the front. Looking at the wound, Lynch bet the round had gone right through the heart, at least caught a piece of it.

The blood under the body was just a leak, a combination of the location of the exit wound and gravity. No smearing around the shoulders or the head. She hadn't thrashed around at all, which people do when they get shot, seeing as how it hurts likes hell, which Lynch knew from experience. She'd been dead when she hit the cement. One smudge just on the edge of the pool of blood, then a footprint on the first step, slight footprint on the third, maybe a smudge on the fifth. Woman's shoe, right foot, slight heel.

Hair was neat, clothes were clean but not new. They looked big on her, like she had lost weight. Nails trimmed, no polish. Minimal makeup. Old shoes with new heels. Dress had ridden up past her knees. Thick stockings, plain slip. Plain wedding ring. Expensive watch, though. Piaget with diamonds around the face. Smudge of something shiny on her forehead, oil probably. Last rites, Lynch bet.

Lynch looked up at Kowalski. "She looks like shit, Sarge."

"Getting shot will do that for you," Kowalski said.

"Beyond that, though. Skin seems loose. Color's bad. Face looks shrunken."

Lynch stood up.

"All right, Sarge, what else you got?"

"Here's what I know. Deceased is Helen Marslovak, seventy-eight, lives four doors down, other side of the street. Looks like a single gunshot to the chest. The priest – he's up in the church – says she finished confession between 3.00 and 3.05 because he starts at 3.00 and she is always the first customer. He figures she probably said a rosary after, which put her out the door about 3.15. An Agnes Weber – she's inside with the father – came screaming into the church at, the father is guessing, 3.22, because he looked at his watch as soon as she calmed down enough to tell him that the victim was splattered on the stairs, and then it was 3.24. Including the priest, three people were in the church at the time of the shooting. Nobody heard a thing. Also, looking at the body, this ain't no contact wound, and judging from the spray – you'll see we got some bits of this and that up top of the stairs – you're looking at a round with some velocity. My guess is a rifle, but we'll let the pocket-protector types work that out. One thing you're not going to like. The father has handled the body, did the last-rites drill before we got here."

"Saw the oil."

"Also, the Weber woman tracked through the blood."

Lynch nodded. "Just the one shot?"

"Looks like. Got all those windows in the vestibule back there, no holes in those. There's a wooden chest sort of thing back by the wall. They probably put bulletins and such out after mass. Round looks to have hit there."

"So one shot center chest, likely a rifle. Purse?"

"Yeah. It was on its side, top step. Not even open. Six bucks and change in the wallet. Driver's license, Social Security card, no plastic. Hanky, keys, rosary. Bout it."

"And she's still got the watch. That looks like a couple of grand anyway."

"Looks like."

"All right. Thanks, Sarge," said Lynch.

Lynch nodded to the crime scene guy, letting him know he could start on the body. "OK I go through here on the right?" Lynch asked.

"Yeah, detective. Close to the wall, OK? Got some shit up here."

Lynch remembered Sacred Heart as looking old school. Dark wood pews in straight rows facing east, broad middle aisle, ornate altar tucked in an alcove on the east wall, racks of votive candles, big statues. Looked like a church, anyway.

Or had. As he pushed through the double doors, he saw white drywall, burnt-orange carpeting and seat cushions, blonde wood pews in a huge, space-wasting semicircle facing the long north wall, the altar on a half-oval riser sticking out of the wall into the pews and something that looked like a life-sized Peter Frampton in a bathrobe hanging from the ceiling on a Plexiglas cross.

"Jesus," muttered Lynch.

"Well, it is supposed to be," said a voice to his left. Lynch turned to find a beefy priest in an old-fashioned button-up cassock. Mid-fifties, Lynch guessed. Gone a little to fat, but judging from the chest and shoulders, some weight work in the guy's past, and not in the distant past.

"Detective Lynch," Lynch said, offering his hand.

The priest took it. "Father Mike Hughes. I'm the pastor. Actually, I'm the whole staff at the moment. Well, for quite a few moments, now. Young men today just don't seem to grasp the allure of the collar."

"Probably need a video game. *Priest* for PlayStation. Kicking the devil's ass for him."

"I'll suggest that to the cardinal."

Lynch and the priest sat at the end of one of the pews.

"Comfy, with the cushion and all," said Lynch.

The priest smiled. "The church was remodeled in the late Eighties. While the liturgical remedies of Vatican II were long overdue, some of the resulting architectural excesses have been less than fortunate."

"Ms Marslovak like it much?" said Lynch.

"No, I doubt that she did. But you wouldn't hear it from Helen. The woman would never breathe a word against the church."

"Know her well?"

"I've been here twelve years. She's been at mass every morning, and I do mean every morning. First in for confession every Friday at 3.00pm sharp. Past president of the St Anne's unit. Tends the garden. Cooks me a roast first Sunday of every month, God bless her soul."

"So no reason you can think of for someone to kill her?"

"No, none."

Lynch sat for a moment. "Look, Father, you were the last person to talk to her. Anything in that conversation that might shed some light here?"

"You mean in her confession?" The priest turned toward Lynch. "Irish boy in a town like this, you've got to be Catholic, right?"

"I don't know how often you've got to get your card renewed. It's been a while."

"Baptized, though?"

"Oh yeah. St Lucia's, 1961."

"Once you're dipped, you're ours for life. And you know the rules. If it's said in confession, it stays there. That secret doesn't just go to her grave, it goes to mine."

"I figured," said Lynch. "Just taking a shot. She have family in the parish?"

"Her husband died three years ago. ALS. Long time going. She's got a son, but he lives up on the north shore. Lake Forest, I think. Eddie Marslovak? MarCorp?"

Lynch nodded. "That's where I've heard the name. They close?"

The priest shrugged. "She loved him, but she didn't approve of him. A couple of divorces, professed agnostic. He'd visit, I know, and they talked. But close? I don't know."

"How about after the husband died. Any gentlemen friends?"

The priest chuckled. "If you knew Helen, detective, you would know how funny that is. No."

"Other friends?"

"Helen was something of an institution, volunteered at the school, helped with everything, really. Gave free piano lessons.

Taught CCD for thirty-some years."

"You're not giving me much to work with here. Listen, Father, looking at her, she didn't look well. Was she sick, do you know?"

The priest paused for a moment. "I hear some things in confidence but not necessarily in confession. Yes. Helen was very sick. Cancer. She was dying. She didn't want anyone to know, not even her son. She said it was her cross, and she was pleased to bear it. There are elements of this that we discussed in confession that I cannot share with you. But she did talk to me about funeral arrangements. So that she was ill, was dying, that I can tell you."

"This stuff you can't tell me, anything in that?"

"Detective, I cannot divulge or even hint at what is said within the seal of confession."

Lynch looked at the priest, but the priest was looking away.

Agnes Weber was just this side of shock. Probably close to Marslovak's age. She was holding a pair of long black gloves, absentmindedly wringing them.

"Mrs Weber? I'm Detective Lynch. Can I talk to you for just a minute here? Then we can get you home."

She nodded slightly, not looking up, still wringing the gloves. "This is so horrible, so horrible."

"It is, Mrs Weber, and I am very sorry. You knew Mrs Marslovak?"

"Helen? Everybody knew Helen. She was... she was... just so decent to everybody. I lived across from her, just across and one house up. I've known Helen for thirty-five years."

"She sounds like a wonderful woman. The father was telling me."

"I can't understand this." Sounding puzzled, and a little angry suddenly.

"Mrs Weber, how did you get to the church today?"

"Oh, I walked. I always walk. I don't like to drive anymore. It's not far."

"About a block?"

"Yes. I was surprised when I didn't see Helen. I usually see her walking back when I'm headed up for confession. She's always there right at three, but there is a show I like that ends then, so I'm a little later."

"Did you hear anything when you were walking?"

"You mean like a shot? Would I have been out when Helen was... Oh my God, oh my God."

"Yes, ma'am. You were probably on your way to the church when Helen was shot. Did you hear or see anything unusual? Loud noises, cars driving away quickly, anything at all?"

The old woman paused for a moment, her face squeezed with concentration. "No. No. Nothing at all."

"Did you see anyone else while you were out?"

"No. Nobody. I'm sorry, but no."

"That's all right, Mrs Weber. I don't need anything else right now. I can get one of the officers to drive you to your house or to walk back with you if you like."

She looked up for the first time. She was crying. "I stepped in her blood, you know. Did the other policeman tell you? I didn't mean to."

"Yes, ma'am. Don't worry about that. That's OK."

"I'm going to have to throw out these shoes, don't you think? I can't wear these anymore. I have to throw them out."

As Lynch walked out of the church, a guy Lynch knew from the ME's office was just getting ready to bag the remains.

"Hey, McCord," said Lynch. "How're your Sox lookin' this year?"

"The stiff here will make the playoffs before they do, Lynch. Gimme a second – we gotta talk."

"What's up?"

"The shooter was up, at least a couple of stories up. The entrance wound was here," McCord said, tapping Lynch on the chest. "Haven't chopped her up yet, but it's looking like he got at least a part of the heart. Exit wound is down a few inches – blew her spinal cord right out. Bullet's lodged in that wood thing back by the wall. We got spray from the exit wound up top of the stairs, so we know she was standing up there when she got hit. The bullet's down better than a foot from where it left her back. OK, the round drilled through her sternum, then through a vertebrae, so maybe we got some Oswald magic bullet shit going on, but I'd bet my ass on a downward trajectory. Get her into the shop and take a look at the sternum – we got beveling, then I'll know."

Lynch turned and looked across the street. First block, parking lot. Beyond that, a park. Beyond that, a neighborhood of single-story bungalows.

"Shot came from over there, right?"

McCord nodded.

"I don't see anything that goes up a couple of stories."

McCord shrugged. "Hey, I just do the science, Lynch. You get to make sense of it."

Back in the car, heading east on Belmont toward the Kennedy, Lynch called in.

"Lynch," answered Captain Starshak. "Please tell me this church shooting is a ground ball. I've already got a call from the deputy chief on it. Nobody likes this one."

"Line drive into the corner, Captain. This sucker's gonna rattle around some. Deceased's name is Helen Marslovak. Sound familiar?"

"Eddie Marslovak? Mayor's asshole buddy? Governor's asshole buddy? President's asshole buddy for all I know?"

"His mother. Gets worse. Single gunshot wound, center chest. Looks like a rifle. Witness on the street at the time didn't see or hear anything. Victim's still wearing a watch worth a couple grand. Nobody even opened her purse. This isn't some junkie getting up a bankroll."

"Son of a bitch. Press there yet?"

"Couple of TV trucks in the parking lot as I was leaving. They don't have the name yet. Better tell the public affairs pukes to gird up their loins, though."

"You call Marslovak?"

"Heading there now. I want my eyes on him when he hears."

Slight pause on the other end. "You saying you like him for this? Something pointing at him?"

"Captain, I don't have shit right now. What I hear from the priest and a neighbor, this lady's up for a Nobel Prize. Eddie Marslovak's the only family left, and he is one of the richest guys in the city. Gotta at least give him a sniff."

"Yeah. Well, step easy, OK? Last thing we need is him down our shorts."

"Sweetness and light, Captain. Hey, can you lean on the lab for me? The sooner we get ballistics back the better."

"Yeah, will do."

Lynch dropped the phone on the seat. It was after four and raining a little now. From the top of the ramp, he could see the Kennedy was crammed. He crossed over the bridge and headed down the surface streets toward the Loop. Turning on the radio, he caught the first report on the shooting. Victim still unidentified pending notification of next of kin. Fun and games.

CHAPTER 2 – CHICAGO

Eddie Marslovak had a big office. A black leather sofa and love seat sat to the right of the door in front of a bookcase full of expensive looking arty shit. Six-seat conference table off to the left in front of a wall of vanity shots – Marslovak with the mayor, Marslovak with Clinton, a cover of Business Week with his picture on it. There was still plenty of room in the back right corner for a granite-topped desk big enough to land planes on.

Marslovak looked like he needed the room. He had Gordon Gecko's haircut and Jabba the Hutt's body. Behind him, most of the Loop and all of Lake Michigan spread out burnished in the low, slanting gold as the late afternoon sun suddenly broke through the clouds. The view looked like one of the temptations of Christ. Except Christ said no; Marslovak, Lynch was betting, said yes.

Marslovak had the phone tucked against his shoulder and barely looked up when Lynch came in.

"You Lynch?"

Lynch nodded. Marslovak waved the back of his hand at one of his guest chairs, then continued on the phone, banging away at a keyboard while a series of charts flashed across three monitors arrayed along the right side of his desk.

"Yeah, yeah, yeah," he said, cutting off whoever was talking to him. "They had their chance to get on board early, now they know they're fighting for scraps. Suddenly they want the deal they could have had two weeks ago. Fuck 'em. They get asset value – $22.3 million. Otherwise, they can try to hang on after I get another deal in town. Yes or no by the end of the day, counselor."

Lynch could hear a raised voice on the other end of the line.

"I got a four thousand dollar watch, course I know what time it is. It's 4.30. Day doesn't end for another seven and a half hours. Find your clients, get me an answer. I don't hear by midnight, then I'm done. That's how these rollups go. They misplayed their hand, now they're sitting at a table they can't afford. Sorry about that." He hung up the phone and turned to Lynch in a single motion, his eyes completely focused, like the conversation he just ended hadn't happened.

Hard to tell with him sitting down, but Lynch bet Marslovak went two-fifty at least, probably more. Some of it fat, but not all of it. Just a big son of a bitch. Meaty face; mean, close-set eyes; hands like rump roasts. He could buy all the French blue shirts with white collars that he wanted, he was still going to look like the neighborhood, like he should be wearing a butcher's apron.

"All right, detective," said Marslovak. "My receptionist tells me it's important, but so is most of the other shit I got to do. Get to it, OK?"

"It's about your mother, Mr Marslovak," said Lynch.

Marslovak froze. "What about my mother?"

"She's dead. She was murdered this afternoon."

The mean went out of Marslovak's eyes, all the meaty slabs drooping, his face going from looking fifty to looking seventy all at once. "What do you... Murdered? Why?"

"I'm sorry, Mr Marslovak. I know this must be a shock."

Marslovak slumped forward, his face in his hands, almost down to the desktop. His voice was muffled, coming through his palms. "Ah, Jesus, it was the watch, wasn't it? Finally get her to wear one nice thing, and some punk snuffs her over a goddamn watch."

"Mr Marslovak, it doesn't appear to have been a robbery. She was still wearing her watch and still had her purse when we–"

Marslovak bolted upright. "You don't mean raped? Seventy-eight year-old woman?"

"No, nothing like that."

Marslovak's brows knit up. "Where was she?"

"Coming out of the church. She was shot on the stairs."

"Sure, of course." Marslovak sounding a little pissed off. Marslovak got up. Taller than Lynch had thought, six three, probably more like two hundred and ninety. Marslovak walked over to a tall cabinet next to his pictures, grabbing a heavy highball glass and a bottle of something dark – bourbon, scotch, Lynch couldn't see the label. Poured a couple of inches, slugged them down, poured some more – half a glass – then dropped into one of the leather chairs surrounding a low glass table, clanking the glass down hard. He just sat for a while, blank.

"You gonna sit down? What's your name again?"

"John Lynch."

"Fuck," Marslovak said. "Just… fuck. Sit down, Lynch, for Christ's sake. And call me Eddie. Everybody calls me Eddie. Cunt with the gossip column who keeps blowing up my marriages calls me Eddie."

Lynch took the chair across from Marslovak.

"What else you need?" Marslovak asked.

"You and your mom close? She say anything that might help? Anybody she have a problem with?"

"God, Lynch, I don't know. Define close. I loved her, her and the old man. They were the perfect parents. It's just, I'm basically an asshole, OK? I'm not nice. I didn't learn it at home, don't really know where I did. And both of them with the religion shit. I don't buy it. Never have. And couldn't keep my damn mouth shut about it either. But problems? Her only problem was me."

"Meaning what?"

"Meaning she says we're here on Earth to get to heaven, and here's her only son, sucking on Mammon's left tit like God's own Shop-Vac. Meaning she's been to mass everyday of her life, taught Sunday school to a couple thousand kids, and the fruit of her womb is a money-grabbing apostate who's taken every one of the seven deadly sins out on the dance floor for a whirl. Most of them more than once. Most of them I got on speed dial. Meaning that. Know what that's like, Lynch? Spend your whole life building all this and none of it means shit? I was a disappointment, OK? And I guess I'm not going to change any of that now."

"Gotta be rough."

"How the fuck would you know?"

"Yeah. Listen, how was her health, she doing OK?" Lynch giving Marslovak a chance to lie.

"Like I'd know. Talked to her a couple times a week. She's sounded a little tired, I guess. But she's pushing eighty and still trying to play Mother Teresa to the whole northwest side, so she should be tired. I haven't seen her in person since Christmas Eve. I told you I was an asshole, right? I mean, I should stop by and shit, but that usually doesn't go real well. Also, I'm trying to stave off divorce number three, and I got the usual couple hundred balls up in the air here." Marslovak slumped forward, elbows on his knees, head down. "So she's dead. That's it. Died thinking I'm going to hell. And in her mind, that pretty much makes her a failure. Wouldn't have killed me, you know, just turn up at church once in a while, go through the fucking motions. Wouldn't have killed me."

"Listen, Eddie, I know you've got things to take care of. Anything else you can think of I should know? She have any money, anything like that? Something somebody might have been after?"

"With what the market's done to real estate, if you figure the house, what's left of the old man's annuity, insurance, whole estate will go $300,000 to $350,000 tops."

"Decent chunk," said Lynch.

"Matter of perspective, I suppose. With the market jumping around like Richard Simmons on Dexedrine, my net worth's moved more than that while we've been talking."

"Really?"

"Really."

"And that net worth is?"

"Neighborhood of $2.3 billion. Give or take."

"Nice neighborhood."

"Until you meet the neighbors, yeah. Anyway, the three hundred grand or whatever – it's all going to the church. My lawyer did the will."

"That bother you, with your religious sentiments and all?"

"Nah. Church will do nice things with it. Feed the hungry, clothe the naked. Long as they don't go clothing any of my favorite porn stars, what do I care? What am I gonna do with it?"

"Could there be some connection to your work? Somebody you pissed off coming back at you?"

"I pissed off pretty much everyone I ever met, Lynch. Some sick fuck got a hard-on for me and shoots my mom? Possible, I guess. Hard to figure. Why not just shoot me?"

"Like you said, some sick fuck. They take some funny angles sometimes. Anybody come to mind?"

"I'm the sickest fuck I know, Lynch. Wasn't me."

Lynch pulled out his card and left it on the table. "If you think of anything that might help, give me a call. I'm sorry, Eddie."

As Lynch headed to the door, Marslovak sat in his chair staring down into his nearly empty glass. "All your life you've got a mother, then you don't," Marslovak said, his voice flat. "It's like God dying. Like there's nobody left to please."

Lynch turned to see Marslovak finish what was in his glass, then set it down on the table. "Get the fuck out, would you please, detective? And close the door behind you."

Lynch drove to the station, started the file, called around to crime scene and the lab. Nothing new yet, but Lynch was feeling juiced. This wasn't another drive-by where they'd haul in one sullen kid or another, it not making much difference whether they had the right one, because whatever kid they hung it on would have been happy to pop whoever had been popped for whatever dumb-ass reason one of the punks would eventually cop to. It wasn't another obsessive ex who'd beat the one-time love of his life to death and left enough physical evidence behind for ten trials. That's how Lynch spent most of his time. Piecework. Spending each day wading through a cesspool of human shit.

It was almost 9.00pm when Lynch got back to his place. He had the top floor on a four-story he'd bought after Katie died. Used the insurance money, leveraged himself to the nipples. Picked the right neighborhood, though – Near North just before it got going. Got a great price because the place was falling apart. But the Lynch family knew tools. Best memories from his childhood were working with the old man. Plaster, plumbing, wiring, whatever. Took Lynch ten years and most of his spare time, but now the place was perfect. Retired cop leased the first floor –bar and sandwich joint, McGinty's – two units on two, two units on three, Lynch on top. Cash flow better than his salary, the building worth better than a million, even after the crash.

Lynch had opened up his floor, exposed the brick on the exterior walls, sanded and finished the wide plank floors. He kept a weight set and a treadmill in the back. Lynch did a couple sets each of benches, military presses, curls, squats. Did a quick twenty minutes on the treadmill. Maintenance. It had been a long day, and it was going to be a longer one tomorrow. Lynch figured he'd read for a while and turn in. Just after 10.00 the phone rang.

"Lynch."

"Hey, John. Elizabeth Johnson at the *Tribune*. How are you?"

"I was fine. How'd you get this number?"

"I'm a reporter, John. I've got sources."

"Yeah, well, I'm a cop, Johnson, I've got a gun. Look, it's late. What do you want?"

"What can you tell me about the Marslovak shooting?"

"Come on, Johnson. You know we got actual PR guys paid to do this shit. They even got badges and guns and hats, so you can quote them as sergeant this or lieutenant that, just like they were real cops. So call the public affairs pukes, will you?"

"And I'm sure they will be very helpful, John. I'm sure you've filled them in completely. Look, you owe me one."

Johnson was new in town. She'd been with some paper in Minneapolis for ten years, and she looked Minnesota. Tall, blonde, Nordic, broad shoulders, long legs. Lynch had talked with her three months before. A couple guys in his division nailed some gangbanger on a series of drug killings, and the asshole's lawyer tried to muddy the water with some made-up crap about payoffs. Lynch's name hadn't been in it yet, but it would have been in time. Lawyer was a media-savvy radical, big on his image as the savior of the oppressed, always quick with the sound bites, the leaks, the dirty tricks. What he really was was a leech attached to the artery of drug money that kept all his underprivileged friends in nine millimeters. The talking heads on the TV had run with the payoff shit, reported the allegations, but Johnson actually checked the facts. Ran a series on the shyster, exposed a mess of scummy trial tactics – blatant race baiting, witness tampering, even a juror who admitted to throwing a case after a series of threats. The lawyer ended up getting his bar card yanked, and the gangbanger ended up getting the full ride – a place in line for the state-sponsored OD. Afterward, Lynch had bought Johnson a drink. Some sparks, but pretty clear they were both fighting that, too.

"Hey, I said thank you," said Lynch.

"John, I was new in town, OK? I should have squeezed you for your marker. But you owe me, and you know it. How about this – we meet for a drink. I buy this time. I tell you what I need, and you decide. That's fair, right?"

Lynch thought for a moment. Not about the case, but about Johnson. He'd enjoyed the drink last time. And he'd seen her around, she'd say hi, he'd say hi, him always feeling a little visceral tug. And he'd heard she left Minnesota after a divorce. Besides, growing up in Chicago, he understood the algebra of favors. His old man had moonlighted as political ward muscle for years. What was it he used to say? "Everybody's gotta scratch a few backs. Otherwise, whole world's got itchy backs. Nobody's comfortable."

"Yeah, OK," Lynch said. "You know McGinty's?"

"Sure. Half an hour?"

"OK, yeah."

Lynch wondered should he change. After fourteen hours, he figured a shower and a clean shirt, at least. Toweling off, he poked through the closet and saw the sweater his sister had sent for Christmas. Strange-looking roll neck kind of faded purple thing he always thought looked a little candy-assed, but he had to admit his sister knew this kind of shit, so he thought what the hell. Threw it on over a pair of jeans, slid his holster back on his belt.

Johnson was waiting at the end of the bar when he got downstairs. She'd gotten her hair cut, he noticed, very short now. Long neck. Black turtleneck, tight. Black slacks. She looked like a million bucks in stock options.

"John," she said, getting up from her stool. "Thanks. Really." Big friendly smile. Lots of straight, white Scandinavian teeth. She put out her hand.

He took it. Big hands, he thought. But his were bigger. He hoped she noticed.

"You are the only person on the face of the earth that calls me John," he said.

"Really? What should I call you?"

"Most people call me Lynch. There are a couple other options, but you'll have to buy more than one drink to hear them."

She slid her hand up to his elbow and turned him into the dimly-lit brick room toward the high-backed wooden booths along the windows that overlooked the river. "Guess we'd better get a table, then," she said. "It could be a long night." Different smile, less teeth, more sly.

When the waitress came, Lynch ordered a double Woodford Reserve. The waitress' smile perked up along with her likely tip. Johnson asked for a Chardonnay.

"You a bourbon connoisseur, Lynch?"

"Hey, you're buying."

"You're really going to get your pound of flesh, aren't you, detective?"

"Pound?" Lynch said, looking up from under his eyebrows with a slight smile. "I'll take all the flesh you care to offer." He watched for her reaction.

She tilted her head a little, small chuckle, then looked back.

"That's a very nice sweater, John Lynch." Another smile. Not so sly this time. That was the smile he was looking for. She took a long sip from her glass.

"So how'd it go with Eddie Marslovak?" Johnson leaned forward, forearms on the table.

"Who says I talked to him?"

"Come on, Lynch. You're the lead on his mother's murder. He's maybe the most powerful man in Chicago. What are you going to do, send him an email?"

"Yeah, OK. I talked to Eddie. This your technique, Johnson, right for the throat? I don't get schmoozed?"

"You want schmooze?"

"You're buying the drinks. Sure. Schmooze me."

Another smile, a look like he'd surprised her a little, like she was happy about that. "OK, Lynch. Tell me about being the Great White."

Lynch's turn to get rocked back a little. Great White: a nickname from his football days at Boston College. White guy – rare for a CB, maybe not at BC, but at most places – decent speed, played strong safety, and tended to leave blood in the water. Little grin from Lynch. Trying not to look too proud about it, the jock thing being a little silly at his age. Still, though.

"So who put you onto that, Johnson? That's going back some."

"Every girl wants to meet a football hero. Third round pick, right?"

"Green Bay, yeah. Blew out my knee in the preseason. That was that. Happened today, signing bonus be enough to retire on."

"Happened today, they'd fix your knee. Miss it?"

"Shit, I'd be long retired by now anyway, Johnson."

"But still?"

"Yeah, OK. I miss it. I liked it. I was good at it. And there is nothing like completely reordering some wideout's worldview when he tries to go over the middle."

Johnson laughed. "So why the cops? Why not coach or do TV or whatever?"

"Dad was a cop. Genetic inertia, I guess. So what else you got? Gonna grill me on my aborted engagement to Cindy

Tremaine back in the third grade?"

"How about Cabrini, 1984? Want to talk about that?"

She'd read the book on him. Lynch turned to the side, looking out the window over the river. Took a long swallow. In his mind, he could still see the muzzle flashes, hear the round thump into Michealson, hear rounds ripping through the sheet metal on the squad. Remembered getting hit, crawling to the front of the car, laying prone, firing from under the bumper. The first black kid going down, holding his gut, feet kicking, rolling over. The other kid running toward the squad, squeezing off shots. Lynch with one round left, knowing there'd be no chance to reload, knowing he'd never be able to anyway, bullet in his left shoulder, his left arm useless. He stayed prone, bracing the butt of the pistol on the ground, lining the kid up, the kid still shooting, but too high, Lynch letting him come, then putting a .38 right through his chest. Michealson making that gurgling noise, Lynch trying CPR, getting nothing out of it but a mouthful of blood.

Lynch took another swallow, held the glass up and wiggled it at the waitress. "I said schmooze, Johnson. Didn't ask for a proctological exam. Pick a new subject." Waitress put down the new drink, Lynch took a pull. Both of them quiet for a minute, Johnson knowing she'd stepped out of bounds.

"So," he said. "What about you? Minneapolis, right?"

"Born and raised. Cop family, too. Dad just retired. Chief of Detectives. Older brother's a captain, younger brother put in ten years on the force, law school at night, comer in the DA's office now."

"So why'd you skip town? Sounds like you had a house full of sources."

"When I said cop family, I meant cop family all the way. Not an easy place for a girl with ambitions beyond marrying one of them. Which I did, which was a mistake. He wasn't too keen on me working, especially for the press. After the divorce, I was on my own, all the way out from under all that macho bullshit for the first time. Liked it. Figured I'd be even more on my own down here."

"So not much use for cops, huh?"

"Don't get me wrong, Lynch. My dad, my brothers? They're good people. Hard to live with sometimes. I've been around cops my whole life. That sense of honor at the core of the whole thing? I like that. You don't get that with your MBAs. But, with a lot of them, after a while, they never take off the body armor."

"Your ex?"

"Yeah. Kevlar man."

"Don't worry, Johnson. I haven't put on a vest since I got off patrols."

"There, you see? We're hitting it off already." Johnson getting another wine.

"Yeah. You give good schmooze. Look, I don't really have shit on the Marslovak shooting yet, and I couldn't give it to you if I did, you know that. Why the call?"

"I'm not looking for a quote here, Lynch. This is not-for-attribution all the way. Just with Eddie Marslovak in the mix, this is going to be front-burner for a while. I don't want to get blindsided by anything."

"OK. Strictly as background. I talked with Eddie. I think he needs a couple of bushels of Prozac and maybe a decade or two of therapy. But if he ties into the shooting, it's going to be sideways – somebody coming back at him out of some deal he screwed them on or something. All I got."

"OK. Thanks. This will not come back to bite you, honest."

They talked for another hour. Lynch filling her in on Chicago politics, the kind of stuff you couldn't know coming in from Minneapolis. The feudal nature of it, the ethnic blocs, the primacy of neighborhood, the mayor's office passed down from Hurley to Hurley like a family title. And the fixers – the city lifers, on and off the payroll – guys who had lines into everything, who could pick up the phone at their summer places over on the Michigan shore and conjure up votes from thin air or graveyards.

Got to the point where it had been time to go for a while, both of them still hanging in.

"Hey, Dickey Regan at the Sun-Times says to say hello," said Johnson.

"You talked to Dickey?"

"I heard you were friends. He gave me the Great White stuff."

Lynch shook his head and chuckled. "Asshole."

"He also told me you were a good person for a cop. Said you had better things to do on St Paddy's Day than get shit-faced with the Emerald Society and plot to undermine our constitutional protections. That's pretty much a direct quote, by the way."

"Yeah, well, Dickey and I go back. You can tell him he's OK, too. For a press weenie."

Johnson finished her wine. Played with her hair a little, like she wasn't used to it being short. Leaned back in the booth, stretched. "God, four glasses of wine. I knew I shouldn't have driven. Now I've got to drive home."

"As a police officer, I would advise against it. I can get a unit to run you home."

Johnson laughed. "Just what I need, covering the cop beat. Some uniform spreading the word he got strong-armed into playing taxi for me."

"We can go to my place for a while, get you some coffee."

"Inviting me up for coffee Lynch? What's the matter, don't have any etchings to show me?" That sly smile again.

"Just an offer in the interest of public safety, ma'am. Although I do have this extensive collection of Seventies album covers."

"Except I don't think you should be driving either."

"Don't have to. I live upstairs."

"Really?" There was a little tone in her voice; not sarcasm. That smile again.

"Still like my schmoozing?" Johnson murmured into his neck as they clinched inside Lynch's door, both of their coats and four shoes on the floor by their feet. Lynch had untucked her turtleneck and slid his hands up her back.

"I knew you had ways of making me talk, Johnson."

"If you're going to keep undressing me, you're going to have to call me Liz."

"OK, Liz." The turtleneck came over her head. Black bra. "Isn't this the time when we're supposed to disclose our sexual histories in the interest of public health?"

"Why?" she asked. "Is yours long and varied?"

"Wife died in '86. Did some tomcatting around for a few years," he said. "Only been back in the pool a handful of times since, though."

"You better have been wearing your trunks," she said.

"Always wear my trunks."

"I was divorced fourteen months ago," Johnson said. "Dipped my toe in here and there, but haven't been doing laps for a while."

Lynch's hands ran back down her back to the waistband of her slacks, and then to the front to the buckle of her belt.

"You like to swim?" he asked.

She pulled Lynch's sweater over his head. "I finished second in the state in the 400 IM in high school."

"I can only dog paddle, but I'm vigorous," said Lynch. "You gonna pull me out if I get in too deep?"

Johnson's slacks dropped to the floor. Her hands ran down Lynch's chest and began to work the front of his jeans. "I can do better than that," she said. "I can give lessons." His jeans dropped. She ran a finger up the long, white welt on the right side of Lynch's ribs, and then kissed the round, puckered scar under his left collarbone.

He unhooked her bra, and she pulled back for a second to let it fall down her arms.

"Last one in's a rotten egg," said Lynch. She smiled again, even better than last time.

There was a moment later, Johnson on top, rocking, neither of them rushing it, the dim light through the blinds falling in gentle curves across her breasts, when Lynch felt something break and shift inside of him, like a bone that had been set wrong being made straight. All those frantic couplings all those years ago, with Katie in the car before they married, and even after, there had always been a savagery to their mating. The cop groupies he'd pick up on Rush Street and the cruel gravity of their need. Now this gentility, this fluidity. He was swimming, and not struggling toward the surface and choking for air. Just swimming. For the first time in his life, he could breathe here.

CHAPTER 3 – RESTON, VIRGINIA

"Yes, sir, we will keep you apprised." Tecumseh Weaver (Colonel, USMC, retired) hung up on Clarke, sat back in his chair at InterGov Research Services and sighed. Fucking Clarke. How a guy got to be where he was with balls as small as he had was still a mystery to Weaver. But he sure had his panties in a bunch now. This little problem of his, it wasn't the sort of thing Clarke could sic an official dog on, though. So he was tugging on Weaver's leash instead.

Weaver'd never liked being on a leash.

The suite housing the offices of InterGov Research Services was not quite in Langley and not quite in DC, which was as it should be. And if the company's internet connections and telecommunications were a little more secure, their staff a little better armed, and their raison d'etre a little harder to discern than those of the neighbors in the generic office park just off of I-66, that was as it should be, too.

InterGov Research Services was a limited liability corporation whose owners were even more mysterious than the company itself, being the figments of some very creative imaginations. InterGov was one of the thousands of small consultancies surrounding Washington that cleared away some of the fiscal bloat of the federal budget every year. InterGov's masters viewed this not as wasteful, but rather as a way of creating financial breathing room outside the prissy auspices of the

House and Senate intelligence oversight committees. Just another form of off-balance-sheet accounting.

And InterGov did provide real and valuable services to its legitimate clients. It had access to the NSA's supercomputers and to some of the CIA's best research talent, so clients like the Department of Agriculture received quick, accurate, and affordable analyses of pressing issues like Uzbekistan's projected wheat yield, trends in Kenyan coffee production, and the statistical likelihood that, somewhere in the United States, the curious little bug that caused mad cow disease was already turning some citizen's brain into so much insentient Jell-O.

But InterGov's most valuable talent pool knew very little about computers, except for those attached to weapons systems. And if most of them were a little larger, a little stronger, and a little more familiar with places like Yemen, Mogadishu, Medellin, or Montenegro than your average Joe, well, that was as it should be, too.

It was the highest and best use of the latter pool of talent that Weaver considered as he waited for Chen to get back in from Reagan National.

Fucking Fisher, thought Weaver. This Chicago thing had his stink all over it. No details yet – Weaver had the techies hacking into the Chicago Police systems and would have those shortly – but there was speculation regarding a rifle.

Ishmael Leviticus Fisher, InterGov's resident sniper – hell, resident genuine USDA-inspected number-one badass – he'd gone off the reservation two months earlier, and InterGov was pretty far off the reservation to begin with. Fisher had been on Weaver's operations team ever since he put InterGov together. Hell, Fisher and Weaver went back all the way to Saigon. Anyway, InterGov had a leak. A lot of your Al-Qaeda types, the ones that hadn't got Hellfire missiles up the ass, Fisher'd been the man who put them down, so he had a little rep in

Arab circles. Just before Christmas, one of the raghead groups who were looking to put Fisher's head on a wall got some intel they shouldn't have and put a bomb in the Fisher family car. Blew up Fisher's wife and kids, but missed him. For a couple of weeks, Fisher stuck with the program, working with the Intel team trying to get a line on the bombers, letting the PsyOps boys poke around his head looking for blown circuits. No evidence of psychotic break, the white coats had said. No apparent disassociation, they said. Somewhat disturbing lack of arousal, they said. Then Fisher disappeared.

At first, Weaver thought maybe the ragheads had gotten Fisher, too. Then he thought maybe Fisher had gotten some intel on his own and gone hunting. Then forty days of nothing.

On day forty-one, somebody put a 7.62mm hole through a dairy farmer in a church parking lot in Door County, Wisconsin. Lots of people get shot in the United States every day, but not many of them get shot with rifles. So when the Wisconsin thing popped up, Weaver took a sniff and caught a funny odor. So he packed Chen off to Cheesehead country to sniff it out.

Weaver's phone rang. Chen was back.

Chen wore a plain black pantsuit over a black silk blouse when she walked into Weaver's office. She stood five feet two inches and weighed, Weaver was guessing, ninety-five pounds. Educated guess, because Chen was a dead ringer for the girl Weaver had stashed in the apartment on Mandalay Road in Hong Kong through most of Vietnam. He'd had to kill that one eventually, though. Still a little twinge when he thought about it. What was it with oriental chicks anyway, Weaver wondered. No tits to speak of, asses like fourteen-year-old boys. Just like chink food, though. Finish with one and fifteen minutes later you're ready for another serving. Not that Weaver had any carnal designs on Chen. Made a run at her when she first came

on board, and the vibe he got was enough to shrivel his sack.
Hoped he never had to take out Chen. She could break an oak
board with either hand, with either foot, even with her head.
And she could get that flat little .25 auto out from wherever
she had it stashed and put all eight rounds through your "X"
ring while you were still wondering whether you should be
scared of her or her cute little gun. Mind like a goddamn Cray
computer, too.

"Enjoy your trip, Chen? America's dairy land, you know.
Try the cheese?"

"Too much fat to justify the protein, sir."

"Of course. So what do we have? It was Fisher?"

"Statistically, Fisher is the logical candidate. The local
authorities suspect that the victim was shot from a snowmobile
from close to the shore. However, the medical examiner's
findings indicate that the wound channel is on a downward
angle, entering just above and to the right of the victim's
heart and exiting through the left side of the sixth thoracic
vertebrae. One of the victim's gloves was on the ground by
the body, the other on his right hand. Their theory is that the
victim dropped the glove and was shot as he bent over to pick
it up. The victim being bent over at the time would explain the
wound channel."

"But that's not your theory?"

"No, sir. I was able to access the local system and examine
the crime scene photographs. Blood spray on the back of the
glove the victim supposedly dropped indicates the glove was
within six inches of the entry wound at time of impact, which
is exactly where it would have been if the victim was putting
it on when he was shot. That means the victim was not bent
over, which means that the round hit at a descending angle.
The shot came from the ice out on the lake, which eliminates
the possibility of an elevated shooting position. The downward
angle can only be explained by distance. For the round to

arrive at an angle matching the wound channel, the shot would have to have been fired from between nine hundred and one thousand meters. With a little more than one hundred meters between the victim and the shore, we must assume that Fisher fired from more than eight hundred meters out on the ice."

Weaver let out a low whistle. "A thousand meters with a weapon that's iffy starting around seven hundred and in a twenty plus crosswind? Don't suppose the locals bothered looking out that far."

"No, sir. They found fresh snowmobile tracks at one hundred ten meters and some sign that the machine stopped on the right line for the driver to take the shot. They confined their search to the first two hundred meters of ice. At eight hundred meters, the ice was only marginally safe."

"And they didn't recover a slug?"

"No, sir. Again, faulty assumptions. They assumed the round was fired from less than two hundred meters, so they assumed a flat trajectory. Therefore, they also assumed the round would have passed through the victim with sufficient velocity to reach the woods beyond the shooting scene. They determined that the round was not recoverable."

"So no slug?"

Chen pulled a small plastic envelope from her jacket pocket and dropped it on Weaver's desk. The thing inside looked like a misshapen lead mushroom. "The slug was in the landscaping bordering the parking lot less than twenty meters from where the body was located."

"And?"

"A cursory examination reveals nothing to dispute the assumption that it was fired by Fisher. It is the appropriate caliber. I could find no evidence of ballistic signature. Fisher is still saboting his rounds."

"OK, so for now we have to figure Fisher took out this dairy farmer out. You get anything on the victim?"

"White male, fifty-nine years old, five-eleven, two hundred and two pounds. Married with four adult children, none living at home. Operated a successful dairy farm located twelve miles from the church."

"Any idea why Fisher did it?"

"The victim had no international ties. His farm has significant value, but he had minimal cash or securities holdings and none of those holdings are tied to likely targets. The victim had never traveled outside the country and had only traveled outside the state three times in the last twenty years."

"So Fisher is wandering the country shooting people for the hell of it?"

"People?"

"Shooting in Chicago this afternoon. Looks like a rifle. Victim was Helen Marslovak, mother to Eddie Marslovak, so big money. Fisher doing private hits, maybe? We need to start looking for money movement?"

Chen shook her head. "It seems unlikely. Fisher made some peculiar tactical choices. The church where the victim was shot was surrounded on three sides by wooded land. Fisher could have taken the shot from wooded cover and from less than one hundred yards. It is almost as though he chose to fire from as far away from the victim as possible. Also, the victim spent long periods of time on his property alone, often before first light and after dark. Yet Fisher chose to take the shot during daylight and in a situation where the shooting would either be witnessed or discovered almost immediately. I would imagine that Fisher had to remain on the ice for several hours after the shot before he could return to shore. Odd choices if he was working for hire."

"Almost like he was bragging. Anybody else we know of could have taken the shot?"

"At that distance, with that weapon and in that wind? No, sir. There are only a few who could have made the shot at all, with anything."

"So he shoots an old lady coming out of church just for kicks."

"A Catholic church?"

"Yeah."

"Had she just attended the Catholic sacrament of reconciliation?"

"Reconciliation? What the fuck is that?"

"The sacrament previously known as confession. The victim in Wisconsin had just left reconciliation."

"Don't know. We'll check. But that feels like something. Fisher had the Jesus bug pretty bad." Weaver stopped for a moment, rubbed his face. It had been a long day, and there was the prospect of longer days to come.

"Anything else?"

"Yes, sir." Chen pulled another small envelope from her pocket. The envelope held two tiny electronic devices: a camera half the size of a pencil eraser and a transmitter smaller than that, two thin wires sticking out of it like antennae. "These are our most advanced audio and video surveillance options. I found the audio transmitter wedged into the molding inside one of the confessional booths in the church the victim had just left. The camera was affixed to the bottom of the last row of pews. The camera was directed at the door of the booth in which the transmitter was hidden."

"You check with Paravola?" Tom Paravola headed InterGov's technical section.

"Thirty sets of these units are missing."

"So we can assume another set is sitting in the church in Chicago just waiting to get us in this up to our asses. Locals tumble on those, nobody's going to think they came from Radio Shack."

"Yes, sir. Their discovery would prove problematic."

Weaver thought for a moment. "Get to Chicago, Chen, but

I don't want you anywhere near that church. Let's get a local on this. Who's that guy we used on the University of Chicago break-in down there? Villanueva? See if we can get to him. This goes south, I don't want our fingerprints on it."

"Yes, sir. I will make arrangements. Is there anything else?"

"Bring Ferguson up to speed, will you? Tell him to get a team together by tomorrow, get the war wagon loaded up. We need to get Fisher inside a body bag before some cop gets his mitts on him. If Fisher decides to start answering questions, well, that would add up to better than thirty years of the wrong sorts of answers."

"Yes, sir."

Weaver sat alone in the office, nursing a drink. Hide and seek with Ishmael Fisher, Ferguson was gonna love this one.

Weaver closed the files on his desk and put them in the drawer. Lease renewal two months out, request from research for another $150,000 in computer shit, open enrollment for the health plan coming up. Couldn't think with all that crap in front of him. Needed to get a line on Fisher.

OK, Fisher was driving almost certainly. Just too hard to hide traveling by air now. Also – ten days between Wisconsin and Chicago, so he was taking his time. If he had slipped his moorings, and Weaver was pretty sure Fisher was well away from the dock at this point, there wasn't anything wrong with his navigation. Everything aboard the SS Fisher was battened down and squared away. Just working off a new set of charts was all. Charts from Mars or somewhere.

Get PsyOps back on it, of course. See if the behavioral witch doctors could get a reading. They were right more often than Weaver expected them to be, but he still didn't trust that psychic hotline bullshit.

Two killings, though. So that gave him two dots to string together. Enough to start looking for a pattern. Weaver punched up the two churches on the computer, plotted them on GPS. Dot two was damn near exactly due south of dot one – within yards of due south of dot one. OK, that's odd. Could be a one-in-360-degree coincidence, but at least it was a place to start. Something about Fisher's moral rigidity and an exact north-south line resonated with Weaver. He sent an email down to research.

Needed to muddy up the waters, too. Dot one was working out. Locals didn't have squat, and they weren't going to find the slug or the electronics now.

He had Eddie Marslovak attached to dot two. Guy with that kind of money, those kinds of connections... Weaver figured they could play the six degrees of Kevin Bacon game with him pretty easy. Wouldn't be too hard to put some stink on him, to get the cops interested. It'd fall apart, but Weaver didn't need a conviction, he just needed time.

Weaver's to-do list was getting crowded. Get research to expand their parameters on the Fisher search. See what they could do about grabbing any public video – ATM cameras, security cameras, toll booth cameras, traffic cameras. Chicago was pretty wired up. Run all that through the recognition software, see if anything comes up. What else? Toss Fisher's place again, couldn't hurt. He must have squirreled away some identities, he couldn't be doing all this on cash.

Weaver wondered what Fisher's old man would have made of all this. Ezekiel Amos Fisher had been Weaver's mentor. Zeke had started in the OSS. After Buchenwald, he'd gone zealot, convinced you had to fight evil with evil. Weaver remembered when he'd joined the team, right after Korea, Zeke going on about the just war doctrine, whatever Catholic shit that was, about how violence was only justified when it prevented a greater harm. For Zeke, Communism was the greatest harm imaginable. Which meant Zeke would do anything as long as it hurt the Reds more than it hurt Uncle Sam. Now Zeke's kid had popped a couple civilians, one of them in Chicago. Zeke Fisher and the FBI COUNTERINTELPRO guys had done some shit in Chicago back in the day, playing ball with Hurley and his Red Squad. There was the Hampton raid, where Zeke helped the FBI tee up the Chicago Black Panther party and let the Chicago cops butcher them in their beds. And there was the other thing. Weaver didn't want to think about the other thing just yet. But Fisher killing people in Chicago? Weaver didn't close this down fast, Clarke would really start wetting his drawers.

Weaver was not just leery of the upcoming Ides of March, he was having his doubts about the entire fucking month. And April was looking very cruel indeed.

CHAPTER 4 – CHICAGO

February, 1971

"Jesus, Stosh, I know you'd stick your dick in a light socket if you thought you'd get away with it, but this is fucking nuts," Riley said, looking down at the bodies.

Hastings Clarke stood by the door watching Riley. Clarke hated Riley. Hated the big, round Irish head, the massive shoulders, the ill-fitting suit, the too-short tie on the slope of the unapologetic gut. He hated Riley as the venial representation of everything wrong with the city. When Clarke came west to join the Hurley dynasty, he found not corruption as a rash overlying the sound skeleton of government but a body politic completely rotted through. Urbs in Horto, City in a Garden, was Chicago's official motto. But Qua Mei? was its operating principle. Where's mine?

Clarke understood self-interest. He'd met David Hurley, Jr at Yale Law and had seen the Chicago opportunity early. The East Coast was complicated. You had Kennedys and Tafts and Roosevelts. Dozens of old-line links to power, all with money and connections, all from the same schools, all looking for a way in. Clarke's family was in the mix, of course, New York money back to the Revolution. But in Chicago, one family ran an entire state. David Hurley was going to be Clarke's shortcut to the head of the class. Clarke went back to Chicago with

David, ran his campaign for DA, served in his office, and now ran his campaign for the US Senate. Clarke would use his family money and contacts to ease Hurley onto the national stage. Then Hurley would back Clarke in Illinois. Maybe a congressional seat next cycle. Maybe Hurley would make a play for governor and Clarke would move to the senate. While his prep-school cronies were still angling for some backwater undersecretary slot, Clarke would be on the lead lap.

Now David was dead. Worse, he was a dead homosexual. Eight years wasted.

Clarke looked back at the bodies. Stosh Stefanski, head of Chicago's Streets and Sanitation Department, the mother-lode of clout, was sprawled in the middle of the floor, naked except for a sleeveless T-shirt. The T-shirt was a mess because Stefanski had been shot in the chest. A lot. David Hurley was slumped in an armchair across the room wearing only his boxers, a bullet hole in his right temple and a bigger, messier hole a little higher up on the left side. Hurley's gun was on the floor next to the chair.

"You did the right thing, kid, calling me," said Riley. "What's your name again? Hasty?"

Clarke could hear the ridicule in his voice, the alpha-male bullshit, Riley having to mark his territory, make sure the east-coast punk knew who was sucking hind tit.

"Hastings."

"Right, Hastings. What is that, some kind of family thing?"

"Something like that," said Clarke.

Riley was over by the far wall, turning off the thermostat. "You wanna open those windows for me, Hastings?"

"Why? It must be ten degrees outside." Almost 10.00pm, and the temperature had been dropping all night.

"Time of death, kid. Stuff happens with stiffs. Don't ask me the particulars, I don't know. But whatever it is, it happens slower if they're cold. Gives us more time to work out what happened here."

Clarke looked at the mostly naked corpses, sniffed the smell of sex in the air. "Don't we know what happened here?"

"Looks like Junior was a rump ranger. Stosh here, well, Stosh'd fuck a toasted cheese sandwich – especially if the sandwich was just working out which way its bread was buttered. Especially if the sandwich wasn't really sure it wanted to get fucked yet. Stosh liked em hurt and confused, liked fucking them, liked fucking them up even better. That way, he'd have em on a string, and he could pull it whenever he wanted. Looks like maybe he pulled a little too hard. Looks like Junior got pissed. That's the rough draft, anyway."

"Rough draft?"

"First shit happens, then history gets written down. Got a guy on his way's gonna look things over, decide what history is."

"He who controls the present," Clarke said.

"Yeah, well, you, me, and Orwell, we're gonna go see the old man." Riley looked over, saw Clarke looking at him. "What, you think I can't read?"

Clarke was thinking, if they put the fix in, I may still have a play here.

Mayor Hurley stood looking out the window of his spacious, spartan office on the fifth floor of City Hall, facing the plaza to the east, where the new Picasso sculpture stood. The wind drove small, scattered flecks of snow through the spotlights that lit the sculpture.

The mayor was so different from the son. Junior had been tall, lean, dark Irish. The mayor was short, stocky, ruddy, yet emanated power like a scent. Clarke had never understood the relationship between father and son. The son was devoted to ending the corrupt politics for which his father was practically the Platonic form. No real emotional connection between them that Clarke could see – no real emotional connection between the mayor and anyone. But the mayor put the full force of his machine behind the son, and the son had an intense personal loyalty to his father.

"Fucking statue, still don't get it," said Hurley.

"Pardon?"

"The Picasso. Junior's idea, you know. Public art, he says, so we can be a great city, like New York or Paris. Like we ain't a great city already. Like I gotta put a fucking steel monkey in the middle of the Loop so we can be a great city."

"Picasso is genius. Subjective as individual works may be, to have his work on so prominent a stage."

"Yeah, yeah, yeah. Make all the art critics in the world gush about us. Course you could move all the art critics in the world into the same damn place and you wouldn't have a city, you'd have a village, cause there's maybe a couple hundred of em, and the village wouldn't need an idiot. And then they'd all starve cause they don't know how to do nothing. What I like about it? The Picasso? I look out on a nice day in the summer, and I see the kids climbing up that slanty part at the bottom and sliding down. Got the parents standing there, trying to figure out is it a baboon or what, and their kids play on it. I like that. Some guy from the Art Institute came to tell me I gotta keep them kids off it, that it was sacrilege or some shit. Scrawny atheist fuck in my office talking about sacrilege. Told him that Picasso might be a drunk and can't keep his pants zipped, but at least he makes a decent slide."

The mayor didn't move, hands clasped in the small of his back, still facing the window, silent again. Clarke couldn't stand the silence any longer.

"I'm very sorry, sir," he said, "about David."

The mayor nodded. "You was his friend, Junior always said that. Said you did good work for him. Said you was loyal to him. You and me, we got our differences. But you were good to my boy. I ain't gonna forget that."

Clarke didn't buy the personal emotions, he knew he was being handled. The mayor was as close to a sociopath as anyone Clarke had ever known. "Thank you, sir. He was a great man. I am proud of what I've been able to do with him."

"Still proud, after tonight?"

"I, eh, I didn't know..."

"About the queer thing? Yeah, I know. I thought about it, maybe over the years. Seen this and that made me think. I wondered should I have said something. But there's things you don't wanna think, not about your own boy. Then he got married, and with the wife and the kid on the way and all, I thought maybe he'd be OK."

"It shouldn't define him, a single weakness. It shouldn't become all he was. It shouldn't be used to tarnish what he stood for."

He could see the mayor nodding.

"It ain't gonna. Nobody's gonna know. Not ever. You understand that?"

"Riley told me."

"I'm not asking did Riley tell you. I'm asking do you understand that nobody's ever gonna know?"

"Yes, sir. I understand."

Another long silence. The mayor spoke first this time.

"Junior was right, you know, about me, about how I run things. Not the way it oughta be. It was different times I come up in. You got your Hitlers and such, and nobody's worrying too much how do you beat the son of a bitch. You do what you gotta do. And then I get this job, and see so much that needs doin' and everybody wantin' to chinwag everything to death. And so maybe I find some corners to cut and strings to pull, and pretty soon, I look back and I got sick fucks like Stosh running things just cause he's got half the city by the balls. And now I gotta live with did I get my own kid killed."

"It does need to change, sir." Clarke was being probed, he could feel it. Hurley could write history any way he wanted, but Clarke would always have the rough draft, so Hurley needed him.

"Such a waste. He was our chance. Move away from all this crap, reach out to the next generation. There's Billy, of course, but he ain't got it, not like Junior did." Billy was the mayor's other son, just finishing college.

Careful here, thought Clarke. "It doesn't need to be a waste, sir."

Hurley finally turned away from the window. "You got something to say, spit it out."

"You need a bridge to the new generation, and you need a placeholder until Billy is ready to take the stage."

Hurley's eyes glinted, almost the hint of a smile, seeing right through to Clarke's play. "You think you're the solution."

Clarke nodded. "You've never really gotten to know me. You saw the Ivy League polish, and you wrote me off as some pantywaist. But you and I have the same ideology."

"Only ideology I got is power," said Hurley.

"Exactly. Whatever it is you want to do, you have to have power first."

"So you want me to slot you into Junior's place?"

"Given recent events, we would have the assurance of each other's fealty."

"You get a ticket to the big show, and I get a pet senator?"

"Within reason."

Hurley walked back to the credenza, pulled a bottle of Jameson's from the cabinet, poured some into a couple of highball glasses, handed one to Clarke.

"Never work. No secret around town how you and me get along. I put you up, you'd look like a poodle on a leash."

"We can get around that."

Hurley put a hand up, shushing Clarke. He walked back to

the window for a minute, sipping his whiskey, then turned back.

"Here's what we do. You declare. You're the independent taking up Junior's flag. Press'll eat that shit up. They love to give it to me in the chops anyway. All those hippie loonies, they'll flock to you. Meanwhile, I pick out some schmuck, run him in the primary. My side takes a dive, we get some of the vote out your way under the table. You're the underdog who takes down the machine. Comes the general election, I got no choice but to back the party side."

Clarke thought for a moment. It was brilliant. But it could also be a ploy. Could be a way for Hurley to buy his silence long enough that Clarke couldn't ever come forward, then cut him off at the knees, have his guy actually win, send Clarke packing. It could be, but it didn't feel that way. There's always a moment when you have to take that leap.

"Smart play. I'll give it a few days, lay low, grieving, get through the funeral. But you announce your candidate first – somebody out of the machine. Then I'm outraged. I have to step forward in Junior's memory."

"Right way to play it," said Hurley, nodding. "Just remember one thing here. We got each other by the balls. I've been at this a long time, had mine twisted before. You try to cross me, I'll rip yours off."

"Yes, sir," said Clarke.

Hurley let out a soft snort.

"What?" Clarke said.

"The assurance of each other's fealty? You wanna make it in this town, you better stop talking like that. Your Ivy League crap don't carry no weight around here."

After Clarke left, Hurley sat in the office with Riley.

"I've been thinking about who we want handling it with the cops," said Riley. "You know that Declan Lynch guy?"

"Up on the northwest side? Does some precinct work and whatnot? Rusty Lynch's brother?"

"Yeah. Rusty can help keep him in line. Also, once he reads the tea leaves, I think he'll smell an opportunity in it."

"Good. Call the commissioner."

"Zeke Fisher called while you were talking to the kid. He's done over there. Wants you to know he's sorry, but it's going to be ugly. What he had to work with, only way he could go. On the plus side, looks like a chance to clean up the rest of your nigger problem. He also wants to know does he need to do anything about Clarke."

Hurley shook his head. "Tell Fisher don't worry about ugly. Junior turned fag, he deserves ugly. And we don't need to worry about Clarke. Clarke's our next senator. We own him and every vote he's ever gonna cast."

CHAPTER 5 – KANKAKEE, ILLINOIS

Present Day

Ishmael Leviticus Fisher lay awake in the anonymous hotel on the frontage road off I-57. He needed to sleep, but the moment kept coming back to him. His wife, the quick smile and short wave out the driver's window of the Blazer as it crunched through the yellowed leaves, down past the short stone wall, past the chestnut tree, angling to the right as it backed into the street.

Andy's face in the back window, the delicate skin around the blues eyes crinkled, that smile that seemed to split his head like a melon full of teeth. Amanda in the car seat past him, just a year old, just a hint of Amanda through the reflection of the white house and the black shutters and the fragile blue of the autumn sky.

Then the white-yellow flash of the Semtex, like diamond lava, and a sound like all the bones in the world snapping at once, the driver's side of the Blazer pitching up, part of the bottom showing, and then the gas tank exploding, a richer, redder fire with a sound like a bass drum stretched with his own flesh and beaten with his own heart.

Picking himself up and running to the burning hulk, half, half, half his son strewn into the street, his head now truly split, brains, not teeth, smiling out. And his wife, thrown out onto the lawn, blood sheeting down her face and a flap of her scalp hanging across one eye, a ragged triangle of gray plastic jutting from her abdomen, her right leg gone almost to the hip, the scarlet, arterial blood arcing out in desperate spurts. Her clawing at the plastic as he reached her, clawing at the invasion into her already crowded womb. And her remaining eye meeting his eyes just once, and her saying "the baby," and her hands falling away from her stomach as that one good eye rolled back and the blood from her leg slowed, no longer propelled by a beating heart.

Fisher closed his eyes, forced the memory away. He got out of bed, pulled on a pair of shorts and a T-shirt, and went out into the night to run.

CHAPTER 6 – CHICAGO

When John Lynch got to his desk, he had a message to call McCord at the ME's office. Got what he usually got, McCord eating something while he talked.

"Sorry to interrupt your breakfast, McCord."

"Brunch, Lynch. Had breakfast couple hours ago. We can't all keep your hours."

"So what have you got for me?"

"You know about the cancer?"

"Priest told me. Bad?"

"Broad's a walking tumor. Got it everywhere."

"She in pain you think?"

"Must've been."

"So I should put out an APB on that Kevorkian, huh?"

"Depends. Can he shoot?"

"So what else?"

"Definitely a descending line on the shot. Had to have some elevation. Like I was saying yesterday, bouncing off all those bones, maybe it just got kicked down, but I got a real clean entrance wound in the sternum, and the beveling on that tells me the round was headed down when it hit her. 7.62mm, so definitely a rifle round."

"Fuck." Lynch trying to picture the scene in his mind again. "You see anything when you were over there? Parking lot, right? Then the park. Bungalows behind that. Anything high enough?"

"Maybe the guy climbed a tree in that park, I dunno. Like I said, I just do the science. By the way, got her in the heart. Pretty much dead center. Guy's either real lucky or real, real good."

Lynch ran through the ME's findings for Starshak.

"How far's that park from the church?" Starshak asked.

"Got the street, parking lot, another street, the trees in off that a bit. Gotta be three hundred yards anyway, probably more."

"Long way. Right in the heart, you said?"

"Yeah." Lynch thinking a minute. "Hey, you used to be SWAT, right?"

"Yeah," Starshak answered.

"What about one of the department sharpshooters? Think one of them might be able to break this down?"

"It's an idea. Let me make a couple calls."

Lynch went back out to his desk. Liz had left his place early that morning, wanting to get home, clean up, change. Lynch feeling funny standing naked in his kitchen, trading phone numbers. Lynch pulled out her card and called her office. Got her voice mail.

"Hey, Liz. It's Lynch. Just thought I should call. Listen, I'm not that good at this stuff in person, so I'm not going to go on to some machine, but if you'd like to get together, get some dinner or something, call my cell. I'm, you know, glad you called last night."

Starshak walked out, handed Lynch a piece of paper. "Guy named Darius Cunningham. He's off today, but he'll meet you over at Sacred Heart at 10.00."

"Thanks, Cap."

"So I hear from McGinty you were out late with some blonde looker," Starshak said with a little dig in his voice.

"Fucking McGinty better learn to keep his mouth shut or he's gonna lose his lease."

••••

Resurrection Hospital was on the way to Sacred Heart, and Lynch hadn't been to see his mom in three days. He parked the Crown Vic outside the emergency entrance, badged the guard, and headed up.

Lynch took a minute to suck it up before he walked into his mom's room on the sixth floor. When the doctors first diagnosed the cancer they gave her six months. That was four years ago. She was down two breasts from the cancer and a foot from the diabetes, weighed maybe eighty pounds. Better to go the way Dad went. Bullet through the head and you're two hundred and thirty-five pounds of morgue fodder.

With his chipper face cemented in place, Lynch stepped in. The first bed was empty. The room was dark, washed with the blue flicker from the TV.

"Hey, babe," he said. "Lookin' hot. Docs still hittin' on you?"

She still lit up when she saw him, but she was down to about a twenty-watt bulb.

"Johnny," she said. She put up her left arm for a hug. The right one had too many tubes in it.

He bent down and kissed her parchment-like cheek. Her arm across his back felt like a piece of rebar in a paper bag. He sat in the chair by the bed.

"So how you doin'? Pain OK? These nurses won't keep you in dope, I got some contacts, you know."

"Oh, stop it. I'm fine." She smiled. "It always does me good to see you, Johnny. You're a good boy. You hear anything from your sister?"

He hadn't, not in a couple weeks. "Yeah, mom, talked to her last night. She'd love to come down, but with the boys and the new job and all, well... Sends her love, though. She's prayin' for you."

"She sent flowers," his mother said, nodding toward the arrangement on the stand by the window.

"That's nice," he said. "She's a good kid."

"I got good kids. You both grew up good. That's the biggest comfort I have. That and your father waiting for me."

"Yeah, well good thing he's such a patient guy, Ma, cause I'm nowhere near done with you yet. Boy needs his mother." He squeezed her hand.

She smiled at him again, then he watched her eyes drift closed and her breathing settle into a sleeping rhythm.

Lynch would wait. She wouldn't sleep long. Besides, WGN was just leading in to the morning news. The Marslovak killing was the lead story.

"That poor woman," he heard his mother say.

"Hey, sleepyhead, back with us?" The motor moaned as she raised the bed.

"Why would anyone shoot a lady coming out from mass?"

"Wasn't mass, Mom. She'd just been to confession."

"Well, that's good, then."

"Good how?"

"State of grace. She died in a state of grace."

They both sat for a minute, Lynch having nothing to say to that.

"You keeping your soul clean, Johnny? You gettin' to church?"

"Sure, Mom. They practically gotta kick me out of the place. You know me." Who was it said children had a duty to lie to their parents? Lynch couldn't remember. Didn't matter. People said a lot of things. Most of it was bullshit.

She drifted off again. Lynch left.

CHAPTER 7 – CHICAGO

Darius Cunningham was waiting on the walk at Sacred Heart when Lynch pulled up. Black guy, six-four, shaved head, wearing brown gabardine slacks and a short-sleeved black shirt. Black Grand Cherokee parked at the end of the walk. Lynch could see a thick web of muscle fanning away from Cunningham's neck and into his shirt. Very thick through the shoulders and chest. Tight end, Lynch thought.

Lynch left his jacket in the car. Couple minutes after 10.00, already pushing sixty-five degrees, sun making it feel hotter than that. March in Chicago – freezing his ass off yesterday, sweating through his coat today. Lynch had stopped at Dunkin' Donuts and picked up a couple of coffees. Least he could do.

"You Lynch?" Cunningham putting out his hand. "Darius Cunningham."

Lynch balanced the two coffees in his left hand. "Yeah. Listen, thanks for coming down on your day off." Taking Cunningham's hand. Tight grip. Maybe not a tight end, maybe a speed rusher, Javon Kearse, somebody like that. Lynch offered Cunningham a coffee.

"No thanks, don't drink it."

"Cop who doesn't drink coffee?"

"No, caffeine gives you the shakes. I get called on some hostage deal or whatever and I end up putting a round through some innocent schmuck cause I got a little wobble in my sight

59

picture, I gotta live with that."

"Hey, more for me."

Cunningham turned toward the stairs. "This is the spot, right? The Marslovak deal? Saw the news last night."

"This is it," said Lynch. "She was head-down on the stairs. Forensics put her on top of the stairs when she got hit."

Cunningham walked up the stairs and turned to face down the walk. A black metal railing ran down the middle of the staircase. "Right or left of the railing?" Cunningham asked.

"Left side."

"She's right-handed then? Figure, grabs the rail like this?" Cunningham took the rail with his right hand.

"I guess so. Does it matter?"

"Probably not. Just figures. Know anything about the round?"

"Haven't got ballistics yet. They pulled the slug out of the bottom of that wooden chest back by the wall. Couple inches up from the floor. ME's guy says the shot came in at a descending angle. Something about beveling in the entrance wound. 7.62mm."

".308 caliber, .30-06. Doesn't help much. Most of your decent rifles will chamber that. Where'd she get hit?"

"Center chest. Through the sternum, through the heart, through the spine."

"Nice shooting."

"Or lucky," Lynch said.

Little snort from Cunningham. "Ever been to Vegas, Lynch?"

"Couple of times, yeah."

"Still believe in luck?"

Lynch thought for a moment about last night. "Sometimes. Sometimes I do."

Cunningham stood for a long time, staring out to the south.

"That shit up there yesterday?" Cunningham pointed to a faded red rag hanging off the phone line across the street.

"I don't know," said Lynch. "Looks like it's been there awhile."

"Got another one over by the park. See it there, on the light tower next to the basketball court?"

Lynch looked. He could barely make out another red rag hanging down from the cross member that held the lights.

"We looking for the guy's laundry here or something, Cunningham?"

"Tells. The shooter hung those so he could get a read on the wind. If you were hoping for some neighborhood yahoo getting lucky with his deer rifle, you better get over it. You're dealing with a pro here."

Cunningham started down the walk toward the Cherokee. "Guess we better head down there," he said, pointing out across the parking lot toward the park.

"Over to the park? You think maybe he was up one of those trees?"

"No. Past that, that factory building."

Lynch looked south. Same view as before. Parking lot, park, bungalows. Looming beyond that, a sprawling cement structure.

"The old Olfson factory? That's gotta be half a mile away."

Cunningham nodded. "Seven hundred meters, give or take."

"Who could shoot somebody through the heart from seven hundred meters?"

"I could," Cunningham answered. "For starters."

The Olfson factory had been empty since the early Nineties. Out front, there was a fading sign with a huge photo showing a kitchen with granite counters and stainless appliances advertised The Best in City Living Starting at Only $315,000. In 2006, a connected developer got the place in some kind of sweetheart deal – hardly any of his own money, big grants from the city, the state, the Feds, tax breaks, the whole enchilada. Mess of people had put money down on units, then the economy cratered, the development went belly up, and most of the buyers got squat. *Caveat emptor*, Lynch figured. Around Chicago, though, you hand your dollars over to some real estate guy who's wired in down at City Hall, you better emphasize the caveat part.

The building ran west-to-east in a kind of zigzag for a couple of blocks. Part closest to the church was on the west end, then a short north-south section, then a longer section running east again. Taggers had covered the cement walls solid as high as they could reach. Lots of gang signs. West end of the building was just across the street from the bungalows. The empty space where the building jogged back was fenced off, overgrown with weeds and concrete-busting little trees. Behind the building, an unused rail spur ran southeast to northwest. A berm behind that, then a strip mall on the other side.

"Start down at the west end, that's closest to the target," Cunningham said. "Those windows up on four, that or the roof. Probably the windows, though."

The building was four stories, each story with long banks of divided glass windows. Almost all the glass was broken out of the first two stories, and large chunks of it were gone out of the third. Most of the fourth-floor windows were intact.

Cunningham went through the building in complete silence and with aggravating patience. Stopping in each doorway, standing for a time, walking over to the windows, sometimes squatting down to look at the floor, touching the glass in a couple of places, sometimes assuming a shooting position as he looked back toward the church. Lynch followed along feeling useless as hell.

The place got some use. Lots of graffiti inside, lots of garbage. Fast food wrappers – lots of Popeye's Chicken boxes. Popeye's was back in the strip mall across the tracks behind the building,

Lynch thinking he should ask over there, see if he could get anything. Lots of malt liquor cans, beer cans, busted liquor bottles – bottom-shelf stuff mostly. Pop cans here and there. One room with an old mattress on the floor and used condoms scattered around. Maybe talk to vice, see if there's a local girl he should check out.

Cunningham had gone through the first wing, back through the north-south section, and was most of the way through the last wing. Finally, he stepped into a room and said, "Bingo." Just like that.

"What'cha got?" Lynch asked.

"This was the room. Smell it?"

"Smell urine," said Lynch. "Gonna be smelling that for a while, I think."

Cunningham walked directly to the right front corner, where the windows looked out toward the church. He pointed to a broken pane shoulder high and two rows in from the wall. "Took the shot through here. See the smudges in the dust here? Him setting his feet. Right-handed. His toes are pointing east. No tread in the tracks, though. Probably wearing booties over his shoes, like they do in the hospital. Didn't want to leave us prints."

"So he sticks his gun out the window there?"

"Rifle, Lynch. Guns are artillery. No, not out the window. Smart boy like this, he's standing back a couple of steps. Shoots through the hole. Almost like a silencer – traps most of the sound in the room here."

"That's why he's in this back section, not up front by the houses? Quieter?"

"Most likely. Brass balls, though, giving up another fifty meters just to cut down on noise nobody's gonna be able to place anyway. Get crime scene to check the window here, probably get some residue." Cunningham taking up a shooting position again, frowning a little.

"What time she get hit? Around 3 o'clock, wasn't it?"

"Quarter after."

"So why this side of the room? OK, this whole face of the building is in shadow because of the step-back layout, but why not tuck back in against the west wall? Be even darker over there. Could even brace against the wall if he wanted to."

"Really matter?"

"This kind of shooting, everything matters. It's like a math problem. For each tactical situation, there is one best answer. So far, everything adds up. This wing to cut down on the noise. Also, it's shaded that time of day. He's two doors from the stairwell on the east end. Close enough to get out quick, far enough away that he's got a little time if he hears anyone coming up. Also, look around in here. Less shit in here than in a lot of the rooms. Not a popular spot for some reason, and, trust me, our boy ain't looking to win no popularity contests. So why does he get all that right and pick the wrong side of the room. Maybe that window was already busted, he didn't want to risk the noise breaking another one."

Lynch walked over, looked at the window, shook his head. "He picked the pane, broke it himself. Most of the rooms we've been in, if there's broken glass, it's in here. Kids throwing rocks through the windows from the outside. This one was broken from the inside. Glass that's left is flexed out. Fresh break, too. When he broke it, he knocked the dust off, hasn't built back up yet."

Cunningham nodded, taking up his shooter's stance again. "Gotta be a reason he picked this side of the room." Cunningham walked along the wall of windows, looking at the floor.

"He's firing a semi-auto, not a bolt action. Worried about his brass. See over here, this gap between the wall and the floor? Brass could get down in there, maybe he can't get it back. So he gets close to the east wall. Brass comes out, hits the wall, it's right there. No gap. You're looking for a right-handed guy shoots a semi-auto. He's under six foot, probably military or ex-military, probably a white guy."

"How'd you know his height?"

"Me? I'm six-four. I'd take out the bottom of the next pane up. He took out the top half of this pane – six inches down. Five-eight to five-ten, I figure. Ex-military because of the time and training it takes to shoot like this. I went into the Corps at eighteen, Lynch. Scout/sniper at twenty. Did that for twenty years. Been on the job here now another ten. Police don't train much for shots at seven hundred meters. We can get closer than that. Now, you're out crawling the brush in your ghillie suit worrying about a combat patrol stepping on your ass, seven hundred meters could be as close as you get."

"Seems like you're channeling this guy, Cunningham."

"I understand what he's thinking."

"Scaring me a little."

"Scaring me a little, too."

Back at their cars, they shook hands.

"Interesting few hours, Cunningham, I gotta say. Thanks."

"No problem. You get the ballistics, give me a call. Number of grooves, left twist, right twist – might narrow the weapon down some."

"Will do." Lynch walked toward his car, then turned.

"Hey, Cunningham. You said a white guy. Why a white guy?"

Cunningham smiled. "Lynch, I spent twenty years in the Corps hanging out with snipers. Lotta backwoods types, dirt farmers, hillbillies. I want to run for president of the Afro-American Snipers Association, only vote I know I got to get is my own." Cunningham opened the door to the Jeep, then stopped, turned back one more time. "Besides, Lynch, you've seen the NBA. Always you white boys who want to shoot from the outside."

First time all day Lynch had seen Cunningham smile.

CHAPTER 8 – CHICAGO

Lynch drove back to the Marslovak house, wanting to give it a closer look. Typical Chicago bungalow, red brick, built in the Twenties or Thirties. Helen Marslovak had lived there the last fifty-two years of her life. In that time, Lynch thought, she should have accumulated more shit.

Place smelled of soap. Murphy's Oil Soap. Just like his mom's house. Living room across the front – parlor she'd called it. White sofa along one wall, one big chair. Sofa and chair looked pretty old. Coffee table, end table – those were newer. Big Zenith console set. That was ancient. Lynch hit the on button, saw the white dot in the center of the screen start to grow, listened to the hum, saw the orange glow of the vacuum tubes through the vented cover in the rear. Took him back. Jesus, where'd she still get tubes for it? Flicked it off just as the picture filled in and the sound started. Big Bible on the coffee table, the leather-bound kind with the family tree page in the front where you could fill in all the communions and weddings and such.

Dining room – table, six chairs, sideboard, built-in corner hutch, some dishes there. White cabinets in the kitchen. Not much food. Not much anything. Floors clean enough to do surgery on.

Just the bed and the dresser in the master bedroom, bed perfectly made. Wedding photo on the dresser. Helen had been a looker back in the day, a little Hedy Lamarr vibe going. Another Bible, smaller one, pages and cover pretty worn. Crucifix over the bed.

A number of old pictures lined the hall outside the bedroom. The husband, mostly. Even one of him with Hurley the First, the mayor's grandfather, the first Hurley to stake out the fifth floor at City Hall. He'd ridden his Southside Irish Bridgeport connections to the top prize back in 1952. Hurley the Third had the fifth floor now. Better than fifty years in the Hurley line and no end in sight.

Couple of pictures of Eddie Sr in his hard hat. Blue, with the city seal on it. Streets and Sanitation guy. Picture of Eddie Sr in his Knights of Columbus getup, with the cape and the Three Musketeers hat. Picture of Eddie Sr with the Cardinal. Eddie looking older in the last two, Lynch betting the ALS had already kicked in before the last one was taken.

Bedroom in the back must have been Eddie Jr's. Old Cubs pennant on the wall, picture of Ernie Banks. Bears' spread on the bed. Picture on the dresser, Eddie maybe thirty years and ninety pounds ago, standing in a football uniform. Scrapbook. Lynch picked it up. Eddie as a baby. Eddie holding up a fish on a pier somewhere. First Communion picture, Eddie and the parents standing on the steps where Lynch had seen the body. Graduation shots, high school and college. Wedding shots – all three wives. First one with the tux, the next two just suit and tie. Newspaper clippings. Eddie making partner at Morgan Stanley twenty years ago. Eddie setting up his own shop. Eddie yukking it up with the current Hurley at some ribbon cutting. Eddie throwing out a first pitch at Comiskey – the old one. Mom was prouder than she let on, prouder than Eddie knew.

An old desk was tucked into a corner in the hallway. Lynch went through it. Checking papers – bank statements, insurance policies, satisfaction of mortgage on the house. All of it pretty vanilla, nothing there. Lynch found a three-hundred-sheet spiral notebook in the center drawer, black cover. A sort of journal, Helen Marslovak's account of her illness. The diagnosis back in October. Metastasized colon cancer. Deciding pretty much right off not to fight it – no chemo, no surgery – docs having told her there wasn't much point. Writing about the pain with a kind of gratitude, thankful to know it was coming, to have a chance to put her soul in order. No self-pity that Lynch could sense.

Lynch went to put the notebook back, saw a piece of cardboard in the bottom of the drawer. He pulled it up. On the other side was an eight by ten photo, black and white, Eddie Sr and Hurley the First in the Hurley box at Wrigley, right behind the Cubs on deck circle. Eddie Sr and Hurley were up against the brick wall, leaning on it with their elbows. Ron Santo was standing on the field to the left of the mayor, Don Kessinger over to the right. Son of a bitch, Lynch thought, one of Hurley's favor shots. Walk into any alderman's office where the guy'd been around during the first Hurley reign, any mover and shaker in the city, you were gonna see his Wrigley shot. And the ballplayers in the shot, they told it all, in a kind of social ranking system as esoteric as any court ritual at Versailles but one that every politico in Chicago understood. Santo, he was Hurley's favorite, even more so than Ernie Banks, because Santo was a white guy, and Hurley the First, he didn't have much use for Schwartzers. Not racism of the white-supremacist type. Just he liked the balance of power the way it was, and the way it was when he took over left the blacks pretty much out of it. You'd see Ernie in a lot of the shots. Ernie had just enough step'n'fetchit in his act to keep Hurley happy. He was the only black guy you'd see, though. Never saw Billy Williams, never saw Fergie Jenkins. If you had Ernie and Santo, that was top drawer. Lynch's old man had a Wrigley shot, Santo and Huntley, which was hot shit, too. But Lynch's old man had hauled a lot of water for the

Hurley family in his day. Now here's Marslovak, Streets and San line grunt as far as Lynch could tell, and he's got Santo and Kessinger? Lynch peeled the photo off the cardboard backing. Date from the developer on the back. July 1971. All these other shots out on the walls, what was this doing face down in the bottom of a desk drawer?

Lynch found an empty manila envelope in the center drawer and tucked the photo inside. Time to drive out to River Forest, to see Uncle Rusty.

CHAPTER 9 – CHICAGO

March, 1971

Detective Declan Lynch couldn't decide. The watch commander told him Riley wanted him on the case, which meant the mayor wanted him on the case, and that was good. But the stiffs were the mayor's kid and one of the mayor's go-to guys, which, if Lynch didn't solve this quick, would be bad.

Wasn't hard to decide about the crime scene, though. The crime scene was a mess.

There was a lot of blood, and not much of it left in the bodies. Stefanski was spread-eagle on the floor, naked except for what was left of a Dago T. There was a shirt on the floor by his head, a pair of pants in the pool of blood next to him, more clothes strewn all over. The fire ax someone had used on him was still buried in his chest – looked like it was buried all the way into the floor. Stefanski's chest was completely open, chunks of meat and rib sticking out. Lynch could even see his spine in a spot. He'd taken a good whack or two to the head as well. Just enough face left to know it was him. Must have thrashed around quite a bit – blood was smeared all around his body, smeared on his arms and legs, like he rolled over a time or two. Guess you would, Lynch thought, guy's chopping you up with an ax. Lynch could see several spots where the ax had bit into the floor.

Junior Hurley was in his shorts, sprawled on the floor at the base of a big wing chair across the room. The top of his head was gone, a bloody wad of skull, hair, and brain lying between the rest of the body and the wall. Some blood on the chair, lots of blood on the floor, Hurley's blood flowing over to mix with the smeared mess around Stefanski. Blood on the walls, too, where somebody'd used it to write BUTCHER THE PIGS. On the other wall, near Stefanski, RAPES THE PEOPLE. A bloody tie was wadded up on the floor near the graffiti. Must have been what was used for a paintbrush.

Footprints in the blood, too. At least three different shoes that Lynch could see. That diamond pattern on those Converse shoes a lot of kids were wearing. A bigger set, looked like boots of some kind. Something smooth-soled that was smeared around pretty good. Converse guy got around. Lynch could see his prints fading out toward the dining room. Looked like boot guy was the poet – good clear set of his prints by the wall next to Junior where the writing was.

A lot of shit smashed on the floor – a lamp in a mess of pieces, books thrown around, Hurley's briefcase dumped out, the papers everywhere.

Lynch turned to the uniform watching the door. "Whole place trashed like this?"

"Yeah. We swept the joint when we got here, just making sure it was empty. Not much blood once you get by here, couple footprints in the dining room, but they ripped everything up pretty good."

"Like they were looking for something?"

"Could be," said the uniform. "More like they just wanted to. You get to the john, you'll see somebody ripped off the toilet seat and hung it over the light fixture. What's the point in that?"

"Anything else?"

"Smelled dope when we got here."

Lynch took a sniff. "Yeah, a little. OK. ME guys are here, so you and your partner get on the canvas, see if the neighbors got anything."

••••

First thing the next morning, Lynch met with Dr Thomas Anthony, the ME. Sitting in the glassed-in office Anthony had off the autopsy room, metal furniture, chemical smell. Anthony was a big guy, bald, huge head, which, Lynch knew, was pretty much full of brains.

"Thanks for turning things around so quick. Long night for you guys, I know," said Lynch.

"At least I'm done for now, detective. I don't suspect you'll be sleeping until you have an arrest."

"I'm hoping you have something to help me out there, doc."

"To start, you've got multiple assailants. Three sets of footprints, definitely contemporaneous because they walked on one another's tracks a couple of times. At least one of your assailants is likely colored, because we've got a couple of Negroid hairs stuck to the ax handle. They were in Stefanski's blood, so they were deposited while the ax was being used. One set of tracks is from a pair of Converse All-Stars, size twelve. One is from a pair of Red Wing work boots, ten and a half. I'm working on the other one. Smooth soles, heel, more like a dress shoe. Smaller, maybe a nine. We found the butts from two marijuana cigarettes in the room."

"Wonderful," said Lynch. "Coloreds and drugs – old man Hurley's head is gonna explode. Cause of death looks pretty straightforward. Standard ax murder. Not that I ever had an ax murder before."

"Almost impossible to tell, actually," said Anthony. "Especially with Stefanski. The damage done with the ax is so severe that if there was any preexisting cause, it was obliterated. There was a mark on one rib, or should I say rib fragment, that didn't seem to correspond with an ax. But the rib cage and surrounding anatomical context were so disassociated that any findings other than death due to trauma from the ax simply can't be supported."

"What are you telling me with this marks-on-the-ribs shit?"

"You saw Stefanski. I don't have a piece of Stefanski's ribs or sternum bigger than four inches, and the pieces I have are badly damaged. However, I have one piece of rib, still connected to the sternum, that has a fresh groove in it that doesn't look like the ax wounds. Again, though, with so much trauma, I can't do anything but report it as an anomaly."

"Groove like what?"

"Like a gunshot, actually, if I had to guess."

"This groove, where was it located?"

"Not on the rib itself, but along the top of the costal cartilage where it connects the third rib to the sternum."

"And a bullet goes through there, it hits what?"

"The heart."

Lynch looked at Anthony for a moment, waiting for a sign.

"You telling me Stefanski got shot?"

"No. I'm telling you that a single anomaly in the evidence could support that conclusion. Arguing against it, I have no soft tissue damage consistent with a bullet wound. Although, if Stefanski were shot prior to the ax wounds, such evidence would have been obliterated. And we recovered no slugs – not from the body, not from the scene."

"Anything else?"

"We're missing a piece of Hurley's skull and scalp from the right temple. It could have stuck to one of the assailants. It could have been tracked out. It could have been taken as a souvenir."

"That a big deal?"

"It happens. I won't say it's common."

"Sounds like there's something else you won't say."

Anthony nodded. "There's this. Most of Hurley's clothing, and Stefanski's for that matter, is soaked with blood. The clothing is lying in the blood, got walked on – it's just a mess. Except Hurley's shorts, which aren't much of a mess because he was wearing them. Which is why I noted a small amount of blood and other fluids in his underwear. Semen. Further examination revealed additional blood and semen in his rectum. I have no way of telling whose, but based on the serology, it could be Stefanski's."

Lynch's turn to be quiet. Anthony just sat, looking at him, waiting.

"You telling me Hurley's kid was queer?"

"I'm telling you he had anal intercourse shortly before his death, possibly with Stefanski."

"Willingly?"

Anthony shrugged. "No bruising not associated with the head wound, no defensive marks. No significant tearing in the anus. Anuses are not designed for sex, so in cases of anal rape, tearing is usually evident."

"So you got a few things making you think," said Lynch.

"It's the combination of them. By itself, the missing piece of Hurley's head? Like I said, it happens. But I've got this weird groove on Stefanski. So, suppose somebody shot him but didn't want it to look like they shot him. So they take the ax, chop him up, dig the slug out of him or maybe out of the floor. Now, you have this transverse ax wound on Hurley. That's a little strange. Usually when bodies come in with head trauma, the blow is descending or at a bit of an angle. That's the natural swing at somebody's head. This is pretty much straight across. Makes sense if you were a baseball. Might even make sense if the wound were to the thorax."

Lynch pictured what the doc was saying. Awkward to swing sideways at a guy's head. "OK, doc, go on."

"OK, so if you are standing up, the only way somebody takes you through the head from side to side with an ax is if they are a couple of feet taller than you. Hurley was over six feet. In this case, it looks as though Hurley was lying on the floor. We've got an ax mark in the floor under his head and wood splinters in his scalp on that side. So the transverse wound makes sense because it was a descending blow to the side of his head while he was lying down. But what's he doing on the floor?"

"Maybe he got knocked down first."

"I don't have any other sign of trauma, and, if our guy had used the ax to knock him down, I would. So there's that. Now, suppose our fictional somebody, he doesn't want Stefanski to look shot, so he does his Jack the Ripper routine on him. Suppose he also doesn't want Hurley to look shot, but Hurley's shot through the head. So he lays Hurley on the floor and cuts his head in half, and picks up the chunk that shows an entrance wound."

"OK, say I play along here. Before the ax work, what I got is one guy shot through the chest and another guy shot through the head, temple to temple. Missing chunk's from the right temple, Hurley's right-handed. Which probably makes it a murder-suicide. Hurley pops Stefanski, then pops himself. You got any powder burn on Hurley? Stippling?"

Anthony shook his head. "No. But if it was a contact wound, then it would have been very localized, localized enough to be on the missing chunk of Hurley's head."

"And with the semen stuff, maybe you have some kind of lover's quarrel. But what's with the ax shit? I mean, Hurley and Stefanski didn't chop themselves up."

"Doesn't make sense, does it?"

"So maybe this. Hurley and Stefanski do the nasty. Maybe Hurley wants to, maybe he doesn't. Either way, it sets him off. He plugs Stefanski, he plugs himself. Somebody walks in, puts it together. Somebody who doesn't want a homo murder-suicide to be the story. So we get the ax and the footprints and the blood graffiti and all of that."

"Makes you sound like a fruitcake when you say it out loud, doesn't it, detective?"

"Little bit, yeah."

"Another problem with that. Time of death. Based on body

temperatures, we've got a time of death right around midnight. You guys got there by 12.30, right?"

"Yeah. We got an anonymous disturbance call. Somebody said he'd heard some shouting, saw three black guys jump in a red Dodge, tear ass off. Call came in at 12.17."

"Thirty minutes, forty five minutes tops, between time of death and you guys coming through the door. Hard to see a murder-suicide, then somebody finding the bodies, and then somebody staging this whole mess in a half hour."

"So your call is what?"

"I go to court, all I can say is that the evidence points to both of them being hacked to death with an ax, time of death around midnight."

"And that's what's in the report?"

The ME smiled. "We've got the report. Of course, sometimes I get a report done, and then I get some other results in, so I file an addendum. It just so happens that I didn't get the results on the semen, blood typing, and what have you in on time for the main report, so that's in this addendum." He pushed a manila envelope across the table to Lynch. "There should be a copy of that with the official report, too, of course. It would be unlike me to forget to file one. But it has been a long night."

"Leaving the ball in my court?"

"You decide it's gotta come out, I'll back you up. You decide one thing's got nothing to do with the other, I see no reason to have young Hurley's reputation destroyed."

Lynch thought about it. "Fucking Stefanski. What I've heard, he always did have trouble keeping it zipped."

"De mortuis nihil nisi bonum," said Anthony.

"Been a long time since my altar boy days, doc."

"Say nothing but good of the dead."

"Gonna be a short eulogy, then, in Stefanski's case."

CHAPTER 10 – RIVER FOREST, ILLINOIS

Present Day

Rusty Lynch lived in one of the big old stone houses set back off Oak Park Avenue just as you drove north into River Forest, place probably going for seven or eight hundred grand. Uncle Rusty paid cash for the joint the month after he got back into town from doing his eleven-month hitch at the Club Fed up in Wisconsin, same Club Fed where Dan Rostenkowski worked on his short game after getting caught with his pinkies in the House Post Office cookie jar. In fact, Uncle Rusty and Rostenkowski had been in together for the bulk of Rusty's jolt. Rusty'd been in on some kickback beef the Feds cooked up when he wouldn't play ball on one of their stings. He'd fallen on his sword for the Hurleys in the sure and certain faith that they'd have his back when he got out. Lynch wasn't even sure Rusty liked the River Forest house. Rusty'd always been a city guy, the type that started breaking out in hives he didn't smell some diesel fumes every ten minutes. Now he's living on a half-acre of oaks pretending to be a feudal lord? Lynch figured the house was more like a fuck you at the Feds who sent Rusty up. The top Fed prosecutor who tried to flip Rusty was one of his neighbors now.

Lynch parked in Rusty's brick circle drive at the end of a line of six cars, the Grand Marquis the princes of the city drove or were driven in. Couple of the cars had drivers lounging in the front seats, listening to the radios. A stretch Mercedes at the end of the line. The driver was a retired cop Lynch knew, guy named Lewis, standing next to the car smoking, guy who'd done his twenty, then gone private. Personal security, that kind of shit. Lynch pulled out a Camel and joined him.

"Hey, Lewis. Riding shotgun for somebody?"

"Hey, Lynch. Howya doin? Yeah. Funny you turning up. Got a call from Eddie Marslovak. Thing with his mother got him freaked a little, I guess, maybe thinking somebody's coming after him. He's gotta nice ride, anyway."

Lynch looked up and down the Mercedes. "Got a bar and everything?"

"Bar, TV, couple a cell phones, some kind of hookup so his computer's on line. Like driving a space shuttle. Hey, you're workin' his mom's case, right?"

"Yeah."

"You out here to see him?"

Lynch shook his head. "Wanted to talk to Rusty real quick. Guess Uncle Rusty's still got the juice, huh?"

Lewis dropped his butt to the bricks and ground it under the toe of his wingtip. "What I hear around the Hall, more juice than ever. Taking the fall on that Fed beef, good career move, far as I can see. Got him out of the county board seat. Doesn't have to play sleight of hand to get paid no more."

"Well, not me, Lewis. Still on the city's clock." Lynch flicked half a Camel into the pine bark mulch along the side of the drive and headed for the door.

Rusty Lynch was what Lynch's old man would have been given another thirty years. Big, hair gone pure white, fine cross-hatch of busted veins over the nose and cheeks, still that sparkle in the eyes that was menace and merriment both at once. Rusty Lynch broke into a broad grin when he opened the door.

"Johnny. Fuck me, it is good to see you, boy. Get your ass inside, say hello to the fellas."

"Rusty," Lynch said, stepping into the slate-floored hall. "You're looking good."

"I'm lookin' like a fat old drunk whose clothes all have enough Xs in them to go into the dirty book business and don't I know it." The old man threw a playful jab into Lynch's gut. "But you're keepin' fit, Johnny, and you always favored your mother anyway. Good on you."

Rusty ushered Lynch into the living room, a long rectangle with a barrel-vaulted ceiling. All the furniture was wood or brown leather. Marslovak and Burke, Hurley's chief of staff, Lynch knew. They sat to the right.

"Some of you boys know my nephew, John Lynch, him being one of Chicago's finest. And, Johnny, I know you know some of the boys. Eddie I know you just met, though not the best circumstances, and you and Dick Burke go back a bit anyway."

Lynch nodded at Marslovak and Burke. Burke gave a short wave.

"Tony Lazzara's the mayor's new money man. Rod Fell's our rising star in congress, up there in Rostenkowski's old seat, and, God help me, these other fine boys are riding herd on him, out from the masters at the DNC, but I can't keep their names straight. Anyway, just wanted to show you off. Is it private business you've got?"

"Just a couple minutes is all I need, Rusty. I can come back."

"Oh, no need of that, Johnny. These sharp fellas can carry on without me for a bit." Rusty draped an arm over Lynch's shoulder and turned him toward his study.

Rusty dropped the hint of brogue and the stage Irish act as soon as he and Lynch got into his office and shut the door. Being in touch with the auld sod was always good practice in

Chicago, but Rusty had been born on the west side, just like
Lynch.

"Interesting crowd," Lynch said.

"I swear, Johnny, I work harder at this off-the-books wise-
man shit than I ever did when I drew a paycheck."

"Still drawing a check, from what I hear."

"Well, I'm doin' all right. I've always told you, Johnny, we
look after one another in this town. You never did want to
hear it, though."

"Just not my game."

"How's your mother? Got down a couple weeks back, she
was still hanging on."

"Gotta be soon, I figure. Not like there's much left they can
cut off."

"Tough thing. You've been good to her Johnny." .

"She was good to me."

Rusty nodded, made a toasting motion with his glass. "So
what brings you out? Not that you aren't welcome."

Lynch pulled the Wrigley shot he'd taken from the Marslovak
house out of the envelope and handed it to Rusty.

"What do you make of this?"

Rusty looked at the photo for a minute. "Santo and Kessinger.
What you put that at Johnny? Give that about a nine on a
scale of ten, wouldn't you? And for old EJ Marslovak. Bet his
boy would love to have this."

"EJ?"

"Edward Jacob. Never did get the whole line score on him.
Crew foreman at Streets and San, know that much. Supervised
a lot of the work when himself ripped up the old Taylor street
neighborhood to put in that UIC campus starting back in the
mid-Sixties. Got himself noticed somewhere along the line,
round about '70, I think. Anyway, word came down from
on high. I gave him some precinct work, some ward work,
bounced him around the north side for a while, tried to work

him in with the Polack crowd on Milwaukee Avenue, but he just never made the grade. Pretty clear the big guy owed him one, and the big guy was pretty insistent on squaring his debts. Not so clear what he owed him for."

"So he was a player?"

Rusty shook his head. "Big guy wanted him to be a player, but EJ didn't have the appetite for it. God, I remember him at the Connemara Ball, this has got to be maybe 1971. He's got on some green tux he picked up at some rental shop. His wife, she's got some silly getup on. You never saw two souls lookin' more lost. Himself comes up, asks Helen to dance, trying to make her at home. Look on her face the whole time, you'd think Satan was trying to butt fuck her. They were out the door by 9 o'clock. Speaking of which, you goin' this year?"

"The Connemara? I don't know, Rusty."

"You should make an appearance, Johnny. People miss you. Your old man, he was well loved, and there's them that would like to make a gesture to his boy. You're leaving a lot on the table, son. You got a whole inheritance waitin' on you. You know I can lay it out for you any time you like."

"Thanks, Rusty. I know you told the old man you'd look out for me. I'm making my way, though."

"Don't get touchy on me now. Nobody's saying you can't pull your own wagon. Just wondering does it have to be uphill both ways all the time with you. You're owed, Johnny. Nothing more than that."

"Those debts seem to go both ways, Rusty."

Rusty gave a little snort. "That they do, my boy. That they do."

Back in the car, Lynch picked up his phone, checked his messages, hoping Liz had called back. Nothing. Little feeling in his gut. Might as well be back in high school. She'd been in circulation better than a year, had a couple of drinks, maybe it was just a thing. Nothing saying a woman couldn't just be looking for a little touch.

"Jesus," he said to himself, pulling his sunglasses off the visor. "Might as well go home and watch Oprah."

Lynch took Harlem back down toward the Eisenhower, then cut east onto Jackson cruising the west side back toward the Loop, heading toward the United Center. His Crown Vic wasn't a marked unit, but it was marked enough for this neighborhood. Lynch watched the look outs on some of the hot corners scurrying ahead, letting the street dealers know five-0 was on the block. Lynch rode with the window cranked down a couple turns, taking in the sights and sounds, just showing the flag a little, letting his chat with Rusty percolate.

Lynch wasn't sure he was worried about Eddie Marslovak being out at the house. Eddie moved a lot of money around town, both on the books and through back channels, so he and Rusty, they'd be dipping their sticks in the same hole often enough. The rest of it – Burke, this Lazzara guy, Pretty Boy Fell – that pointed to some official deal, not something related to the shooting. Interesting that Eddie wanted some security, though. Lynch would think about that.

Lynch was more curious about Rusty's quick spiel on Marslovak. Usually, Rusty was slow, patching things together, stopping to think about this guy or that guy, rummaging around the fifty years of hardball politics that cluttered up his head. So his rehearsed version of the EJ Marslovak story had Lynch wondering. Either Rusty'd been thinking about Marslovak himself – which was natural, given Helen's murder – or somebody had tipped him off that Lynch might be asking.

Just as Lynch swung north onto the Kennedy, his phone rang.

"Lynch."

"Hey, John Lynch." Liz. Son of a bitch. "Thanks for calling this morning. It meant something. Saved me thinking all day.

You know, was it just the booze or something."

Lynch paused, wondering how far to go with this. Fuck it. Just roll with it. "Wasn't just the booze, Johnson."

"Not very macho and cop-like, Lynch. You OK?"

"Fine. Thinking about trading in my nine, maybe getting a nice .22. One of those little chrome plated automatics? Mother-of-pearl handle? Later maybe get my legs waxed."

"Now you're sounding better. You scared me there for a second. Nice to know that you managed to squeeze in a thought about me, though."

"A couple, yeah."

"Nice thoughts?"

"Well, not PG nice, but nice."

That chuckle. Already falling for that chuckle. "Still want to take me to dinner?"

"Yeah."

"Like a real date? I go home and change and you pick me up and everything?"

"Yeah, like that."

"You going to open the doors for me, help me with my coat?"

"Don't need a coat. It's nice out."

"Help me pull up my zipper then?"

"Help you pull it down, even."

"So a full-service date?"

"Yes, ma'am."

That chuckle again. "Pick me up at 7.00, John Lynch. And bring me flowers."

Lynch checked his watch. Half past one.

CHAPTER 11 – CHICAGO

Lynch went straight to Starshak's office. Starshak was wearing what he always wore – a solid navy blue suit, white shirt, simple tie, half a pound of crap in his hair keeping everything locked in place.

Starshak's office was always neat. He didn't like shit out. Desk, low filing cabinet along the right wall, tall cabinet back in the corner. On the low cabinet he had a line of framed photos – his wife, the two daughters, one family shot that had the dog in it, big Collie, the kind with the darker hair. A fern hung in front of the window on the left. Thing was huge, and Starshak was always futzing with it, picking off dead leaves, spraying it with the squirt bottle he kept in his desk. On top of the tall filing cabinet, Starshak had a glass case. Starshak made model airplanes. In fact, he was some kind of hot-shot modeler, even had some plaques on the wall near the cabinet. Every month or so he'd rotate a new plane into the case. Lynch had been out to his house a couple of times, holiday things Starshak's wife would put on for the squad. Whole basement was walled with display cases holding Starshak's planes.

Lynch was pretty sure the plane in the case was new.

"New plane, boss?"

Starshak looked up. "Yeah. German. FW200 Condor. Scourge of the Atlantic. Long range recon mostly. Tracked conveys and called in the Wolf Packs."

Lynch nodded.

"So how'd it go with the SWAT guy? He any help?"

"You're gonna love this. He says the guy took the shot from the old Olfson factory. Fourth floor, east end. Told crime scene, they got the mobile lab down there, they're checking it out. Looks right, though."

"That's like what, halfway to the Loop?"

"Half a mile, give or take."

"This just gets better and better."

"Gave me some good stuff, though. Kind of a profile. Been lots of traffic in the old Olfson place, too – lot of garbage, lot of tagging. Based on the graffiti, looks like some offshoot of the Vice Lords hangs out in there. Gave the gang crimes guys a call, see if they can get me any names. Be somebody to talk to anyway. Took a better look around old lady Marslovak's house, too. Found this." Lynch handed Starshak the Wrigley shot.

"So Marslovak's old man had some clout?"

"Talked to my uncle about it. He says Hurley the First owed the guy for something and tried to square it by wiring him in, but it didn't take. Something about the whole thing seems off. Also, Rusty had some conclave going on out there – Eddie Marslovak, Burke from the mayor's office, that new finance guy, Lazzara, Pretty Boy Fell, couple of DNC guys. And Marslovak's got Pete Lewis riding shotgun for him now."

"So where do you want to go with this? I mean, you start rattling those cages, we both better get our Kevlar shorts on cause somebody's gonna try to rip our nuts off."

"I know. Don't even know if there's anything there. But what am I supposed to do, not look?"

"Nobody's saying don't look. Just look careful."

Lynch nodded. "Slo-mo around?"

Shlomo Bernstein was a new detective in the district. Came from a rich family on the North Shore, decided he wanted to be a cop when he was six. Parents humored him. When he wanted to go to the academy out of college – *summa cum laude* from Princeton – his dad made him a deal. Do graduate school. Keep your options open. If you still want to be a cop, fine. So Shlomo took second in the MBA class at the U of C in about ten months and went straight to the academy. Made detective in record time. Probably be commissioner in another six, seven weeks.

Starshak called out into the room. "Slo-mo, my office."

Bernstein was about five-six, needed his boots and winter coat to go to one hundred and fifty. Good looking guy, though. Very sharp dresser, like some junior-sized male model.

Bernstein walked in the office and looked at the plane in the case.

"Condor, right? Focke-Wulf 200?"

Starshak smiled. "Yeah. Just finished it."

"You went with the Arctic markings. What, the Murmansk run?"

Starshak laughed. "Bernstein, why don't you get your ass on *Jeopardy*, make a couple million? Say, what's on your plate right now? You got time to help Lynch with this Marslovak thing?"

Bernstein's eyes lit up like a fourteen year-old finding his dad's *Playboy* stash. "Hell, yes. What do you need?"

"Couple of things," Lynch said. "First, looks like our guy took the shot from better than seven hundred yards. Can't be too many guys around can put a hole through somebody's heart from that distance. Get me some background, see what you can find."

"Like Wimbledon Cup winners, that sort of thing?"

"This ain't tennis," said Starshak.

"Wimbledon Cup is the national thousand-yard shooting championship," said Bernstein.

"Jesus, Slo-mo," said Lynch. "You got a long gun at home? I gotta put you in the mix for this?"

Slo-mo shrugged. "Just read it somewhere."

Lynch shook his head. "OK, the other thing. Unlimber that underpaid MBA brain of yours. Take a look at MarCorp, last few years. See if something jumps out at you, somebody that might want to come back at Eddie Marslovak. Somebody that would know where to find this kind of talent."

"OK. Am I gonna get in the field on this at all, or are you gonna keep my ass parked behind the computer all day?"

"Who knows, Slo-mo. Find me something nice, and I might take you out for ice cream later."

"Yeah, yeah. Gonna get calluses on my ass. Could have done that at Merrill Lynch for another couple hundred grand a year. All right. I'll see what I can get. Then I'll go home, dust my gun."

"Tell you what, Slo-mo. You get me something nice, and, after ice cream, how about we go roust some bad-ass homies, tune em up a little, maybe cap some nines on their asses?"

Slo-mo smiled. "Double dip, Lynch, with sprinkles. Then we go roust some goyim."

Back at his desk, Lynch found a stack of messages. Mess of reporters. Two messages from crime scene, one from McCord, all three marked urgent. He called McCord's cell.

"What do you got?" Lynch asked.

"I'm at your factory, Lynch, checking on your shooting site. Also heard you wanted gang crimes to check on who might be hanging out here. I think your shooter may have found your gangbangers already. We got us a clearance sale on stiffs."

CHAPTER 12 – CHICAGO

1971

Hastings Clarke lived in one of the older high-end buildings along Lake Shore Drive, just north from Oak Street Beach. Dark paneling, heavy furniture, thick oriental carpets.

"Nice place, Mr Clarke," Declan Lynch said as Clarke ushered him in.

"Thank you," said Clarke. "And please, call me Hastings. How can I help? I'm very anxious for David's killers to be found."

"Let's start with the obvious, given the ugly nature of the crime scene. Was David getting any threats?"

"David could be very forceful discussing the issues – you've seen that. But he was also a very fair-minded man. You've heard what he's had to say about his father's politics, yet his father and that whole political machine enthusiastically supported him. I couldn't have imagined anyone wishing harm to David – he devoted so much of himself. Still, something like this happens, and then you start to think…"

"Think about what?"

"Detective, you understand what a volatile issue race is in this city, hell, in this country. And David was one of the few honestly race-blind people I' have ever known. Absolutely without prejudice. A close friend of Dr King's, in fact. That was central, vital, to his campaign. I think that's what gave him the moral authority to speak out against some of the more radical elements in the colored movement. There were a few people, a very small minority, on the fringes of that movement who resented him – some, in fact, who I believe find exacerbating racial strife to be in their best interests. We did get some ugly mail – calling David just another white massuh, that kind of thing – from those people."

"Anyone in particular come to mind?"

"There's a group called the AMN Commando, AMN standing for Any Means Necessary. A lot of its members used to be associated with Fred Hampton and the Panthers. And I want to make it clear, detective, that I am not equating the two. Hampton may have been a polarizing figure, but he did a lot of good for his community. His extra-judicial murder – and I know that may offend you as a policeman in this city, but that's what it was, and David agreed with me on that – that's driven some in the Negro community in dangerously radical directions."

"So you think these AMN guys are worth a look?"

"I didn't say that, detective. You asked about threats, and I wanted to be up front with you. My real fear, to be honest? The mayor, Riley, men like that, they'll seize on this to push their agenda, solve their problems. I hate to inject race into David's murder when he's been such a champion of the colored community. That the bigot element might seize on David's death for their own ends, that would be intolerable."

"That why you're thinking of running? I hear maybe you're throwing your hat in the ring."

"It is a consideration. I will wait and see who the Hurleys bring forward. But I am committed to seeing David's ideals represented in this election. I am willing to make that sacrifice if necessary."

Sacrifice, Lynch thought to himself. The bullshit you had to listen to out of these people. "OK, let's change gears here a bit. Can you tell me what David was doing at Stefanski's? Can you fill me in on the timing there?" Lynch watching Clarke, seeing a little tightening around the eyes during the question.

"The mayor wanted David to talk with Stefanski about some local political issues. Let's face it, as much as David was committed to change, he understood he needed to be elected if he wanted to change things. He couldn't ignore the Democratic machine's ability to deliver votes. It's my understanding that Stefanski was the connection to some of the city workers that drive turn-out efforts. As distasteful as David found some of the local politics, at least he grew up in this climate. He knew these men, even if he didn't always approve of them. He had a way of pressing his concerns without damaging those relationships. So he met with Stefanski regularly. I did not attend those meetings. My presence in certain circles seems only to inflame things."

"So David was spending a lot of time with Stefanski?"

"As I said, detective, I didn't attend David's meetings with Stefanski. Certainly, he'd meet with him from time to time." Clarke seeming less and less comfortable.

"He have a decent relationship with the guy?"

"I really don't understand your focus here." Clarke sounding a little short now.

"The murders happened at Stefanski's place and they were pretty ugly. You see that level of violence, lots of times that points at something personal."

"I don't know how to respond to that, detective. I've heard stories, of course, about Stefanski. A bit of a reputation. I suppose this could have been something aimed at him, something David got caught up in."

"Kind of a late night, though, wasn't it? Midnight?"

"Nature of the beast in an election."

"OK, another thing. I understand that David owned a gun."

A little laugh from Clarke. "Quite a row about that, actually. His father insisted, after Bobby Kennedy's assassination, and after King's. He wanted David to be able to protect himself. Silly, really. I mean, look at those shootings. What good would a gun have done either man?"

"It was a Walther, a PPK?"

"I wouldn't know, detective. We used to do some skeet shooting, summers out on the Long Island, so shotguns I can tell you something about. Pistols are beyond me."

"Small automatic, the kind from the James Bond movies."

"That would be David. He did have a sense of style."

"He carry it?"

"He did that night, actually. I saw it in his briefcase that afternoon, for all the good it did him."

Not at the crime scene, Lynch thought, so somebody took it. The gun turns up, that will help.

CHAPTER 13 – CHICAGO

1971

Five men were in the conference room at City Hall when Declan Lynch arrived shortly after 9.30am.

"Sorry I'm late," said Lynch. "Just got word to come down when I got to the station."

"No problem, Lynch," said Riley. "Thanks for coming."

Riley had his coat off, over the back of his chair, and his cuffs turned up over his wrists. Two almost identical guys in black suits sat across the table with a tape deck sitting in front of them. Crew cuts, that tight-ass look Feds usually had. Bob Riordan, head of Hurley's Red Squad – an informal police team charged with tracking peaceniks, Reds, the Weatherman, Black Panthers and, Lynch figured, probably Republicans – sat at the near end of the table. At the far end sat a compact man, perhaps five feet nine inches, in a tan summer suit, three-button natural shoulder, a white shirt, and red and blue rep tie.

Riley waved around the table. "Gentleman, this is Detective Declan Lynch. Lynch, Riordan you know. Over here we have agents Harris and McDonald, FBI COUNTERINTELPRO. They coordinate with Riordan on, well, whatever needs coordinating. And over here we have Ezekiel Fisher. Zeke, you wanna tell Detective Lynch what you do?"

"No," said Fisher.

Riley chuckled. "It's alright, Lynch. Same answer I always get. It's OK. He's a friend of Hurley's. Anyway, he helps out."

"So what's the drill here, Riley?" Lynch asked.

"Couple things. First off, it's the mayor's kid we're dealing with here, so he called J. Edgar, told him he wanted some help on it. Hope you don't mind."

"Fine by me," said Lynch.

"Second, papers are already going bat shit with this, and you know how the old man feels about press, especially around his family. So he wants to play this real tight. Wants to keep it to the players here in this room until we need something else."

"Again, fine by me, but my captain's gonna wanna know what I'm up to."

"Commissioner's talking to your captain now. You need anything from him, you got it, but he don't need to know shit," said Riley.

"Gonna make things ticklish for me, just so you know."

"Lynch, this turns out, you can get your ticket punched any way you like. It don't, Captain's the least of your problems."

Lynch paused a minute, stared Riley down. Not like he didn't know that, didn't mean he had to like it.

"OK," Lynch said finally, "so what are we doing today?"

"The old man, he was telling me that Junior was catching some shit from this one nigger group – the AMN Commando. Panther types. Wanted that looked into."

"Yeah," said Lynch. "Interviewed Hastings Clarke yesterday. He brought them up. Seemed like he wanted to raise the radical black angle and shoot it down at the same time."

Riley nodded. "Junior was a little sensitive about race stuff. It's all the rage with these guys, brotherhood of man and all that shit. So Clarke wants to keep the coloreds on his side. The thing, though, is the old man, he hears maybe some of these guys had a hard on for Junior, he checks em out, calls Riordan, who runs things past our buddies from Washington here, and God knows who Zeke runs things past. Thing is, this comes up," Riley nodded his head at the tape deck, "and we thought you should hear it." Riley nodded at the Feds, and MacDonald clicked the tape on.

Negro voice, sounded like anyway. Giving a speech in front of a pretty raucous crowd. "We ain't waitin' no more. We ain't askin' no more. Rights ain't some scraps we wait for from the massuh's table. We don't need them from nobody – we own them. We was born with them. All we need to do is keep Whitey from takin' them away. Pursuit of happiness? You ask any Black man wants to work for what any white man gets for free. They be takin' it away. Liberty? You ask our brothers locked up in white jails because they march for their rights or fight for their rights. They be takin' that away. Life? You ask Fred Hampton bout that when you see him, shot in his bed by the Chicago pigs. Butchered in his bed. They be takin' life away. But we gonna let them take ours? No. By any means necessary. Fight in the streets if we gotta. By any means necessary. Butcher the pigs if we gotta. By any means necessary–" The Fed clicked the tape off.

"Butcher the pigs?" said Lynch.

"Thought that might ring a bell," Riley answered.

"Who's on the tape?"

Zeke Fisher sat forward in his seat, folded his hands in front of him on the table. "He calls himself Simba now, which is Swahili for lion. His real name is Harold James, Jr. Born August 3, 1948 to Rosa and Harold James in Mobile, Alabama. Moved to the south side of Chicago in September of 1955. He was a player with the Black Panthers here, mostly with some of the social programs they were running around the South Side. After the Hampton shooting, he turned severely militant."

"He's organizing the gangs," Riordan said. "We got some informants on the inside of that. Hampton had that supposed gang truce, all that crap about the niggers gotta stop fighting each other, gotta fight us instead, so this James guy knows that crowd. What's he's doing now is trying to turn that into his own little army."

Harris, the FBI guy, spoke up. "We've obtained tapes of other speeches in which this butcher the pigs rhetoric has come up. He's very hostile to the police – to any authority, really."

Lynch felt like he was sitting through a sales job – everybody in the room adding his piece to the pitch.

"The thing is," Lynch said, "why would some guy who's known for this butcher the pigs line go and paint it on a wall?"

"That's a valid question," said Fisher. "I don't think we can look at this like a traditional crime where the intent is to avoid detection. This was a political act. I believe that James wants to create a direct conflict with the political authority, and especially with the more liberal politicians that, in essence, are his competition. He wants to create an unbridgeable barrier between the radical movement and traditional political solutions. In essence, he wants a rebellion."

"Sounds like a death wish," said Lynch.

"Hey, he wants to die, I want him dead, I got your racial harmony right here," said Riordan.

Lynch stopped Riley in the hall outside the conference room. "Listen, couple of things I want to run past you without the audience."

"OK," said Riley, pushing open the door to the men's room. "Step into my office."

Riley walked over to a urinal and started taking a leak. "So what's up?"

"ME found something on Hurley once he got him in the shop. No easy way to put this. Looks like Junior was a fag. He had semen in his ass. Stefanski's semen, so far as the ME can tell." Lynch was watching closely to see how Riley took this.

Riley kept pissing. Finished, zipped up, turned around.

"This on paper?"

Lynch decided to play a little dodge ball on that one. "Not in the ME's report. He wasn't sure this had anything to do with the murder. Didn't want it out there if it doesn't need to be. Kind of a hard thing to overlook, though."

"Yeah. Jesus. Fuckin' Stefanski. I mean, I knew he was a goddamn pervert, but a turd burglar? Damn."

"I know. So this colored shit? Could be. But then I got this fag thing, and I gotta wonder."

"Yeah. I can see that. So where you going with it?"

"Gotta run it out."

"Yeah. Old man know?"

"Haven't told him."

"Let's hope you don't have to. He's got a little kill-the-messenger streak in him."

"Anyway, wanted you to know, just so nothing comes at you out of leftfield. You can decide what the mayor needs to know. Speaking of which, you want me to fill in the Fed twins or your pet spook?"

"The Feds are just here to help out with the nigger shit. Don't tell them nothin' on this other stuff. Fisher? Don't even talk to that bastard you don't talk to me first. That son of a bitch makes my sack shrivel up. As far as what the mayor needs to know, I ever gotta tell him the kid was taking it up the ass, we're both screwed."

Later, Riley and Ezekiel Fisher walked through the plaza, past the Picasso statue.

"ME got the fag stuff," Riley said.

"We had to figure that was possible," said Fisher. "Is it being pursued?"

"This Lynch guy, he's got the bit in his teeth. I'll leave that with you."

"I understand," said Fisher.

CHAPTER 14 - CHICAGO

1971

Declan Lynch pulled up the alley behind the house on Neenah and parked the Impala next to the garage. He was working on the upstairs bathroom with his boy and had all kinds of crap in the garage. His wife Julie was kneeling down, facing the house, working at the strip of flowers she always kept along the wall. Her butt sticking out at him in a pair of tight plaid Bermudas.

"Damn, yard looks better already, long as you stay bent over like that."

She sat back on her haunches, flicked her dark hair out of her face, and turned to look at him over her shoulder.

"You are just a fiend, Declan Lynch."

"Trust me on this one, doll, I'm way down on the fiend scale."

She got up and walked across the small yard, meeting him at the gate, quick hug and peck.

"So, big shot, how's life down at City Hall?"

Lynch blew out a long breath. "Baby, month from now I'm either gonna be commissioner or I'm looking at life on traffic duty."

She gave him a quick squeeze, just letting him know how things stood with her. Felt good.

"You should get upstairs and see the kids. They've got a surprise for you."

"That good or bad?"

She smiled. "I haven't checked yet."

Lynch walked past Missy, their old black lab, sleeping against the fence next to the dog house he and Johnny had built a couple years back, went in the side door and up the stairs. House was the typical quasi-bungalow that filled up the whole northwest side. Upstairs had one big unfinished room when he bought the place, with two bedrooms, kitchen, one bath, and a parlor down. Last summer, he'd roughed in the plumbing to put another bath upstairs, Johnny working right there with him. Kid had a real talent for it, picking up stuff just watching. Through the winter, he and Johnny had roughed in the walls, turned the rest of the upstairs space into the new master bedroom, put the shower and toilet and sink in. All that was left was getting the tile down on the bathroom floor and painting.

As Lynch went up the stairs, he could hear Johnny talking to his sister.

"That's it, Collie. Just run that rag along there and get that extra grout up before it dries on the tiles. You're doing great."

He heard Colleen giggle. "It's cold."

At the top of the stairs, Lynch could see the boxes from the tile place, couple of corner pieces Johnny had snipped off sitting in an empty box.

"Fe, fie, fo, fum," Lynch rumbled, turning the corner toward the bath. "I better not find things screwed up by no bums."

"Daddy!" Colleen squealed, running out of the bathroom. She was only seven. Johnny walked out behind her, wiping his hands on a shop towel. Smile on his face told Lynch all he needed to know – kid had done things right.

"Hey, Dad."

"How's it going, buddy?"

"Got the floor in. Collie's just helping me finish up. Gotta seal the grout tomorrow."

"Let's have a look."

Lynch stuck his head in the door. Floor looked perfect. Couple more cut-up tiles outside the door than there should have been for a floor this size. Figured the kid measured wrong, or they cracked on him. But that's why you got extras, and that's how you learned.

"Damn. Looks real nice."

"Didn't we do a good job, Daddy?" asked Colleen.

Lynch scooped her up. "You did a great job, Collie. Your brother teach you how?"

Great big smile spread across her little round face. "Yep."

"Is he a good teacher?"

Suddenly, she looked serious. "Daddy, he is the best brother in the whole world."

Lynch reached out and tousled John's hair. "Guess I'm a lucky man." He buried his face in Colleen's neck and blew a loud raspberry. She squealed again, Johnny smiled, and Lynch heard his wife coming in the back door.

"If the construction crew will come downstairs, I've got a great big bunch of weeds I've pulled out ready for dinner."

Colleen laughing. "Mom, we can't eat weeds!"

His wife shouting up the stairs, "Well, I might have something else for the picky eaters."

Johnny smiling at him like he got it, like he understood how much it meant to be part of all this. Lynch thinking so what if he got traffic duty for life.

Later, Lynch was in the kitchen grabbing a beer from the fridge when his wife called him from the living room where she was watching the news.

"Honey, you better get out here. You're going to want to see this."

Lynch walked into the living room just in time to see Simba or whatever his name was standing on the street in front of several of his followers almost screaming into a row of microphones, looking a little washed out in the lights for the cameras.

"White fear-mongers tryin' to incite hatred, say it's the Black man you have to fear. It's the Black man gonna break into your house, gonna kill you in your sleep, gonna rape your women. When Fred Hampton tried to say the Black man don't have to live in fear, don't have to live in shame, it wasn't no Black man came for him. It was the white cops come and shot him in his bed. The white pigs come and murdered him and then walked away smiling while the white judges and white DA all say, 'Yah suh, dat's fine. You go on and shoot down that black dog.' And now I hear dey coming for me, saying I killed the mayor's pet boy, pretty boy walking around talkin' how only the fine white man can save us poor Black folk. You pigs all come on. But don't expect me to be lyin' asleep in my bed. You want war, we be warriors." He thrust his fist into the air, holding it there, and the line of black men behind him did the same. "By any means necessary." All of them shouting in unison. Then he turned and walked back through the middle of the pack.

He was wearing a pair of black Converse All-Stars.

CHAPTER 15 – CHICAGO

Present Day

When John Lynch got to the Olfson plant, the mobile lab was pulled up near the east end. Meat wagon from the ME's office after that, couple more units from technical services. Somebody'd set up a generator near the door, buzzing along like a power mower, couple of lines running inside. Lynch saw one of the lab guys coming out the door. Skinny guy with glasses and hair that was always falling in his face. Lynch trying to think of his name, then it coming to him. Novak. Kind of a grump. Lot of the guys called him No Sack because he'd lost a nut to testicular cancer a couple years back.

"Novak, how's it going?" Lynch asked.

"You sure can pick em, Lynch. There's like a billion square feet in this place."

"Room work out? This the place?"

"Looks like. We got fresh gunshot residue on the inside of the window. Not much else. No prints that we can find, at least not upstairs. McCord call you about the stiffs?"

"Yeah. What's that about?"

"The gangbangers you were looking for, ones that hung out here? Found four of them in the basement."

"I'm assuming dead?"

Little smile from Novak. "Why don't you go on down and

have a look. Hate to spoil it for you."

"OK. Hey, where're we at with ballistics from yesterday?"

"You know, Lynch, I was going to check on that this morning, but then I got a call about how I had to get out here and toss an entire abandoned factory. Then it turns out we got a multiple in the basement, and, with the factory being the likely shooting location and being better than half a mile from the DOA yesterday, that gives me a crime scene about the size of Rhode Island. Ballistics is working on it. You want to call in, be my guest."

One of the lines from the generator ran up the stairs. The other snaked down the hall and into a doorway on the left. Lynch followed the second line down the basement stairs. The tech guys had shop lights set up every twenty feet. Long hallway, doors leading out, all on the right side. What was left of some old furnaces, couple of rooms with machinery in them. Where the building turned in was a large room. Somebody'd set up some furniture down here. Green plastic chairs, a beat up old table with a big ass boombox on it. Three of the chairs were knocked over. Couple of ice chests under the table. Popeye's wrappers and quart Beck's bottles everywhere. Lynch saw three of the numbered yellow plastic tents the crime scene guys liked to set out to mark stuff. One was just to his left, inside the door. He could see a piece of brass on the floor next to it. Lots of gang graffiti. At the far end of the room was a dark area that ran back under the wall. Just outside that, four body bags were lined up on the floor. Lynch had seen plenty of the ME's bags, these looked different. McCord was crouched near the end of the last bag on the right, had the zipper open. He looked up.

"Hey, Lynch. Welcome to Pee-wee's playhouse."

Lynch nodded. "You guys get new bags?"

"Nope. Perp must have bagged them for us. These look

military. Bagged the bodies and shoved them back up under the wall here. Figure it's that Keep Chicago Clean shit Hurley's always pushing. Even your criminal element's getting with the program."

"Got a perp with his own body bags?"

McCord just shrugged.

"See we got some brass. They shot?"

"Haven't unbagged them yet, figured you'd want to see everything in situ. But we've got no blood on the floor, no splatter on the walls. You want to help me unwrap them?"

Lynch pulled on a pair of latex gloves and helped McCord slide the bags out from under the stiffs. Four black males. As McCord and Lynch worked the last one out, his head lolled around like it was attached to the body with a piece of string. Two 9mm Smiths clanked in the bottom of the bag under the body.

"So these the gangbangers you were looking for?" asked McCord.

"They got the right tattoos, they're wearing the right colors, looks like my boys. Guess they won't be answering any questions. How long you think they've been down here?"

"They're limp, so rigor's come and gone. Bags kept the bugs out, so we didn't get any help there, but based on some of the discoloration, a couple days anyway. Your guy must have run into them while he was casing the joint and decided he didn't want their company."

While McCord looked over the bodies, Lynch slipped a pen through the trigger guard of one of the pistols and sniffed the barrel. Fired recently. Tried the other. That one, too. He checked one of the pieces of brass on the floor. 9mm.

"Sure nobody got shot? Somebody got off a few rounds in here. Cement walls, had to be like a fucking pinball game."

"No gun or knife wounds on these guys. Number four, clearly a broken neck. Way broken, completely dislocated. Number two here? Got some blood from the nose but not much. You've heard of that shoving a guy's nose into his brain shit? Think somebody may have done it. This nose is way out of whack, and that should have bled like hell. Unless, of course, you die and somebody lays you on your back. Bet I find a mess of blood in his sinuses. Number three here, he almost looks like a strangulation. You got your cyanosis and such, but no ligature marks on the neck. Do got what looks like blunt trauma to the throat, though. Somebody may have crushed his trachea for him. Number one here? Not a clue. I don't see a thing."

"Somebody threw some shots down here."

"We'll test these guys for residue. Maybe they were shooting while your guy was busting them up."

"Some guy walks in here, takes on these four – and they all look like they've been in a few scrapes – snaps the one guy's neck, shoves the other guy's nose up his head, crushes a trachea, and, what, scares this last guy to death, and they're shooting at him, and he walks out?"

"I keep telling you, Lynch, I just do the science."

"You wanna switch jobs?"

"That mean I get to date that reporter chick you took home last night?"

"That on CNN or something?"

"Or something."

"No. I keep the reporter chick."

"Fuck it, then."

Lynch stripped off the gloves and shoved them in his pocket. "OK, I'm outta here. I'll tell Novak to go ahead and process the room. Once you get anything solid on our friends here, let me know."

CHAPTER 16 – RESTON, VIRGINIA

"Fisher's first mistake," said Chen, handing Weaver a manila file.

"He doesn't make them," said Weaver.

"The Post Office's mistake, actually," said Chen.

"OK. What have you got?"

"We found a bill for a post office box rental from a UPS store in Fredericksburg at Fisher's house."

Weaver shook his head. "That's a plant. Fisher wouldn't leave anything he didn't want us to find. And he stopped his mail service before he took off."

"This item was delivered to the wrong address. One of Fisher's neighbors found it in their box and dropped it in his slot after Fisher stopped his mail service."

"You check the envelope?"

"Prints and DNA. Fisher never touched it."

"OK. So what did we get?"

"We checked the box in Fredericksburg. Fisher closed it the day he left town, but it has not been re-rented. One piece of mail was left in the box. Based on the postmark, we believe it was delivered the day Fisher closed the box. A promotional mailing from American Express to Thomas McBride. This is not an identity Fisher pulled together in recent weeks to support his current activities. He has been building McBride for years. It is his failsafe."

Weaver flipped through the file. McBride owned a townhouse in Reston. He had an account with Citibank. He'd filed tax returns for the past eleven years. He had the Amex card and a Visa. Virginia drivers license and a US passport, both with Fisher's picture on them. Some activity on the Visa after Fisher's disappearance but prior to the Wisconsin shooting. Nothing recent on the Amex. But Fisher had made electronic payments to keep the accounts alive.

"He hasn't been using these since the shootings started. He has to be using something."

"Paravola theorizes that Fisher has established some one-offs, accessing the cash lines for some, using the others for one or two days, then switching. We are researching that now."

"But if he feels us getting close, he'll switch to McBride."

"Yes, sir."

A failsafe. You were in this business long enough, then you built one. Weaver had a couple. If they could put some pressure on Fisher, then he'd revert to the McBride ID, and when he did, they'd have him. It was the first piece of feel-good news Weaver had had in days.

CHAPTER 17 – CHICAGO

Lynch stopped by Bernstein's desk. "Getting anything?"

Bernstein looked up. "I'll give you a printout, pictures of semi-auto sniper rifles. Helps that it's semi-auto, because as far as I can tell most of these things are bolt action. Germans have a few, couple different H&K models. Swiss have a couple Sig Sauer models. Then you've got your Israeli Galils, and there's a Russian gun, Dragunov, though these last two are maybe less likely. Accurized assault rifles, not sniper rifles per se. Anyway, you'll know what you're looking for. I'm pulling up a list of guys who have won this or that for target shooting at your range or better. Probably a waste of time, though. I mean, you're still thinking this is some kind of hit, right? For-hire job?"

"Best I can do for now."

"I can't figure somebody who hires out wants his name on a trophy."

"Still..."

"Yeah, I know. Gotta run it out. Also getting you a list of anybody official that uses this kind of talent. FBI HRT guys, Special Forces, SEALs, Marine scout/sniper. Overseas you got your SAS... Hell, you start looking overseas, and we'll be at this awhile. Of course, most of the semi-autos are from overseas."

"Any restrictions on these or can anybody buy one?"

"None of them are fully automatic, so as far as I can tell, you got your FOID card and you know where to shop, you can pick one up. I don't think you're going to find any of these up at Farm and Fleet, though."

Lynch nodded. "OK. Let's start with the domestic groups. Find out who to call. See if anyone washed out or got pushed out for being hinky."

"OK."

"What about Marslovak?"

"Did get some interesting shit there. Couple years back he finished a big-ass roll-up in the waste hauling industry."

"What is this roll-up crap? Heard him say that on the phone."

"Find an industry with fairly standardized operations but that's segmented geographically. Waste hauling is perfect, right? I mean, picking up garbage is picking up garbage. Do it the same in Miami as you do in Seattle. You start buying out a couple big players in major markets, consolidate your back-office functions – HR, marketing, finance. Probably set up an HQ somewhere and shut down admin facilities everywhere else. Now you've got economies of scale, so you start undercutting the market on price, even working at a loss at first if the Feds don't get after you for going predatory. Cripple all the local mom-and-pops cause their cost structures are top-heavy, then you buy them out cheap. Also inverts all your vendor relationships. Suddenly, GM or whoever is selling you a thousand trucks instead of two. So you get to beat them up on the price. Once you own the market, you ratchet your prices back up where they were, and bingo. Guy like Marslovak? He's not interested in running the thing. Face it, operations is too much like work when you're used to being the house in a roulette game. Probably sells as soon as he hits critical mass."

"So you make a pile and put a lot of other people out of business and out of jobs?"

"Not quite that simple. Companies that catch the wave early

usually sell at a premium, so they do OK. But yeah. Basically you're driving inefficiencies out of a fragmented national or regional market model, one of those inefficiencies being people's jobs. You also wipe out a lot of companies."

"So that's gotta piss some people off."

"In this waste hauling gig, it's interesting who he might have been pissing off, too. People equal garbage. Businesses equal garbage. So the Big Apple is sort of the Shangri-La of trash. Biggest market in the country. Also, mobbed up to its frontal lobes. Cost structures there were completely out of whack because mostly you had the mafia taking out your garbage, and they don't work cheap."

"And Marslovak rolled it up anyway."

"Big time."

"That's good work, Slo-mo. Get what details you can. We'll go down tomorrow and drop this on Marslovak, see how that shakes out. Get your butt out of the office for a while."

"What, no ice cream?"

"Buy you a cone on the way back." Lynch took a step away and then turned back. "Hey, Slo-mo. You dress nice. Think you could maybe give me some pointers?"

Bernstein turned in his chair, gave Lynch a careful look.

"You look OK. Little GAP-commercial generic maybe, but OK."

"Yeah, but I was thinking of upgrading a little. You seem like you put some effort into this."

"I'm a Lilliputian Jew, Lynch, not an ex-jock. We're supposed to use money to get chicks, and I went with the cops instead of the investment bankers. If I don't at least dress up, bris would've been the last time anybody touched my unit. So, you want to push the old sartorial envelope? You got a date or something?"

"Something like that."

"OK. When?"

"Tonight."

Bernstein laughed, shook his head. "It's almost 4.00 Lynch. How much time you got?"

"Picking her up at 7.00."

Bernstein pulled a planner out of his desk. "I'm going to call my guy at Barney's, over on North Michigan. Andre. And yes, Lynch, he is gay, so don't sap him or anything when he measures your inseam, OK? He'll set you up nice. You're at least gonna have to get some pants hemmed, which means he's gonna have to push it through alterations for you, so slip him a little something. Otherwise I look like a schmuck."

"What, like a five?"

"Like a twenty."

"Jesus, Slo-mo. Maybe you should be working there."

"Be a twenty-grand bump in pay if I did."

CHAPTER 18 – CHICAGO

March, 1971

Lynch jerked awake in bed, looked at the clock. A little after 3am. Dog barking. Not Missy, neighbor's dog. Somebody shouting, Lynch not able to make it out. Tires squealing in the alley.

Julie sat up in bed.

"What's going on?"

Lynch getting out of bed, grabbing his short .38 from the nightstand.

"Don't know. Get downstairs, keep the kids in their rooms." Lynch stepping into his slippers and heading for the stairs.

Lynch stepped out the back door, wearing his pajama bottoms and a T-shirt. His next-door neighbor was out on the porch, trying to calm his mutt down, the mutt still yapping.

"What's going on?" Lynch asked across the fence.

"Mess of coloreds out back by your garage, Declan. They jumped in some red beater when I come out, hauled ass down the alley."

"Get a make on the beater?"

"Dodge, it looked like."

Red Dodge. Lynch headed down the fence toward the garage, whistling for the dog. Nothing. Let himself out the gate, walking around the side of the garage into the alley.

Missy lay on her side in front of the garage door, throat cut, blood pooling around her head and shoulders. Someone had dropped a blood-soaked wad of newspaper next to the dog. Lynch looked up at the garage door. "Butcher the Pigs" smeared in blood on the door.

And just on the edge of the pool of blood, part of a heel print. The distinctive diamonds from the bottom of a pair of All-Stars.

All sorts of things going through Lynch's head. Like if everybody's playing this so tight, how come some radical asshole knows who I am, where I live? Like if he does, and he's such a fucking warrior, what's with knifing an old, half-blind dog? Like either way, Lynch and this Simba fucker, they were gonna talk. And depending on what Lynch got, he was either gonna take down this Simba and his fist-pumping friends, or he was gonna take down somebody else. He didn't care how Junior Hurley felt about it, Lynch was about done taking it up the ass.

Lynch went back in the house, grabbed the phone, and called the all-hours number he had for Riley. It rang five times before Riley picked up, Lynch hearing the sleep in his voice. Good, thought Lynch. Would've made him think had Riley been up, waiting on a call.

"What?" said Riley, clearing the gunk out of his throat.

"It's Lynch." He told Riley about the dog and the garage. "Call Riordan, get the troops up. We're gonna go roust this Simba bastard, get some answers. Got the feeling he ain't in bed anyway."

The Feds said Simba was holed up in a two-flat on the west side just south of the Eisenhower off Central. Lynch met Riley and Riordan and his squad in the north parking lot at Chicago Stadium. Riordan had ten cops with him, big guys, every one of them carrying a pump gun along with his sidearm. The FBI twins were there, too, in their raid jackets.

"Your buddy Fisher not coming?" said Lynch.

"He's more an advise and consent guy," said Riley.

"Good, because I'm pretty sure he's got no police powers. And you know you're not coming, right?"

Riley held up his hands and shook his head. "Fuck, no. News tonight is as close to any rabid armed niggers as I wanna get."

"Good." Lynch speaking up. "We are doing this by the book, gentlemen. I need this son of a bitch Simba alive to answer questions. I don't need his head on a wall next to Hampton's. OK? Riordan, what do you got?"

"Our guy tells us probably four, maybe five, guys in the place," said Riordan. "This Simba, he sleeps in a room on the first floor in the back so he can get out quick if he's gotta. Empty lot to the west, and the building east is an abandoned three-flat, so they ain't gonna do any roof-to-roof crap. All of em gonna be armed, and we gotta figure all of em are willing to shoot it out after Simba's little pep talk on the news tonight. I don't care how many dead niggers we got, I don't want any dead cops."

Lynch interrupted. "All we end up with is dead coloreds, we don't get any answers. Don't forget we're dealing with Hurley's kid here. We're gonna surround the place, we're gonna announce, and then, when they don't come out, and I figure they don't, we're gonna gas em and wait it out."

One of Riordan's goons shook his head. "I ain't gettin' shot over no nigger– "

"Hey," Riley shouted. "Mayor wants to know what happened here. This is Lynch's case, and his rules."

Lynch looked around the group. "OK, here's how we do this. Me and the Feds here, we're taking the alley in the back. Layout of the place is there's no door straight back and only the one door on the side of the house they can come out toward the back. Got the two doors up front, one for the upper and one for the lower. Riordan, you line your boys up across the front, get a couple on each corner that got a clear view down the sides. Let me make this real clear. I'm not telling anybody not to shoot back, but I see anybody, and I mean anybody," Lynch looking right at Riordan, "pulling any crap, I'm gonna cuff em myself. I want the Feds to do the bullhorn work. They can tell this Simba they're here to make sure nobody gets trigger happy. All this guy is at this point is a guy I wanna talk to. I don't want nobody doing anything out of line. Remember that you're cops, not some dickhead rednecks runnin' around with sheets over your heads."

Lynch looked the group over, holding the eyes each time until they looked away.

"Let's go."

Riley got back into his city car, reached over to the walkie-talkie on the seat, and clicked the send button twice.

For Zeke Fisher, it felt like the old days in France – or in Korea or Laos or half a dozen other shitholes, for that matter. And the west side of Chicago was about as deep a shithole as any of them. He wore black fatigue pants, a black turtleneck, and a black watch cap. He had burnt cork rubbed onto his face and thin black gloves on his hands. The Walther PPK he'd taken from Stefanski's house and two extra clips hung in the shoulder holster under his left arm. In his right hand, he held a small penlight. He was flattened in an alcove of the wall of the building immediately east of the two-flat where the AMN Commando were hiding, watching the side door, waiting for his signal. He heard the walkie-talkie in the pack click twice. Time. He pointed the penlight toward the side door of the house and flashed it.

The door cracked open. A hand stuck out the door and showed three fingers. Three targets in the house besides Fisher's guy.

Fisher stuck the penlight into the cargo pocket of his fatigue pants. In two steps, he reached the waist-high chain link between the properties. He put his left hand on the top of the fence, braced, and swung his legs up and over, landing without a sound. One step and he was at the door.

Amos Jones waited there, watching Fisher move from the wall to the fence to the door like a damn ghost.

Jones was a career loser and small-time thief. He'd started hanging with the radical black crowd in '68 at the convention because it was a good way to meet white college chicks who thought screwing black guys absolved their racial guilt. He'd been in the building when Hampton got killed, Hampton half out of his bedroom, shot but not dead, when some cop just popped him right in the head, easy as that. Getting laid didn't seem like near enough all of a sudden.

The cops had smacked him around pretty good, both on the scene and on the way to the station. At the station, they'd left him cuffed to a bench in some cold-ass cement room for a couple of hours, just in his shorts, cause that's what he'd had on, not even any socks or nothing.

Then some white guy, guy in a suit and tie, nice looking hat, but lean and with the deepest no-shit eyes Jones had ever seen, walked in the door. He took one look at Jones and then called out into the hall.

"Officer, please uncuff this gentleman and get him some clothes. I'd like to speak with him."

Ten minutes later, Jones was wearing some jail-issue coveralls, sipping on a cup of coffee, and sitting across the table from this guy. Jones was still pissed. He got this thought, just for a second, toss the coffee in the guy's face, jump the guy, take his chances.

The guy smiled across the table at him.

"Mr Jones, if you throw that coffee at me, I'm going to kill you with the cup. I'm not going to tell you how and ruin the surprise, but trust me that it will be unpleasant."

Jones figured he should just drink the coffee, see what the man had to say.

"Mr Jones, let me provide you with a quick philosophical context for our discussion. I have no enmity toward you or your people. I will not abuse your intelligence by trying to convince you that racial enmity played no role in tonight's proceedings. It did. But it is immaterial to me. I am not a member of the Chicago Police Department or, really, an official appendage of any governmental body, yet I can assure you that I have served this country for nearly thirty years directly at the behest of persons whose power and influence are far beyond your experience. Are we clear so far?"

Jones knew the guy was talking over his head on purpose, trying to make him feel like shit, but he caught the gist of it. Jones nodded.

"Good. I also believe that, in the words of Abraham Lincoln, this nation represents that last best hope of mankind. I will do anything necessary to preserve that hope. I believe that Mr Hampton was an honorable man. He believed what he said and fought for what he believed in. But, quite simply, he was on the wrong side of history. His insistence on an adversarial approach to the resolution of racial issues at a time when that approach provided aid and comfort to our Communist enemies amounted, in essence, to treason. And so he was dealt with as a traitor."

"Bullshit," said Jones. The guy stopped and looked at him, waiting. Jones couldn't think of what else he wanted to say.

"As difficult as it may be to rebut that well-reasoned argument, Mr Jones, allow me to continue. You are, of course, free to disagree, this being America and your rights being of such paramount concern to me." The guy stopping for a second to give Jones this cold smile just in case Jones didn't know bullshit when he heard it. "As I said, I considered Mr Hampton to be an honorable adversary. I do not extend that opinion to you. You, sir, are not an honorable man. You associated yourself with Mr Hampton for the social cachet attached to the movement. You found that being a revolutionary afforded you a degree of respect not attendant to your former activities as a thief and small-time criminal."

Jones put up his hand and opened his mouth as if to interrupt, and the white guy stopped, raising his eyebrows. But Jones could think of nothing to say.

"Yes, quite," said the white guy. "As I was saying, you attached yourself to the movement not out of any real sense of injustice or commitment but simply for your personal benefit. What I am now going to propose, Mr Jones, is that you act again for your personal benefit."

The white guy stopped and looked at Jones expectantly. Jones was pissed, this guy basically calling him a Tom. Jones wanted to scream, get pissed. Mostly he wanted the guy to be wrong. But Jones knew he wasn't.

"I'm listening," said Jones.

"Excellent, Mr Jones. No tantrums, no half-hearted protestations of bravery or character. Straight to business. You show a very clear grasp of your circumstances. Let's consider them in particular. At this moment, you have two options. I can wash my hands of your situation and return you to the kind ministrations of the gentlemen who brought you in here. I don't believe they will kill you in custody, as this evening's events have created sufficient concerns of a legal nature, but I do believe they will conduct a rather energetic interrogation, which will eventually compel you to confess to some charge along the lines of attempted murder of a police officer, as it is important to the officers just now that someone go on record as having shot at them first. You'll spend what will likely be a very short life in prison. Does this align with your perspective?"

The man stopped again, the same expectant look, like he actually wanted to hear what Jones had to say. Jones nodded.

"Then our opinions of your situation coincide. Your second option is this. You walk out of here now, with me. You will be released back into the wild, as it were, as a hero, the only man to escape the ambush of Fred Hampton, the only witness who can bear the truth to his brothers. No one else will believe you, of course, because the police will swear you were never present. But amongst those of your race, you will be a new hero. You will use the status this grants you to ingratiate yourself to other radicals in the city. From time to time, I will reach out to you, and you will inform me as to their activities and their intentions. In exchange, I will ensure that you do not become a target of Chicago's finest and that you live in a style you had not heretofore imagined possible. What say you?"

Jones thought about it. Sell out himself and his brothers for a get out of jail free card and a pile of cash. But the fact was, he'd been selling out himself and his brothers for a couple of years just for the occasional piece of pussy. Figured with the new rep and the new dough, he'd still get the pussy.

"Guess I say yes," said Jones.

When Fisher got to the door, he saw that Jones had remembered his instructions. Jones held one finger to his head and pointed to the room in the southwest corner. Simba was in the back room, alone. Jones held two fingers to his chest and pointed to the room in the front of the building. Two more were up front. And then he pointed to the corner of the small foyer inside the back door. The black Converse All-Stars Jones had worn to Lynch's house earlier, and to Stefanski's house before that, were on the floor. Fisher nodded and then tilted his head toward the open door. Time for Jones to go.

Fisher stepped aside to let Jones pass. As Jones cleared his right shoulder, Fisher's right arm flashed around Jones' neck and his left hand clamped to his own right wrist. Fisher tightened the bones in his arm against Jones' throat, squeezing the ceratoid artery, choking off the blood to Jones' brain. He held the position until Jones passed out then slowly slid Jones to the floor. He pulled the Walther out of the holster, got Jones' prints on it, put it back. He picked up one of the All-Stars and dropped it outside the door. He wanted to make sure at least one of the shoes was found in good shape.

The two guys in front had the couch turned to face the front windows, small black and white TV on a coffee table in front of them, late night movie on, something with a mummy. Guy on the right was bigger, almost a head higher on the couch than the guy on the left, real broad through the shoulders.

"Egypt in Africa, right?" the one on the right said.

"Yeah," answered the other guy.

"Then I'm pulling for the mummy."

"Mummy gonna lose, fool."

"Hey, mummy's a brother."

Fisher slid out his sap, a leather tube filled with sand, less than a foot long. Two quiet steps, his arm already swinging, the sap catching the big guy just behind and below the right ear, the guy slumping forward, out cold. Fisher's arm moving right through, banging the sap hard off the other guy's forehead. Fisher's arm shooting past, then swinging back backhanded, catching the smaller guy again on the side of the head, the guy not out but stunned, dropping off the front of the couch to his knees. Fisher swung his leg up, rolled over the couch onto his feet, stepping around behind the guy just as he started to open his mouth to yell. Fisher locking the chokehold on him, pinning his voice in his throat, squeezing him out of consciousness. Fisher propped him back up on the coach, next to the big guy. One more good whack with the sap, behind the ear, to make sure he stayed out long enough.

Fisher walked back to the corner room, slid the door open,

could see James on his side in the bed facing him, blanket half off, his smooth chest rising and falling in the light from the kitchen. Fisher stepped to the bed and sapped him hard, twice, then rolled him off the bed so he'd be under the window. Then Fisher picked up the .45 automatic from the nightstand next to the bed, grabbed both pillows, wadded them tightly against the muzzle of the .45. He fired three shots through the window into the wall of the garage at the back of the property near the alley, and two more into the edge of the window frame. More noise than he'd like, but with the vacant lots around the building, it should be OK. He put the gun down on the floor, put Simba's hand over it.

He returned to the front room, found a heavy-framed .38 revolver on the couch next to the big guy. He still had the pillows from the bedroom and picked up the small pillow from the couch as well. These guys had the front windows open, so he didn't have to shoot out the glass. Fisher emptied the wheel gun through the pillows and the screen, making sure he hit the tree out front and the car parked across the street. Other guy had a .45. Fisher took five shots with that, hit the wall inside the window, put one in the front door. Three more holes in the screen. He dumped the two guys on the floor by the window, stuck the guns in their hands. Then Fisher shut the windows. Holes in the screen wouldn't make sense with no holes in the glass, but the windows would be gone soon. In the meantime, he needed them to hold the gas in.

Fisher stepped into the kitchen, pulled the stove away from the wall, and slid his combat knife from the scabbard sewn into the right cargo pocket of his fatigues. Reaching behind the stove, he sawed at the gas connection until he felt the knife bite through and heard the gas start to hiss. Fisher slipped off the small pack and pulled out the walkie-talkie.

"Ready here," Fisher said.

"On their way," Riley said. "Lynch will be in the back."

Fisher put the walkie-talkie away and headed down the basement stairs, leaving the door to the basement open behind him. The gas, lighter than air, should stay upstairs. Simba's boys had painted over the basement windows, didn't want anybody seeing downstairs. Which made sense, because downstairs looked like an armory. Fisher took out his penlight, found a crate, and set it by the window facing the back, sliding the window open just enough for a field of fire. He picked up a .45 from a shelf, checked the magazine, and slid the gun in his fatigue pocket. Then he pushed once on the fake panel in the east wall and felt it pop open to reveal the tunnel to the vacant building next door. The tunnel he'd told Jones not to tell Riordan's guys about. Fisher was ready to go. He got up on the crate to watch the back.

At the intersection east of the building, Lynch and the Feds turned down the alley while the three squads with Riordan's team went straight toward the front of the house. Lynch had told Riordan to pull up quiet, no lights, then, when Riordan saw Lynch's lights and bubble go on, to turn on the lights and bubble tops out front.

Lynch pulled his squad up behind the house, the Feds pulling their plain sedan in next to him. Lynch hit his lights and bubble, the Feds hit theirs, and Riordan's team lit up the front.

Lynch got out of his car, staying behind the door, and nodded to the Feds. They got out behind the doors of their cars, and one of them pulled out the bullhorn.

"Harold James, this is the FBI. We are assisting the Chicago Police. You are wanted for questioning..."

Fisher watched from the basement of the house while Lynch and the Feds moved into position. He had Hurley Jr's Walther out. Fisher liked the PPK. He'd used them in Europe during WWII.

Smooth action, good velocity, nice flat trajectory at this range.

Lynch was staying behind the car door, which complicated things, but Fisher had a good angle. Didn't want to shoot through the glass if he didn't have to, funny things could happen. Let the Feds start with the bullhorn but don't let them talk long. This Simba had set himself up as a hothead; he wouldn't hesitate.

"Harold James–" The Feds starting in, Lynch sticking his head up a little to get a better view of the house.

Fisher fired.

The FBI guy on the bullhorn heard the crack and saw Lynch drop straight down, not moving again. Two more shots smacked into the door of the Feds' car. The special agent dropped down behind the door and yelled into the bullhorn.

"Riordan, we are taking fire. Lynch is down. Light em up, and get some gas in there."

Both FBI men trained their revolvers on the back window – Simba's room, and opened up. Up front, they could hear all ten guys firing, and the phoop of the tear gas gun.

Fisher ran toward the front of the house. On his way past the basement stairs, he tossed the Walther up so that it landed next to Jones. He pulled the .45 from his fatigues, popped the penlight once to get a line on the front basement window, and then emptied the entire clip out toward Riordan's men. With the bushes out front, they wouldn't see the flash in the basement, but they'd hear the fire, and the rounds ought to hit something. Once the .45 was empty, Fisher moved quickly into the tunnel, closed and latched the door behind him, ran through the basement of the building next door, up the stairs on the east side, over the fence by the next property, and through the next two lots to the street. He was gone.

••••

Riordan heard the first shots out back, one and then three more, heard the warning from the Feds, then heard fire coming from the front of the house.

"Tear the fucking place down, boys," he yelled, and the squad started up with everything they had.

The first two gas canisters crashed through the screens and window in the front room of the house, but the third wasn't slowed down by any glass or screen because both were pretty much shot out, and it had a slightly higher trajectory. It cleared the couch and bounced into the kitchen, which was now densely packed with gas. The canister set off the gas, and the explosion blew out the back windows and side door, leaving the house in flames.

"Shit!" Riordan got on the radio to call in the fire department. As the house burned, some ammo inside started cooking off, more as the heat in the basement started to rise. Riordan and the Feds backed off, watching to make sure nobody left.

Nobody did.

Three hours later, Elsie Anthony, the ME's wife, woke up in an empty bed. Tom had said he'd be late, but it was after 4.00am. She walked over to the bedroom window and looked out at the driveway. Tom's car was parked in the drive. She threw on a bathrobe and went downstairs. He wasn't in his office, wasn't watching TV in the den. She walked out to the car. She could see her husband slumped over the steering wheel. She yanked open the driver's door and reached inside, feeling his neck for a pulse. She'd been an ER nurse for ten years before she married Tom. She knew a corpse when she touched one.

CHAPTER 19 – CHICAGO

Present Day

Lynch dropped nearly a grand on some damn comfortable loafers, toffee-colored slacks made out of some lightweight wool that Lynch couldn't pronounce, a black silk crewneck top that was almost like a hologram – it had this subtle pattern that looked different every time you switched angles – and a lean, three-button jacket, faint check, little olive, little black, lot of the toffee color from the slacks. Waiting for the jacket and slacks to get back from alterations. The Andre guy even had them letting out the side seam in the jacket along the hip, make room for Lynch's gun. Have to get a dress gun, Lynch thought, flat little .380 or something.

. "How about some underwear, detective?" This Andre guy, he didn't quit.

"That's OK, Andre. Got plenty of shorts."

"Not like these." Andre holding up some silk boxers, fifty bucks a pop.

Lynch laughed. "I'm not dropping fifty bucks on something nobody can see."

Andre tilting his head a little. "I don't know detective, you came to see me looking like that, I'd want to see your shorts."

Lynch laughing again. Liked this Andre guy, couldn't help it.

••••

Lynch got to Johnson's place at five after seven, Wrigleyville, Pine Grove and Addison, just off the Inner Drive. He had a Sonata in the garage back at his building, but also a British Racing Green Triumph TR6 he'd bought with some of his dough when he'd been drafted. Didn't drive it much, but he kept it pristine. Temperature had gone up all day, seventy right now, supposed to stay up in the mid-Sixties all night. Lynch figured what the hell, cruise the Drive with the top down, dressed like movie star, why not?

Johnson answered the door wearing leather pants that fit like a tattoo and a metallic silver top that draped like water, sweater tied loose around her neck. Deep scoop in the top. With her heels, she was Lynch's height.

"Wow, look at you," she said.

"Rather look at you. No dress? Thought I was supposed to help you with your zipper."

She grabbed his hand and ran it up the front of her pants. "These have a zipper, see? Some detective you are."

Lynch headed south on the Drive, swung through Grant Park on Columbus, cut south of the Loop and took Taylor Street west out toward the UIC Circle campus to a little Italian place in an old brownstone set back from the street, patio in the front behind a wrought iron gate. Only ten tables in the place. Lynch knew the owner and had called ahead. Got the little booth in the corner, tucked into a nook next to the fireplace. Expensive, but once you've dropped a week's pay on clothes, Lynch thought, what's a couple hundred for dinner?

They talked easily all through dinner, Lynch telling her stories he hadn't told anyone in years. Even talked about his mom a little, Johnson putting her hand on his during that just right, like a balm. Her telling him about doing a year as the TV weather bunny in a station in Duluth just out of school, how the sports guy used to grab her ass and she'd finally broken his nose. Lynch couldn't believe it when they'd finished the wine and he looked at his watch and it was almost 11.00.

Lynch waved down the waiter.

"If we could get our check please? Thanks."

The waiter smiled. "No check tonight, sir, compliments of Mr Wang."

Lynch looked back over his shoulder. Paddy Fucking Wang. Must have been in the private room in the back. Lynch hadn't seen him on the way in.

Johnson's eyebrows went up. "You know Paddy Wang?"

"Everybody knows Paddy Wang," said Lynch. "Thing is, he knows me. We better go say hi."

Paddy Wang looked like an understuffed children's toy. Chinese, though he claimed to be part Irish, barely five feet tall, shaved head, wispy white goatee, always dressed in green, sort of a Mao suit this time, but only if Mao had had his handmade from a couple grand worth of watermarked silk. What looked like brocaded scarlet slippers on feet about the right size for a Barbie. Two of his interchangeable minions with him, Chinese guys in black suits, white shirts, black ties.

"Paddy," Lynch said, putting out his hand.

"Johnny," said Wang, a broad smile. "Too long. Too long. You never come see me."

"I know you're a busy man, Paddy."

"A man so rich in business as to be poor in friends is a poor man indeed," said Wang. Wang looked expectantly at Johnson.

"Paddy, this is Liz Johnson. She's a reporter with the *Tribune*."

"Intimate dinners with the press, Johnny? You are full of surprises."

"John and I are also friends, Mr Wang," said Johnson, putting out her hand.

Wang took it, bowed, kissed it gently, then covered it with his other hand. "Then you have been twice blessed by the gods, my dear. First with this celestial beauty, and then with Mr Lynch's friendship. Neither are gifts to be taken lightly."

A smile from Johnson. "Mr Wang, I see your reputation for charm is well-deserved."

"Christ, Paddy," said Lynch. "A little thick isn't it, even for you?"

Wang with his inscrutable smile.

"Johnny," said Wang. "You will come to the ball this year." The Connemara Ball, Paddy's annual St Patrick's Day shindig. Lynch got his invite every year, but he'd only gone twice, couldn't even say why, except that the air there just never felt right in his lungs.

"I dunno, Paddy. You know I'm not really part of that crowd."

Wang shook his head. "I'm afraid I must insist, Johnny. It is the year of the horse. Your sign, and your father's as well. And please do bring Ms Johnson. She shall be a new star in our firmament." A short bow from Wang, then his minions formed up at his sides.

"Jesus," said Johnson as they set out in step through the restaurant and out the door. "Paddy Wang."

"Long story," said Lynch. And then he told her.

Anybody used to the Newtonian physics of democracy, even the rough and tumble kind, found out the normal rules didn't apply in the Windy City. There was the usual interlocking web of favors and debts and racial algebra and ethnic loyalty and clout, but everything was relative and relatives. Chicago politics was a world unto itself. And Paddy Wang was the big ball of magma at the center of that world.

You didn't see him. He didn't loom over the landscape like the Hurleys – Senior, Junior, or the Third – the divine right of kings by way of the Chicago mayor's office. But Paddy Wang made the Hurleys. He moved all the continents around.

Lynch's first memory of Paddy Wang went back to his

eleventh birthday, his first after his father was killed. Uncle Rusty coming to the house, loading the family into his car. Lynch's birthday falling on Chinese New Year, Uncle Rusty taking them down to Chinatown for the parade, telling Lynch he had a surprise for him.

Not real cold for February, sunny day, lots of people on sidewalks. Rusty driving right down Wentworth, past the police barricades, pulling up to the parking lot next to the Emerald Pagoda, Wang's restaurant that soared over Chinatown on the east side of the street at 23rd Place. The entrance to the lot was blocked by a line of young Chinese men in period costumes, green silk mandarin jackets and black pants. Rusty leaning out the window, waving to them, the line of men parting, letting the Impala through, a simultaneous slight bow.

Outside the restaurant's front door was a line half a block long of people hoping to get in. Rusty marched Lynch's family right to the front of it and in the door, another bow from the young Chinese woman there, the one with the fine black hair down to her ass and the green Suzy Wong dress.

The inside of the Emerald Pagoda completely redefined young Lynch's sense of the possible. Reds, greens, yellows, seemingly no straight line in the place, everything curving away, always the sense of something fantastic just out of sight. Lanterns everywhere. Silk banners a hundred feet long and hand-painted with fantastic scenes hanging from the ceiling in the central atrium. A two-story waterfall tumbling into a stone pond full of large, colorful fish with billowing fins. What seemed like a thousand tables on a thousand levels, the place looking like a cross between an Escher drawing and something by Dali.

Lynch grabbed the tail of Rusty's jacket as Rusty waded right into the room, Lynch feeling like he was following an explorer into an unknown world. He was afraid to let go, afraid that, if he lost sight of his uncle here, he would be lost forever.

And then Paddy Wang was striding out to meet them, two retainers in black suits a step back on either side.

Wang was wearing a green robe that went down to his feet. The front of the robe was decorated with an intricate dragon rendered in more colors than Lynch knew existed, rubies sewn to the robe as the dragon's eyes and a line of emeralds as big as lima beans running down its spine. A palpable sense of awe, like the pressure wave and wake of a boat, surrounded Wang as he walked toward them. Wang walked right up to Lynch, not even looking at his uncle, stopped, and made a deep bow.

"Young Master Lynch, you grace us at last." Wang's face opened in a radiant smile, he took Lynch's hand.

"Come, come." Wang led him off, Lynch looking back over his shoulder, Rusty giving him a nod and a grin and a thumbs up, receding back into the riot of colors that was like camouflage, that gave you so much to see you couldn't see anything at all.

Wang led Lynch through the main floor of the restaurant, then through a set of huge red lacquered doors. The hall in the back was not as dazzling but almost more opulent in its way. The walls were lined with elaborately carved wooden screens in front of rich silk panels, the parquet floor lined with a succession of deep oriental rugs. Finally, Wang turned Lynch into a small room where two young women, seeming duplicates of the woman at the door to the restaurant, waited. Wang said something to them in Chinese, and they turned to Lynch, smiled, and bowed. Wang squeezing him on the shoulder then, saying, "I will see you soon, young Lynch," and disappearing into the hall.

One of the women opened a large armoire and removed a green silk robe Lynch's size, adorned with the same dragon as Wang's, though without the jewels. Together, the two women raised the robe over Lynch's head and lowered it onto him. Lynch stuck his arm through the belled sleeves. The women took off his penny loafers and slid on a pair of black slippers. Then, each taking a hand, they led him back into the hallway and farther into the building.

Wang, the two Chinese men in the black suits, and at least a dozen Chinese men in the green and black outfits the men in the parking lot had worn waited by a door in the back.

"Excellent, excellent, young Lynch. Come." Again Wang took Lynch's hand, the entire retinue falling in behind them.

The doors opened before them, and Wang and Lynch stepped into a narrow alley behind the restaurant. In the alley was a parade float in the shape of the dragon on the two green robes. Two of the men in the green and black outfits rolled a wheeled set of stairs like those to an airplane up against the side of the dragon. Wang led Lynch up the stairs. At the top of the dragon was a hollowed out area with a sunken floor, and in the middle of the floor were two gold chairs with red cushions. Lynch thought they looked like thrones. Wang motioned to the chair on the right, and Lynch sat down. Wang sat to his left. The two women who had dressed Lynch in the robe climbed up the stairs and stood behind the chairs.

Wang shouted something in Chinese, and Lynch heard a truck engine start under the float. The float drove down the alley and turned left onto Wentworth.

More people than Lynch had ever seen lined the sidewalks and the edges of the street. Even more hung out of windows along the upper floors along the route. The street was full of dancers and acrobats and young men running paper dragons in serpentine patterns. Fireworks exploded everywhere. Gongs banged, and people shouted and laughed.

Lynch heard his name. "Johnny! Johnny! Over here!"

Lynch looked to his left. His mother and Uncle Rusty stood right in front, outside the Emerald Pagoda, Mom holding his sister's hand. His uncle had his hands cupped around his mouth, making a megaphone.

"Happy birthday, buddy!"

Wang pressed something into his hand. Lynch looked. It was a coin, bronze, half the size of Lynch's palm. There was a square hole in the middle of it, with Chinese characters on either side.

"Happy birthday, indeed, young man. This is your father's legacy. Never lose it. It is magic. It can buy anything." It was the happiest Lynch had been since his father's murder.

At 5.15am Lynch and Johnson sat in her kitchen, drinking tea, Johnson in her panties and an old Golden Gophers sweatshirt, Lynch showered, dressed again, figuring he'd have to head straight to work.

"You never told me if it works," said Johnson.

"Jesus, Johnson. It works, OK? Needs a little rest now, though." Lynch giving a little laugh.

"I know that works, Lynch. The magic coin? Does it work?"

Lynch fished out his keychain. The coin was threaded onto the metal loop. He set it on the table. "Tried it once, my senior year at Mount Carmel. I was, I dunno, sort of a jock punk then. Not really, I guess. I was never comfortable with that, but that was the crowd I hung with mostly. Anyway, spring break that year, some of us got to talking shit like guys do. You know, I know this guy, my old man knows that guy. So I say I know Paddy Wang. Which gets me a big bullshit from everybody. I mean, they know my old man had been a kind of quasi-ward boss on the side, but they figure that's Triple A ball at best, and Paddy Wang, well, Paddy Wang is the big leagues."

"So you figure you have to show them, right?"

"Yeah. I figure we drive down to the Pagoda, flash the coin, maybe we get comped a meal. Maybe Paddy even comes out, says hello. Anyway, we're driving down Cicero, just north of Chinatown, and Mutt Warren – he was this big slob of an offensive tackle, complete asshole – he sees the Manila, titty bar used to be down that way, another joint Wang owned. It was pretty infamous. He says, you're tight with Paddy Wang, you get us in there."

"Hey," Johnson said. "This is getting good."

"So we park, we're walking up to the door, and there's this guy, looks like Oddjob from the Bond movies, standing there, and he doesn't even talk to us, just makes this shooing gesture. So I hold up the coin. Guy kinda freezes, give this little nod, and opens the door. So, anyway, I made my case. Coin works." Lynch took a sip of tea, feeling kind of sheepish.

"Oh, no you don't, Lynch." Johnson pulled her feet up onto the chair and wrapped her arms around her knees, leaning her head forward. "You have to finish this story."

Long exhale from Lynch. Sip of tea. "OK. Place is pretty seedy, really. Got the big runway down the middle, couple of Asian girls up there, supposed to be in pasties and G-strings, but they're not. Not real crowded. It was a weeknight, and it was early yet, at least by the standards of that sort of joint. Some guys at the tables, they're probably mostly OK, you know. I mean, a little loud, a little drunk, but mostly guys in their twenties just not grown up yet. But the guys lining the runway? I knew right off I never wanted to be one of those guys, staring up into these anonymous crotches like they'd just found God. I tell the guys I made my point and let's get out of here, and I think most of them were ready to go. But Warren, Jesus, he's turned into one of the guys at the runway already. Says we're all fucking pussies, must be gay, and that turns the group's whole mood around. Nobody wants to be the guy when we get back to school Monday who gets the rap for chasing us out of the Manila. Thing is, though, we're all standing there, trying to be cool, not one of us has any idea what we're supposed to do. Do we get a table? Do we go join the mouth-breathers at the runway? Then one of Paddy's Suzy Wong girls walks up, and I'm thinking this has to be one of those girls who stuffed me into that robe when I was eleven, but it can't be because it's been seven years. I think he must clone them or something. Anyway, she walks up, takes my elbow, says, 'Mr Lynch, gentlemen,' and she ushers us through this beaded curtain and into this room off to the right. Mess of food on the table, appetizer-type stuff. Beers on the table. And four of those girls, like up on the runway."

"Meaning naked?" Johnson asks.

"Yeah. Meaning naked. So we sit down, and these naked girls are serving us food, serving us beers. Suzy Wong standing in the doorway like a chaperone. Warren pawing at the girls. They don't actually say no, but they're pretty good at avoiding him. Finally, he says to me, 'Hey, Lynch, use that coin, man. I bet we can do these chicks right here.' This whole thing's got me pretty weirded out already, and now it looks like it's going to get ugly. And I say, 'That's it, we're out of here.' And this time, the other guys are with me. They pretty much jump up out of their seats. Warren sees it's going against him and is just kinda pouting. And then fucking Warren, he grabs this one girl from behind, got his hands all over her, and instantly that Oddjob guy is behind him, peeling his arms off her like they're pipe cleaners. And the Suzy Wong chick, she steps forward, says if I give her my keys, she'll have the car brought around. So, we're out on the walk, car's waiting. Just as I'm walking around the back, this stretch Lincoln pulls up, back window slides down, and there's Paddy Wang.

"'Young Lynch. What a surprise to see you again,' he says. I'm thinking I should apologize or something, and all I get out is 'Hi.' He says, 'Do you know the story of Jack and the Beanstalk, young Lynch?' I say yeah. He says 'In which a man trades his magic beans for a cow?' I say yeah again. He says 'Seems a waste of magic beans, doesn't it, young Lynch?' And the window goes up, and the Lincoln glides off, and I get to drive home, car full of guys carrying on about how they grabbed this and grabbed that, and Warren saying how he should have kicked the Oddjob guy's ass, and I'm just hoping this doesn't get back to my mom, and I'm feeling stupid and dirty and not grown up at all."

"So the coin works." Johnson looking a little sad for him, Lynch amazed how well she understands, falling more for her all the time.

"Need to be real careful what you wish for," said Lynch.

CHAPTER 20 – CHICAGO

Jose Villanueva sat at one of the plastic tables outside the pastry joint on Wabash, drinking his coffee, eating his chocolate croissant, and trying to find a way out of his current fix. An L train crashed and banged along overhead, but the noise didn't bother Jose.

Jose was a professional creeper. Best alarm and second-story guy in the city. You wanted something out of somewhere you weren't supposed to be, you wanted Jose, especially if that somewhere was wired up. Jose's workload was increasingly by referral. Work-for-hire stuff. Private collectors looking for a certain piece, industrial espionage, some work coming out of divorces. Once, some fat cat sent him into a house up in Lake Forest. All he wanted was a painting of a cocker spaniel. Wife got it in the settlement, so he was going to take it. Jose telling the guy that was going to point right back at him. Jose telling him that he'd better take some other shit, make it look good. The guy saying take all the shit you want, just get me the damn picture. Guy paid him five grand for the painting; Jose made another fifteen on the other stuff he grabbed.

No, the El didn't bother Jose. What was bothering Jose was that Magic Mel hadn't been at his joint down on Halsted, not for almost a week. Magic Mel had been Jose's main fence for going on six years now. Jose still did some traditional residential work on his own. Got leads through a bent realtor. Guy'd see some nice stuff going through houses, get the addresses to Jose. And Jose'd take the shit to Magic Mel so Mel could turn it into cash.

Magic Mel was a discreet guy, working out of the back of his plumbing supply store, big ticket goods only. Didn't attract attention handling watches and jewelry from street heists. Tied into the Italians, everybody said. Got you a decent price, got it pretty quick.

Magic Mel owed Jose for some shit he dropped off last week. No big deal. Couple of pieces, maybe two or three grand on Jose's end. But Mel wasn't around, and nobody seemed to know where he was. First couple of days, Jose thought maybe Mel had pissed off the Italians, maybe he'd turn up in the Cal-Sag channel in a day or two. But then the Italians had sent someone to see Jose, asking did he know where Magic Mel was. Then Jose started hearing whispers maybe the Feds had Mel, that they were milking him for stuff on the Italians. And if they were, Jose figured, then Magic Mel might just give them Jose, too. Fuck, probably give them Jose instead.

Jose thinking maybe he should try to get out in front of this, go see his lawyer. That's when a small Asian woman pulled out a seat.

"May I join you, Mr Villanueva? I am sure you remember me from our previous business." She set a briefcase down on the sidewalk beneath the table.

Jesus, thought Villanueva. It was the chink chick from that U of C job back – what, three, four years ago? He had some bad nights sleeping after that. Guy was some hot-shit professor in town for a lecture at the U of C. She told Jose all she needed was the guy's laptop. Simple job, guy was staying at the Westin downtown. Then, two days later, the guy gets popped on the Midway. Cops writing it off to a street robbery, but Jose feeling different about it. Job paid good, though. Ten large just to take a laptop out of a hotel room.

"Hey," said Jose.

"Are you interested in another easy job?" she asked.

"Depends. Going to kill anybody after this one?"

Chink chick sat unmoving, looking dead into his eyes. "It is good to take an interest in your work, Mr Villanueva. It is unhealthy to take too much of an interest, however."

"Yeah, sure," said Villanueva. "Look, I got a lot on my plate right now."

"Worried about your fence, Mr Villanueva? Magic Mel?"

That shook up Villanueva. "I don't know any–"

"Of course you do, Mr Villanueva. Halsted Plumbing Supply. Let's not waste our time, shall we?"

Jose took a sip of his coffee, took a bite of the croissant. Jesus, this bitch scared him.

"OK," said Villanueva. "You got something to say, say it."

She pulled a piece of paper from her jacket pocket and slid it across the table. Villanueva looked at it. Pictures of a very small camera and an even smaller bug. Definitely top-end shit, both because of the size and because you just figured this chink chick, she wasn't here about some retail crap.

"Surveillance shit of some kind," he said. "I haven't seen it, and I've seen most of em. If you want me to beat this shit, you're gonna have to get me some schematics or something."

"I don't want you to beat them, Mr Villanueva. I want you to collect them."

Villanueva took another sip from his coffee, looking at the chick, trying to get some kind of read. Nothing.

"Collect them from where?" Villanueva asked.

The woman slid him another piece of paper with an address on it. Jose looked at it. Sacred Heart Church. Shit. The Marslovak shooting.

"The transmitter should be inside one of the confessional booths. The camera will be secured to the bottom of one of the pews, pointing at the confessional. Find the camera first.

It will show you which confessional to search."

Villanueva set the papers down on the table. "I know what happened at the church," he said.

"Just think of cats, Mr Villanueva. Think of curiosity and cats. Now, we understand that you are a professional and, as such, are entitled to your fee. We propose twenty-five thousand dollars. In addition, we will ensure that no difficulties befall you resulting from the unfortunate situation involving Mr Mel. You understand, of course, that we will require absolute confidentiality."

"Shit, lady, I don't even know who this 'we' you keep talking about is. When you need this done?"

"Tonight."

"When I get paid?"

The chick slid an envelope across the table. "In advance. We're going to trust you. We're going to assume you don't want to deal with our collections department."

"You wanna set up a drop? I mean, I'm assuming you want your toys back."

"You can take them to Mr Mel's, as is your habit," said the woman. "They will be tended to." She picked up her briefcase from under the table and stood up, raising her hand to flag down a yellow cab heading south on Wabash. "Mr Villanueva?"

"Yeah?"

"Don't get caught, don't get curious, and don't get careless. I don't think you'd care to meet me under less collegial circumstances." She turned, walked off, and slid into the back of the cab, and it pulled away.

Villanueva slid the envelope into his coat pocket, thinking for a second should he open it, count it, then thinking what difference would it make. He swallowed the last of the coffee and left what was left of the croissant on the table. Not much of an appetite all of a sudden.

CHAPTER 21 - CHICAGO

Lynch grabbed Bernstein at the office, and they headed over to MarCorp to talk to Eddie Marslovak about the waste hauling deal.

"Might want to bring up Andes Capital, too," Bernstein said as Lynch flipped off some guy trying to muscle a Land Rover into their lane.

"What's that?"

"Venture capital firm down in Miami. Seems to stick cash into MarCorp's deals pretty regularly. I called a friend over at Morgan Stanley. Nothing official, but the Feds have started looking at Andes for money laundering. Think it might be washing dollars for the Medellin crowd."

"Running a laundry for the Columbians and you call the place Andes Capital? Takes some cojones."

"Or just dumb."

"Yeah," said Lynch. "Or that."

Bernstein looked over, little crooked smile. Second or third time Lynch had seen that.

"Fuck's up with you? Don't like the clothes? Blame your friend Andre, he picked em out."

"Hey, they look great. Just didn't think you'd still be in them when you got to work the next day. Guess the date went OK."

"Shut up, Slo-mo."

"Hey, I'm a detective too, remember."

••••

Marslovak was already out from behind the desk when Lynch and Bernstein walked into his office, already on the black sofa, already with a drink. Marslovak dressed casual today, khaki slacks, deck shoes with no socks, white cable knit tennis sweater, probably a 3XL and stretched on him like a sausage casing.

"Thanks for seeing us on Saturday," Lynch said.

"Told you I was trying to stave off divorce number three, Lynch. Whole secret to marital bliss is avoiding your wife." Marslovak didn't look happy. "Who's your little friend?"

"Shlomo Bernstein," said Bernstein. "I'm sorry for your loss."

"Yeah, yeah. Everybody's fucking sorry, nobody wants to leave my ass alone." Marslovak gestured toward a second man. "This is Steve Heaton. He's my attorney. I've invited him to join us for today's festivities."

Lynch looked at Heaton. Blond, six-two, eyes like a Stolichnaya bottle that had been in the freezer for a while. Navy chalk-stripe suit, extremely white shirt, red tie. Even his skin looked clean and pressed.

"You don't need a lawyer, Eddie," said Lynch.

"Such reassurances are always so comforting coming from legal authorities whose personal whims decide whether and to what extent the considerable resources of our government will inject themselves into a citizen's life, detective," said Heaton. "I will be present today and at any subsequent meetings. Clear?"

"Clear and remarkably articulate, counsel," said Lynch.

"Thank you," said Heaton with a cold smile.

"So?" said Marslovak.

"When we talked the other day, you said you couldn't think of anybody off hand that might have a thing for you," Lynch said.

"Didn't say I couldn't think of anybody," said Marslovak. "Said I couldn't think of anybody in particular."

"Not even the anybody attached to the waste hauling rollup in New York?" Bernstein asked.

"Checking me out, Lynch? Waste hauling," said Marslovak. "Few too many guys named Luigi. Few too few dollars in some of the pension plans when you work the books. Somebody'd blown my fat ass away during that a couple of years ago, I'd say you might have your boys. But wait till two years after the deal's done, then blow away my mom on the stairs of the church? Make sense to you, Lynch?"

"It could," said Lynch, "if there's something you're not telling us."

"I think this interview is close to over, detective," said Heaton. "My client is being fully cooperative, and now you are questioning his veracity. I warn you, I had better not start seeing hints in the paper about mob ties to MarCorp. Mr Marslovak's enrichment resulting from the ensuing civil actions would strain your imagination."

"So let's talk about Andes Capital instead," said Bernstein.

"Why?" said Marslovak.

"They've contributed capital to your last six deals," said Bernstein. "Thirteen deals overall."

"So what?" said Marslovak

"Feds are sniffing around them about money laundering," said Lynch.

Heaton stepped between Bernstein and Marslovak.

"First of all, that's immaterial," said Heaton. "Since you've only heard they are being investigated for laundering money, I will assume they have not been convicted of, much less charged with, laundering money. Therefore, MarCorp has no reason, not legally and not even ethically, to consider that possibility. Second, it is not the responsibility of MarCorp, again, either legally or ethically, to investigate or enforce the laws regarding money laundering. We comply fully with all applicable reporting requirements. That is all we are required to do. Third, I can assure you that Andes' various investments, which, if memory serves, are generally between $250,000 and $750,000, were made through appropriately documented channels. No one named Pedro showed up here with a suitcase full of twenties, detective."

"So you're saying that the money laundering charge against Andes may or may not be bullshit, but, in any event, it's got nothing to do with you," said Lynch.

"To paraphrase incompletely and less than wholly accurately, yes," said Heaton.

"OK, look. Nobody's saying Eddie did anything. This looks like a professional hit. That generally means money and criminal contacts. Eddie's got one, some of the people he's done business with have both."

Heaton shrugged. "Detective, I assure you, if Mr Marslovak had an idea, you'd know. If he gets an idea, you will know. Now, are we through?"

Lynch nodded. "A pleasure, counsel. You know, you sure do talk pretty. You got any tips for me, anything I can do to raise my level of discourse?"

"A rose smells as sweet no matter the name, detective. And a buffoon sounds as coarse."

"What do you think, Slo-mo," said Lynch, looking at the lawyer. "Am I the rose or the buffoon?"

"I thought you were the ice cream man," said Bernstein.

Lynch moved the Crown Victoria through the North Michigan Avenue traffic around Marslovak's office like a blunt instrument. Bernstein was trying to time sips on his coffee with Lynch's lane changes.

"How'd you like Eddie's lawyer?" Lynch asked.

"Have to call my parents, see if they're still looking to breed their Rottweiler. Pretty sure the vet said it can't screw any lawyers, though. Not without a condom."

"Yeah. So what's your read on Eddie? Anything?"

"Definitely have to say he didn't hire anyone to pop his mom. Seems too, I don't know, volatile to set this up. Could see that lawyer doing it."

"Get the sense he was holding anything back on the waste hauling thing or those Andes guys?"

"Got the sense the next time he holds something back will be the first."

"Yeah," Lynch answered. "Man, I wish I knew what she said in that confessional."

"You Catholics and your secrets."

"Careful, Slo-mo. Don't make me bring the Cabalists into this."

Back in the office, Lynch and Bernstein ran down what they got from Marslovak, which was nothing.

"Not nothing," Starshak said. "You did manage to piss him off. I got a call from the deputy chief, who got a call from the chief, who got a call from the mayor. Eddie telling them you all but accused him of being a mob guy and a drug dealer."

"That's bullshit," said Lynch.

"Course it is," said Starshak. "Still like to keep it off our shoes, though."

"I got nothing left to rattle his cage about, so I guess we're OK there," Lynch said. "What's with the lab? Still ain't got ballistics."

"Called while you were out," Starshak said. "Guy wants you to stop down."

A lab tech named Pfundstein met Lynch by the elevators. Pfundstein looked about thirteen, wearing glasses that probably weighed as much as he did.

"I'm sorry to take so long with the results, detective, but I've been having some trouble with this one."

"Slug went through her sternum and her spine and dug into a piece of oak," Lynch said. "Figured it was pretty fucked up."

"Oh, it is. Fucked up, I mean." Pfundstein pushing his glasses up his nose. "If you were hoping to be able to match this to a weapon, forget it. I've got the metallurgy for you, and it's not your garden variety stuff, so that might help a little."

"So what was the trouble?"

"Even as messed up as the slug is, it should still have marks, right? I mean it's like fingerprints. Lots of times you get partials. Maybe not enough for a match, but at least you get something. This slug? Nothing. Can't tell you the number of grooves. Can't tell you left twist, right twist. Nothing."

"So what? Smooth-bore weapon of some kind?"

"At that range? Hard to see it. I'm thinking maybe it was saboted."

"What's that?"

"Take a bullet. You coat it with something like cellulose, some kind of resin maybe. Coating picks up the spin from the rifling, so your slug stays accurate, but the coating burns off, both in the barrel and in flight. Only way I can think we get a slug with no marks at all."

"Sounds a little James Bond. This happen much?"

"I've heard of it. Never seen it. I asked around, nobody else has seen it either."

CHAPTER 22 – CHICAGO

Jose Villanueva drove up to Sacred Heart. The church had one of those Saturday evening masses where you could get the thing out of the way, sleep in Sunday. Or be ready for the Bears game, whatever. Anyway, the chink bitch wanted the job done tonight. Villanueva figured he'd do the mass, get a look at the layout. Grab a bulletin, too. Make sure that nothing was going on in the church later, that he didn't break in in the middle of an all-night novena or something.

He sat in the middle about halfway back. He could see the confessionals on the east wall. The pews were laid out in a sort of semicircle, so only the ones on his far right had their backs straight to the confessionals. After that, they started curving away. Camera should be on the bottom of the last pew in that far right section.

Confessional layout was pretty basic. Two sets of three doors. Middle door for the priest, doors on either side for people to come in, spill the beans on themselves. Middle door on the second set of three had a little name plate over it, so Villanueva figured he'd check that set first. Could be they brought a priest in from one of the other parishes to help with confessions, but figured the parish guy was here every time.

He'd walked past the vestibule on the south side on his way in, recognizing it from the news. That was where Eddie Marslovak's mom got it. Bad set up, though. Easy to see from the street, streetlight at the end of the walk. He'd come in to mass through the main door, but that sucked, too. No cover at all. Also, it was a big-ass door, maybe ten feet high, three or four inches thick. Couple of locks on it that he could see, one of them some real old fucker that he'd have to fiddle with some because he was pretty sure he hadn't worked one like that before.

After mass, he walked out the vestibule and looped around the building, cutting up the narrow walk that ran around the north end of the church. Not a lot of room between the north end and the bungalow behind it. People in the bungalow had planted a tall hedge at the back of their property. No leaves yet, so it wouldn't be much help if he had a flashlight on, but there should be enough ambient light to see.

A set of cement stairs ran down parallel to the walk to a door into the basement of the church. Villanueva took a quick peek up and down the walk. Nobody looking. He took the stairs. Fairly deep basement, twelve steps down. Stairs forming a dark well. Villanueva figured he could use a penlight down here no problem. Nobody'd see that unless they were right on top of him. Standard metal security door, wire mesh embedded in the window. Schlage lock. Rinky-dink residential alarm he could bypass in about twenty seconds with a pocket knife and a couple alligator clips. Getting up into the church ought to be easy once he got into the basement.

Back in the car, Villanueva ran down what he'd need. Just the small set of picks. Christ, he could do a Schlage in his sleep. Wear the black Adidas warm-ups. He could park a couple blocks up, jog around the neighborhood a little, make sure everything looked cool. Do the job around 10.00, maybe 10.30. Funny how people thought 3am was the best time to break in somewhere. Everybody looks suspicious at 3am. Ten o'clock, people are still out, walking their dogs or whatever. Still some background noise, some traffic.

Also, better take the .38 with him, keep it in the jacket pocket
of the track suit. Villanueva hated to work with a gun. Take
a bust with a gun, the time you're looking at really balloons
on you. But he had a bad feeling about the chink bitch and a
worse feeling about whoever sent her.

CHAPTER 23 – SCHAUMBURG, ILLINOIS

Lynch and Johnson were in the middle of what Lynch figured was their tenth circuit of the Ikea store in Schaumburg, Johnson showing him all sorts of end tables and shelves and shit she thought would look good in her place. She had good taste, little quirky maybe.

"So this is your idea of fun, huh?" Lynch said.

"You're forgetting, Lynch, I'm not a Chicago girl. I grew up in white-bread country, home of the largest mall in America. This isn't the main event, though. We're going over to Woodfield next, walk the mall, maybe see a movie." She'd called him just after he got back from Marslovak's office, told him it was her turn to take him out.

"Jesus. We gonna eat bad pizza in the food court?"

"Bet your ass."

"Chick flick?" "Yep."

"We gonna at least sit in the back so I can feel you up?"

"That's the idea," she said.

Halfway through some movie about some young, good-looking chick dying of cancer, Lynch caught himself smiling. Christ. He was having fun. Sitting through a bad movie, wandering through a mall, out in the freakin' suburbs, and he was having fun.

Johnson sniffled next to him. "I need your hanky," she whispered.

"Don't have one."

"What kind of man takes a girl to a movie like this and doesn't bring a hanky?"

"Sorry, out of practice."

Johnson nudged her head into his shoulder, and he put his arm around her head. He slid his hand down, gave her breast a little squeeze. She slapped his hand.

"I'm trying to watch the movie," she said.

A minute later, Lynch felt her hand rubbing his thigh.

"Thought you were watching the movie," he said.

"I am," she said, "but you're not."

Lynch smiling again. God, this was fun.

After the movie, Johnson drove to one of the restaurants ringing the mall. Houlihans, TGIF, Chili's, Lynch couldn't remember without looking at the little plastic dessert menu. Bennigans.

"I know this will sound stupid, but this place reminds me of home," Johnson said.

"Why? Your dad like to make up stupid names for drinks?"

Johnson laughed. "Just growing up. Out with my friends, we'd always end up in some place like this, you know? Talk about who was going out with who and how far they were going. Just comfortable, that's all."

They just sat for a while. Lynch was drinking a black and tan, which he'd had to let stand for five minutes before it got any separation, but still, a black and tan. Johnson was having some drink named after a cartoon character. Nice they could just sit, drink, play a little footsie, nobody feeling like they had to talk all the time.

"Are you doing OK, Lynch? Having urban withdrawal?"

Lynch smiled. "This is nice. You keep doing that with your foot, and I'm not going to be able to stand up, though."

"So, when was the last time you were out of the city?"

"Berwyn count?"

"No."

"Cicero?"

"No place where Al Capone used to hang out."

Lynch laughed. "I guess Christmas. I drove my mom up to my sister's. Right before she got real bad."

"Where's that?"

"Milwaukee. She's some big-shot VP with Northwestern Mutual. Her husband is a surgeon. Got a couple kids, getting up to junior high now."

"Are you guys close?"

"Not like we should be," Lynch said. "Guess I'm supposed to lie about that, right? Used to be, when she was little."

"What happened?"

"Hard to say. Everything changed after my father was killed. I tried to be dad, she resented it. Nothing horrible, but we just... People say drifted right? That sounds so stupid. I mean, I call sometimes, she calls sometimes, and it's, you know, how are the kids? They're fine. How's work? Work's good." Lynch took a sip of his beer, looked out the window. Wind shifting around, starting to pick up. "I miss her. Funny, huh? She's not dead or anything, but I miss her."

"That's got to be hard now, with your mom."

Lynch shrugged.

The waiter came by, asked if they wanted dessert.

"I think we're going to have that somewhere else," Johnson said, looking at Lynch, her foot sliding up his leg again. "I've got a taste for something I don't see on the menu."

It was colder walking out to the car. The wind was out of the northwest now, Lynch smelled rain in the air. Johnson drove south on 355 toward the 290 extension that ran east toward the city. She drove fast, weaving through the moderate traffic.

"You're quiet, Lynch," she said.

"Thinking about the Marslovak case."

"And you're afraid to say anything to me?"

"Yeah, well, you're still the press, Johnson. I mean, this is your beat."

Johnson cut right around a slow-moving SUV, ran up behind a semi in the right lane with a panel truck next to it, cut two lanes left around them and then back across all three lanes and onto the 290 ramp.

"Jesus," Lynch said. "Good thing I'm not working traffic."

Silence again, and not comfortable.

"This could be a problem for us," said Johnson. "If we can't talk to each other."

"Yeah."

Quiet again for a while.

"How about this, Lynch. Unless I say otherwise, everything you tell me is off the record. Not just not-for-attribution, not just background, it's strictly between us. Can you trust me that far?"

Lynch thought for a second. He'd only known Johnson at all for a few months, only known her personally for three days. But you either trust somebody or you don't. He could think of guys he'd known all his life he'd trust about as far as he could dropkick a floor safe.

"Yeah. I think I can."

"OK, then."

They drove in silence for a while, Lynch knowing it was a kind of test now. He'd have to say something. She wanted him to say something.

"It's the confession thing," Lynch said. "I can't get past thinking that Marslovak said something in that confessional, and whatever she said, that got her killed."

"And the priest won't say?"

"Can't say," said Lynch. "You're not Catholic, are you?"

"Lutheran, I guess. You hear people say they're cultural

Jews? I guess I'm a cultural Lutheran. My family didn't go
to services much. Christmas, Easter, stuff like that. Gives you
a place to have weddings and funerals, though, almost like
being in some kind of club."

"I'm pretty much in the same boat now. We went growing
up. Every Sunday, every holy day. Catholic schools, altar boy,
the whole thing. I just... I don't know. I don't believe a lot of
things I used to believe. I don't do a lot of things I used to do.
I guess church is one of them."

"Lose your faith, Lynch?"

"Makes it sound like a quarter under a couch cushion
somewhere. I believe there's a God," Lynch said. "Hard to know
what to believe beyond that. I can't help feeling sometimes
that if I ever meet him, I'm not going to like him much."

"So what's with the confession thing? Priest really can't
say?"

"Rules are the priest can't reveal anything said within the
seal of confession."

"Even though she's dead?"

"Doesn't matter."

"Then how could anyone know? I mean if he didn't say
anything—"

"Oh, shit." Lynch grabbed his cell phone off his belt and dug
a small notepad out of his jacket pocket. He found the number
for Sacred Heart and dialed it. Father Hughes answered.

"Father, Detective Lynch. I know it's a little late. I hope I
didn't wake you."

"Actually, I just got in from the hospital, detective, visiting a
parishioner. What can I do for you?"

"The crime scene guys, did they look inside the church at
all?"

"Not much."

"You going to be up in, say, half an hour?"

"I could be, why?"

"I'd like to take a look inside the church."

"All right, detective. I'll see you around 10.30 then."

Lynch flipped the phone shut, dropped it on the seat.

"Get over to 294 north, we're going to church. And stop driving like an old lady, will you? Let's make some time."

Jose Villanueva cruised past the church. Lights were out. Weather had turned some, a misty rain just starting, wind picking up a little. He saw one dog walker a block past the church. Guy had his collar up, head down, pretty much dragging some poodle-type rat dog along. Villanueva looped back to the east and parked his Explorer in the lot of a convenience store near Belmont.

Villanueva jogged the six blocks back toward the church. Tracksuit on, use the die-hard exercise addict disguise. He had his picks, a Swiss Army knife, and a mini-Maglight in his left-hand jacket pocket. The short-barreled .38 bounced, zipped in the right-hand pocket. Also had several different lengths of coated wires with alligator clips on the ends. The rain was picking up and coming sideways, but the black Adidas warm-ups were Gore-Tex, so it wasn't too bad. As he came to the church, he was tempted to cut right up the narrow walk on the north side, get in out of the rain, but he ran past, circled the block. Nobody was out. Visibility was getting bad, too.

He checked his watch as he came up on the narrow walk the second time. 10.14. Good a time as any. He didn't vary his pace, just turned up the walk like it was a short cut he used all the time, then trotted down the cement stairs to the basement door of the church.

He turned on a penlight and held it in his mouth. Then he took the pocket knife, opened the blade, and carefully sliced back the coating on a couple of wires attached to the alarm on the door. He pulled the wires out of his jacket, picked two that were the right length, and clipped them to the exposed spots on the wires. He looked at his watch. 10.19.

He put the extra wires and the pocket knife back in his jacket and pulled out the narrow black case that held his picks. It took him less than thirty seconds to rake the tumblers and turn the lock. He was in.

Johnson pulled up in front of the rectory at 10.41. Father Hughes pulled the door open just as they walked up. He was wearing black pants and a heavy turtleneck. Johnson and Lynch stepped into the foyer.

"Guess spring is over already," the priest said.

"You Chicagoans are such wimps," said Johnson.

"Father, this is Liz Johnson," said Lynch. "Liz, Father Hughes." Johnson and Hughes shook hands.

"Your partner?" the priest asked.

"Friend," said Lynch. "We were out when I had a thought I should have had a couple days ago. I'm still thinking all this goes back to whatever Mrs Marslovak said in confession. But that only makes sense if someone knows what she said."

The priest put up his hands. "I didn't say anything, and I'm not going to."

"I know. You wouldn't have had time anyway. But somebody heard."

The priest's mouth dropped open. "You mean—"

"I mean I think somebody bugged your confessional, Father."

The priest pulled a ring of keys off a rack by the door. "We'll go in through the basement. Light switches are down there."

Villanueva needed a few minutes to find the camera, longer than he expected. He was lying on his back, shining the penlight along the bottom of the pew, when he finally spotted it. Whoever had placed it had put it right up against one of the supports. Damn, it was small. Villanueva had never seen one so small. He slipped the pocket knife blade under the adhesive holding the unit and pried it loose. Villanueva pulled a small Ziploc bag out of his pants pocket, dropped the camera in, sealed the bag, and shoved it back into his pocket. The camera had been pointed at the set of doors with the priest's name on the plate over the middle door.

The confessionals took a while. He started with the priest's booth, figuring if you had good pickup on the unit, you might get stuff from both the other booths. Checked under the chair, checked the molding around the doorjambs and around the little sliding screens into the other booths. Checked along the baseboards and the molding in the corners and the juncture between the walls and the ceiling. Nothing. Did the same in the booth on the right. Nothing again.

Villanueva had gone through the entire third booth and was getting pissed off. If the camera was that small, then the bug was probably even smaller. Must have missed it. He'd have to start over in the priest's booth. He checked his watch. 10.44. He'd already been inside for twenty-five minutes. Church was quiet, and he had no reason to expect company. But this whole job seemed queer from the start, and Villanueva wanted to get out, get home.

He was about to leave the booth when something caught his eye, just a sliver of something sticking out from behind the molding on the right side of the sliding screen that opened into the priest's booth. Could be a hair or even an antenna from a cockroach. Villanueva held the light in his mouth and carefully slid the knife blade up behind the molding. Bingo. Bug wasn't much bigger than a fat grain of rice, couple wires leading out of it. He put it in the bag with the camera. 10.47.

Lynch put his hand on Father Hughes' shoulder just as the priest went to put his key into the lock in the basement door. Hughes looked back. Lynch put a finger to his lips and pointed up at the bypass wires rigged into the alarm at the top of the door. Lynch motioned the priest back toward the stairs.

"I left my cell phone in the car," Lynch whispered. "I need you to get back to the rectory as fast as you can. Call 911, tell them you have a break-in at the church. Tell them there is an officer on the scene who needs back-up. Go."

The priest scurried up the stairs and back up the narrow walk. Lynch edged along the wall and back to the door. He reached up under his jacket, sliding the Berretta 9mm out of the hip holster. Standing on the last step with his back flat against the wall of the church, Lynch reached down and slowly turned the doorknob and pulled. The door moved. It was open. For just an instant, in his peripheral vision, Lynch thought he saw light in the door's window.

Villanueva had just gotten back down the stairs to the basement when he saw the door move. Just a fraction, but it moved. Instantly, he shut off the penlight. His eyes took a second to adjust to the darkness, but Villanueva spent a lot of time in the dark. He was used to it. Slowly, he unzipped the right-hand pocket on the warm-ups and pulled out the .38.

He saw part of a head slip into view through the door's window, just for a second, then pull back. The head had come down into the top left corner of the window, so somebody was standing on the stairs, leaning down to peek in. Villanueva knew the person wouldn't be able to see him inside in the dark. He edged over to the wall, made his way along the wall to the corner, then worked along that wall toward the door.

Villanueva pictured the situation in his head. He had his back to the interior wall to the right of the door. Whoever was outside probably had his back to the exterior wall on the other side of the door. Difference being, Villanueva knew where the guy on the stairs was. That guy had no idea where Villanueva was.

Villanueva ran through the possibilities in his mind. Could

be the priest, janitor for the parish, somebody like that. Maybe the guy noticed the bypass on the alarm, maybe he noticed the door was unlocked. Either way, he'd probably be on his way back to the rectory, probably be calling the cops about now. But Villanueva didn't think he'd take that peek back in the window. And if it was somebody like that, then they weren't there now. Sooner he got the hell out the better.

Could be the person saw the door a while ago, had already called the cops, now the cops were waiting for him. No. Cops would come in and get him, be on the bullhorn, have the whole place lit up.

That left the chink bitch or someone working for her. She said she'd find him. Maybe this was her plan. Pop him right on the stairs, leave the bugs on him, set him up for the Marslovak shooting.

Thing was, any way he looked at it, his situation wasn't going to get better. The door was still open a fraction. He was just a step from it. Get the gun up, hit the door with his shoulder, come through ready to start shooting up the stairs. Hope he didn't see anything. See anything, a shoe, a leg, start pulling the trigger. Best chance he had.

Villanueva took a couple deep breaths, tried to relax some of the tension out, raised the gun, and slammed into the door.

Lynch leaned down to take a peek in the window, pulled his head back instantly. Stupid move. Dark out here, but even darker in there. All he'd do looking through the glass was silhouette his head in the window, give the guy a shot at him. Lynch flattened back against the wall. Could have sworn he'd seen a light. Gone now. If somebody had just shut off a light in the basement, then he'd probably seen Lynch peek in the window. Guy might head back upstairs, try to get out another door. Lynch started sliding back up the stairs, keeping his eye on the basement door as he went up. Figured he could get down to the end of the walk, watch the basement stairs and the vestibule door, cover two exits anyway. Guy ran for it, Lynch would just have to trust he could run him down.

Lynch was halfway up the stairs when the door slammed out, wanging against the cement at the back of the stairwell. A man in dark clothes flew into the cement well, arms extended, a loud crack and a muzzle flash as he fired into the stairs where Lynch had just been. The round hit the step below Lynch's feet, throwing up cement chips. Lynch felt something cut into his right leg, just above the ankle. Lynch brought his gun up and fired, but the guy had kept moving left, across the stairwell, bringing his gun up higher, seeing Lynch further up the stairs. Lynch's round punched into the steel door, sparks flying. Another round dug into the wall just in front and to the right of Lynch's head, bits of cement stinging Lynch's face, Lynch feeling some blood, his right eye clouding up. He heard another shot, but didn't feel anything. Guy was running out of options down there, trying to back into the corner now, trying to get behind the door, trying to bring the gun right. Lynch started squeezing off rounds as fast as he could, aiming for the space between the door and the wall. The sound of the shots in the cement well punched into Lynch's ears like nails, the strobing of the muzzle flash revealing the man in the dark tracksuit as he was slammed back into the wall, the graceless spasmodic jerking as Lynch's rounds tore into him, one more flash as the man pulled his trigger again, the round ricocheting off the floor and whining up the stairs and into the night.

Lynch felt the hammer in the Beretta click down on an empty chamber. Instinctively, he thumbed the clip release, the top note of his brass still tinkling off the cement as the empty clip clattered down the cement stairs. Lynch tore the spare clip from his belt, slapped it into the Beretta, pulled back the slide, and brought the gun back to bear on the target.

The man was crumpled in the corner of the stairwell, a short-barreled revolver on the cement near his left leg. Lynch went down the stairs carefully, keeping the Beretta level, then flicked the revolver away from the man with his right foot. Lynch could smell blood, could see it beginning to spread around the man. The man's hand moved a little, and he heard the man trying to say something. Lynch leaned down.

"Fucking chink," the man said, the words rasping and bubbling through the blood that spilled out of his mouth and down his chin. "Fucking chink."

Lynch sat on the gurney outside the rear of the ambulance. The EMTs had bandaged his leg where a bullet fragment had punched through his calf, wrapped a turban around his head and taped a piece of gauze over his right eye. Another bandage was on the right side of his neck. They'd cut his right pant leg open past the knee and stripped off the sock and shoe. The pant leg was soaked with blood. Lynch had also bled down the right side of his jacket and shirt. One of the EMTs gave him a blanket. Lynch draped it around his shoulders. Rain had stopped, but it was getting colder.

"You're gonna need to get some shit picked out of your face, get that leg wound cleaned out, get everything sutured up," one of the EMTs told him. The guy peeled off his latex gloves and started packing up his material. "Somebody's got to take a good look at the eye, too. I'm not messing with that. You should be OK. Face is gonna look like shit for a while."

"Hey," Lynch said. "You should see the other guy."

"I did. His face looks fine."

Captain Starshak walked over. "He about ready to go?"

"Yeah," the EMT said. "Soon as you guys say, we'll take him in."

"OK," said Starshak. "Give us a second here."

The EMT walked around to the front of the unit.

"How you feeling, John?"

Lynch shrugged. "Like I got shot a couple times and mainlined some adrenaline."

"You're a lucky son of a bitch, you know it? Looks like the guy got four rounds off from about six feet inside a cement box, and all you picked up were some fragments."

"Yeah. Remind me to grab some Lotto tickets on the way home." Lynch gave a little grunt, shifted on the gurney. "The OPS guys happy?" Lynch had already given a quick statement to the office of professional standards investigators who looked into all officer-involved shootings. They had his gun.

"Far as I know," said Starshak. "Hard to see where they can have a problem. Priest backs up your story, crime scene matches up. They wondered a little did you have to shoot the guy so much. You put eight rounds into him between his belt and his collarbone."

"Yeah, well, he was shooting at me. I got a little excited."

"What I told em. Right before I told em to go fuck themselves. You know who you popped?"

"Didn't get a great look. Dark down there, and he was spitting up a lot of blood."

"Jose Villanueva."

"The second-story guy?"

"That's him."

"He's doing churches now, boosting chalices? Seems a little low-rent for him."

"Wasn't after the chalices. Had a baggie in his pocket with some hi-tech crap in it. Priest told me what you were thinking about the confessional being bugged. Looks like you were right."

"The electronics point anywhere?"

"Sending them down to the tech weenies, see what they can make of them." Starshak let out a long exhale, his breath clouding in the cold, damp air. "Fucking cold. You don't figure he shot old lady Marslovak? Coming back to pick up his stuff?"

Lynch shrugged. "Toss his place, I guess, see if you find a long gun. Be for-hire if it's him, but I don't remember him doing anything like this. And he would have had to learn to shoot somewhere. He ex-military?"

"Slo-mo's checking."

"More likely somebody hired him to clean up."

"You mean after they hire somebody else to pop the Marslovak woman?"

"Yeah."

"Lotta hiring. Jose didn't work cheap, either."

Lynch nodded. "He said something right before he died. Said 'fucking chink.' Said it a couple of times."

"So?"

"So somebody says fucking chink in this town, who do you think of?"

"Paddy Wang?"

"Yeah. Did I tell you he turned up where I was eating a couple nights back? Picked up my tab, told me I gotta show up at the Connemara Ball this year."

"Think we should haul him in, shake him up a little?"

"Shake up Paddy Wang? With what? A nuke? Nah. Let me think on it. I'll figure some way to come at him." Lynch saw Father Hughes and Liz Johnson standing across the street by the curb. Her face was red and her eyes looked puffy. She gave a little wave, uncertain. He waved back, smiled, which made his face hurt.

"OK, Lynch, get yourself patched up. I'll see what we can make of Villanueva. So that the blonde from McGinty's?"

"Yeah."

"Think now that your face is all messed up she might be looking for a replacement?"

Lynch flipped him off. Starshak smiled, clapped Lynch on the shoulder, and gestured to the EMTs. They came back, strapped Lynch to the gurney, and rolled it inside the unit. Lynch watched through the back window as the ambulance pulled out, the flashing lights washing through the rain-dampened branches of the trees and into the sky, staining everything red. Lynch was tired suddenly, and feeling empty. And cold.

At Northwestern, the ER docs irrigated and sutured the wound on his leg, picked nine bullet and cement fragments out of his head and neck, and removed a shard of cement from his eye. It was almost 3am when they were done.

"All right, detective. We're going to have to keep an eye on that leg, make sure we don't get an infection." The doctor handed Lynch two bottles of pills. "The antibiotics should help. You've had some here. Take four when you wake up, then two every four hours until they're gone. The other bottle is for pain. No more tonight. We've shot you up pretty good. You're going to hurt in the morning, though. Same deal, two every four hours. Also, you need to keep that eye covered for at least three or four days. Any questions?"

Lynch shook his head. He felt groggy. His leg was throbbing faintly. He couldn't feel it clearly. It was more like a premonition. The side of his head was still numb from the local they'd injected before they went to work.

"You got a ride home? Got somebody to stay with you tonight?"

Lynch tried to focus. "One of the uniforms'll get me home, I guess."

"OK," the doctor said. "You've got some people waiting for you out front."

A nurse wheeled Lynch to the waiting area. Starshak and Bernstein were standing by the door. Johnson was sitting in a chair.

"He gonna be OK, doc?" Starshak asked.

"Lucky man," said the doctor. "The fragment in his neck came real close to his carotid, and the eye could have been a lot worse."

Bernstein squatted down next to the chair. "How you feeling?"

"How do I look?" Lynch asked.

"You look like shit."

"Feel worse," Lynch said.

"You want me to get you home?" asked Bernstein.

Johnson stood up. "I can get him home."

Bernstein looked at Johnson, then looked back at Lynch.

"Yeah," said Lynch. "Thanks anyway, Slo-mo, I got a ride."

The doctor walked over to Johnson. "Can you stay with him tonight?"

Johnson looked at Lynch, he nodded. "Sure," she said.

The doc pulled her aside. "He's a macho guy, isn't going to ask for help. Keep him warm. Keep him quiet. Liquids are good – orange juice, water. No booze. Food is fine in the morning. This probably hasn't all hit him yet, but it will. Be there for him for that."

"I will," she said.

Johnson got Lynch home and stripped the ruined clothes off him. She found a big mixing bowl in the kitchen and filled it with warm water. She got a washcloth and some towels and soap from the bathroom. She laid the towels out on the big easy chair in the living room and helped Lynch into it. Then she carefully washed the blood and sweat from his body, drying him gently. She found an old Boston College sweatsuit in a closet and helped Lynch put it on. Then she slipped her arm under his and helped him walk back to the bed. She tucked him under the covers and pulled a chair up next to him.

"Guess I ruined your date," Lynch said.

She shook her head. "I can wait on dessert."

"Good thing," Lynch said. "Kitchen's closed for repairs."

Johnson started to laugh, but cried instead. "I was so scared," she said.

"Me too."

She nodded. Tried to speak, couldn't.

"I'm glad you're here," he said.

She kissed his hand again, held it to her. "You sleep," she said. "I'll be here. I'll be right here."

Johnson slept in the chair, waking as Lynch tossed. Around 5.00, he bolted up in the bed, throwing off the blankets and lurching to his feet. His eyes were wide and panicked, and his face glistened with sweat. He swung his right arm wildly, then stumbled on his bad leg, banging into the wall near the door. He was shouting something, but the words were choked and garbled. He froze for a moment, his eyes seeming to clear, then staggered toward the door, panting, starting to retch.

Johnson ran after him to the bathroom. Lynch was down on his knees, his forearms along the sides of the toilet seat, as he vomited violently into the bowl. Johnson knelt next to him, her arm across his back. He stopped, finally, collapsing against her, a string of mucus hanging from his chin. She wiped it from him with her hand and held him against her. She felt his head pressed against her breast. She felt him start to shake. She stroked his hair and held him to her tightly. Finally, the rigidity left him. His body slackened and he sank into her. Johnson sat on the tile floor with her back against the wall with Lynch curled like a child in front of her, his head on her lap, and he wept.

CHAPTER 24 – RESTON, VIRGINIA

In the generic conference room at the back of InterGov's suite, Weaver was trying to be patient while Tom Paravola, InterGov's technology director and research guru, ran down what he had thus far unearthed. Ferguson, Weaver's top ops guy, was at the table along with Chen and Nancy Snyder, chief witch doctor from the PsyOps group.

"We've hacked into all the major credit card issuers, and we have a program sorting through all cards issued based on applications received since Fisher's family was killed," Paravola droned. "We're sorting them by the demographic parameters Fisher could likely use. White, male, age range forty to sixty-five just to be safe. That's still way too many cards. OK, we also have in place programming that cross-references these cards with existing credit histories. Here's how that works. We assign algorithms to–"

Weaver waved a hand. "Tom, could you skip the tech wizard shit? We don't care, and we don't understand. Skip to the bottom line, OK?"

Paravola looked disappointed. "OK, but this is some pretty elegant stuff we've done, and it's got some great potential applications–"

"Paravola, you're starting to piss me off. I'm sure it's great shit. That's why we pay you what we do. It's also why you're here and not doing time for that child porn rap we got your ass out of. Now give me some fucking data."

Paravola blanched and took a swallow of water. "OK. We've got about 51,100 new cards that make sense. Of the ones that have been used, most have heavily localized usage patterns away from the north-south line we're focusing on, and many have been used at dates and times that coincide with Fisher's known activities, but in locations far removed from those actions."

"You mean while he was blowing people's hearts out through their spinal columns," said Weaver.

"Yes, then. That still leaves better than 20,000 cards. Most of those haven't been used at all, so those don't help. OK, that leaves 735 cards that have been used on or near Fisher's line at least once on dates that fit our profile. Of that set, 541 have other charging patterns that eliminate them from consideration, and 107 others have charging patterns that put them within five percent of being eliminated by our current probability matrix. Of the remaining 83 cards, one interesting pattern has emerged.

"A Paul Reynolds, forty-seven, used a Discover card in and around Door County, the first shooting scene, for two days before and on the day of the shooting. That card was not used before nor has it been used since. Charges include a hotel room, meals, and some clothing.

"A Joseph Huss, fifty, used a MasterCard in the northern suburbs of Chicago, again for three days, two before the Marslovak shooting and the day of the shooting. Room, board, and gas. Again, not used before or since.

"And, the pièce de résistance, a Bill Wilson, forty-six, has used a MasterCard for the last three days, first to check into a Motel 6 in Kankakee, Illinois, and to eat at a Denny's, then to buy some shoes at a local sporting goods store, and, just this morning, to buy breakfast at a diner in Onar–"

Paravola stopped talking to duck the water glass Weaver had thrown at his head. The glass shattered against the white board behind Paravola.

"You dumb fuck." Weaver was standing now, leaning toward Paravola, his hands on the table. "You waste our time with your goddamn algorithms and charge-pattern run-downs when you have something close to real-time intel? When did you develop this?"

Paravola was shaking. "Just in the last hour. The last charge was only made a few hours ago."

"What's that town again?"

"Onarga."

"Fergie?"

Ferguson already had a map up on his laptop. "On our line, boss. Maybe an hour or so south out of Kankakee."

"You ready to roll?"

"Got my team," Ferguson said. "Me, Lawrence, Capelli, and Richter. Gave Chen my load-out list yesterday."

"Everything is at the hangar, sir," Chen said.

"Four guys enough?" Weaver asked.

"Best we can do, unless you want to call Langley, get some extra bodies," Ferguson said. "Figured you'd want to keep this in house."

"You figured right. Fergie, get out to Andrews. Beep your team. I want you wheels up ASAP. Get set up in Effingham. You already made arrangements there, Chen?"

"Yes, sir. Ferguson has the details."

"Good deal. Chen, I don't know what we can do in the way of local stringers in central Illinois, but if we have some or can get some, get them out. Hotels, gas stations, you know the drill. Get somebody into Kankakee, see if we can get a make and model on whatever Fisher's driving."

"Yes, sir. Can I contact any other agencies?"

"No. We need to contain this, people. Fisher is our guy. He's our problem. It's a post-9/11 world. Already a lot less handwringing on the Hill when our more legitimate friends

need to color outside the lines a little. This is not the time to
be calling Langley or the feebs looking for help. This sort of
outside-the-box shit is why we exist. If we can't clean this up,
what good are we. Anything else?"

Dr Snyder, who had spent the meeting doodling on a legal
pad, looked up.

"Actually, Colonel, if you have a moment, you and I should
chat."

"Your office," said Weaver. "Rest of you get moving."

The higher-ups at InterGov were left to their own devices when
it came to decorating their offices. Most emulated Weaver's
spartan army-surplus look. But Dr Snyder's office was damn
near opulent.

Two walls were covered by bookcases. The cases were full,
and Weaver had no doubt Synder'd read all that shit. An
exquisite hand-tied rug from northern Afghanistan covered
most of the floor. The pattern was dense and intricate, with
red the predominant color. It had been darker red the first time
Weaver had seen it because Ferguson had picked up a body the
lab needed to look at and had used the rug for packaging on
the flight from Islamabad to DC. Thing was, Fergie'd had to put
a couple 9mm slugs through the body in order to convince it to
lie still, so the body had a couple of leaks. They were going to
toss the rug, but Snyder had asked if she could have it. She got
some restoration friend of hers at the Smithsonian to clean it
up. Still had some stains, but you had to know where to look.

Weaver sat down in one of the wine-colored leather wingback
chairs that flanked a butler's table with brass accents. Snyder
was futzing around in the back.

"Would you care for a cup of tea, Colonel?" she asked.

"Doc, every time I come down here, you ask if I want a cup
of tea. Every time you ask, I tell you no."

"I'm going to have some tea, Colonel. Propriety demands

the inquiry, even given your predictable response." Dr Snyder settled into the other chair, setting a small white china cup and saucer on the table.

"So you unscramble Fisher's eggs for me, doc?"

Snyder smiled. "Alas, like the lamented Humpty Dumpty, Mr Fisher's eggs cannot be put back together again. I do believe, however, I can offer some insight into what might be on his menu."

"Gimme," said Weaver.

"First, Mr Fisher, like most of the gentlemen in your operations department, evidences numerous psycho- or sociopathic tendencies – lack of empathy, lack of guilt, considerable cunning."

"For Christ's sake, we have you test for those qualities when we recruit. Look, Doc, I understand if you're running the local Walmart those qualities might put you off a candidate. But they're all big pluses for me."

"True. Mr Fisher is an interesting case, however. He did consent to examination after his family was murdered. I had expected him to be enraged and focused on revenge. Psychopaths generally hold grudges and do not bear insults of any kind lightly. Fisher was curiously unaroused. In response to questions in this area, he indicated that his family was in paradise. They had all been to the Catholic sacrament of confession that morning, so Fisher was convinced they had died in a state of grace and were thus ensured immediate entrance into heaven. I understand that his father was devout as well?"

"Zeke? Yeah. I did a job in Kenya with Zeke, back during the Mau-Mau shit. Son of a bitch got me out of the rack at dawn one Sunday so we could drive through the bush for better than an hour so he could make mass at some cholera-trap mission."

"So a paternal bond, our Mr Fisher sharing his father's spiritual and vocational faiths. As to the issue of this geographic line that so interests you and Mr Ferguson, that smacks of ritual. Now, mental illness is a maddeningly esoteric affair, so such rituals are often very difficult to decipher. However, if Mr Fisher has become a serial killer, although I suppose one could argue that he has been one for years after a fashion, but if he has become a serial killer operating on an agenda other than the one which you control, then there is almost certainly a ritual involved. In his case, I would guess that this ritual will have religious, specifically Catholic, underpinnings."

"You gonna give me any more guidance on that, or am I just supposed to operate on the assumption that he's become some kind of religious whack job?"

"We are well into the area of supposition, Colonel. But not, I don't think, wholly unfounded supposition. Let me ask you, how many people has Fisher killed?"

Weaver gave a shrug. "Couldn't say for sure. Specific targets on missions I assigned? Better than a hundred. Collateral deaths in those missions? Maybe another hundred. There was Vietnam before that."

"And how would you characterize the men Fisher killed?"

"Scumbags, mostly. Terrorists, drug dealers, third-world thugs. Why?"

"Colonel, Fisher is not, I don't believe, what you would characterize as a primary psychopath – not utterly remorseless, certainly not incapable of forming real attachments. His attachments to his family were authentic and quite strong. I believe he is a secondary psychopath. Ordinarily, the only hope for anything like a cure for a psychopath is an epiphany of some kind. Some event that so undermines their egocentric worldview that they ameliorate or even repolarize their behavior of their own volition. I believe that watching his family die was such an event for Mr Fisher. Unfortunately, the shock of this event was such that it did not redirect Mr Fisher into more normal channels. Instead, it has redirected him into another pathology entirely. As I said, one psychopathic characteristic that Mr Fisher evidenced was a lack of remorse. He was capable of killing in cold blood without allowing his conscience to interfere with his ability to continue to do so. When his family was killed in front of him, when he had his epiphany, the cumulative guilt attendant to all those previous killings must have been extraordinary, compounded by the guilt of not being able to save his own family. He was able to exonerate himself of the latter guilt by taking refuge in his religion – by assuring himself that his family was in paradise. If he had found no mechanism to relieve the guilt of failing to prevent – and, really, since the act was almost certainly targeted at him, of likely causing – the death of his family, the death of the only persons with whom he had an authentic attachment, I don't believe he would have been able to function. Therefore, he has not only found refuge in his religion, he has become imprisoned by it. However, Catholicism compounds the guilt attached to his prior bad acts. The men he killed, by the standards of Fisher's religion, were almost universally evil. Thus, he not only killed them, by killing them when they were not in a state of grace, he damned them. God, in his church's teaching, desires that all souls find their way to him. Fisher had, thusly, subverted God's will."

Weaver leaned back in the chair. He'd learned long ago that you couldn't rush Snyder. She'd get to her point when she got to it. He wasn't sure what would happen if he threw a glass at her, but he was pretty sure she wouldn't wet her drawers like Paravola.

"This is all real interesting, doc, but where's it get us?"

"Colonel, don't you see? The two people he's killed so far were both killed immediately after being absolved of their sins by a Catholic priest. Fisher purposely killed them while they were in a state of grace. He sent them to heaven."

"Christ, doc. You telling me he's trying to balance the books?"

"I believe so, yes."

PENANCE

"Then he's got a couple hundred people to go."

Dr Snyder tilted her head a little, looking amused. "That, dear Colonel, is your problem. There's one more thing, Colonel. I happened to take a peek at that map Mr Ferguson accessed. Your assumption is that the killings will be roughly equidistant from one another along this north/south axis?"

"It's a stretch, but it's all we've got."

"If you look just south of Effingham, you'll see a town called Moriah." Snyder paused expectantly.

"And?"

"Think of your Old Testament, Colonel. When God calls on Abraham to sacrifice his only son, he tells Abraham to take him to a place called Moriah and to make the sacrifice on a height that God will point out. I think the symbolism will be compelling to our Mr Fisher."

"God stops Abraham before he offs the kid."

"Yes," said Snyder. "Abraham sacrifices a ram in the child's stead."

"Not much chance of that happening this time."

Snyder just raised her eyebrows and took another sip of her tea. Weaver got up and headed back up the hall.

An hour later, Weaver stood in a closed hangar at Andrews Air Force base watching Ferguson oversee the former Air America guys as they loaded his team's gear into a Gulfstream IV.

"What are you bringing, Fergie?"

"Got the Remington 700s for me and Lawrence. Scoped 16s with the extended mags for Capelli and Richter, let them handle any hose jobs. Suppressed H&Ks in case we need to take things inside. Everybody's got their personal weapons. Also, I'm bringing a couple of the Barretts."

The Barretts were .50 caliber weapons with ten-round magazines and an effective range of almost a mile. They could shoot through walls, through cars. They could throw armor piercing slugs, incendiary rounds, you name it.

"Jesus, Fergie," Weaver said. "The fucking Barretts?"

"A lot of open country down that way, boss. Might catch him in a vehicle. Frankly, I want to have the bastard out-gunned. Gets to a shooting match, I'll feel a lot better if we're out of his range. Anyway, better to have it and not need it–"

"Yeah, yeah, yeah. Than need it and not have it. OK, Fergie, it's your show. Just try to keep us off Nightline." Weaver clapped Ferguson on the back. "Hey, Chen around?"

Ferguson nodded up at the Gulfstream. "Already on board."

Chen was sitting in the back of the cabin looking at her laptop.

"Playing solitaire, Chen?"

"I had Paravola link me into his tracking program. I'm running a few alternative searches. Will you be joining us?"

Weaver walked down the aisle and sat in the seat facing Chen.

"Yeah. Got some good shit out of Snyder. You heard about Villanueva?"

"Yes, sir."

"Not your fault, Chen. I told you to send the spic. My call. Anything heating up there?"

· "The detective on the case has identified the spot where Fisher took the shot, and another investigator is asking military and law enforcement contacts for names of snipers. We have to assume Villanueva had the electronics on him when he was killed, but I haven't seen anything regarding those in their system yet."

"What's this detective's name?"

"John Lynch."

"He any good?"

"He has an excellent clearance rate on his cases," Chen said. "This is also the second time he has been involved in a gun battle. When he was a rookie, he killed two men and was wounded when he and his partner were ambushed in a housing project."

"So this Lynch guy could be a problem."

"It is possible, sir."

"You think on that then, Chen. Let me know if it looks like we've got to make his life interesting."

"Yes, sir."

"Pull up your map for a second," Weaver said. Chen pressed a few keys and turned the laptop so both she and Weaver could see the screen. "Snyder thinks Fisher will head to a town called Moriah. Some biblical bullshit."

"It's here," said Chen, moving the cursor.

"Gimme some detail."

Chen zoomed in on the town.

"Jesus," said Weaver, "Welcome to Mayberry. They got a Catholic church?"

Chen switched out of the map program and into a local directory. "Holy Angels. Hill Street."

"When they do confessions there?"

"The next scheduled time is 3pm tomorrow."

"Go back to the map, show me the church. Switch to topo," said Weaver.

Chen pressed another key, bringing up a topographical map of the area. Weaver took one look at the dense concentration of curved contour lines and let out a low whistle.

"Fergie's gonna love this," he said.

Richter popped into the cabin, followed by Ferguson, Lawrence, and Capelli. Weaver got up. He went to clap Chen on the shoulder, habit, just what he did with the troops. But he stopped. Every time he touched her, he felt like he'd just put his hand in a snake pit and gotten away with it.

Weaver walked to the front of the plane wondering if he should ask Snyder about Chen, then thinking he'd be more comfortable not knowing.

CHAPTER 25 – CHICAGO

While Lynch slept, Johnson went out and bought food. She could hear Lynch in the shower when she got back. He came out from the bedroom in a pair of khakis and a white T-shirt just as she set breakfast on the table. Eggs, sausage, bagels, grapefruit, coffee.

"Thought you'd gone in to work," said Lynch.

"I'll have to, after we eat. How are you feeling?"

"Leg hurts, but not too bad. Head itches. Listen, thanks for last night. Hope I wasn't too much of a wuss."

"I don't think you've got much wuss in you, Lynch."

"Still, bawling in your lap. Not my usual move on a third date."

"I give all my boyfriends a pass when they get shot."

"Wasn't the getting shot. Second time I've had to kill somebody. Doesn't sit too well with me."

Johnson reached across the table and took his hand. "You might have a little wuss in you after all. But it's the good kind."

Lynch pushed his food around on his plate.

"What are you going to do with yourself today?" Johnson asked.

"Figure I'll visit my mom, then I need to get over to her place. She's been in Resurrection for better than a week. Better start getting shit in order over there. Not sure if she's going to get back home again, but she hasn't been able to keep on top of things for a while. Doesn't feel right letting the place go."

"Well, don't push things. You did get shot last night, in case you forgot."

"Shot's when you get a bullet in you. I just got peppered with some shit."

"Guess you're not a wuss after all."

"Don't worry, I have to move any furniture or anything, I'll give you a call."

After breakfast, Johnson looked at Lynch and made a face. "We've got to do something about your hair." The emergency room staff had shaved off three patches of hair on the right side of Lynch's head to get at the bullet and cement fragments.

He gave her a lopsided smile. "You think?"

She took him into the bathroom and draped a towel over his shoulders. She trimmed the hair back to stubble with scissors, then used his razor to shave it off. She carefully peeled the gauze from over his eye. She opened a fresh gauze pad, spread ointment on it, and taped it down.

"I've got a present for you," she said, opening the white bag she had brought back that morning. She pulled out a black eyepatch, and Lynch laughed. She lifted the towel off his shoulders and shook it out into the bathtub. Then she wiped his scalp with a warm washcloth and, stretching the elastic over his head, fitted the patch over the gauze pad on his eye. Lynch stood up and looked in the mirror.

"Won't Bernstein be thrilled," he said. "I look like Moshe Dayan."

CHAPTER 26 – MORIAH, ILLINOIS

Fisher finished fueling the truck. The line was established. The electronics were in place, and Weaver would know to look for the signal by now. With each sacrifice, Weaver would know more. It was time.

Fisher pushed the nozzle of the gas pump back into the pump housing, walked into the station, and placed the American Express card on the counter. The attendant ran the card through the machine and passed it back.

"Thanks, Mr McBride," the attendant said. "Come and see us again soon."

Fisher just smiled.

CHAPTER 27 – ABOVE KENTUCKY

The Gulfstream was cruising over eastern Kentucky, and Weaver had settled into the starboard seat in front with a glass of Macallan's and a Cohiba. Technically, smoking was forbidden. Of course, technically, he wasn't supposed to be in a plane full of armed thugs plotting a murder, so he lit up the cigar.

Things were looking up. Chen had gotten a call from Kankakee. They had a positive ID on Fisher. He was holding the line. Still didn't know what he was driving, though. But the Moriah thing felt right. And it was a small town. Population 328. Shit, Fergie'd packed enough hardware to take it right off the map.

Weaver finished the scotch and was thinking about a nap when someone tapped his shoulder. Chen.

"Yeah?"

"The McBride identity has surfaced, sir. Fisher just used the American Express card at a gas station."

"Where?"

"Moriah."

Weaver smiled. He could smell blood. He stood up. "Gentlemen, listen up. We have confirmed that Fisher is on the ground in the target area. Fergie? You seen the map?"

"Yes."

"And?"

"And he'll have more hides than crab lice on a crack whore, boss." Some general laughter with that one.

"Tough terrain, Fergie, I'll grant you that. Everybody be ready to roll when we touch down. We are not loitering in the LZ. Chen, you've got recon. Check the church for electronics then take a drive around, see what you can pick up. Richter, Capelli, you've got the trail maps for the state forest. Give me a sweep around that ridge. Fergie, you and me and Lawrence are gonna work up some tactics. Big day tomorrow, boys and girls, and not a lot of sleep tonight. We've got ninety minutes before landing. I'm sacking out."

Weaver sank back into his seat and, in the habit of soldiers everywhere, was out in seconds.

Chen pulled her rented Toyota in the lot in front of St Holy Angels just before 5pm, parking just long enough to let her cell phone run through the frequencies Paravola had programmed in. In a couple of seconds, she picked up some video from inside the church. Fisher had been here. He was ready.

The ridge around the church concerned her. Too much ground and too many potential hides for Fisher. They'd have to wait until Fisher took the shot and be ready for a counter-sniper action. That could get ugly.

Capelli and Richter parked at one of the trailheads north of the church and walked through the woods to the top of the ridgeline that overlooked the parking lot. Sight lines through the woods varied but were not as bad as they could have been. A fair amount of low brush grew in clumps, but the trees were well established, oak and maple mostly. There wasn't much secondary growth, and the ground evidently got some traffic. The state maintained an extensive network of marked trails through the area, and numerous other footpaths were worn into the ground. The late sun drilled down through the bare

trees, dappling the ground. Richter and Capelli didn't expect
Fisher to be in the woods now, but they both wore silenced
H&K MP5s on slings under their coats. They worked up the
back of the ridge abreast, fifteen yards apart. Richter would
move forward while Capelli provided cover, then Capelli
would leapfrog him and work ahead.

At the crest of the ridge, they fanned out, Richter taking
the ridge as it curved north and east, Capelli following the
ridgeline south. Both took range readings to the church from
likely spots along the ridge. The ranges from the top of the
ridge varied from seven hundred and fifty to nine hundred
and twenty meters. They marked on the map spots from
which Fisher could not shoot. The northeastern end of the
ridge provided no angle to the church's main doors, and there
was no door on that side. Just south of the center of the ridge,
a copse of tall oaks blocked a clean shot at the front of the
church. Capelli found an area toward the south end of the
ridge that was heavily overgrown. It would be an excellent
hide if the shooter didn't have to move quickly. Of course, if
you got in there and took fire, it would suck big time. A handful
of other locations were bad – too steep, trees blocking sight
lines, no cover. By the time Richter and Capelli got back to the
trailhead for the drive back to Effingham, they'd eliminated
almost half of the ridgeline and targeted fifteen likely hides.

Weaver, Ferguson, and Lawrence drove the Suburban up
I-57 to the west end of Effingham, where most of the hotels
clustered along Fayette Avenue. Chen had booked six rooms
at the Days Inn.

Ferguson unfolded a large-scale US Geological Survey map
on the round table in his room, and the men clustered around
it.

"Got to figure he's going to park north at one of the trailheads
and walk in," said Ferguson. "He comes from the south here,

he's either got to park at the church or in this mess of homes here. Either way, people are going to see him."

"So we stake out the trailheads?" Lawrence asked.

Weaver shook his head. "Too many. You got four on this stretch right behind the ridge, which would leave you guys one-on-one. Get up around this curve here, there's three more. If he's willing to hump it a-ways, Christ, then he could park anywhere."

Ferguson nodded. "I'd do the trailheads if I had, say, fifteen guys. No. We're going to have to get him at the church."

"Gonna be a bitch," said Lawrence. "Got, what, almost a mile of ridgeline up there? All of it wooded?"

"We'll see what Capelli and Richter find. You know some of it will be shit," said Weaver.

Lawrence ran his finger along Hill Street up to the church and along the south verge of the church lot. "Can't take him from the south. Nothing there," he said. "Be looking right into the sun that time of day."

"Too close to the houses anyway," said Weaver.

"Church got a tower or anything? Best bet is to be on his line," said Ferguson.

"Too risky," said Weaver. "Odds are we aren't going to get a read on his position until he takes his shot. So we got a body out front and cops on the way. Even if we suppress one of the Remingtons, somebody out front would hear it. Even if they don't, we'd have somebody stuck up there until the cops got done. Maybe they decide to take a look. We gotta stay mobile."

There was a knock at the door. Weaver pulled a slim automatic from the inside-the-pant rig beneath his right kidney and walked over to check the peephole. When he opened the door, Capelli and Richter walked in with three large pizza boxes and a bag full of water bottles. They pulled out their maps and gave them to Ferguson, who started transferring the markings onto his map.

"Gimme a minute here," he said. He sat at the table and rested his chin on his hands while the rest of the crew ate.

After ten minutes, Ferguson sat up straight. "OK, I think we got a plan. We go in at him from behind. Capelli, Richter, tell me about this shit in here." Ferguson pointed to the area at the back of the ridge that ran downhill toward the trailheads.

"Got a sort of funnel," said Richter. "Pretty open for woods up the middle, not a lot of secondary growth. North and south here it gets shitty. Steep, more brush." Richter ran his finger up the ridge on the map. "You can see where the trails coming in bunch up about halfway up here, then fan out again."

"That's what I'm thinking," said Ferguson. "After the shot, he's hauling ass. Ain't gonna be like Chicago, locals are going to know the shot came from that ridge. Still, he's not gonna bang through that shit on the sides like a fucking greenhorn. He'll come down that funnel, not on one of the paths, but through that funnel. Figure on the verges, right or left."

"So how do we set it up?" Weaver asked.

"Me and Lawrence take the top of the funnel, either side. We should hear the shot, so we'll have a line on him. Capelli and Richter get in the shit on either side of the narrow part. Let him get halfway between our positions, then they start hosing. Maybe they get him. They don't, either he heads back up the ridge into me and Lawrence and we take him out, or he's gonna try to get cover between him and Capelli and Richter, which is gonna leave his ass open to us and we take him out anyway."

Weaver looked at Lawrence. Lawrence nodded.

"Could get loud," Weaver said.

"What do we got across that narrow part, Capelli? Looks like fifty, sixty yards?"

"Something like that," Capelli said.

"Have Richter and Capelli stick with the H&Ks," Ferguson said. "They're suppressed, and they're accurate for that distance. Lawrence or I take a shot, probably only be the one, and we're shooting down the ridge and we're a good couple hundred yards beneath the ridgeline anyway. Sound ain't gonna be much back by the church. Oughta be OK."

"What time do we insert?" Weaver asked.

"Chen said this confession shit at the church starts at 3.00, right?"

"Yeah," said Weaver.

"Gotta figure Fisher is going to set up early. We want to make sure he's in position before we move in. Be a real clusterfuck if we all walk in at the same time. Lawrence and Capelli can insert at this trailhead on the right, work up the right side. Richter and I will work in from the left. Say we start making our move around 1pm. We're going to wanna go in real slow and real quiet."

"How about extraction?" Weaver asked.

"Chen can take the Suburban, cruise the area starting around 2.00. We're going to have to pack Fisher's body out. We can call her in when we're ready."

Weaver looked at Capelli. "Good by you?"

"Hey, Fergie's the man. He says it's the plan, then it's the plan."

"Richter?" Weaver asked. Richter had taken out a combat knife and was running a whetstone along the blade.

"Whatever, man. Tag em and bag em. It's all rock and roll to me."

"Richter," Ferguson said. "Gets to where you gotta show Fisher your knife, you might as well cut your own throat with it. Because he will take it away from you and open you up like a tuna can."

Weaver was wishing he didn't have to use Richter. He was good, former SEAL, but he wasn't as good as he thought he was. Weaver was thin on ops guys, though. Had a couple of teams in Europe taking out Al-Qaeda targets the Agency pukes couldn't get enough shit on for arrests, another team in South America.

"You guys need to understand what you are up against," Weaver said. "Fisher is good. He is very, very good."

"He's old, and he's nuts," said Richter. "And we're good, too. And there are four of us."

Ferguson looked Richter in the eyes. "Fisher is better now than you are ever going to be, Richter. Nuts or not, old or not. I've worked with him, you haven't. He's better than I am – way better. And I'm better than you."

Richter sat back. This was not a community in which anybody admitted second-class status. "Yeah, well, still. Four of us, one of him. Is he four times better?"

"Guess we'll find out," said Ferguson.

At 12.15am, Weaver was alone in his room, still looking at the maps, turning Ferguson's plan over, trying to find something he didn't like. Seemed solid. He heard a tap at his door. He pulled out the Walther again, checked the peephole. Chen. She was still wearing her black pantsuit, looking like she got dressed fifteen minutes ago. Weaver opened the door and waved her into the room.

"What's up?" Weaver asked.

"Contingency plan, sir."

Weaver nodded and sat back down at the table. No matter how much he liked Fergie's plan, it was still Fisher they were trying to take out. Which meant there was still a decent chance that this time tomorrow, Fisher'd be headed for points south and Weaver'd have a state forest full of dead guys to explain.

"OK, Chen, what do you have?"

"I have placed traces of crystal methamphetamine and fifteen thousand dollars in cash in one of Richter's personal bags. A number of crystal meth labs have been discovered in rural Midwestern communities. Paravola is ready to replace

NCIC files on four known crystal meth dealers with the ops team's data."

"Nice touch, Chen. I think I can actually get some sleep now."

CHAPTER 28 – CHICAGO

As soon as Lynch walked into his mother's hospital room, he knew death had spun out of the final turn and gone to the whip. Her complexion had gone from pale to waxen to almost corrupt. Her breathing was the sound of a rasp on cheap plywood. He pressed his lips to her cheek, and it felt like something from the deli counter.

"Johnny," she said.

"It's OK, ma." He brushed a strand of hair away from her mouth.

"Hurts," she said.

"I know," he answered. "I know."

He remembered the bungalow up on Neenah. Summers, his mom in the plaid Madras shorts she liked and the sleeveless blouses, the smoke from the grill, the neat row of rose bushes along the chain-link fence between their yard and the Garritys's. Mom singing show tunes as she flipped the burgers. Dad in the dark chinos and the Dago T, the nylon web yard chair sagging beneath him, a gold Miller High Life can in his massive paw. Lynch's sister, maybe three or four, climbing up the old man's legs and into his lap. Mom still something of a looker, like Jackie O, the way she'd sit on the wood stairs in the back, legs crossed, one sandal just dangling off her toes. The sound of the neighborhood kids – the Garrity twins, Tony Campanaro, Sean Haggerty getting up a whiffle ball game in the ally. Wandering across the yard to the gate to join them, his ma's voice strong and high and sweet behind. Knowing supper was coming and there was no better place in the world.

"You made us a good life, ma," Lynch said. "Couldn't have done any better. I love you. I'm going to miss you."

Lynch watched one tear roll down his mother's desiccated cheek, then saw her eyes roll up. It wasn't sleep anymore. Lynch wasn't sure what it was, but it wasn't sleep. The rasping went on and on.

After a while he couldn't listen to it anymore, and he left.

Lynch went to his mom's, cleaned out the fridge, collected the mail. Grass was starting to grow. He went out to the garage, but there wasn't any gas for the mower. Might be a little much today anyway. Trying not to give in to the leg too much, but it was barking at him some. He looked up at the little attic his dad had made in the rafters, plywood nailed over the cross members. Knew there was some shit up there, old Christmas lights, scrap. Knew it was coming, the day he'd have to clean all that out. The house didn't bother him – he had a whole history with his mom in the house after his dad. But the garage felt a little like a mausoleum.

On the way back to his place, Lynch drove past Sacred Heart and found Father Hughes sweating through a Notre Dame sweatshirt next to a pile of flagstones. Lynch could see where the priest had dug out the outline of a walk leading to the Marian grotto. He'd laid down a crushed limestone base and had just started laying in the fieldstones.

"Tell me this is some kind of new Lenten penance, Father, and I'm turning Baptist," said Lynch, coming up the walk.

"I like the eyepatch. You OK?"

"Itches some. Otherwise I'm good."

"I was just ready for a lunch break," said the priest. "Care to join me?"

"What are you serving?" asked Lynch.

"Peanut butter and jelly and milk."

Lynch laughed. "No cookies?"

"Can't abide the store-bought ones and can't bake to save my life," answered the priest.

"Tell you what, Father, I had a burger up at that bar off of Belmont last week, and it didn't kill me. Can a lapsed altar boy stand you to a beer and a bite?"

The priest smiled. "I'd never dream of depriving a man of the chance to perform a corporal work of mercy. Bless you, my son."

They settled into a booth in the back. Lynch ordered a grilled ham and swiss. The priest went with the tuna melt. They each had a black and tan.

"Father," said Lynch, "I want to ask a favor."

"If you're planning on laying a walk, I think I'm retiring after this one."

Lynch smiled. "It's my mom. She's dying. Should be any day now. We'll have the funeral up at St Lucia's, but she's been in and out of the hospital for over a year now, and the priest she knew up there died. Couple of young guys on the staff now. Nothing against them, but I don't know them. Actually, you're the only priest I do know now. I need to get the funeral together, and, I don't know, I'd just like somebody familiar to see her off."

The priest reached across the table and squeezed Lynch's forearm. "Tough thing, detective, burying your mom. Dad gone?"

"Years ago," said Lynch.

"I'd be honored to do the service. Just call when it's time. I'll talk to the parish up there and set things up. Any other family?"

"Got a sister up in Milwaukee, nephew I don't see enough.

We, I don't know, just kind of lost touch. Used to be close."

"Have you called her? She'll want to be down before your mom goes."

"Yeah," said Lynch. "I gotta do that. I gotta do that right now." Lynch pulled out his cell phone, got his sister's secretary. He had to lean on her a bit to put the call through.

"Colleen, it's Johnny. It's about mom. It's any time now. You better come down."

Lynch and his sister agreed to meet at the hospital at 7pm.

"It'll be hard for her," the priest said. "Not having been here. She'll feel guilty."

"Yeah," Lynch said. "Hard thing to watch, hard thing to miss."

Lynch stood in the cold, sucking on a Camel and watching the cars turn off into the hospital parking lot. When he saw the cream-colored Lexus with the Wisconsin plates swing in, he flicked the Camel into the street and started walking toward the car. Always touchy enough seeing his sister without catching shit about smoking right up front.

Colleen Lynch-Kettridge stepped out of the car in a Hillary Clinton-type pant suit, except Hillary didn't have Collie's ass.

"Hey, Collie," Lynch said.

She stopped, looking at him, taking in the shaved head and the eyepatch. "What happened to you?"

"Occupational hazards. I'm OK. Any trouble getting down?"

"Christ, Johnny," she said, "I've been down before. I know how to get here. Don't fucking start, OK?"

Lynch put his hands out, palms forward. "Take it easy, will you, Collie? I didn't mean anything. Just the traffic can be a bitch is all."

She stepped forward and Lynch hugged her, but it was like squeezing a pile of lumber.

"I'm sorry, Johnny. It's just I know you think I should get

down more, and I think I should get down more. But I just flat can't, you know? I mean, I just can't."

"It's good to see you, Collie. Really it is."

"Yeah, OK, Johnny. It's good to see you, too. Guess we better go in, huh?"

"Yeah." Lynch turned with her toward the door. She was just a shade shorter than he was. He'd have never figured she'd get so tall, not when she was a kid and he was running her down the alley on his shoulders. He'd been like a god to her then, her tagging along with him everywhere. And he didn't mind. Liked it. Liked being the big brother, watching out for her, making sure she understood how everything went down. Not much he could tell her anymore.

"Just so you know," he said as they stepped on the elevator. "It's not pretty. She's really gone downhill the last week." His sister just nodded.

As they cleared the doorway to his mother's room, Lynch heard that same rasping noise. Shorter strokes now, like a file working against the grain. A real hard pull to get the breath in, then it just kind of leaking out. For a flash, just a flash, Lynch wanted to pull that thing out of the bed, brace it up against the wall, and beat it till it was pulpy and ruined and couldn't make that noise anymore.

Lynch stood back and let his sister take the lead. She went around to the far side of the bed and squatted down, getting her head level with her mother's, her right hand coming up and stroking the sunken cheek.

"Ma, it's Collie."

No response, maybe a little catch in the breathing.

"We're here, ma," she said. "Johnny's here too. You just rest. We'll be right here."

Rasp. Rasp. Rasp.

Collie looked up at him, and he saw the tears running down both sides of her face. It caught him off guard. He hadn't heard the crying in her voice. It was his kid sister's face again after all these years. She stood up and came to him, and he held her and heard her talking into his chest.

"God, Johnny, I don't know if I can do this again. After Daddy."

"It's OK, Collie," he said. "I'm here this time. I'm right here. I'm always going to be right here from now on, OK?"

He felt her nod, felt her shake against him, felt the tears soaking through his shirt. In the background that fucking rasp rasp rasp. Then rasp rasp no rasp. Something that had been beeping stopped and started to whine, and Collie spun away from him. She was at the bed, taking the corpse in her arms, pulling it up against her, saying not yet, not yet, not yet.

Lynch putting his hand on Collie's shoulder, making some pointless shushing sound, her turning to him looking as hurt as anyone he'd ever seen, saying, "She didn't even know I was here, Johnny. God, Johnny, what kind of bitch am I?"

Lynch holding her again. "She knew, Collie. It's OK. She knew."

Feeling his heart go out of him. Feeling something important slip away that he would never have back again. Feeling his sister against him like an extra lung, like it was the only way he could breathe just then. Like it was the only way either of them could breathe. And his own breath coming then in that same fucking rasp, hard to get it in all of a sudden, through the tears.

Lynch drove his sister to an all-night diner on Huron, down toward the Drive.

"I feel like shit, Johnny, dragging you out to eat, but I haven't had anything since breakfast."

"What, you think mom would want you to starve?" Their mother was always shoving food at them whenever they'd visit, always saying they looked too thin.

A little laugh out of Collie. "No, mom wouldn't want that, now would she?"

She ordered a cobb salad. Lynch ordered a Reuben.

"So," she said, "you gonna tell me what happened to your head?"

"Got shot a little."

Collie bolted upright in her seat. "Jesus, Johnny, what do you mean a little?"

"Guy hit a wall near me, I caught a few fragments. Gonna be fine. Itches like hell, though."

"And you were gonna tell me about this when?"

"Just happened, Collie."

"I do worry about you, you know. Though I gotta say, the eyepatch kind of works for you."

The waitress dropped off the food. Most of the salad looked like it had been shipped in from California by slow train.

"Nice place," Collie said. "You still know how to show a girl a good time."

"Speaking of showing girls a good time…"

Collie raised her eyebrows. "My god, John Lynch is seeing somebody?"

"Only been a couple of dates, but it feels right."

"So spill."

"Name's Liz Johnson. She's a reporter with the Tribune."

"And?"

"And what?"

"She hot?"

"Smokin' hot."

"Well, she better treat you right or I'm coming down and kicking some ass."

"Cool," Lynch said. "Girl fight." Collie threw a piece of wilted lettuce at him.

They worked on the food a bit, Lynch actually having to walk to the kitchen to get somebody to bring out more coffee.

"Guess we need to talk about the details," said Collie.

"Yeah. Figure what, Thursday for the wake – have that at Fitzpatricks – Friday for the funeral?"

"I guess," she said.

"Talked to a priest down here. He said he could do the service, handle that end of things."

"I hate leaving it all on you, Johnny."

"Jesus, Collie, you got a family. I just got me. Nothing I can't handle."

"I know, just this last year, I know you had to take up a lot of slack with mom."

"You did what you could, Collie."

She looked out the window for a long moment, Lynch knowing she was fighting tears, not wanting to let him see just then. She'd grown up tough.

"We can talk about the house and whatever later," Lynch said, "but I was thinking I could buy out your end if you want, rent it out. Finished with everything there is to do at my place a few years ago, and God knows mom's place could stand some updating. Give me something to do."

Little smile from Collie. "Maybe I could come down some day, help with the tile."

Lynch smiled back. "That's the extent of your training, as I recall, wiping up grout. Bring Tommy down with you. I could show him a few things. Really don't see you guys enough."

"Yeah. Let's do that. Let's make sure."

"Anything out of the place you really want?"

"Her old sewing table. I'd like to get that."

"Sure. We'll go through the place, see what we want."

They finished their meals, had some bad pie, talking easier than they had in years, Collie not heading home until after two.

Back at his condo, Lynch poured one stiff drink into a highball glass, then screwed the top on the bottle and put it back up

in the cabinet over the stove. One stiff one was OK, but
he wasn't going to leave the bottle out and swim in it. Not
tonight. There'd been a message from Liz on his machine, and
he wanted to call, wanted her to come over, wanted her. But
he didn't feel like he should go from his mom to his sister to
her like that, not that quick. Didn't want to think about that.
Didn't want to think period.

Lynch sank into the big chair. He picked up the remote,
then put it down again. His head itched, and he needed to
change the gauze pad over his eye. He just couldn't get right
tonight. All your life you got parents, suddenly you don't. He
remembered telling Marslovak about his mother, Marslovak
saying it was like God dying, Lynch knowing now what
he meant. For some reason, he felt like nothing meant shit
anymore.

CHAPTER 29 – EFFINGHAM, ILLINOIS

Weaver had everybody muster in his room at 9am. He'd run out early, picked up a mess of Kripsy Kremes, little noblese oblige, prove he was one of the guys. Weaver wished there was a Dunkin' Donuts in town. Krispy Kremes were good warm, but he'd take a Dunkin' at room temperature any day. What he really wanted was a coffee, but the boys would be shooting today, so coffee was out for them, and he wasn't going to drink it in front of them.

"Everybody get some grub here," Weaver said. Ferguson and Chen grabbed the other two chairs at the small round table, Chen opening up the laptop that was practically part of her. Capelli and Richter took the two beds. Richter was wearing a black T-shirt with a smiling skull on the front. The caption under the skull read "You Can Run, but You'll Just Die Tired." A pile of Farm & Fleet bags were stacked between the beds.

"Chen's got the uniform of the day for you. Commercial hunting cammies, standard woodland pattern. Not perfect, I know, but we can't have anybody turning up in a ghillie if things go south."

"Jesus, Colonel," Richter said. "Gotta go out dressed like Jethro?"

Weaver just gave him a look. Chen's laptop gave three quick beeps. She hit a few keys.

"Fisher has used the McBride ID again," she said.

"Where?" asked Weaver.

"Comfort Inn, three blocks west of here. He used the automatic checkout at 6.17am, but the desk didn't process it until seventeen minutes ago."

"OK, good, so we know he's on site. Anything, Fergie?"

"Just glad I didn't know he was that close last night," said Ferguson. "Don't think I would've slept well. If he's been outbound since 0617 hours, we should probably pack up and roll. Take a little more time on the set-up, give everybody a chance to recon the site. Get your cammies on. Check the batteries on your radios. We'll do com checks en route."

Weaver stood by the door, clapping everybody on the back as the team filed out, feeling old. He missed this shit. On the other hand, playing games in the woods with Ishmael Fisher was the type of thing that played hell with your life expectancy. Weaver even gave Chen a pat as she walked past. Closing the door, he felt as though he'd had an ice-water enema.

Chen dropped Ferguson and his team off one at a time at the trailheads along the road at the back of the ridge behind Holy Angels. By 11.30, Ferguson had scouted the funnel and placed his men. They did one more quick com check. Everybody's radios were online. Now it was just a matter of waiting.

At 12.07, Ferguson heard Weaver through his ear piece.

"Yeah?" Ferguson answered.

"Change of plans, Fergie. Chen got another hit on the McBride ID. Fisher charged a couple energy bars and some water at Moriah Marathon just after 8am this morning. Chen's scouted it out. Fisher's car is still there. Guy says Fisher asked for a brake job, wanted the car ready by 3pm. Brakes are done, car's still there. Get this. Fisher said he was going to go hiking until the car was done. I want you guys over at that station."

"We're set up here, boss. Sure we want to make the move? You know I don't like the other team calling my plays."

"It's your op, Fergie, so it's your call. Do me a favor, though, and check the site. Map handy?"

"Yeah."

"OK. Look at the road Chen dropped you at. Now follow that about six clicks west. See the curve to the north?"

"Got it."

"See that flat spot on the north side of the road just before the curve?"

"Sitting in the bottom of the bowl? Yeah."

"That's the spot. Tell me you don't like that terrain better."

Ferguson looked at the map. He remembered reading about the Union cavalry commander who'd been the first Union officer at Gettysburg. He'd taken one look at Cemetery Ridge, dismounted his troops, and dug in until Meade got there. Later, he'd said a cavalry commander's job was to find some land worth dying for and that had been it. This gas station was perfect. Flanking overlooks on three sides. Let Fisher get into the bowl, they'd have him in a fucking Cuisinart. Get Lawrence up high on one side, get himself up on the other, take the Barretts, they'd have a clean shot down the road either way for at least a few hundred yards if Fisher somehow made it to the car. Nothing was perfect, but this was close.

"Time's gonna be tight," Ferguson said. "Get everybody back down to the road. Have Chen drop us at the trailhead three, four clicks north of that station, up around that curve. Get down to that bowl, scout out sites. Gotta switch weapons, too. Capelli and Richter are gonna have to trade the H&Ks in for the scoped 16s. Lawrence and I are gonna need the Barretts. Chen got them in the truck?"

"She's got them," Weaver answered. "You got to go or no-go this now, Fergie."

Ferguson'd never really liked the idea of trying to take Fisher in open ground on the back of the ridge. It was the best option under the circumstances, but he felt it was about a sixty-forty

play. This bowl, that was ninety-ten if they had time, probably
still eighty-twenty rushing it.

"Let's do it," Ferguson said. "We don't have time to disperse
the pickup. Have Chen pull into the trailhead she dropped me
at. We'll all meet there. We're out."

By 2.40pm Ferguson had his team in place. Ferguson was at
the top north end of the bowl where it jutted out into the road,
just where the road curved around to the north. The station
was a single cinderblock building set back from the road. There
were two pump islands out front, four pumps. To the east of the
station was a small paved lot. Fisher's Tempo was parked at the
east end of the lot, away from the building. Back of the bowl
was the high ground, but it was no good. The station blocked
too much of the view to the lot. Ferguson had Lawrence at the
top of the east side of the bowl with the other Barrett. He had
a clear shot at the car, at the lot, and down the road to the east.
Capelli and Richter were spread out on a ledge on the east side
of the bowl about one hundred and fifty yards up from the lot,
maybe two hundred yards down from Lawrence.

The plan was simple. Let Fisher get in, pay, and head for the
car. When he was in the open in the lot, Capelli and Richter
would open up with the 16s. They should cut him down
before he even heard a shot. Lawrence would start pumping
.50s from the Barrett into the Tempo's engine just to make
sure that, if Fisher makes it to the car somehow, it ain't going
anywhere.

Ferguson had one hardball round and then five incendiary
rounds on the top of his ten-round clip. Soon as he heard
Capelli and Richter cut loose, he would put one round through
the phone junction outside the shop, put the landline out.
Guy inside could have a cell, but the reception was spotty in
these ridges. Down in that bowl, a cell wasn't calling anybody.
Ferguson had even had trouble with the radio until he got on

top of the bowl. Once the phone was down, Ferguson would put the incendiary rounds through the Tempo's gas tank, set that off, and then take out Fisher if he wasn't down yet. If Fisher made it back into the building somehow, Lawrence and Ferguson would slap in armor piercing clips and start pumping rounds through the building's walls and roof while Capelli and Richter moved in. Ferguson knew better than to count his chickens, but this sure smelled like a bucket of extra crispy to him. Fisher was on a short clock.

Ferguson used a pile of dead brush facing the station as cover for him and the long barrel of the Barrett. There wasn't much cover facing the road to his left or behind him, but if he had to take that shot, Fisher would already know it was coming. Ferguson pulled out his binoculars and surveyed the other side of the bowl. It took him a few minutes to find Lawrence. He could barely make out the end of the barrel poking out from behind a fallen tree. Ferguson keyed the throat mic on his tactical radio.

"Lawrence," he said.

Ferguson heard a single click in response. Affirmative.

"Pull back about six inches. I can see your barrel."

Another click.

"How am I looking?" Ferguson asked.

"Got your left foot," Lawrence said. "Don't think it's visible from the ground."

Ferguson gave the mic a click.

Ferguson scanned down to Capelli and Richter. They were on a larger, flatter ledge with heavy cover. It took a couple of minutes to pick them out.

"OK, everybody, let's settle in," Ferguson said.

Fisher had been prone in his ghillie suit since 9.45am. They had come in from the northwest, using the trail that ran by the back of the bowl. He heard three men walk past his position,

could hear another one cut south. He gave them thirty minutes
to settle in before he moved.

Slowly, Fisher raised the Dragunov. He'd be firing through
a lot of cover, so he was careful picking his line. He'd take the
three on the east side of the bowl first. He found Lawrence
near the top of the ridgeline. He had good cover in front of
him, but Fisher had a quartering shot at the base of the skull.
Range was under four hundred meters. Fisher let out half a
breath, let his mind clear, let the mil dots settle, slowly started
squeezing the trigger. The Dragunov twitched with a low
cough. Through the scope, Fisher saw a puff of red and gray as
the top of Lawrence's head disintegrated. Fisher slowly moved
the Dragunov down and to the right.

The next target was easier. Less brush in the way. But he
would have to work quickly. These two targets were only
twenty meters apart. He didn't know them. Younger guys. They
were set up closest to the lot, both carrying M16s with scopes
and extended magazines. If he didn't get them clean, Fisher
would have a mess of incoming fire. The first target was prone,
closest to Fisher. The second had a good sitting perch between
two trees. Farther guy was the tougher shot, and he could roll
into cover easily. Take him first. Fisher didn't see any bunching
to indicate body armor but didn't want to risk a chest shot. A
branch hung down across the top of the target's head. Fisher
sighted in on his throat and fired and then quickly swung the
rifle to the left. The prone target was rolling and bringing his
M16 up toward the back of the ridge. Guy processed the shot
quick, Fisher thought, figured the angle. Fisher took a snap
shot at center mass and the target lost his weapon, curling into
a fetal position. Still some movement, though. Fisher centered
his sight picture on the side of the target's head and fired.

Ferguson watched the station and waited, trying to gauge the
odds of somebody driving by or stopping for gas at a bad time.

Traffic was sparse. One couple arrived in separate cars, left one for service and drove off together. Only one other car on the road in the fifteen minutes he'd been watching. Guy must do service business mostly, Ferguson thought. Maybe more traffic in the fall, once hunting season opened. Lots of deer signs in the woods.

Ferguson was trying to stay focused. The terrain was perfect, but he didn't like throwing an op together this fast. Something was eating at him. Ferguson tried to think what was missing. But, shit, the terrain was perfect. Suddenly, Ferguson keyed his mic.

"Chen, you on line?"

"Yes."

"What's the next closest service station?"

"One moment," she answered. "It's on the east side of town, at the end of the ramp off the Interstate. From your position, 6.1 kilometers."

"Son of a bitch," said Ferguson. That's what was wrong. Why would Fisher put himself in this bag if he didn't have to? Just for a brake job? With another station six clicks away in a public space with good sight lines? "Tell Weaver we are bugging out. Meet us back at the trailhead. Out."

Ferguson thought he saw something and knew he heard something. He thought he saw lateral movement at the top of the ridge directly behind the station. Peripheral vision. When he looked directly, nothing. But he knew he heard a click, like someone activating a throat mic. Ferguson clicked his. No response. "Lawrence," he whispered. Nothing. Movement again, turning his way this time. Ghillie. A gun in a ghillie. He could see the suppressor. Ferguson tried to swing the Barrett, but he had only cleared a field of fire for the station and the road. The Barrett hung up in the brush. Fuck this, he thought, and rolled off the ledge down the loose rock scree toward the road.

••••

Fisher's sight picture settled on Ferguson just as he tried to turn the Barrett. Fisher knew Ferguson. He had worked with him, had eaten at his house, knew his children. Fisher paused. Just a fraction of a pause. As Ferguson rolled toward the edge, Fisher fired. Ferguson disappeared, his Barrett hung up in the brush at the top of the ledge, and then slid butt-first over the edge. Fisher wasn't sure on Ferguson, but he had done what he had set out to do. He had warned the Philistines.

Fisher pulled the green duffle holding the rifle case out from under the brush and looped it over his shoulder

Fisher made his way east along the edge of the ridge. He stopped as he passed Lawrence's position. Fisher took the Barrett and slipped the bandolier of spare magazines off the corpse and into the duffle. The Barrett's barrel stuck out a long way. Half a mile east of the station, he cut across the road and south, uphill toward the ridge overlooking the church.

In the woods along the ridge behind the church, Fisher stripped off the Ghillie and left it on the ground. He wouldn't need it anymore. He pulled the duffle off his shoulder and set the Dragunov inside. He took the stock off the Barrett and separated the barrel assembly. Now it fit in the duffle.

The red pickup was parked in the far corner of the parking lot close to the ridge. Confessions had started, but Fisher was not doing God's work today. He was in the City of Man. He opened the truck cap, set the duffle in the back, and then drove across the lot, down Hill Street, down Main Street, and back to I-57. The sign at the exit read North Chicago.

Back to the City of God.

Ferguson rested for a minute on the shoulder of the road at the base of the rocky incline he had just tumbled down, letting the trivial pains – the cuts, scrapes, and bruises – settle out so he could focus on any major damage. Nasty cut on the back of his head. He could feel blood running down inside his collar.

Right shoulder hurt like hell. Looking at it, he could see a furrow through the jacket, the shirt, and the flesh on the top of the shoulder. Fisher had come pretty close. Ferguson tested the range of motion. Not separated. Nothing felt broken. Maybe a rib. Might be a cracked rib. Right hip was stiffening up in a big hurry where his radio had been smashed into uselessness. Other than that, just garden-variety pain, a feeling like he had been put in a dryer with a laundry basket full of rocks.

The Barrett had clattered down a few feet to his right. The objective lens in the scope was cracked. Ferguson picked the weapon up and worked the action. A shell ejected and the next shell in the clip fed into the chamber. Nothing jammed. He set the Barrett in the shallow ditch between the rock face and the road.

The big question was this: Was Fisher coming for him? He reached inside the cammie jacket where he had a Browning Hi-Power 9mm in a shoulder holster and pulled the pistol free. He slipped off the safety and chambered a round, then switched the Browning to his left hand. He could knock out the X-ring with either hand from fifty feet, and he still wasn't real sure about his right arm.

The road had been cut into the rock intermittently along this stretch. Just ahead, a shoulder of rock jutted out, cutting off Ferguson's view around the corner back to the Marathon station. He got to his feet. No light-headedness, no sudden failures in the ankles or knees. He made his way to the edge of the rock outcropping. Decision time. If Fisher was waiting, Ferguson would be dead as soon as he stuck his head around the corner. Of course, if Fisher was stalking him to confirm the kill, then he would be dead in the next few minutes anyway. He had no way to contact Chen. He needed to get back to the trailhead, but that would take twenty minutes at least, probably thirty at the rate he'd be moving now. No time for that. Better get inside the station, use the landline, see if

Weaver had a plan to come back from this shit.

No point being coy. Ferguson slipped the Browning back into its holster, walked around the corner and across the blacktop toward the station. When he was still alive after the first two steps, he knew Fisher was gone. Ferguson remembered what Winston Churchill had said, that nothing was quite so gratifying as having been shot at and missed. Thing was, this didn't feel real special. Used to. Sad goddamn thing when living through the day didn't float your boat anymore.

Ferguson could see a man in a blue work shirt behind the counter. He could see the man's eyes widen when he saw Ferguson. He could see the man pick up the phone and dial a number. Without breaking stride, Ferguson drew the Browning, brought it up, and snapped three quick shots through the window and into the blue shirt. The shots knocked the man backward into a wire rack of cigarette cartons. The man and the cartons tumbled down behind the counter.

The door had a bell over it that jangled when Ferguson walked in. He walked around the counter and stepped over the body. The receiver to the phone was on the floor, the cord snaking up to the wall unit. Ferguson grabbed the cord and put the receiver to his ear. Dial tone. He hit the redial button. Three tones. 911. He hung up and called Weaver's cellular.

"Weaver."

"He set us up," said Ferguson. "Had a suppressor on the Dragunov. I just caught a sense, took a header off my hide. Radio's smashed to shit. I'm on the land line from the station. Owner got a call in to 911 before I popped him. Gotta figure we got heat on the way."

"What about the other three?"

"They're dead. Either that or you're betting Fisher missed two shots in one day."

"Fisher bug out?"

"I had to walk across thirty meters of open asphalt to get in here. He's gone."

"OK. Chen's on the way. Figure two minutes from the trailhead."

"OK. Sorry, Colonel. I screwed the pooch on this one. Should have seen it coming."

"Fuck, Fergie, we all should have. And seeing things coming is my job. You didn't screw the pooch, just gave the old boy a hand job is all. See you at the hangar."

Ferguson hung up the phone and walked back out the door toward the rock face. Figured he'd better get the Barrett.

Ninety seconds after Ferguson walked out of the station, Chen came around the rock face from the north and pulled into the lot. As Ferguson walked toward the black Suburban, a purple minivan pulled into the station from the south and rolled up to the pumps. A plump blonde soccer mom got out and reached for the pump handle. She froze when she saw Ferguson. Chen climbed out of the Suburban.

"Hi," the soccer mom said.

Chen whipped her little .25 from behind her back and shot the soccer mom through the forehead. The woman slumped back against the side of the minivan and slid to the pavement. Ferguson heard a siren coming fast from the north. A sheriff's car came around the rock face. The cop saw the body against the van, Chen with the gun in her hand, Ferguson in his cammies, blood on him. The cop pulled a perfect bootleg skid, sliding the car around to put it between him and the Suburban. Chen was already putting rounds through the cruiser's windshield with the .25, but the cop had his door open and went out low, getting the engine block between him and Chen.

"Chen," Ferguson called. He pulled the Browning from the holster and tossed it. Chen caught it with her left hand while she took the last shot in the .25 with her right. Then she started lighting up the front of the squad car with the Browning.

Ferguson grabbed up the Barrett, swung the barrel down, pulled the butt back into his damaged right shoulder (and wasn't that going to hurt because the Barrett kicked like a couple hundred angry Rockettes), lined up the hood of the cop car, and cut loose.

The Barrett didn't sound like a rifle. It sounded like the voice of God, and like God was really pissed off. Ferguson wasn't aiming the first round. The .50 slug tore through the front quarter panel and into the engine block, rocking the cruiser on its suspension and ripping something loose that caused a jet of steam to shoot out the front of the hood. Metal scrap must have blown down into the tire, because it blew out and the cruiser settled toward Ferguson. Ferguson remembered the incendiary rounds. He swung the barrel toward the rear of the cruiser and fired.

The back of the cruiser erupted in a yellow-orange flash, the car leaping up on its front tires like a horse trying to throw a rider and then smashing back down. The cop rolled away from the front of the car, his clothes on fire. Chen took careful aim and put two rounds through the side of his head. Ferguson was ready to climb into the Suburban when he noticed Chen walking toward the minivan. In the back in a car seat was a kid, no more than two, pink coat. The kid was screaming.

Ferguson leveled the Barrett at Chen.

"Chen," he called. "Leave the kid."

Chen turned, saw Ferguson with the Barrett pointing at her across the hood of the truck.

"It's a sterile mission, Ferguson. No contagions."

"It's a fucking baby, Chen. It's not a contagion. Kid can't even talk. Weaver wants the kid, he can come out here and do it himself. Release the clip, pull back the slide."

Chen paused for a second. Then the clip fell to the pavement, and she ejected the round in the Browning's chamber. She walked to the truck and put the Browning on the hood.

"Get in," Ferguson said. "You drive."

As she climbed into the truck, Ferguson set down the Barrett, picked up the Browning, slapped in a new clip, and chambered a round. He opened the rear passenger door and tossed the Barrett over the seat into the cargo area. Ferguson climbed into the back, sitting behind Chen, still holding the Browning.

"Let's go," he said.

Chen drove past the burning cruiser and the purple minivan, out onto the two-lane road and east toward the Interstate. A mile later, two sheriff's cars shot past them, headed west. Ferguson felt the adrenaline starting to wear off and the pain setting in. His shoulder was the worst of it, but it had competition. He pulled the first-aid kit from the back and took out a bottle of painkillers. The bottle said two every four hours. He took four. By the time they cleared Moriah, he was starting to feel better. Hell of a thing. Three friends dead. OK, two friends and Richter, never did much like Richter. Killed some poor fuck just trying to run a gas station. Helped kill some soccer mom and incinerate a cop, and he was starting to feel better. He hoped they didn't run into anymore shit on the way to Effingham.

Ferguson really didn't feel like killing anyone else today.

CHAPTER 30 – ABOVE INDIANA

As the Gulf Stream streaked east toward Washington, Weaver sat back in the leather seat and swirled his Macallan around in the leaded highball glass. Chen had patched up Ferguson. He was sleeping in the back row.

Weaver remembered his first kill. Some Burmese agitator friend of Ho Chi Minh's looking to expand Minh's influence. Hot night. Alley behind the pussy bar in Bangkok littered with colored patches where neon reflected off the puddles. Smell of rain. Smell of fish. The feral look in the mark's eyes when he'd seen Weaver, seen the knife. Slant fuck tried some of that chop-sockey shit, but the boys at the agency's little spa out past Quantico had taught Weaver some chop-sockey shit of his own. And the mark only went about one hundred and forty pounds. It hadn't taken long. Hadn't really been his first, though. There were all those Chinese up and down the Korean peninsula, mostly around Chosin. But Korea was different. Korea was as stand-up fight.

Weaver had his highball glass most of the way to his mouth when he saw Chen standing next to him.

"Yeah, Chen?"

"Sir, I've extrapolated our line on the assumption that today's action is a continuation of Fisher's pattern. If so, his next stop will be between Memphis, Tennessee, and Huntsville, Alabama."

"I know what state Memphis is in, Chen."

"Yes, sir."

"Huntsville, too, for that matter. Killed a man in Huntsville."

"Yes, sir."

"Doesn't feel like a pattern anymore, does it? Feels like date rape. Feels like Fisher asked us out and then gave it to us up the ass. Anyway, we're not going anywhere right now. Don't have the horses. Christ, if Ferguson were a horse, I'd be thinking about putting him down. We'll have to regroup in DC. We're going to have to borrow some bodies. Who's the least pissed at us at Langley these days?"

"Intelligence or operations, sir?"

Weaver turned in the chair to stare at Chen. "We need to take this rabid bastard out, Chen. What do you think?"

"Aqulia would be your best bet in operations, sir."

"Isn't he still pissed at us about Costa Rica?"

"I assume so, sir."

Weaver nodded. "OK, see if you can shake a couple teams out of Aqulia, then see if you can narrow down this Memphis-Huntsville deal a little. I'll talk to Snyder, see if she's got a thought."

"Yes, sir." Chen continued to stand in the aisle. Weaver looked up.

"There something else?"

"Sir, Ferguson left a civilian alive at the station. There was a child in the minivan that pulled in for gas. I was going to eliminate it, but Ferguson threatened me with his weapon and forced me to leave the child alive. We were operating under sterile mission parameters, sir, and the protocol is clear. No contagions."

Weaver was getting that ice-water feeling again, and not just in his rectum. "How old was this kid, Chen?"

"Younger than two, sir."

Weaver nodded. "I guess that will be OK, then. Not like the kid's going to ID us."

"Yes, sir. I just thought you should know."

Weaver nodded, and Chen returned to her seat. Shit, Weaver thought. Better talk with Ferguson.

Ferguson shifted in his seat, and the resulting pain woke him, drove him up through the murky depths of the drugs like a swimmer struggling toward the shimmering light for breath. Opening his eyes, he could see Weaver and Chen talking in the front of the cabin.

Ferguson hurt. He felt... well, he felt like he'd been shot and fallen off a cliff, both of which he'd done before, but never on the same day. Though last time he'd been shot he was gut shot, and this was just a little hickey, so on balance he figured he was ahead of the game – if the game was seeing how much you could fuck yourself up without getting zipped in a bag for the ride home. And wasn't that just a stupid fucking game to be playing in the first place.

And then he realized he'd been dreaming, which was a surprise because he didn't dream. Or at least he never remembered his dreams, which was the same thing as far as he was concerned. But he had been dreaming about the kid in the van, the kid strapped in the car seat. He dreamt that she was still sitting there, probably crying because it was dark and she couldn't see her mother. Mom wasn't far away, of course. Mom was lying right outside, ambient temperature by now, stiffening up, probably starting to take on that blue color. In the dream the kid sat and sat and sat while the sun went up and down and up and down and the mom rotted away.

And that's when Ferguson decided he was through. Now he just had to decide what that meant. What it didn't mean was walking up to the front of the cabin and asking Weaver for his pension, because that would just mean finishing the ride in a body bag. It meant no more sterile ops, though. It meant that for damn sure.

••••

Weaver saw Ferguson was awake and headed back, carrying his drink, taking the seat on the aisle.

"How you doing, Fergie? Need a shot? Chen's got the bag up front."

"Doing better than Lawrence," Ferguson said. "Better than Capelli and Richter for that matter."

"Yeah," said Weaver, "well, you were better than them. That's why you're still here."

Ferguson shook his head. "I wasn't better. I was just on the opposite side of the bowl. If Fisher hadn't put his round through Capelli's throat mic, I'd have been staring at that Marathon station while Fisher decided what part of me to perforate."

"You earn your luck, Fergie, you know that. If anybody had a draw to an inside straight coming, it was you."

"Luckier than that cop, too. And the lady in the van. And the poor bastard in the station."

Weaver turned to look directly at Ferguson now, Ferguson still staring straight ahead, focusing on the seat in front of him, not wanting to look at Weaver, not in the eyes, not now.

"This wasn't your first rodeo, Fergie. You got a problem we need to discuss?"

"No sir, Colonel, sir."

Weaver took a long pull on his scotch. "Goddammit Fergie, don't you go soft on me, not now. I got nobody left I can count on." A sigh, another pull on the drink, sinking a little lower in the seat. Silence for a while.

"I know that was hard today, Ferguson. And I know you don't want to hear it right now, but that was good soldiering. The lady, the cop, the grease monkey? Collateral damage. That's all. You know what we do. You know the kind of shit that could fall down on people like those poor bastards if we weren't in the way. And you've been in the way longer and better than most. Jesus, Fergie. Think about New Orleans. The shits you took out in January. We played by the rules,

they would've got to the Superdome during the big game and
suddenly the WTC would look like choir practice. I'm not
saying it's always easy to stomach. I am saying it's got to be
done. Three hundred million people in this country, Fergie.
Every so often, a couple of them have to help pick up the tab."

"Yes sir, Colonel, sir." Ferguson sounding a little choked.
"Thing is, I keep asking myself who we were saving today and
I don't see any stadium full of people or any nutjob with a
WMD. I just see our guy and our nasty little secrets. I don't see
where the flag is big enough to hide behind, not on this one."

Weaver looked down. Clapped Ferguson once on the knee.
"It's a tough call, Fergie, I'm not going to argue that. And,
frankly, I gotta admit I'm glad I wasn't there today. Hard
thing to see, hard thing to do. Hell, Fergie, we don't push the
envelope, we're the guys you call when the situation is all the
way outside the postal system. Look, you're busted up, you're
doped up, and you've got some healing to do. You rest up and
let this shit go for tonight. My op, my orders. The civilians are
on my tab."

Ferguson just nodded. Weaver got up to walk back to the
front of the cabin.

"Colonel?"

Weaver looked down. "Yeah, Fergie?"

"What about Chen? Think she's wishing she could be glad
she wasn't there?"

"I don't think Chen does glad, Fergie. I'm not even sure how
she'll know when she's dead."

Weaver walked up the aisle, grabbing a seatback when the
Gulfstream hit a little bump. He plopped down in his seat
and poured a couple more fingers of Macallan's into his glass.
Fergie was a good man, and Weaver had to admit he'd hung
him out today, hung him out trying to keep InterGov's ass out
of the fire, nothing more. Fergie was right, no hiding behind

the flag on this one. Weaver tried to picture the scene that afternoon – having to drop the station owner, watching Chen pop the soccer mom, frying the cop. He wanted to feel worse about it, but he couldn't get it in his head.

"Hey, Chen."

"Yes, sir."

"What kind of minivan the soccer mom driving?"

"Dodge Grand Caravan, sir. Purple. A 2003."

Now Weaver had a picture in his head, the mom sprawled outside the driver's door, the police cruiser burning in the foreground. He imagined seeing the kid in the car seat, the figure distorted through the heat and smoke from the burning cruiser but clear enough for you to know it was screaming.

Weaver felt for a moment like he might cry. Then he remembered he didn't do that anymore.

CHAPTER 31 – RESTON, VIRGINIA

Weaver's driver pulled the green Jaguar sedan into the brick circle drive in front of Ferguson's nondescript four-bedroom in a development of nondescript four-bedrooms at a quarter to eight the next morning. Ferguson was sitting on a bench in his front yard, reading the paper. He was dressed preppie – khaki slacks, light green polo, blue blazer. Weaver thought Ferguson looked OK walking to the car. Still stiff, probably half a dozen bandages on under the preppie getup, but OK. Weaver wasn't surprised that Fergie was out in the yard. He didn't like Weaver coming into his house, never had.

Ferguson got in back with Weaver, and the driver quickly moved through the side streets onto the Interstate and west. They cleared the suburban sprawl. Trees pushed down near the shoulder, some budding, some with those tiny first leaves, their green still vibrant, electric, alive, not yet diffused through a range of experience. Pretty in a generic way, but life knew how to knock the pretty off.

"Nature's first green is gold," Weaver said. "You ready any poetry, Fergie?"

"When it comes to slaughter, well you'll do your work on water and you'll lick the bloomin' boots of him that's got it," Ferguson said.

"Kipling? Not much in vogue these days. White man's burden and all."

"Some other one I remember, guy trying to get into this girl's pants, telling her worms will have at her if she waits too long. Something about time's winged chariot drawing near."

"Marvell," said Weaver. "To His Coy Mistress."

"Thing is, I've been hearing that chariot myself. Fisher's driving it. I take it the Judge called you."

H Dickens Reynolds had been a Brigadier General, a Federal Appeals court judge, and then, for seven years, the Deputy Director of Operations at the CIA. Now, at eighty-one, he was a country gentleman, graciously ensconced on one hundred and fifty well-coiffed acres of horse land in the Virginia countryside. He was also as close to an official liaison as InterGov had with the sanctioned intelligence community.

"Little pissed about you calling the Judge, Fergie, gotta tell you," said Weaver. "End running me like that. You know we gotta keep our shit in house."

"Had my say last night. I have to hear from the umpire on this one if I'm gonna keep playing ball. I understand this is the big leagues, and I understand we play hardball, and I understand every so often somebody pulls one into the stands. Just feel like we're playing the whole game in the bleachers all of a sudden."

"OK, Fergie. We go back. Anybody's earned a free shot at me, it's you. Judge'll sort this out. Fair enough?"

"Leave it with him," said Ferguson.

An hour later, Weaver's driver guided the Jag down a long drive flanked by freshly painted three-rail fences beyond which chestnut horses gamboled on a flawless pasture in the slanting morning light. He parked in front of a portico big enough to hold Bill Clinton's libido.

Weaver followed protocol with the butler who answered the door. The butler was six-two, weighed about two-twenty, wore a 9mm Beretta in a shoulder holster under his suit coat, and knew a half dozen ways to kill a man without taking it out. And he had friends in the house. Weaver and Ferguson followed him into the study off the entry hall.

Reynolds looked good for eighty-one. He looked about average for sixty-five. He was still wearing a plaid Pendleton robe over black pajamas.

Weaver pulled up when he saw Chen sitting in a chair flanking the desk where Reynolds sat. "What is this, an intervention?"

"Perhaps the best possible characterization of this, Colonel," said the Judge. "After I talked with Ferguson last night, I became increasingly concerned about the direction of this operation. About the entire unit, actually. I called Chen and asked that she come out early this morning to debrief me, which corroborated and even exacerbated my concerns. Let's review, shall we?

"Fisher's family was killed in January. Your PsyOps people saw no cause for concern. Then he disappeared. There was the Wisconsin shooting. Three days ago, your research team captured data regarding a shooting in Chicago. Your systems guy put together a profile on likely credit purchases, and you tracked Fisher to downstate Illinois. Clearly, this was an ambush. It was not subtle. Reports I've gotten have six dead. Police recovered two scoped 16s with extended mags and a Barrett, none of which had been fired, all from your guys. Got a cop car that looks like it got hit with an antitank weapon. What's wrong? You guys didn't have time to call in air support? Maybe some armor? Christ sake, Weaver, it looks like the Israelis were chasing Arafat through the place."

"I was the guy on the ground, sir," said Ferguson. "It's my bad."

"Not your choice, Fergie. Bad rolls up hill. Weaver made the call. That's his bad. And Weaver's my boy, so we've got some guys at Langley who figure it's my bad. OK, the good news. Chen did some prophylactics, just in case things went south, set up your team to look like druggies. Locals are buying it for now because there's nothing else on the shelf, but they are asking themselves why somebody was killing druggies on a hill behind a gas station, and why the druggies were going up there armed to the gills. I trust you've got somebody making sure this doesn't track back?"

"I'm on that, sir," said Chen.

"OK. The locals have already called the Feds in and we can get some rhythm with the Feds, so we can probably pull enough strings to keep this from biting us on the ass. But changes need to be made. Weaver, I'll be very direct. You're out. This in no way diminishes your previous service and is not meant to be a reflection on your character. It's just become apparent that you've become too inured to the ramifications of your unit's actions. I blame myself to a large degree. We've been too free with the extra-legal latitude. Difficult to ask anyone to work in that kind of gray area that long without losing their bearings."

"I understand," said Weaver, his voice level, his face a mask.

"I know this is difficult, and I assure you'll be taken care of. Your service record has been adjusted so that you qualify for the maximum possible pension, military and also foreign service. Full access to health care, all of that. Anything else you need, please do call."

Weaver nodded. "Am I dismissed?"

"Yes, Colonel. Please do not challenge this. You have had your time. Just fade away."

Weaver turned and left the room. After a moment, Ferguson saw the Jaguar winding down the drive.

Reynolds got up and walked over to a sideboard on the right wall, poured a cup of coffee from a silver pot there. "You two want anything, coffee?" Chen and Ferguson declined. Reynolds settled back behind the desk. Then, "Ferguson, I want you to take over InterGov."

"Are you sure that's the right move, Judge? I've been a field guy all my life."

"And you haven't lost your conscience doing it. Weaver was an ops guy when he took over, too. And you've got help. Chen, you OK with this?"

"Yes, sir."

"OK. Final point, but this is vital. We need Fisher in a bag ASAP. Any idea where he's heading?"

"I'd guess Chicago, sir," said Ferguson. "Last killing was there. Fisher grew up there. Evidently Zeke did a few things there, late Sixties, early Seventies. Trying to get some detail on that, but it seems to have been on-loan stuff to the Hurleys. Some kind of tie with them and with Paddy Wang, of course."

"Damn Chinaman's older than I am, far as anyone can tell. He still active?"

"Very."

"You talk to him on this yet?"

"No. But that's up on my list. The more I thought about this last night, the more I think it's Chicago. That Door County shooting, that one was a red herring. Fisher threw it out there to set up this line. Bet he GPS'd the church in Chicago, then started looking for one due north and one due south. He knew we'd pick up on that. So he takes out the dairy farmer up north, then gets his one free shot in Chicago. He knows how we operate, knows we'll be looking for him, and knows we're thin on troops. Figures he culls the herd some, we need time to regroup, and he can get back to whatever the hell he's up to. He's got some kind of agenda. I bet he takes down somebody else in Chicago soon."

"Get going, get on the ground in Chicago. And try to keep the body count down."

CHAPTER 32 – CHICAGO

Tommy Riordan knelt in the last pew at Our Lady of Martyrs feeling like he always felt, like a minor Kennedy. He looked like a Hurley – the tall, handsome, dark Irish kind. The Hurley mayors all fell into the other Hurley mold – the stocky, leprechaun-gone-to-seed model. Tommy's mom was a Hurley. His dad had headed up Hurley the First's quasi-secret Red Squad. So Tommy Riordan had his Hurley credentials. He wasn't a front-page guy, though. He was a side-of-the-podium guy, one of the schmucks on the edge of your TV picture on election night clapping and gazing adoringly at the anointed.

Not that it got him much. There was the Streets and San job, which was a cushy hundred Gs a year because showing up was pretty much voluntary unless there was some ghost payroll probe in high gear. Then he had to keep his ass in the office, but he could do his drinking in there, so it wasn't too bad a deal. And there were the consultant scraps come elections. Couple grand here, ten grand there for gopher work – leaning on precinct captains who were letting turnout slip, stopping by shops that had the wrong signs in their windows, doing his regular-guy stump speech at some of the union halls. And his family got to use the Hurley summer place over in Michigan, the Hurley version of Hyannisport, but they were pretty much hind tit in that line. Usually got early June, late August, primetime going to the real players.

So yeah, being a minor Kennedy meant he was set for life
if he didn't raise the bar too high, if he didn't mind eating
scraps. Thing was, he minded. Fifty-two years old, he was no
kind of man and he knew it.

And the Catholic thing, too. Being a minor Kennedy
meant keeping that up as well, not that he could really shake
it. Grade school right here with the sisters at Martyrs, high
school with the Jesuits at St Ignatius, grandpa's clout getting
him in at Notre Dame and making sure he didn't flunk out.
And his old man was big on the rules – the take off your hat in
church rules, the fishsticks on Fridays rules, the Holy Days of
Obligation rules. The old man was a little slack on some of the
other rules, the thou shalt not stuff – adultery, stealing, false
witness, even the thou shalt not kill if you believed the rumors
– and Tommy had picked up on those habits early.

Which was why he was kneeling in the back of the church.
Communion at least once a year during the Easter season.
That was the rule. And if you were gonna receive, then you
had to be in a state of grace. That was the rule. And that meant
confession. So each year, Tommy Riordan tried to work out
what it was he was sorry for, which was a lot, did the "bless
me, Father, for I have sinned" routine, and tried to keep his
nose clean until Easter so he could take Communion. Or his
prick clean, actually. Nose wasn't his problem.

Thing was, he was pretty sure he didn't believe any of it. He
was pretty sure the whole thing was a scam. Couple years ago,
he faked it. Told the wife he was heading down for confession,
spent a couple hours at the High Hat Tap instead. Come Easter,
he went right on up, took the host. Two hours later he was
puking up ham and deviled eggs like he was never gonna stop,
and that night he had the dream about Sister Mary Theresa –
the dream where she's got him bent over some wooden bench,
he's naked, and she's got that Samurai yardstick the sisters all
carried, and she's flaying his ass with it, and it's hot and dark

where they're at, and Tommy knows that this is hell and this shit, it's just gonna go on and on and on.

He remembered some philosophy class at ND, that Pascal guy and his wager. So, OK, confession once a year, get his annual minimum adult requirement of grace and such at Easter mass, and hope he didn't die in between with anything on his rap sheet that called for more than ten to twenty in purgatory.

So Tommy knelt in the pew and ran down the commandments. Number one? False gods. There was the Bushmills just for starters, and Riordan had to admit he had way more faith in Bushmills than he had in anything else. Lord's name in vain? Ten, twenty times a day, minimum. Keep holy the Sabbath? Bears games count? Honor thy mother and father? Turned out pretty much like Dad, can't give more honor than that, right? He was OK on number five, hadn't offed anybody yet. Coveting? Stealing? Lying? Yeah, yeah, yeah, cop to all of it. But number six was the big one. Thou shalt not commit adultery. Some trouble there. Always had been some trouble there.

Riordan hauled himself to his feet and headed for the confessional. He made his confession, but he didn't have the words to cop to all of it, didn't even know how to phrase the extent of his depravity. He headed for the door of the church, knowing his soul was supposed to feel clean but feeling like it was some bed sheet that hadn't been changed in thirty years. There was some shit that just wasn't gonna come out.

Ishmael Fisher watched the doors to Our Lady of Martyrs through the scope of the Dragunov from the living room window of a fourth-floor apartment five hundred and seventy meters away. The building had no other units on this floor, and the unit on the floor below was vacant. The woman who lived in the apartment had left at 8am and returned just after 5pm on the three days Fisher had watched the building. It was 4.15pm.

Fisher watched Riordan step through the tall wooden doors and then stop as they closed behind him. Riordan looked down to find the bottom of the zipper on his leather jacket. Fisher centered the sight picture on the middle of Riordan's chest and fired.

Edith Jacobs had just stepped into the lobby of her building when she heard a noise. A door slamming, or a piece of furniture falling upstairs somewhere. Whatever it was, it wasn't helping her headache. She'd left work an hour early because of the migraine, and the pain hadn't eased. She started up the four flights of stairs.

As Fisher watched through the scope, the force of the round drove Riordan back into the doors, his back hitting just where the two doors met. His arms flew open. They hit the doors just above the two long brass poles that served as handles. As Riordan slid down the doors, his arms caught the tops of the poles and he hung – seemingly crucified – against the door. Fisher watched for a couple of seconds. When he saw no blood pulsing out of the entrance wound, he knew that Riordan was dead.

Fisher fit the Dragunov into the case and was about to close the cover when he heard feet outside the apartment door, heard the jangle of keys. Fisher flattened against the wall to the side of the door.

Edith Jacobs opened the door and took one step into the room before she saw the rifle case open on the floor. Then the door swung closed behind her. She turned and saw a lean man with short, iron-gray hair wearing a black, long-sleeved T-shirt and tight black leather gloves. She thought to scream, meant to scream, but the man put a surprisingly slender finger to her lips, and then closed the hand over her mouth, spun her around, and pulled her back against him. The force of his grasp was gentle yet certain. And she knew she was going to die.

"Oh my God," she mumbled into his hand, "I am heartily sorry for having offended thee..."

Fisher listened to the Act of Contrition, sensing its perfection, let the woman finish. Then he slid his right hand under her chin and snapped her neck. She will be with Him today in paradise, he thought.

Fisher looked through the gap in the blinds to the church. A crowd had gathered around the body, and a patrol car was just pulling up. He would have to move quickly. He set the woman down gently, closed the lid of the rifle case, picked it up, stepped out the door, and walked down the stairs.

The 54mm casing from the round Fisher had fired lay under Edith Jacobs' right scapula, which would have been uncomfortable, had she been alive.

CHAPTER 33 – CHICAGO

Ferguson was in Chicago, unpacking in his room at the Palmer House on State Street, when Chen walked through the connecting door between their rooms and handed Ferguson a piece of paper.

"Another person has just been shot leaving confession. I picked up the Chicago PD radio traffic. Here is the address."

"So he had this lined up before he even left for downstate," said Ferguson.

"It would appear so."

"OK. I'm going to go scope this out. Run the victim, see what we get. Also, get on the horn with Snyder, get the straight shit on what she told Weaver, see if she can update it any based on recent events. And find out what we've got on Fisher's dad. This all ties back somehow."

"Yes, sir."

Ferguson turned toward the door.

"Chen, do we have a problem? Over the Moriah shit?"

"Our orders were for a sterile op, which meant killing the child in the van. Your interpretation differed from mine. We took it up the chain of command, and the chain of command came down on your side. I have no issue with that."

"And killing the kid, you would have had no issue with that?"

"No."

Ferguson just nodded and left.

CHAPTER 34 – CHICAGO

Crime scene already had a tarp over Tommy Riordan when Lynch got there.

"He really crucified?" Lynch asked McCord, who was eating a hot dog out by the curb.

"Just stepped out the door when he got hit," said McCord. "Basal reflex threw his arms out, round hitting his sternum knocked him backward, and he ended up hanging from his pits from the door handles."

"Press get that?"

"Oh yeah. Your buddy Regan got here awful damn fast with a photographer in tow. That's gonna be the cover of the *Sun-Times* tomorrow for sure. One of the TV guys already did a quick standup. Your guy's got a name now – the Confessional Killer."

"Great," said Lynch. "Rifle?"

"Haven't got him off the door yet, but you gotta figure."

A sergeant Lynch didn't know walked over. "You the guy they called in on this?"

Lynch put out his hand. "John Lynch. I caught the first one up at Sacred Heart."

"Got six people were on the street out here when Riordan got popped. They're all inside. Can't decide whether they heard anything or not. Nobody saw nothing. He's standing outside the door, suddenly he's doing his Jesus impersonation."

"OK, thanks. I'll get to them. You got a timeline?"

"4.15 damn near exactly."

"Anybody check for electronics like we had at the Marslovak scene?"

"Crime scene guys already got those. Same stuff, they tell me."

"Great, just great."

Cunningham walked up. "What's with the hair, Lynch? Going skinhead on us?"

"Whole Michael Jordan thing looked so good on you, thought I'd give it a try."

"White boys got ugly heads. Like the eyepatch, though. The pirate thing is cool."

Cunningham took a few minutes to recon the site, then identified the shooter's likely hide. Fifteen minutes later, Lynch and Cunningham stood in the fourth-floor apartment looking through the window toward Our Lady of Martyrs. Behind them, the crime scene guys were taking pictures of a corpse on the floor.

"Same deal," Lynch said. "No rock this time. Glass cutter. Cuts a hole in the glass and shoots through it."

Cunningham nodded. "She's got these thick drapes, too, and he's got them pulled most of the way shut. Help keep the sound down, and anybody looking back this way isn't going to be able to see anything inside."

"How hard a shot?"

Cunningham shrugged. "Little closer, little more wind today. Figure a wash. No stretch for our boy."

"They're saying he got him through the heart again."

"Looked like."

Lynch turned to look around the room while Cunningham stood at the window. Cunningham took out his scope again, looking toward the church with the same view the shooter had.

Hadn't been any kind of fight. Small room, maybe thirteen feet from the door to the window. The woman had been some kind of unicorn nut, glass and ceramic unicorns everywhere. Must have been a couple dozen of them in the tall, skinny curio cabinet to the right of the door, couple of them on the coffee table in front of the sofa, more on the end table. Nothing knocked over, nothing on the floor.

Looked like she barely got in the door. She was stretched out on the other side of the coffee table from the sofa. She must have walked in on him after he took the shot. Way she was lying, he wouldn't have been able to stand and line himself up with the hole in the window. Neck was broken. Lynch didn't need the ME to tell him that. He could smell urine, too, and shit. Lots of times that happened, dead people not being real big on muscle control. Pissed Lynch off, her having to lie there like that, stinking in her own filth. You could look at the place and see she liked things clean, could see she took the time to bleach her blouse and starch the crap out of it. And she had to end up on the floor, her pants full, while guys took pictures of her.

"Hey Lynch, get over here."

Lynch stepped around the corpse and joined Cunningham by the window. Cunningham handed him the scope and pointed toward the east edge of the crowd. "Cubs cap, khaki jacket, shades. Standing next to the garbage can. See him?"

Lynch picked out the guy. He was drinking a can of Dr Pepper. "Yeah, I got him."

"I've seen that guy before, Fort Campbell. Turned up a couple of times when Gulf War I was getting going. Had an agency smell on him."

"You sure?"

"Scout/snipers, we got paid to notice things and remember them. And shoot them."

"OK, let's scoop him up."

Lynch got on the radio to the uniform sergeant handling the crowd. "We got a guy we'd like to talk to. Six foot, one-eighty or so, Cubs hat, shades, tan jacket, blue jeans. East end of the crowd, north side of the street, standing by the garbage can next to the bus stop. Be cool. Don't want to spook him."

Lynch watched the sergeant call a uniform over. Nobody pointed, but the uniform took a look as he crossed the street. Soon as he did, the guy in the jacket dropped his soda into the garbage, turned around, and headed around the corner. The uniform took off running, going around the building maybe twenty seconds behind. Too long. The guy was gone.

Lynch called down to the sergeant again. "Get that garbage can sealed off. There's a Dr Pepper can in there, should be right on top. I want the prints off that."

In the apartment, the crime scene guys were getting ready to roll the body over. When they did, the piece of brass the woman had lain on stuck for a moment, then fell to the carpet.

"Maybe caught a break here, Lynch," a crime scene tech said. More photos of the brass, then he bagged it.

"Let me see that," Cunningham said. He took the plastic bag, held it up. "Son of a bitch."

"Son of a bitch what?" Lynch asked.

Cunningham kept looking at the casing. After a moment, he handed the bag back to the tech.

"Nothing."

"Didn't sound like nothing."

"Thought I saw something, but it was just the light."

Lynch looked at Cunningham, who was working hard at looking at anything but Lynch.

"What'd you think you saw?" Lynch with a little edge in his voice, pushing it.

"Didn't see nothing. Thought I did, didn't. OK?" Cunningham was over the surprise of whatever it was now, staring Lynch down. Lynch knew he wasn't going to get anywhere with it, but he knew Cunningham had seen something. Lynch thinking, a cop? Somebody from Cunningham's unit?

CHAPTER 35 - CHICAGO

Lynch had just gotten back in his car when his cell buzzed on his hip. He snatched the phone up.

"Lynch."

"It's Liz Johnson at the *Tribune*."

"A little formal, Johnson, considering I've seen you naked."

"This isn't a social call, Lynch. I just heard about Riordan, wondering if you have anything for me."

"Nothing I can give you."

"But something you can give Dickey Regan?"

"What's that supposed to mean?"

"You see Regan's story today? 'Mystery of the Olfson Factory and the Magic Bullet'? All this inside forensic shit on the Marslovak shooting and the whole mess in the basement there? And I got people around the office knowing I'm seeing the lead on the case and wondering why I'm getting my ass handed to me by your buddy Regan. So maybe I'm a little sensitive, wondering, you know, am I mostly good for taking you home from the hospital and cooking you breakfast."

Lynch took a breath, not sure where to step. "I haven't talked to Dickey in weeks, first off, so if he's getting shit, it isn't coming from me."

"He's getting it from somebody." A little tone in her voice said she wasn't sure.

"And somebody's gonna be unhappy when I find out who."

Lynch was pissed now, not needing this. "And I wasn't calling anybody yesterday on account of I was busy watching my mom die."

Silence. "Oh Jesus, John, why didn't you call me?"

Lynch feeling like shit, having put the knife in and no way to take it back.

"Look, I'm sorry, Liz. It was late, I was with my sister. Then I got the callout on this first thing. Probably shouldn't even be on this. Honest to God, whatever Regan's getting, it's not from me."

"Oh Jesus, Lynch, I guess I knew that. I was just pissed."

"Look, Riordan's old man used to run the Red Squad for Hurley the First – might make an angle for you, not that it's a secret. And you can quote an anonymous source saying it's the same guy."

"John, I just... I feel like shit."

"Me too. Look, I got to go."

"Yeah. No harm no foul?"

"Sure. We're good." Not sure they were.

Lynch thought for a moment after Johnson hung up. No way McCord was leaking shit. Novak. He'd have the info, and he felt right. Lynch scrolled through the directory on his phone, found Regan, hit dial.

"Hey, Lynch," answered Regan. "Hear you're sleeping your way through the press corps. Hope you're not looking to get in my pants, too."

"Why would I want to when Novak's already in there?"

Little pause, all Lynch needed to hear. "What the fuck you talking about?"

"Just tell me why I shouldn't have the asshole canned, Dickey."

"Canned for what? You ain't got shit."

"Got all I need. Better start shopping for a new snitch. I'm shutting his act down."

"Whatever, Lynch. Hey, saw the video feed from the Riordan shoot. Like the Kojak look. You just need a little lollipop."

"Fuck you, Dickey."

"Right back at you. You gotta buy me lunch soon."

"Sure," said Lynch. "I ever get my head above this crap, I'll give you a call."

CHAPTER 36 – CHICAGO

Cunningham ran steadily along the bike path by the lake shore. Cool night, breeze out of the north pushing a little drizzle. Kind of night that kept the crowds down. Kind of night Cunningham liked. And the running helped him think.

It was a 54mm casing, that was the thing. Only one long gun Cunningham knew of chambered a 54. The Dragunov SVD. Standard Soviet sniper rifle starting back in Nam and for a while after. Not really a top-drawer weapon. It was based on the AK-47, even looked like a stretch version of one. Meant more for infantry support. Have one guy in the weapons squad, train him up, he can give a unit longer-range capability. But, even with training, five hundred yards was good with the Dragunov. Now you got some guy taking two targets dead through the ten ring, one from nearly six hundred, the other from better than seven hundred. And he was saboting his rounds, which wasn't making the shot any easier.

That, and even through the plastic bag, Cunningham could tell the casing wasn't off-the-shelf. Somebody had taken some time on the neck, turning it, making sure the slug would get a nice, clean release. No way to tell in the time he had, but he'd bet the primer hole had been deburred as well.

So a pro. Knew that already. But the Dragunov? Not the type of thing a pro would choose.

Except one.

You didn't spend twenty years playing scout/sniper for the Corps without getting out some. Cunningham had been out some. Wondered one time if he could get through the whole alphabet – Angola, Beirut, Cambodia, Djibouti... Sometimes things you might hear about on the news – Lebanon, Somalia. Most of the time, though, places nobody'd ever know he'd been, doing stuff nobody'd ever know he'd done. Sometimes you were wearing the uniform, lots of times you weren't. Lots of times you were dressed up like a Bedouin getting chauffeured around Eritrea in a twenty-year-old Land Cruiser by some guy who said he was Agency for International Development, except he was packing a 9mm with custom grips and had Agency stink on him so bad you couldn't get it out with a bottle of Febreze.

OK, so Cunningham wasn't a super-spook. Most of his fun and games, that had been early on. Usually in Africa cause a kaffir who can shoot, there's always a place for one on the dark continent. But Cunningham, he'd done a few things. And he hung around guys who'd done a few things. And these guys, you'd trust them with your life – hell, trust them with your daughter, even if she was liquored up. So he'd heard things.

And he'd heard about the Dragon.

First time was around 1980, just when Afghanistan was heating up for the Reds. Arms dealer in Peshawar named Abdul the Fat, an honest one, which pretty much made him Mother Teresa in that neighborhood. You name it, he could get it. SAMs, Stingers, C4, Claymores, M-whatevers, from Garands to 14s to 16s to 81s. Probably had more Lee-Enfields in his shop than the Brits had in the Raj when Kipling was stomping around. You made a deal, it stayed made. You set a price, it stayed set. Didn't matter if you were Mujahideen, Ivan the Red, some Agency puke, a Kurd with a bug up your ass. Abdul the Fat was the honest broker, the market-maker for mayhem. Among certain circles, he was probably the best-loved man between Riyadh and Delhi.

What Cunningham heard was the Agency wanted Abdul the Fat out so that the Islamic whackos who were getting their rocks off playing with the Ruskies would have to get out of the open market and start swapping their unswerving fealty to US policies for every case of bang-bangs the US could send their way. But leaving Uncle Sam's fingerprints on Abdul the Fat's corpus delecti would be beaucoup bad PR. So the Agency pukes, they set up a trap for this Russian Spetsnaz shooter who'd been leaving lots of dead Mullahs around the Hindu Kush. They took him out real quiet-like, and they turned his Dragunov over to this hot-shit trigger jockey who had earned his bones doing really whacked-out shit in Nam the last couple of years. So this guy pops Abdul the Fat right in the middle of a handoff to some of the local ragheads. Slug gets tied to the same barrel that's been leaving the dead Mullahs all over, the whole thing gets charged to Moscow's account, and the Agency corners the market on selling arms to Fundamentalist Islam – which, and this was the part Cunningham had to admit got hard to believe, actually seemed like a good idea at the time. Typical Langley three-rail shot.

OK. So that was so much fun, they start using the same gun and the same guy on lots of hits that make the Politburo look like they have their heads up their zhopas. He plugs some Solidarity guy in Gdansk, pretty much handing the keys to the Warsaw White House to Wałęsa. Couple dozen hits on priests and other lefty troublemakers in a fruit salad of banana republics in Central America. People start calling the guy the Dragon. Thinking is he's Soviet, or ex-Soviet, but either way he's got Ivan seeing, well, red.

Then the wheels came off the Big Red Machine. Nobody needed a fake Russian anymore. But the shooter? He gets some weird religious attachment to his Dragunov. He is doing God's work, and the Dragunov is God's instrument – some such shit, like it's Excalibur or something.

Dead guys start turning up with clean rounds in em. No rifling, no nothing. Word among the Fort Campbell types was that the Dragon was saboting his rounds so he could keep using his toy.

And now you got people pierced by magic bullets turning up outside churches in Chicago. You got a 54mm casing that somebody who loves bullets more than he loves his mother has honed like a fucking scalpel. And Cunningham had to decide what he was going to say and to whom.

On the one hand, it was a no-brainer. Cunningham was a cop and anyway you sliced it, this was murder. On the other hand, Cunningham had, by the legal definition, murdered people before – and done so on the orders of the sort of people who might be ordering these kills, if it really was the Dragon at work.

But why would they be ordering these? Hard to see Riordan as Al-Qaeda or anything. Harder still to see the old lady who caught the first one. But Cunningham had been around a lot of funny-shaped blocks.

What he had to do, he figured, was call in. Had to be somebody he knew still far enough inside that they could talk to somebody and get the word back. And if the word was national security, then Cunningham would have some thinking to do.

Cunningham turned, headed for home, spit a wad onto the trail. Still had a bad taste in his mouth.

CHAPTER 37 – CHICAGO

Bernstein waved Lynch over as soon as he got into the office the next morning.

"The prints from your pop can? Got a hit."

"About time we caught something. Who?"

"You're going to love this one. Ferguson, James R., USMC."

"A Marine?"

"Yep. All sorts of shit you're gonna like. Enlisted in 1968. Couple of tours with a long-range recon unit – and they are, from my research, gentlemen of some account. Nominated for the Silver Star twice and the DSC once. Got the second Star. Four Purple Hearts, and not those John Kerry band-aid jobs, either. Took a round through his right lung. Another one through his left leg. USMC long-distance shooting champ in '70, again in '72. Graduated from the scout/sniper program in '72, then his records get a little fuzzy – gotta figure he got lent out to one of those special operations groups you hear about."

"Son of a bitch. Home fucking run. We got a photo?"

Bernstein handed Lynch a formal USMC portrait from 1973. Better than thirty years old, but it was the guy.

"That's our boy. Anything more recent?"

"Not likely. Nothing after '73. Records have him as KIA. They planted him at Arlington."

Lynch just stood for a second, looking at Bernstein, then rubbed his face. "So how do prints from some guy who's been

237

dead since the Nixon administration end up on a pop can in yesterday's trash? I watched this guy drop the can in the garbage. I watched our guy take the prints."

"An interesting question."

"So somebody screwed up. Run em again."

"Already did. Got the same record, and the prints are way past a legal match – every loop, every whorl."

"Some kind of computer screw up?"

"These didn't start out digital. What I've got is a digital copy of his paper record. The prints are on the same piece of paper as his photo, and you're telling me the photo looks like the guy. Computer could pull up the wrong record, but it couldn't mismatch the photo and prints – they're all part of the same image. If the records were more modern – prints and photos residing as separate pieces of data – then, sure, it'd be possible to screw up the search, get the data mismatched. But this? I don't see how."

"Maybe a vampire?"

"Maybe he's Hindu."

"What?"

"Reincarnation."

"Thought they came back as cows or something."

"Varying levels of incarnation reflecting their growing enlightenment until they achieve Nirvana."

"That Cobain guy achieved Nirvana. Look where it got him."

"Nirvana the state of being, not Nirvana the band."

"So God's not a grunge rocker. This is seriously fucked. We got a possible perp matches up every way we need him to, and we got some computer in Washington telling us he's been dead for better than thirty years. Is it just this system says he's dead? You check anything else?"

"In 1974, armed forces insurance paid off the only living relative, a spinster aunt, Ellen Grinde, who kicked off in 1980. Arlington checks out. They've got a James R. Ferguson buried in the fall of 1973. Ran a credit check using all his info – nothing. The James R Ferguson with these prints hasn't filed a tax return, used a credit card, applied for a loan, engaged in any reportable financial transaction of any kind since July, 1973. This guy hasn't popped up anywhere he shouldn't have until yesterday."

"Cunningham put me on to the guy. Said he turned up at Fort Campbell just when Bush the First was taking his swing at Saddam. Said he thought he was CIA."

"So we got some operative out of a Tom Clancy novel, and the CIA fakes his death so it can send him around shooting old ladies and Democratic party hacks from outrageous distances?"

"You got a better explanation?"

Bernstein smiled. "You ever hear of Occam's Razor?"

"That a Gillette product?"

"Philosophical principal. States that, all else being equal, the simplest explanation for any given set of facts likely is the right explanation."

"And?"

"The Tom Clancy scenario? So far as I can see, that's it." Bernstein pulled a couple of pages out of the pile on his desk and handed them to Lynch. "Something else we ought to think about, too. We got two people in a row shot coming out of church now. The press thinks it's a serial killer ritual thing – this Confessional Killing shit – not some kind of payback for Marslovak. Maybe they're right."

"Thinking the same thing," said Lynch. "You run a search?"

"Had a shooting little over a week ago in Wisconsin. Guy coming out of confession. Also, you see the news last night, big shootout downstate?"

"Thought that was some drug deal."

"Maybe, but we don't get that many people shot with rifles from long distances, and a couple of those guys were, so I Googled around on that a bit." Bernstein handed Lynch a map. "Got your Wisconsin shooting here, north shore of Door County, just about two hundred thirty miles north of the Marslovak shooting. Thing is, it is due north, I mean exactly. Now, you got this mess downstate, town called Moriah, a bit southeast of Effingham. Damn near exactly two hundred thirty miles south."

"Due south?"

"Off by a mile or so. But there's a Catholic church near the downstate thing, and it is due south. Exactly."

"Guess I better make some calls," said Lynch.

Lynch called the sheriffs in Wisconsin and downstate. Door County sheriff was sticking to his story – he had a case on a jilted husband, and he didn't want to screw with it. Said he'd take a look at the church for the bugs, though.

Guy from downstate, Buttita, he wanted to talk.

"We get out there," Buttita said, "and we got the station guy dead – three 9mm center chest through the window. We got the cop and a housewife in the parking lot. Housewife's on the ground next to her minivan, two year-old kid in the back seat bawling her eyes out. Housewife's got a .25 through the forehead. Cop's got a 9mm in the head and is burned to a crisp. Somebody'd put a couple of .50s into the squad car. Got some .25 holes and 9mm holes in the squad. That's got to be at least two, maybe three people – two different hand guns and a big-ass rifle. So we're working that scene for a while when I notice we're getting a lot of crows up on top the ridge east of the station. We get up there, this is maybe 200 yards out, we got two more stiffs, dressed in cammies, both got nines in shoulder holsters, both got M16s next to them, none of their weapons are fired. One's got a hole through his chest and a hole through the head, the other's got a hole through the throat – all 7.62mm rounds, rifle rounds. So now I've got two different hand guns and two rifles. Another little ways up that hill, we got a third guy missing the back of his head."

"Let me play psychic here and guess that you can't get any ballistics on the 7.62s," Lynch said.

A long pause on the phone. "We haven't let that out."

"Got a couple of shootings up here, same thing."

"Drugs?"

"Not so far."

"The cammie guys? They got IDs on them, so we run that, find out they stayed in the Days Inn over in Effingham. Got a duffle in one room, got traces of meth in it, also a mess of cash. Ran these guys through the system, they all got a history in the meth trade. We were thinking a drug thing some way or another, but still damn weird. Dead guys up on the hill, dead people in the parking lot. Got a blood trail off the cliff on the west end. Just a clusterfuck."

"Let me make it weirder for you. You got a church near there, Holy Angels?"

"Not far away, yeah."

"I'm gonna fax you a picture of some electronics. You may want to take a look over there and see if you can find anything like them in or near the confessionals."

An hour later, Buttita called back. "OK, Lynch," he said. "It's officially weirder."

It was dark when Lynch left the station. When he was halfway to his car, Cunningham stepped out of the shadows and into the blind spot created by Lynch's eyepatch.

"Let's take a walk. You and me gotta talk."

Lynch turned. "Reason you couldn't call me?"

"Maybe."

"You gonna keep being real mysterious like this?"

"Till we get up on the street, in with some people and background noise where I'm pretty sure nobody can keep a parabolic on us and get anything, yeah."

"Being a little paranoid, aren't you?"

"Bet your sweet ass," Cunningham said.

Lynch and Cunningham walked up onto a main drag, mixed in with the evening pedestrian traffic.

"OK, Cunningham, what's up?"

"That casing. I did see something, but I had to check a few things before I talked with you. Especially on top of seeing that guy on the street."

"So what do you have?"

"Ghost story," Cunningham said. "Or maybe a spook story." He told Fisher about the Dragon.

When Cunningham was done, Lynch stopped, turned and eyeballed him for a minute. "You wanna explain why it is you have to talk to your old Corps friends before you talk to me?"

Cunningham held Lynch's eyes, didn't look away, didn't blink. "I get to where I think I gotta explain myself to you, I'll let you know."

The two men stood like that a minute, then Lynch turned and started back up the street.

"That guy you saw at the Riordan scene? Was that this Dragon guy?"

"Don't know. Heard about the Dragon, never saw him. But I got passed around a little today through the Corps grapevine. Guy I finally talked with – and I'm not giving you any names here, so don't ask – he's a little freaked. Some weird shit happening in DC. Lot of churn all of a sudden over on the spook side of the street, chain of command getting juggled, and suddenly there's a big market for shooters. Somebody needs triggermen ASAP. Don't know who, don't know why. Also, that shit downstate? Word is that was our boy. Guy I talked to says Fisher – can't remember his first name, some kind of weird biblical thing he thinks, but he's pretty sure on Fisher."

"We got a hit on the prints from the Riordan scene," Lynch

said. "That guy you saw, his name's Ferguson. He's ex-Corps, too. Thing is, system says he was KIA in 1973."

"Heard they do that sometimes – clear the history on somebody."

"So maybe somebody wiped this Ferguson's record, changed his name to Fisher?"

Cunningham walked for a minute, thinking, then shook his head. "I don't think so. Timeline seems off. This Ferguson, he goes back in Nam a-ways. The Dragon, he would have still been a little green then. And if the shooter's Fisher, I don't picture him hanging around after he takes his shot waiting for us to eyeball him."

"You telling me we got two Agency sniper types running around?"

Cunningham nodded. "Two yeah, but not Agency. Whatever's going on is totally black. This isn't going to trace back to anybody with a government business card. I think maybe this Fisher's slipped his leash. An old lady? Some half-ass city pol? Not the type of targets you waste that kind of talent on. And both of em you could have taken out without the sniper shit. That kind of thing attracts attention. Sniping is always plan B. You got another option, you use it."

"So you think Ferguson's here for Fisher?"

"Yeah."

"Which leaves one question."

"What?"

"Why is Fisher here? Slipped his leash or not, he's got an agenda."

CHAPTER 38 – CHICAGO

Lynch drove back to his place, whipped, just wanting to sleep. When he stepped through the door, Ferguson was sitting in the leather chair across the room holding a slim automatic with a sizable suppressor.

"Little gun," said Lynch.

"Hush puppy," said Ferguson. "I could shoot you from here and you'd barely hear it. Just a .22, but there are ten in the clip, and I can put all of them inside a quarter from this distance."

"Good thing I'm not carrying any change," said Lynch.

Ferguson smiled. "Couple things. First, take off your jacket, take the nine out from under your arm, left hand, carefully. Take out the clip, rack the slide, and set everything on the table by the door. Don't worry, I wanted you dead, you'd be there. I just don't want your mind cluttered up with any how-do-I-get-my-gun-out thoughts while we're chatting."

Lynch took out his gun, emptied it, set it down.

"You don't carry some cheap-ass little throw-down in an ankle holster or anything, do you? You say no and I see one when you cross your legs, I'm gonna take exception."

Fisher hiked up his pants legs and flashed the argyles at Ferguson.

"Nice socks," said Ferguson.

"Trying to up my sartorial game," said Lynch.

"Christ, you start dating a writer and look at the shit comes out your mouth."

Lynch tried not to show anything.

"Yeah, I know about the reporter," said Ferguson.

"Know a few things myself, Ferguson." Lynch throwing the name out, looking for a little edge. "Like how you died back in '73."

Ferguson let out a little snort. "That or how?"

"Both. Friendly fire. Nice touch."

"OK, we all through impressing each other, or we gotta get our dicks out?"

"Hey," said Lynch, "it's your meeting."

Ferguson twitched the gun toward the couch on the far wall. "Why don't you go on over have a seat, get comfy, so I can set this thing down. Really don't need to keep it on you the whole time, do I?"

"Sure," said Lynch. "Nice and friendly, except for the whole B&E part. But what's a felony among friends, right?"

"I knew you'd be a reasonable guy. OK, we – we being you and us – have been butting heads over a little matter, and that's not productive. Some guys I work with – it's not just me, and you know that – were maybe a little hard-assed about this whole thing. But, gets down to it, we're on the same side. You've got a shooter you'd like off the streets. We'd like him off the streets, too."

"This we, do I get an antecedent to go with the pronoun?"

"Let's just say elements of the national security apparatus, shall we?" Ferguson pulled a pack of Dunhills from an inside pocket. "Mind if I smoke?"

"Actually, yes," said Lynch.

Ferguson shrugged, flicked open a well-used Zippo, and lit up. "Mind if I do anyway?"

"Since you put it like that," said Lynch.

Ferguson took a long pull, blew a stream of smoke up toward the ceiling.

"How'd you get my name? Cunningham spot me?"

"Down by the church. We pulled your prints off the Dr Pepper can you dropped."

Ferguson nodded. "Fucking prints. They were supposed to swap those out years ago. Let me ask you this. You work out who you're looking for yet?"

"Getting close."

"You get close to this guy, you'll get dead."

"I'll give you he's a scary SOB. Still gonna run him down, though."

"And then?"

"And then it's his play. We bring him in or we put him down."

"And that's where maybe we can play ball," said Ferguson.

"Play ball how?"

"Let's just say the put him down part sounds good. The bring him in part? Not so much."

"Surely a guy who'd break into a cop's apartment and hold him at gunpoint isn't suggesting that we subvert a citizen's constitutional guarantees? You guys have heard of due process, right?"

"Got our own version. Look, it's your town, and you're good. You've gotten way closer to this than I would have guessed, and you've gotten there fast. Fact is, if you bring him in, you're gonna have to put a hole in him first. No way in hell he just gives up. So it's ninety to ten the thing goes our way anyhow. I'm just asking you to give up the ten percent so that we can pool our resources and get this thing over with. He's not going to stop, you know."

"Didn't figure he would," said Lynch.

"So how many people you ready to write off just so you can make sure you color inside the lines?"

"We could save a lot of time by just popping every gangbanger we have on file, too. Or maybe just round em up and stick em on a train and take em out somewhere and gas em. Maybe you'd like to help with that."

Ferguson frowned, shook his head. "Great, two minutes into our little chat and you're already playing the Nazi card. Look, nobody likes this thing, but it got away from us. This guy you're looking for, he's a friend of mine, OK? Or I'm as close to a friend as he's got. I don't know what his deal is right now, but whatever it is, it means killing a lot of folks who don't have it coming. He's our Frankenstein's monster. We made him. I'm asking for some help taking him off the board before he runs up the body count. And I'm asking that we keep things quiet. He starts telling tales, it's going to be bad for the whole fucking country. You got no idea how many stiffs have his fingerprints on them. And these are some high-profile stiffs going back a long way. I don't know how much attention you pay to the news, Lynch, but this ain't Mr Rogers' Neighborhood anymore, if it ever was. There're a couple million yahoos out there who'd like to pop a nuke off here and then piss on the rubble. We have to play a little rough, then we do. If you're waiting for me to apologize, then pack a lunch."

Lynch clapped a couple of times, quietly. Golf gallery clapping.

"Wow. Nice speech. You got a neocon hymnal you memorize shit out of?"

Ferguson shrugged. "Got some lines I can riff on. Never know what's gonna work with somebody."

"OK, so your shooter. You're saying instead of you just giving us what you've got, letting us do our job, you want me to make sure we execute the son of a bitch for you?"

"What am I supposed to do, Lynch? Walk down to the station and introduce myself to your boss? I'm dead, remember? The people I work for aren't on anybody's org chart."

"Cut the bullshit. You got channels. Use them."

"Meaning get somebody legit to front the info for us? Not

going to happen. You don't get it, Lynch. Not existing is our whole deal. We don't just need this guy off the streets, we need him out of history. He was never born."

Lynch held Ferguson's eyes a long moment. "Fuck it. I don't see this going anywhere. So what's your end game here? I don't sign up, you gonna pop me? If so, get to it. If not, get out."

"Not gonna pop you, Lynch. Least not yet. Maybe we'll chat again later."

"OK," said Lynch.

"Another thing. You've started poking around in a couple other deals, one up in Wisconsin, another one downstate. Just so you know, that mess downstate? That wasn't my call. But I'm running the show now, and I'm going to keep it as clean as I can."

"Breaking in and holding a gun on a cop, this is what you call clean?"

Ferguson got up, slipped the .22 inside his jacket. "I can't remember the last time I pulled a gun on somebody and didn't shoot them. You're already way ahead of the game."

CHAPTER 39 - CHICAGO

Next day, early. Lynch couldn't sleep, turning the whole mess over in his mind, trying to get a handle on it, getting nowhere. He decided to drive over to his mom's place, finally deal with the garage. The sun was getting up, going to be warm, big clouds floating, the birds back, those yellow flowers his mom had put in along the back of the house bursting out. Daffodils? Jonquils? Lynch couldn't remember.

He backed his mom's old Taurus out, pulled the lawn mower out and left it on the side of the drive. Maybe mow the lawn in a couple hours, gets late enough he's not going to wake anybody up. Some old lawn chairs, not worth keeping. Those he took to the curb. An ice chest, one of the old metal ones, still good. He'd take that home with him.

The bike he'd bought his mom probably ten years ago was leaning against the two-by-fours his dad had nailed into the framing to make a ladder up to the little loft he'd built. Pulled that out of the way. Grabbed a two-by-four. Thirty-six years since he'd been up that ladder. Hadn't put his hand there in thirty-six years.

Lynch pulled his way up, could feel the stitches in the leg tugging a little, then stuck his head up over the edge of the loft, looked around.

Roll of leftover trim pieces from when he and his old man had done the upstairs, the quarter round for the floor and the chair rail, tied neatly with twine like his dad always did. Lynch making a note to look through the house, find any spots that were dinged up. He could use these, swap the bad parts out. A box from that old tile store that used to be on Devon on the stretch south of California heading down toward Western, all Indo-Pak groceries now, falafel joints. Place his old man had bought the tile for the upstairs bathroom, the tile Lynch had put down the day his father was killed. Three decades of dust on the box.

Lynch took the box down the ladder, set it on the hood of his mom's car, and opened it.

An old manila envelope sat on top of a couple left-over tiles, the paper stiff with age, the envelope sealed. Lynch opened his pocket knife and slit the top. ME's report – an older form. It was from the Hurley case back in '71. Autopsy reports on Hurley Jr and Stefanski. He'd read them before, pulled the paper years ago right after he got on the force. But why would his father have a copy, and why would he hide it in the garage? Lynch scanned down the report. Everything matched up with what he remembered. Then an addendum, the serological info on the semen found in Hurley jumping out at him. Semen? That had never come out. That wasn't in the ME's report he'd seen.

Behind the report were several pages of loose leaf paper covered with his dad's precise Palmer-method hand. Notes on the Hurley case, all dated, all written in the three days before his father's death. Marslovak, Riordan and the Red Squad, Zeke Fisher. Lynch felt flushed, and he slumped against the car. My God, all the names were the same. More than three decades later, and all the same names. Lynch read more – the Feds, the AMN Commando, his father's theory for a murder-suicide and cover up, Riley.

Lynch thought back to that last night, the last time he'd seen his father. Something happening outside, tires squealing, barking, his dad going out the back, his mom coming down, bringing Collie into his room, keeping them in there. His dad back in the house, on the phone, Lynch not able to hear it all but knowing his dad was pissed.

The sound of his dad upstairs, closet and drawers opening, quiet for a while, then the old man coming down into Lynch's room.

"Listen, guys, I've got some bad news," the old man said. "Somebody was tearing down the alley. Missy must've got loose out back, and she got hit."

Collie sounding shaky. "Is she going to be OK?"

"No, honey. I'm sorry, but she's dead." Collie was crying now, her head buried in her mom's chest, Lynch seeing his mom look at the old man and the old man look back, Lynch not knowing what was up, but knowing that what the old man said, that wasn't it.

"Now you guys get back to bed. It's really late. Stay out of the alley. Couple of officers will be by to check on some things, see if we can't find out who did this. I have to go out for a while. Something's come up I have to take care of. You two be good for your mother now."

Lynch remembered watching his father straighten up. His mom putting Collie down on the bed then standing. His dad hugging her and her hugging back and there being more to it than usual. Collie scrambling across the bed, latching onto Lynch. His mom finally letting go of the old man, running her hand down his face.

"You be careful," she said, which she never said. The old man just nodding. The old man bent down and picked something up off the floor – the tile box from upstairs. Lynch figuring his father was taking the box out to the garage on his way, feeling good for a minute because that meant the old man figured the floor was done, he wasn't going to sneak back in and fix something he thought wasn't done well enough.

Remembered the old man walking out, the door on the garage going up, the car pulling out after a little while, the car stopping, the garage door going down, then the old man pulling away down the alley.

It was a while before Collie stopped crying and his mom got her back to her bed. His mom stuck her head into his doorway on her way back upstairs, just looking but expecting Lynch to be asleep.

"Mom," Lynch said.

"Johnny, it's late," she answered.

"What's going on?"

"It's just your daddy's case, honey. He had to leave. You know that happens sometimes."

"OK." Lynch letting it go, knowing he wasn't going to get the whole answer.

His mom closed his door, and he heard her walk up the stairs. A couple minutes later, Collie nudged the door open and crawled into Lynch's bed. She was still there a few hours later, when Lynch heard the doorbell, heard the hushed voices, heard his mother scream.

Lynch remembered, later that day, that guy Riley showing up, making a big fuss about what a hero his old man was, about how he'd solved the case. Riley telling his mom over and over again that she had no worries, that the mayor would never forget what her husband had done, that, if there was anything he could do, she should call him, any time, day or night. And asking, by the way, did your husband have any papers around, anything that might have something to do with the case? His mom telling him they'd be in the desk in the bedroom if he did. This Riley guy asking did she mind if he took a look, and his mom saying OK. The Riley guy upstairs, going through every drawer, Lynch sneaking up the stairs and just sticking his head up to watch. Riley pulled one file out of the big drawer on the bottom, flipped through it, nodded, and took that one with him back down the stairs.

"He just had a couple things," he told Lynch's mother. "Isn't really supposed to have this at home, but I know they all do it. I'll just get it back down to the station."

His mom nodding.

"You need any help right now, any cash, anything?"

His mom shaking her head.

"OK. But you call. Anything you need, you call."

His mom just nodding.

Riley looking down at Lynch. "You should be proud."

Lynch sticking out his chin a little. "I am."

"You gonna be a cop like your old man?"

"Yes," said Lynch.

He remembered Riley smiling at him and nodding, then heading toward the door. Lynch pretty sure that his mom didn't like the guy, knowing that he didn't.

Lynch sat at his mother's kitchen table, going through his dad's old case notes, checking off the names.

The day his old man was murdered, that morning, EJ Marslovak had come to see him at the station. He'd told the old man what he'd seen a few days before Hurley and Stefanski were murdered – he'd seen the two of them going at it in a Streets and San trailer down near Taylor Street during the UIC campus construction. Marslovak saying no one had seen him. He'd just stopped at the trailer to check some plans, but had seen the two of them through the window and backed off, waiting to see Hurley leave before he went back up.

The whole Marslovak angle starting to make sense now. EJ must have gone to someone else after Lynch's dad was shot. Word got filtered up, and Riley or somebody got him to keep his mouth shut, probably convinced him that Hurley's personal life wasn't germane, convinced him to keep it quiet, and then started with the favors, trying to ensure his silence.

Marslovak was dead a few years now. Then his widow is shot through the heart by some government super-spook.

Bob Riordan. Head of the old Red Squad. At the scene thirty-six years ago when Lynch's old man was murdered. Riordan was dead years ago now – '85 maybe, '86? And now his kid, Tommy, just your basic political hack, he gets it through the heart, same shooter.

This Zeke Fisher working on things with Riley, and old hand from the sound of it, not a kid even then. But Fisher was the name Cunningham had thrown out, the guy he'd ID'd as the shooter. File that under what the fuck for now.

Some of the other names in the file he'd have to check on. The two Feds, Harris and MacDonald? Almost certainly be retired now. Might be able to track them down. Riley? Lynch knew he was long dead, have to see if there were any kids, somebody who might have memories.

Lynch pulled out his cell, went to hit speed dial for Starshak's office, then thought better of it, scrolled down, found Starshak's cell.

"Lose the office number?" Starshak answered.

"We gotta talk. Not at the office."

A pause. "Not gonna like this, am I?"

"Bring the files from 1971 - my Dad's murder, anything else on that AMN group."

"So that would be a no," Starshak said.

Lynch looked at the file one more time. One name he didn't have to check out, Hastings Clarke. Lynch knew exactly what Clarke was up to, knew where to find him. Hastings Clarke was President of the United States.

CHAPTER 40 – WASHINGTON, DC

Weaver still couldn't believe this. The Judge giving him that old soldiers just fade away bullshit? Throwing him a bone with the pension, like it was about the fucking money? Like a guy in Weaver's gig wouldn't have enough socked away to live any way he damned well pleased for as long as he wanted? Ferguson punking him out. Chen imprinting on her new master like a baby goose. Jesus. What the hell did the judge think? Weaver was just gonna roll over, gonna show his ass?

Of course, the Judge didn't know about Weaver's hole card. Always the big mistake in this line of work. You're privy to so many secrets you forget maybe there's something you don't know.

Skeffington Young liked to walk, Weaver knew, liked to get out of the West Wing, take a little stroll, usually during lunch. Skeff was almost thirty years younger than Weaver, an up-and-comer, one of the Yale lackeys Hastings Clarke surrounded himself with. He'd just been bumped up to assistant national security advisor.

Weaver waited, sitting on a bench in Lafayette Park. Saw Young heading up Pennsylvania. Weaver took an angle, cut him off.

"Hey, Skeff."

Young turned with a start. "Jesus, Weaver. You scared me."

"I'm a scary guy, Skeff. Listen, you need to get a message to

255

the boss. I need to talk with him."

"Weaver, I've heard from the Judge. It does sound like you got a bit of a raw deal, but, really, if you think the president is going to intervene–"

"I'm not looking for the president to change the Judge's mind for me, Skeff. I'm looking to save the president's ass. Some shit went down a long time ago. Chicago shit. It's about to come back and swallow old Hastings whole. I can help, but I need to talk with him."

"Really, Weaver, if I tried to set up a personal meeting with the president on such a shallow pretext–"

Weaver reached into his jacket pocket and pulled out an envelope, handed it to Young. Young opened it, slid out the photo. Black and white shot of Stefanski lying dead on the floor, half naked, gunshot to the chest. Photo taken before Zeke Fisher's boys had gone to work with the axe. A little lever Fisher'd held on to. A rough draft of history.

"What the hell is this, Weaver?"

"Just show it to the boss, Skeff. Tell him I gave it to you. Tell him we have to talk. And remember whose star you've got your wagon hitched to. Boss doesn't play ball, he isn't going down in flames, he's going supernova. This thing blows, you'll go up with him. Nobody who's ever touched him will be able to get far enough away."

It took until the next evening, Weaver watching a CNN blurb on the Riordan shooting, getting itchy, knowing Ferguson would already be on the ground in Chicago. Knowing that if Ferguson cleared this before Weaver got back in the game, then Weaver was fucked. But the phone rang, and now Weaver was sitting in the president's private study, upstairs at the White House, the picture of Stefanski on the desk.

"I assume there are more," said Clarke.

"Of course."

"Doesn't prove I was there. Doesn't prove I knew."

"You wanna play it that way, then I suppose no. We've got the addendum to the original ME's report, proves your David was taking love suppositories from Stefanski. We got the photos, proves the cover up. Then, of course, we've got the four dead black guys and the dead cop, which makes it a cover up plus five murders. And we got you as the primary beneficiary of the entire exercise. In the strictest legal sense does this put dick in the wringer? I'd guess not. Not sure on statute of limitations issues. I think the clock on murder runs forever, but I don't think they can get you for that. Don't know about the conspiracy stuff, or the aiding and abetting stuff. Or even that they can prove you knew. So, does this mean you're going to the joint? I was a betting man, I'd bet no. But that's not the real problem, is it? It comes out your whole career was built on killing some guys, including a cop, well, getting a hummer from an intern gonna look like small ball."

Clarke sat looking at the photo. "All these years, I've waited for this to come back. I didn't run, you know, for president – not the first couple times it would have made sense. Afraid of this, afraid someone was holding out, waiting."

Weaver just sat. Thing he'd learned interrogating people, turning people, when they're busy torturing themselves, don't interrupt. He'd let Clarke drop all the way to the end of the rope, let him feel the tug.

Finally, Clarke looked up. "Why now? Just over your job?"

"Name Zeke Fisher mean anything to you?"

Clarke shook his head.

"That's who took the picture. Ezekiel Amos Fisher. My mentor, actually. That's who Riley called to clean up little Davey's mess. Well, not Riley, Paddy Wang. Riley called Wang, Wang called Fisher. You know Wang, right?"

Clarke nodded. "Still do, talked to him last week, trade agreement with China."

"Well, Riley needed somebody but figured this was a little over his head, so he called Wang, and Wang called Fisher. And less than ninety-six hours after you found the bodies, Fisher had the whole thing wrapped up tight in a bow of dead radicals."

"I was horrified, you know, when I heard. My god, five dead, including that cop–"

"Not so horrified you didn't run for senate, though. Not so horrified you didn't start talking up David Hurley like he was the white Martin Luther King. Not so horrified you didn't ride his corpse into office."

A tired, sad smile from Clarke. "Not that horrified, no."

"Anyway, Fisher took the photos, and he held on to the paperwork. Guess he figured having a pet senator might be a good idea someday. He was still regular Agency back then, back before the Church Committee, back when the Agency could color outside the lines. He kept these in his private files. Anyway, things changed, and guys sitting in your chair found out they got their hands tied maybe a little tighter than they liked, and they set up the group I run, or ran. Zeke ran it first. He bought it in Laos, in 1978. And I took over. And this," Weaver reaching out and tapping the photo, "was part of his legacy. But there's another part. There's Zeke's kid. Ishmael. That name you know. The story you don't." So Weaver told him. The family history, the car bomb, the murders in Chicago, the clusterfuck in Moriah, the whole thing.

When Weaver had finished, the president got up and walked over to the sideboard against the wall, poured a couple of inches of whiskey into a glass, then sat back down.

"So this Ishmael Fisher is trying to clean up his father's mess somehow?"

"Can't say for sure," said Weaver. "Fits with what our shrink worked out."

"And if he's taken alive, he knows?"

"About you, sure. And about better than thirty years of other shit we need to keep in the dark."

The president took a long pull on his drink.

"So what do you need?"

"I need InterGov back. I need somebody to keep the Judge off of me. I need shooters. Ten of them. Good ones. And one last thing. It's likely to get loud and messy the next week or so. We won't leave any fingerprints on anything that points back easy, but I need to know somebody's got our back here. It's too late for nothing to come out. Press'll be chasing lots of shit, but we'll be able to muddy the water up well enough they won't be able to make any of it stick. But we need to close ranks here. People start pushing, I need to know somebody's gonna push back, hard, not get all weak at the knees."

That tired smile from Clarke again. "My character, actually, is more in the weak at the knees camp. Always have known that about myself, and have always tried to keep too much stress off my knees as a result. But I don't suppose I have much choice this time, do I? You'll wrap this up quickly?"

"Yeah, but you gotta move fast," said Weaver. "Start making your calls now. I need to be up and running in the morning. Then I'll wrap it up just like last time. In body bags."

Weaver's alarm went off at 4am. If Clarke was playing ball, Weaver would know by now. He picked up the phone and called the ops desk.

"It's Weaver. You guys get word?"

"Yes. You're back in charge."

"OK. What's our disposition on Fisher?"

"Ferguson and Chen are on the ground in Chicago. Ferguson said he'd send for shooters once he reconnoitered. Just got a roster on the QT out of Langley fifteen minutes ago. We have some reinforcements coming in. Should have them by 1200. I told Langley to send them straight to Andrews. Didn't figure they'd do us much good here." "You told them right. Have everybody muster at the hangar. I want us wheels up by 1500."

"Chicago?"

"Yeah."

"I'll notify Ferguson."

"Negative. He or Chen been in touch at all since I was put back on top?"

"No, sir."

"Keep them out of the loop."

A pause on the other end. "Yes, sir."

"But get ready to pull the plug on them – phones, credit cards, the works. Ferguson got the willies on this one. Thing like this, I need a team I can trust to go to the mat. We're gonna put them on the sidelines."

CHAPTER 41 – CHICAGO

Ishmael Fisher took a quick reading with the range finder from the planned location of his next hide.

Fisher had planted cameras and mics in seventeen churches, all over the city. Once Weaver picked up the signals, he'd have to start running intel, matching possible targets against locations, trying to ID shooting hides, trying to set up ambushes. He wouldn't have enough bodies or enough time. And he wouldn't get a signal here. Not until the chosen day.

This was the last target, the third of the trinity. The last clean soul attached to his father's sin.

CHAPTER 42 – CHICAGO

Lynch, Slo-mo, Starshak, McCord and Cunningham were crammed in a corner both at McGinty's. 10am, the place not open yet, McGinty in back cleaning up.

Starshak had the paper from 1971, files on the Hurley case and the raid on the AMN Commando. Lynch brought what he'd found in the garage, papers scattered around the table. Lynch ran down what he knew, and Cunningham filled them in on the spook angle, on Ferguson, the Dragon, Fisher.

"This shit has all got to tie together," Starshak said. "Too many intersections."

"Whatever happened back in '71," Lynch said, "this Fisher's got the facts. And he had them before we did."

"But why now?" said Starshak. "Been forty years."

"Doesn't matter in a way," said Bernstein. "We've got enough to start putting a murder case together for 1971."

"Murder case for who?" Lynch said. "Riley's dead. Old man Hurley's dead. Riordan's dead. I checked on the ME from 1971. Anthony? Guy who put the serology together? Died of a heart attack the same night my dad was killed."

"Convenient," Starshak said.

"You want more convenience? The two Feds in my dad's notes? The ones at that meeting? One was killed in action in 1975. The other one died in a car crash in 1977. This Zeke Fisher? If he's not dead, he's gotta be a hundred years old. And

I can't seem to prove he was ever alive."

"Except now we have somebody half that age with the same name running around the city shooting people," Bernstein said.

"Got the beginnings of a conspiracy case against Clarke," Cunningham said.

"Obstruction maybe, statute's run out on that," said Starshak.

"Tie him to the murder, then the clock keeps ticking," Cunningham said.

"Except we can't, not with what we've got."

"One thing we could do, exhume the bodies," said McCord.

"Which ones?" said Bernstein.

"Hurley Jr and Stefanski. Lots of advances since '71. Might be able to get some physical evidence. Anthony, too. Heart attack my ass."

"But where's that get us, except more evidence for a case against dead guys?" said Lynch.

"Might shake the tree a little," said Starshak. "Somebody's got a bug up his ass about this stuff. He sees somebody taking a look at '71, maybe he makes a move we can spot."

"It's an idea," said Lynch. "What about Fisher? Any thoughts on who else he might wanna shoot?"

"Gotta throw the mayor in the mix," said Starshak. "Guy seems to be going after survivors."

"And the president," said Bernstein.

"Shit," said Cunningham. "We notify the Secret Service, they're going to want to know why. We tell them why, we're sticking our heads up a little higher than I want to right now."

"It's all been Chicago so far," said Lynch. "Maybe we can hold off on the president, at least until we have more evidence he was actually in on it. Everybody who got it so far is tied to somebody who was in on it for sure."

"But the mayor's a lock," said Starshak.

Nods from everybody.

"Still gonna be putting our heads up," said Cunningham.
More nods.

"Anybody else?" asked Lynch.

"Stefanski never had kids, so far as I know," said Starshak.
"Kind of a notorious skirt hound, though, so who knows?
Tommy Riordan's got a sister and a couple kids of his own, so
that's possible. There's Eddie Marslovak. Riley's kid croaked
from cancer, and his wife's dead. Got a nephew that's an
alderman."

"We start going out to nephews and such, we'll be in the
hundreds," said Bernstein.

"OK, so I at least gotta get on the phone upstairs, tell them
about the mayor," said Starshak.

"Maybe I ought to do that," said Lynch.

"Why?" asked Starshak.

"Because I'm on the list, too. If this ties to '71 and Fisher is
targeting the descendants. Officially, the rest of you are out of
this. I'd like to keep it that way."

"I'm not hanging you out to dry, Lynch," said Starshak.
"We all get in it, the jig's up. They know they can't take us all
down."

"But once they know we're in, then they're going to start
covering their tracks. Nobody knows we're looking back to
'71. I let em think I'm playing ball, just me, maybe I can still
sneak up on somebody. I'll call Paddy Wang."

"Risky play," said Starshak.

"I've been living with the fact my father was murdered for
most of my life, but always thought the guys who did it went
down at the same time. Just found out they didn't. Worse than
that, just found out they set him up. Risky or not, I'm in."

"Just keep an eye out," said Starshak.

"An eye's all I got left right now," said Lynch.

CHAPTER 43 – ABOVE VIRGINIA

Weaver was sitting next to Nancy Snyder on the plane heading out to Chicago, the new troops in the back.

"Your Moriah tip didn't play out too well, Doc."

"Our Mr Fisher has an impressive mind, Colonel. I believe he anticipated us understanding his motivations in general and so looked for an opportunity to add an element of religious symbolism upon which we would seize. It fit in very nicely with all the data that you believed, I might add."

"I'm not playing gotcha here, doc. We all fucked up. You still think this all souls go to heaven angle is the right one?"

"It might help if I had more context. I am not one of your shooters, as you like to call them, but I have to assume that choosing to shoot people only immediately after they attend the Catholic sacrament raises considerable tactical complications for our friend. If he could shoot whomever he wanted where and whenever he wanted, then you wouldn't even know where to look."

"You got me there, Doc."

"So I still believe that the victims being in a state of grace is a central feature of Fisher's pathology. However, he has moved away from the geographic line, which we now assume to have been simply part of his ruse. And he has returned to Chicago, where he was raised. And, if I understand correctly, his father did favors of a certain sort for the ruling family there."

"Yep."

"In all likelihood, then, these killings are meant, in some way, to expiate familial guilt for some previous action, either by Fisher or by his father."

"Makes sense."

"So, Colonel, if you would kindly share with me whatever details you have been hiding about these activities, then perhaps I can provide some meaningful assistance."

"Who says I'm hiding something, Doc?"

"You are always hiding something. It is your nature. And you used something to undermine the Judge."

Weaver thought for a minute. And, strange as it was, he trusted Snyder. "OK, why not. My ass is hanging out so far now, it's not going to matter."

He gave Snyder the entire story – what happened in '71, the current investigation, what happened between him and Ferguson, everything.

"My, what a tangled web we do weave," said Snyder when he had finished. "I assume that we have the president's blessing."

"We've got the president's nuts in a vice is what we've got."

"Along with yours, if I read things correctly."

"Doc, my nuts have been in a vice since Vietnam. I'm used to it."

"I think, then, that Fisher's motivation is fairly plain. He is not, as I previously assumed, trying to balance his books, as you put it. He is trying to clear his father's account. You've said before that Fisher and his father shared not only their religious zealotry but also their patriotic zeal. I now believe that killing bad men did not and does not trouble Fisher. But what may trouble him is that his father killed a good man. One can assume in the context of the Fishers' shared patriotic mania that the black activists framed for the old murders were acceptable victims – political apostates, if you will. But the detective, this Lynch? He was a truly innocent party. Beyond innocent, even. Actually heroic. And so Fisher is harvesting innocent souls connected with Lynch's murder and offering them to God as a holocaust in penance for his father's sins."

"Great," said Weaver. "Mess of guys involved in that. How do we narrow it down?"

"The victims have to be religious. As I understand it, confession has fallen out of favor with many Catholics, so that should help. After that, some direct ancestral involvement with the act itself."

"Marslovak barely qualified."

"But she did. Her husband maintained his silence in order to benefit from the act. And when Fisher took Marslovak, he was also baiting his trap. Riordan would have been more overt, so he was harvested after your little tête-a-tête downstate."

"Fisher is a tricky bastard."

"You have to remember, Colonel, that his motivation, however demented it may appear to you, makes perfect sense to him. His pathology in no way compromises his cognitive skills or his training."

"Swell."

Snyder and Weaver rode in silence. Just as the plane began its descent, Snyder spoke again.

"Colonel, I am in no way competent to offer what you would consider tactical advice, but I did have a thought."

"Shoot."

"How droll. In any case, you told me that a Darius Cunningham is assisting Lynch the younger with his inquiries."

"That's who ID'd Ferguson."

"Darius is an odd name. It sounds as though he may be an African-American."

"He is."

"And I assume that, with your usual passion for detail, you have a dossier on him?"

"Most of it. His father was a Kenyan national, immigrated

during the Mau Mau business – seems his name was on somebody's chop-chop list. Settled in Chicago, went into social services, got pretty political during the whole civil rights deal. Real pain in the ass for the Hurleys. He wasn't one of the Panthers, more in the work-inside-the-system crowd, but he sure as hell played footsie with them. He was real wired in with King and the SCLC people during their fair-housing shindig in Chicago in '66. Got roughed up pretty good during one of their marches, some kind of back injury, never came all the way back from it. Our Darius enlisted in the Marines in1968, eighteenth birthday. His old man died in '71."

"The same year as Lynch's father."

"Same month."

"And Cunningham is a contemporary of Lynch's?"

"Same age? Give or take."

"Colonel, I assume that, in addition to addressing the Fisher situation, you would like to provide an alternative explanation for the killings so as to divert an investigation?"

"Ideally, yeah. But I'll settle for Fisher in a body bag."

"Don't you see, Colonel? Lynch is seeking to avenge his father. Yet four other men, black men, also innocent by legal standards, died that night. Given Cunningham's race and your talent for adjusting history, it should not be difficult to establish that Cunningham is also seeking to avenge a murder – if not his father's then some other connection to the radicals killed in the raid. Given his father's history, that should not prove overly difficult."

Weaver turned and looked at Snyder for a long moment. "And Cunningham is one of the few guys in town with the skill set to have done these church killings."

"Exactly," Snyder said.

"Blame the whole thing on the nigger with the gun?"

"It is the American way, Colonel."

••••

The plane landed at O'Hare and taxied to a hangar used by the local Air Force Reserve unit. As the team unloaded, Weaver pulled aside four of his new recruits. He had to admit Clarke had gone all out, cashed in some heavy markers. These guys were on loan from Mossad.

Weaver handed a couple of files to Uri, the team leader. "Got a special job for you four. I know you don't have much background on this whole situation, but we had a command breakdown a couple days ago. Two of our people went rogue. They still think we're on the same side, and I want them to keep thinking that right up until you take them out. They've got tac support from us – money, comm. We can use the credit cards to track them and the phones to GPS em. Paravola'll get you what you need for that. I want them off the board by tonight. Pictures, background, it's all in the files."

"They any good?"

"Damn good."

The Israeli smiled. "So are we."

CHAPTER 44 – CHICAGO

"Young Lynch, after all these years, finally you honor me," said Paddy Wang, standing behind his desk in his dark, intensely ornate office. The young Asian woman who had ushered Lynch in backed out, bowing. A tough-looking young guy in the black suit of Wang's people stood next to the desk, eyeballing Lynch.

"Something I needed to run past you, pretty sensitive. I thought you might be able to offer some guidance," said Lynch. "Be better if we talked alone."

Wang turned, said something in Chinese. The man walked out past Lynch, walking closer to him than he had to, radiating threat. Wang waved toward one of the chairs in front of the desk.

Wang, sitting down, chuckled at his aide's behavior. "To be so young and with so much need to prove oneself. Is that a blessing or a curse?"

"Probably both, like everything else," said Lynch.

Wang laughed. "Are you sure you're not Confucian?"

"Just don't tell the Pope."

"I have not yet met the new Pope, but I shall keep your secret when I do," said Wang. "So, what concerns you, young Lynch?"

"I never know what you already know, Paddy, so I usually just figure everything," said Lynch. "You know I'm working on these sniper shootings?"

"I have heard," said Wang.

"The thing is, a pattern may be emerging."

"The religious involvement?"

"A historical pattern. A potential relationship with the murder of the mayor's father."

"This I had not heard. How disturbing. There is evidence of this?"

"Nothing direct. Riordan's father, of course, was very involved, helping to identify the Black Panther wannabes. The widow Marslovak? Her husband worked very closely with Stefanski at the time."

"Ah, the man that the blacks killed along with Hurley."

"Right. So what's concerning me is that these shootings – so far, we have two – both have this tie back to figures associated with the killings. Clearly, the shooter has some kind of agenda, possibly a pretty powerful psychological agenda. If his target profile really is driven off that event, then the mayor may be on his list – the mayor or others close to him."

"I understand your concern. But why come to me?"

"Come on, Paddy. I go through channels with this, it's on the news by the weekend. I know how the Hurleys are about family. I don't need that aggravation."

"And it does involve your father," said Wang. "You may be in danger too, young Lynch."

"I thought about that. Won't be the first time a cop had somebody come after him. I'm taking precautions."

"I am glad. And the mayor will be as well. The Hurleys have always felt indebted to your family."

"Anyway, I figured you'd know who to get word to and how to get it there. I solve crimes, I don't create dirty laundry."

"I appreciate your sensitivity, young Lynch."

"I was also wondering if there was anything you could add that might shed some light. Any other potential targets?

The mayor we got. Riordan's sister, Eddie Marslovak we got. Stefanski or Riley have any relatives we should watch out for?"

"Alderman Riley is a nephew, of course, and he has a family. Sadly, Riley's son died very young, and his wife is long dead. Stefanski was a bachelor."

"Heard he sowed his share of wild oats, though. Anything ever come of that?"

"So long ago, young Lynch. Certainly nothing that I recall."

"OK, well get the word to whomever, and let me know if there's anything I need to watch."

"I shall, young Lynch." Wang rising from behind the desk to show Lynch out. "And now, of course, you must attend the Connemara Ball."

"Come on, Paddy, you ever going to give up on that?"

"It is the algebra of favors. You have asked for my intervention. Only for the good of my friends, granted. But now I ask that you and your striking new companion grace my festivities tonight. I must insist."

CHAPTER 45 – CHICAGO

Uri, team leader for Weaver's lend-lease Israelis, sat in the rented Ford watching the blips for Ferguson's and Chen's phones on the nav application that Paravola had uploaded onto his phone. They were booked into adjoining rooms at the Palmer House on State Street. Chen was in her room, or her phone was anyway, and she was online. Paravola was working on hacking her feed, but she was doing some kind of non-standard encryption, backing up what InterGov already had. Paranoid little bitch. Weaver said they were good.

Ferguson had been out since the team arrived, GPS from his phone bouncing around the south side. But now it looked like he was headed back to the hotel. So the Israeli waited. Better to take them both at once.

Uri watched the side mirror, saw Ferguson coming down Wabash on foot. Must have parked in the garage up the street, keeping his transportation separate, not wanting to rely on the valet. Uri let Ferguson pass, let him get to the intersection. Ferguson was stuck, waiting to cross the street, waiting for the light to change. Uri got ready to move, just waiting for a bus to pass the car, give him a little cover.

Uri watched the bus, watched Ferguson, didn't see the bicycle messenger speeding along the edge of the parked cars, going against the one-way traffic. As Uri swung his door open, the bike messenger slammed into it, bike crashing over, the messenger taking the spill in a roll, popping back up on his feet, coming at the Israeli.

"Fuckin' tourist," the messenger yelled, extending his arms, locking them to shove Uri.

Ferguson had just started across the street when he heard a crunch behind him. Didn't turn his head to look, too many years of tradecraft. Instead he checked the reflection in the big plate-glass windows that lined the arcade of shops on the ground floor of the hotel. In the reflection, he saw the bike on the ground, the open car door, saw the messenger roll up, spring at the guy getting out of the car. The guy slipped the shove easily, quick move, great balance, then an elbow into the bike messenger's ribs as the momentum of the shove carried him past. Krav Maga move – that home-grown shit the Israelis taught all their guys. Mossad move. Three other guys had gotten out of the car, too. All the right age, right size.

Four Mossad guys popping out of a car behind him? Ferguson didn't know what it meant, beyond nothing good. Meant they were waiting for him, though. Which meant they knew he was coming. Probably the damn phone. Probably Weaver.

Ferguson continued across the intersection, watching the window. The Mossad guys were spreading out, two heading north up Adams, two continuing after him. Not hurrying, trying to look casual.

Ferguson kept on Wabash and then turned into the retail arcade on the ground floor, below the lobby, saw a guy coming toward him carrying a shopping bag. Face wasn't a good match for him, but the guy was the right size, was wearing the same type of nondescript raincoat, same color hair. Ferguson dropped his phone into the guy's shopping bag and then ducked into one of the shops, turned behind a display.

He saw two of the Israelis come through the revolving door

into the arcade, scanning. They stopped. The taller one, the one who had dropped the bicycle messenger, pulled a smartphone out of his pocket, checked the screen. Guy scrunched up his brow, nudged the other guy, and they went back out the door. Turned north. Same way shopping bag guy had gone.

That proved it.

"Fuck," said Ferguson.

"May I help you?" A voice behind him, a little disapproving.

Ferguson turned. Little, nattily dressed guy, maybe five and a half feet, might go one hundred and twenty-five with a pocket full of change. Gelled hair, manicure.

"No," said Ferguson. "No, I don't think you can."

Uri and his wingman were most of the way up the block, Uri splitting his attention between the screen on the phone and the pedestrian traffic. Sidewalks were crammed. Had to get a good look more than a couple of people ahead. Then he saw the guy in the raincoat. Short, salt-and-pepper hair, right size. Could be. Sped up. Drifted left. His wingman knew the drill, drifted right so they'd come at Ferguson from both sides. Only a couple yards back now. Readout on Uri's screen said he was right on top of Ferguson's phone and pacing it. But he was close enough to see this guy wasn't Ferguson. Fucking bike messenger. Should have killed the son of a bitch.

He stopped, punched the team button on the phone. The other two should have been coming in the west end of the arcade just after he left the east.

"You guys see Ferguson go out that way?"

"No. He didn't come west."

The Israeli thinking Ferguson was probably gone. Probably got a sniff because of the damn bike messenger, planted his phone on this schmuck for cover and took off. But the Israeli still had numbers and firepower on his side. Attack, always attack. That was the Israeli way. Both at once was better, but one was better than none. Get Chen, then run Ferguson to ground.

"OK, screw Ferguson for now. We take Chen. Cover the arcade, both ends, watch the elevators and escalators. Looks like she's still in her room."

The Israeli and his wingman jogged back toward the door.

Ferguson figured the other two would be spreading out to cover the arcade. Best move would be to break contain, get outside, get clear. But only if he wanted to sacrifice Chen. Figured it was time to decide whether he believed his own bullshit. Called out Weaver because he'd lost his moral compass, such as it was. Now he had to decide. Did he throw Chen under the bus to save his own ass or did he stand up?

Big crowd coming, trade show group or something, all in suits, those lanyards with name tags hanging around their necks. Ferguson used them as cover to cross the arcade, got into the knot of suits, went up the staircase to the lobby. He was all in now. Only way back out was through the Israelis. One of the suits split left, texting away on his BlackBerry, heading for the men's room. Ferguson needed comms, trailed the guy into the john, gave him an elbow across the base of the skull as soon as they cleared the door, dropped him to the floor like a bag of flour. Grabbed the BlackBerry, hoping to hell Chen was online. He knew she used some kind of tech voodoo to keep her connections secure, mostly just to piss off Paravola. Didn't know whether that would help with an incoming message, but it was the only chance they had. Ferguson started texting.

014. Her room number backwards, that was their emergency identifier, let her know to answer.

Go
Blown 4 Mossad
In house?
Yes

Your 6

Lobby

Roger

All he could do. Ferguson dampened a paper towel, wiped down the BlackBerry, dropped it next to the guy on the floor, the guy just starting to moan. Ferguson slipped back into the lobby.

Good hide in the corner – big ass planter, out of the traffic flow, with a view of the elevators.

Chen worked quickly but knew better than to hurry. She slipped her laptop into her backpack, along with the operational cash – ten thousand dollars in twenties. Then she twisted the silencer onto her .25, dropped that into her right hand pocket, put the 9mm in her shoulder holster, slipped on her jacket, grabbed the backpack, flipped it on, adjusted the coat so the 9mm didn't show, made sure the backpack straps were clear in case she needed to draw.

She picked up two small black boxes from the desk, peeled the strips covering the adhesive patches off the back, stuck one on each side of the door, and threw the switches. Next she picked up the landline in her room, dialed the ops desk, and set the phone down, leaving the line open. Went through the connecting door to Ferguson's room, walked across the hall listening at doors. No sound at the first door, but TV noise from the room directly across from hers. She tapped on the door.

"Yes?" A man's voice. Good.

Chen remembered to smile, how supposedly people could hear that in your voice.

"Hi, um, this is kind of embarrassing, but I think I left my key down in the locker room after my workout. I called the desk, they said they'd send somebody, but it's been like fifteen minutes. I'm going to be late for an appointment. I was hoping maybe I could borrow your key? Or you could just run down there with me?"

Heard movement, the guy walking to the door. She looked up at the peephole, made sure to put a little flirt in it. She put her hand in her jacket pocket.

The man's voice. "Sure."

The door opened, the guy stepping back, letting Chen in.

"I'll just grab my key," he said.

He turned into the room. Chen pulled the .25 from her pocket, shot him through the back of the head. She closed the door behind her and watched through the peephole. The Israelis would be there soon.

Uri knew the Asian woman should still be on the fourth floor. He had one team covering each other up the stairwell and one man watching the elevators. Uri stayed behind to cover the lobby, watching the stairs and escalators, just in case.

Ferguson had to be gone. Only tactical play for him. So get the woman at least.

Beep on his smartphone. He checked the text. Paravola. The landline had just gone active in her room. She was there. Called the guys in the stairwell.

"Her landline just lit up. She's in the room. You up the stairs?"

"Holding at the fourth-floor door."

"Three doors down, right hand side. 410. Go, go, go."

Ferguson watched from his hide as three of the Israelis entered the lobby. One took a covering position, the guy leaning on one of the ornate pillars, straight line of sight to the elevators. The other two went straight to the stairs. Ferguson scanned for the fourth guy, Krav Maga guy, couldn't see him. Wall to Ferguson's right blocked his view that way. Guy was probably back there, in front of the stairs and the escalators, covering the exit to the ground level.

Ferguson slipped out the hush puppy. Long way across the lobby with a .22. Had to be thirty yards, lots of crossing traffic. Ferguson braced his hands on the top edge of the planter, sighted, squeezed off one shot, taking pillar-guy right at the base of the skull, pillar-guy crumpling straight down. Then Ferguson heard a muffled explosion. Chen.

Chen watched the hallway through the peephole. The two Israelis edged open the stairway door, eyed the hallway, then stepped out. They stayed to the right against the wall, not wanting to show through the peep hole in 410, just in case. That kept them clearly in Chen's view. The first one ducked down, below peephole level, went to the far side of the door.

They nodded to each other. The first pulled out an electronic pick, slipped it into the lock, waited for the click, then spun and hit the door, driving the door handle down, the other guy pivoting to follow.

The door opened into the room, crossing the beam between the flashbangs Chen had stuck to the doorframe. She closed her eyes and clamped her hands over her ears. Lots of noise and light, some smoke, no real damage, but enough to disorient anyone close. Chen stepped into the hall, the .25 already level. The second guy hadn't been all the way in, hadn't caught as much of the blast, had enough operational training to be spinning, looking for a target, but his eyesight was shot, his hearing shot. He was just bringing his gun up when Chen shot him twice in the forehead. The first guy was further into the room, still staggering. Chen gave him one to the back of the head, walked across the hall, gave each of them a double tap to be sure. She swapped to a full magazine, then headed for the stairs.

Uri saw his guy drop by the pillar just as he heard the explosion. Son of a bitch. Tried the upstairs team, no answer. Had to assume they were off the board, too. He turned, walked fast down the escalator, headed for the car. Nothing else to do.

Weaver was right. These two were good.

Turning out of the hotel, he saw the bike messenger still holding his ribs, walking his bike up the street, looking down at the ground. Fucker'd screwed this whole thing, cost Uri three men. As the guy passed, Uri said, "Asshole."

The guy looked up. Uri drove the straightened fingers of his left hand into the man's neck, felt the trachea go. Quick, close, nothing anybody would see. The bike messenger fell to the ground, grunting out that "ach, ach, ach" noise people make when they can't breathe.

Uri loved that noise. Made him feel a little better.

CHAPTER 46 – CHICAGO

Lynch and Liz Johnson walked into the Connemara Ball shortly after 8pm, the party in full swing, Johnson in a strapless floor-length jade-green silk number, tight to mid-thigh then flaring out, Lynch in a black tux and green tie.

"Any idea how hard it is for a girl to find a green formal on twelve hours' notice, Lynch?" Johnson said under her breath.

"You found the right one. Every guy in the room is staring at you."

Johnson smiled. "They are, aren't they?"

At least one of them was. Rodney "Ramjet" Williams, one of the Chicago Bears still making a living off being a Super Bowl champ more than twenty years earlier, walked up as soon as he saw Lynch.

"Hey, if it ain't John Lynch, Mr too slow for the show," Williams said, talking to Lynch but leering at Johnson. "Almost didn't recognize you with this new haircut of yours. Love the eyepatch. Is it talk like a pirate day again already?"

Williams had been a wideout at Miami when Lynch was at BC. Faster than shit, lots of talk about him being a top-five pick. Middle of Lynch's senior year, BC played Miami. Word on BC was they were a step slow in the secondary, so, first series, Williams went deep, blew past the corner. Lynch had deep help on that side, cut toward Williams. Decent throw and it would have been an easy six, but the Miami QB put too much air under the ball, and Williams had to slow down to make the catch. Lynch timed his hit perfectly, launching himself from two yards out like a helmet-tipped missile, hitting Williams high just as he tried to bring in the ball. Williams went down like he'd been shot, the ball popped into the air, Lynch rolling to his back, making the grab for the pick.

Williams got back up but, for the rest of the game, he was too busy looking for Lynch to look for the ball, his arms getting a little short every time a ball came downfield. Teams got the message. Rest of the year, first time Williams ran a route, somebody'd put the wood to him, even if it meant picking up a flag. Ramjet's numbers dropped way off, some of the scouts giving him a new nickname – AA, short for Alligator Arms because he wouldn't reach for the ball anymore, too afraid of what might be coming, and also because Williams had picked up a couple of DUIs down in Miami. Come draft day, Williams fell down the board into second round, where the Bears finally grabbed him. Still fast as hell, and he grew his balls back eventually, at least outside the hashmarks, turned back into a deep threat. Never could count on him over the middle.

"Rodney," said Lynch.

"Damn, boy, you finally a player? Look at you, ol' gumshoe Lynch at the Connemara Ball. And with this fine specimen here." Williams draping his arm around Johnson's shoulder. "Ramjet's just one nickname, my lovely. You get tired of your little-league date, you want to learn some of my private talents, you just look me up."

Johnson shrugged off Williams' arm. "I already know your other nickname, AA."

A little crowd had gathered, watching the show. Williams throwing his hands up, pretending good humor.

"Whoa, baby, you want to get personal, let's do that in private."

Lynch took Johnson's hand, walked past Williams. "Always good to see you again, Rodney." Then he leaned in, quieter voice in Williams' ear. "Don't make me hit you again."

The Emerald Pagoda was the same visual feast that Lynch remembered from his childhood, only more so because of the crowd and the ball.

"This place is amazing," said Johnson.

"Thank you, Ms Johnson." Paddy Wang sneaking up from the right, Mayor Hurley with him. "Detective Lynch, Elizabeth Johnson, the mayor asked that I introduce you personally."

Hurley was thick through the shoulders and chest, too much booze in the face, looking a decade older than his thirty-eight years. Green tux jacket, green tie over black pants.

"Detective, I can't tell you how pleased I am finally to meet you. Your family, your father, they are real heroes to me. Every year, Paddy tells me he's gonna get you to show up, and every year I'm disappointed."

Lynch shook Hurley's hand. "Mayor, nice to meet you. My father was a hero. I'm just a cop. Glad to finally get to the party, though. Quite a show. This is Elizabeth Johnson. She's a reporter with the Trib."

Wang interjected, "Don't worry, your honor. Ms Johnson understands that the ball is off the record, start to finish."

"Ms Johnson." Hurley shaking her hand now. "All reporters looked like you, I'd change my opinion of the press."

"Thank you, your honor."

Wang started to usher Hurley away, flesh to press, but put his hand out to Lynch.

"Thank you, young Lynch, for coming. You have made my night a success."

Lynch shook the hand, felt a small square of paper pressed into his palm. Opened it after Wang had walked away.

Stefanski had a daughter. Born March 13, 1964.

"Love note?" Johnson asked.

Lynch stuffed the paper in his pocket. "Something like that. We'll talk later."

Lynch knew he could trust Johnson, knew he should level with her, but wanted it straight in his head first. This thing with Stefanski was another free radical. Before he handed anything off, he wanted to be sure she knew where to look. And who to look out for. He took her elbow, turned her toward the dance floor.

"Care to dance?"

Johnson smiled. "I'd love to. But I thought tough guys didn't dance."

"Usually we don't. But it's common knowledge that dancing is just ritualized sex. Gets chicks hot."

Weaver was working his way through a couple of inches of scotch digesting a bad day. The Palmer House thing, that was a clusterfuck, but the Mossad guys had come pre-packaged with paper that set them up as Al-Qaeda types if the shit hit the fan, so he had a net over that. Problem was it left Ferguson and Chen on the field looking to get even. Swell.

Other problem was this Lynch fuck. Paravola was still tied into the Chicago PD systems, tracking the sniper investigation. Looked like Lynch was starting to sniff around his old man's murder, might be making the wrong connections.

Just my fucking luck, Weaver thought. Fisher goes psycho and the Chicago version of Sherlock Holmes gets the damn case instead of some fat-ass donut muncher. Lynch was one more complication Weaver just didn't need. Time to see how Clarke's knees were holding up. Clarke was an old Chicago boy, after all. He had always been the Hurleys' man in DC. If the President of the United States can't get a cop from his home town yanked off a case, what good is he?

CHAPTER 47 – CHICAGO

Next morning, Lynch walking into the office, dragging some. The Connemara Ball was everything he'd heard. After three when he and Johnson left, the party was still going on as far as Lynch knew.

Starshak stuck his head out of his office door. "Lynch, need to see you."

Lynch walked in. Starshak's face was tight, his jaw clenched.

"You don't look happy," said Lynch.

"I'm not. We're off the Hurley case. Word from up top. You're too close to it they say, what with this stuff from '71 now. And with your mom's death, they're afraid you won't be focused. Bullshit like that."

"You surprised?"

"This clusterfuck? Wish I was. Feds are running it now. They've set up a taskforce. Desk tells me they badged their way in here in the middle of the night, took all our files."

"You know this is fucked."

"I know."

"The stuff I found in the garage, any of that in our official files yet?"

Starshak shook his head. "Taking my time on that."

"You tell the Feds about it?"

"Wasn't here, nobody to talk to."

Lynch pursed his lips, looked around the squad room.

"That strike you as a little strange? No hand-off meeting?"

"How it strikes me is maybe they've already decided how this turns out. Like they figure they don't talk to anybody, then they don't have to chase down anything that doesn't fit their theory."

Lynch nodded.

"By the way," Starshak said, "you see the news last night? Shootout at the Palmer House? Brave Feds save Chicago from a terrorist plot?"

"Saw it, yeah."

"Thoughts?"

"Giving up thinking for Lent. It's not getting me anywhere. Look I'm gonna take a few days, OK? I got the wake tonight, funeral. Guess I'm not supposed to do any real cop work."

Long look from Starshak. "Yeah, fine. But behave, OK? And watch your ass."

Lynch drove out to Rusty's.

"Can't say I'm surprised to see you Johnny. Hear it's been a rough morning."

"Had better."

"Good to see you at the ball last night."

"Yeah. You left early."

"Getting old, my boy. Connemara Ball takes a year off your life, you do it right. Makes me about a hundred and forty."

"I can see that. Little tired myself this morning. Listen, I got a question for you."

"Thought you might. About Stefanski's kid."

"So you know about the note."

"Wang gave me a heads up. Said something about tectonic shifts, paradigms, usual Wang smoke and mirrors."

Rusty stepped out of the doorway, let Lynch in, walked him back to the kitchen, bottle of Jameson's open on the counter, glass half full next to it.

"Little hair of the dog," Rusty said. "Breakfast. You want any?"
Lynch shook his head. "Just what you got on Stefanski."
Rusty grunted, sat down on a stool at the counter.

"Stefanski, back in the day, used to go through a couple secretaries a year. Either they put out and he got bored with them, or they didn't and he replaced them. But there was this Italian chick, Tina Delatanno. This is mid '63. Before when Kennedy got shot. Word was Stefanski knocked her up. That had happened before. Stosh knew this doc, and usually that's how it got taken care of. But this Tina, she wasn't having that. She stuck around till she was showing a little bit and Stefanski canned her. So anyway, it figures there's a little Stosh or Stoshette running around somewhere."

"Stoshette. Wang said daughter. And Delatanno had the kid on March 13, 1964?"

"Don't know how Wang got the date. Be about right, though."

Rusty took a sip, grimaced a little as it went down, Lynch wondering what was up with the short answers, what happened to the Rusty who usually wouldn't shut up.

"You wanna save me a step here, Rusty? I know you can run this down."

Rusty raised his head, strange look on his face.

"Give me a minute." Rusty walked into the next room. Lynch could hear him on the phone, couldn't quite make out the conversation.

Rusty walked back into the room. "Gave birth at County. Put the kid up for adoption. What I'm told, she maybe got leaned on a little about how this had to be done on the QT, so the adoption ended up going through some Jewish group, whole different circle there, put a little distance between the kid and Stefanski. Far as I go."

"Got a name on the kid? Know what became of this Delatanno?"

Rusty just shook his head. Lynch staring him down, Rusty taking another sip of the whiskey, looking at his hands.

"OK," Lynch said. "Listen. I'm running into some stuff about dad's murder. You ever hear anything at the time made you think something was off?"

Rusty looked up slowly, his eyes red, wet, looking old and frightened. Shook his head again.

"Like I said, Johnny, far as I go."

Lynch looked at him, knew he knew. Not everything, probably, just something. Or at least that there was something, Lynch wondering what it's like spending half your life sitting on your own brother's murder, thinking he should be pissed but just feeling sad, sad and tired.

"OK," Lynch held Rusty's eyes. The old man looked away, Lynch needed a drink all of a sudden. Picked up Rusty's glass, downed it, set it down. Rusty looked back up.

"I probably won't be stopping by for a while," Lynch said, saw the old man's face sag like Lynch had put a knife in him.

"I..." the old man paused, his eyes wet now. "See you tonight, though, if I'm welcome." Lynch's mother's wake.

Lynch just gave a short nod, turned and headed for the door.

The old man called to his back, "Johnny, watch your ass. You don't know these guys like I do."

Lynch didn't turn to face him:

"Hope I never do, Rusty."

CHAPTER 48 – CHICAGO

Back at his building Lynch ran into McGinty, McGinty holding out a piece of paper.

"You piss in somebody's coffee, Lynch?"

Lynch looked at the sheet. A Notice of Violation from the city building department. So it was going to be like that.

"I'll straighten it out," Lynch said, and headed up the stairs.

When he opened his door, he saw Ferguson sitting in the same chair as last time, holding the same gun on him. Tiny Asian woman standing in his kitchen, a laptop open on the counter in front of her.

"Should I just get you a key?" Lynch asked. "Save you some time?"

"Wouldn't save me that much time," said Ferguson. "You've got a shitty lock."

"Matter if I got a better one?"

"Not really."

"So who's your friend?"

"Friend might be pushing it. She's a sociopath that works for me. Say hi to Lynch, Chen."

Chen nodded.

Lynch nodded back. "OK, Ferguson, what do you want?"

"Wondering if maybe you've had any second thoughts about my last offer."

"Why? Something changed?"

"You got pulled off the case, for one thing. Can't be real happy about that."

"No."

"Thing is, I got pulled off, too. You might have heard about it. Little thing at the Palmer House?"

Lynch paused a moment at that.

"Guess when your guys pull, they pull a little harder."

"Think of it as an early retirement offer. I declined."

Lynch held his coat open, showed Ferguson his gun. "I gotta take this out again, break it down, all that shit? Or can I just sit down?"

"Old friends like us? Just have a seat. You do anything I don't like, Chen'd kill you before I could anyway."

Lynch sat on the couch.

"So, your offer," Lynch said. "Yesterday you were offering the full if unofficial cooperation of the United States intelligence community to augment an official investigation by the Chicago Police Department. Now, I'm off the case. You're off the case. So now you're offering what? You and a tiny Chinese sociopath augmenting, basically, just me. I got that right?"

"Pretty much."

"Guys from the hotel still trying to kill you?"

Ferguson raised his face, his eyes hard.

"Guys from the hotel are dead."

"Point taken. To rephrase, whoever sent the guys from the hotel still trying to kill you?"

"Seems likely."

"They gonna send more guys?"

"Probably."

"And if I'm around, they'll kill me, too?"

"Could be we kill them."

"Always nice to have that to fall back on," Lynch said. "You want to explain to me why I want in on this?"

Ferguson sighed, his voice getting pedantic, like Lynch was

a deliberately willful student.

"Because you're pretty sure that whatever is going on now has something to do with your father's murder. And you're pretty sure that if the Hurleys and my bosses have their way, it all goes back under the rug."

Lynch leaned forward, elbows on his knees.

"I thought you wanted it under the rug. Wanted it buried with your shooter. Fisher, right? Ishmael Fisher?"

Ferguson raised his eyebrows. "So you got the name." Turned to look at Chen. "Told you he was good." Chen just nodded. Ferguson turned back to Lynch.

"Yeah, under the rug looked pretty good up until they tried to kill me. Now my only shot at living through the week is to bring the whole thing down around their ears."

Lynch turned to Chen. "That your position too?"

Chen nodded.

"OK," said Lynch. "How do we do it?"

"Get all the info you can to your reporter friend. Once her editors hear about this, they'll start having visions of Pulitzers and book deals, and the calls will start. Gonna take them a while to run things down, check facts, but word will percolate, and that will keep the pressure on the other team. Puts them on a tighter clock. Keeps them from spending much time looking for me, for one thing, because they'll know they gotta close the book on Fisher ASAP. More pressure we put on, the better the chances that somebody makes a mistake. Meanwhile, we find a way to get Fisher and my ex-boss and all his boys in the same place at the same time."

"I might be able to help with that," Lynch said. "Theory we've got right now is this Fisher is targeting descendants of people tied to all this from 1971."

Ferguson nodded. "Pretty much the theory we got right now, too."

"There's someone most people don't know about who'd be

way up on his list."

Ferguson raised his eyebrows. "Yeah?"

"You know Stefanski had a kid?" Lynch asked.

"No," Chen said.

"She can speak?" Lynch asked.

"Doesn't often," Ferguson answered. "Tell me about this kid."

Lynch told Ferguson what he knew about Stefanski, Delatanno, the adoption. As he talked, Chen started clicking away on her laptop.

"But you got no name?" Ferguson asked.

"No."

"Give me another minute," Chen said. More clicking.

"Don't suppose you need my WiFi password?" Lynch asked.

Chen looked up for a moment, the typing paused, shook her head, then looked back down at the keyboard.

"Adoption records will be sealed," Lynch said. "That's not going to be on a public server anywhere."

"Neither is your banking information," Chen said without pausing. "You currently have $5,412.34 in checking."

Chen kept banging away, jotting the occasional note. Finally, she looked up.

"Pearl Spritzen. Born March 13 1964. In and out of foster homes, juvenile record, then several arrests through the early Eighties. Drugs and prostitution mostly. Died of AIDS on August 6, 1989. She had a daughter, who was adopted out of Catholic Social Services. Andrea Manning, born November 30, 1980. She lives on the north side at Broadway and Sheridan. She is, apparently, a Catholic. The closest Catholic church is Saint Mary's. Manning is listed in the current church bulletin as a lector and the director of their religious education program, so we can assume she is devout and therefore attends confession."

"It's Holy Week," Lynch said.

"So?" said Ferguson.

"You're Catholic and you're the confession going type, the one day of the year you're probably going to go is Good Friday. Check the church, Chen. I bet you they've got a penance service on Friday."

More clicking. "11am," Chen said.

The room went quiet for a minute.

"Target, time and place," Ferguson said.

"Do we figure Fisher knows?" asked Lynch.

"Every time we figure he doesn't know something, we get our ass kicked," said Ferguson.

"And do we figure Weaver knows?"

"We can make sure he does," said Chen.

"So you'll have everyone you need in the same place," Lynch said.

"Right."

"And then?"

"Then we shoot them."

Clean up after one bloodbath by arranging a new one? Lynch thought. But he figured he'd keep that to himself. Still had time to find an angle, work this out some other way. In the meantime, he needed Ferguson and Chen on his side. He looked up and saw Chen staring at him like she could read his mind.

"You two want to get out of here maybe?" Lynch said. "I got my mother's wake tonight, got some personal business to tend to."

Ferguson just nodded, stood up, slid the .22 into his coat. Chen closed the laptop and the two of them walked to the door.

"We are sorry about your loss," she said reflexively as she passed him, the words coming out of her like they were preprogrammed and somebody'd hit the right button. The bullshit official phrase of condolence. Lynch thought back on all the times he'd said that, families of victims, friends of victims. Hoped he'd managed a little more sincerity, a little more feeling.

Be hard to manage any less.

CHAPTER 49 – CHICAGO

"We sure on this?"

Weaver was talking to Paravola, pushing back on some new intel that might point at Fisher's next target.

"I've hacked it all the way back to the womb. This Spritzen was Manning's mother, and Spritzen's mother was Tina Delatanno. Hired at Chicago's Streets and Sanitation summer, 1963, and fired a few months later. She was Stefanski's secretary. Intel on Stefanski we already have says he used to screw all his secretaries, so yeah, she matches up every way I can match her. I got hospital records, adoption records, Chicago employment records, Social Security. Now, Stefanski knocking this Delatanno up, that lead came out of your people. Still, if this is accurate, then you're going to love this next bit..."

Another one of Paravola's dramatic pauses. Weaver huffed. Paravola, always with the theatrics, always needing affirmation. Guy really ate at Weaver's nerves.

"Spit it out, Paravola."

"What your people had, this Delatanno, she goes to work for Stefanski, he pops her cherry, she starts showing, that starts some talk around City Hall, so Stefanski fires her and that's the end of the line. Nobody paid much attention because Stefanski pulled this kind of shit a lot, so nobody kept tabs on Delatanno, and the next known address I have on her is out of state. Des Moines, Iowa in April of '64, little over a month after the kid is

born. No record of where she was between getting canned and
turning up in corn country. Thing is, birth certificates, they
gotta show an address, right? And the address on the birth
certificate is 6412 West Palmer, Chicago."

"That's that Marslovak woman's house."

"Yeah. Her husband, that EJ guy, he was Streets and
Sanitation, too. Worked with Delatanno. What we got on him
and the old woman, all the nice church lady crap, I'm betting
they took her in until the kid was born."

Weaver thought for a minute. They had some other possibles,
Mayor Hurley probably on top of the list, that Lynch fuck on
the list. But with the Marslovak tie, this Manning chick, she
was number one. With a bullet.

"One other thing," Paravola said. "She looks like a hardline
Catholic. I grew up like that. If she's gonna go to confession
any time soon, it's gonna be Friday. And her church is having
a little penance party Friday morning."

"OK. Good work. Send it out. Full packages to everybody."

Weaver needed a break to get out in front of Fisher, now
maybe he had one. Turned into the room, used his command
voice.

"All right people. We got a solid line on Fisher's next
target. Andrea Manning. You're all getting a data dump from
Paravola. I want a full court press. Surveillance, intel, photos.
Twelve hours from now, I ask you what her dirty panties smell
like, I want an answer. And get me a tactical solution. Our
guess is this chick hits the confessional on Friday. We got the
date, we got the time, we got the place. I wanna know where
Fisher's gonna be and how we're gonna take him down."

CHAPTER 50 - CHICAGO

Pushing 8pm, the main viewing room at Fitzpatrick's Funeral Home was only half full. Lynch eyeballing the crowd, looking for faces. Part of the deal, being a cop, there were always asses in the seats. Wakes, weddings, whatever, like the guy or not, you showed up. Just part of having everybody's back. But they weren't showing up tonight. So the word was out. Which meant somebody'd put the stink on Lynch, at least for now, and anybody that was worried about it rubbing off was staying away. The violation from the building code people, that was just bullshit, but this stung a little.

Starshak was there, Bernstein, McCord, Cunningham. A few other cops, guys he went back with, guys he'd gone through doors with, but some who normally would have shown, some of the upstream guys, some of the brass, hell, some of the guys from his own squad, suddenly they had better things to do.

With the cop numbers down, the crowd was trending old. People from the neighborhood, the ones that were still alive, retired cops who knew his dad, didn't have to worry about promotions anymore. Some of the political crowd was there, just a few, guys who weren't quite sure whether pissing off Rusty was worth snubbing Lynch.

Rusty'd been late, half in the can when he got there. Keeping his distance, sticking to a corner in the back where he could hold court, get his ring kissed.

Half the crowd was from Milwaukee, friends of his sister's. Made Lynch a little sad, not so much the numbers as the realization that she had this whole life up there that he'd missed out on. Lynch burying his mom, his sister next to him in the black dress, the only other person in the room who could look at the body lying there with the over-done hair and a couple pounds of make-up and know that the first thing his mom would have said if she could look in a mirror would be "My God, would you look at this, I look like the Whore of Babylon." His sister there and she's almost a stranger to him.

Liz walked in, rushed, hair a little messed. He'd dropped her at her place after the ball – she had to take off for Springfield at dawn, had to cover some special session down at the state capital, some pissing contest over pension funding, the latest game of political chicken between the downstate Republicans and Hurley's machine. Must have driven up from Springfield as soon as the day's session ended, and must have broken some traffic laws doing it. Hadn't gone home first to change, hadn't worried how she was going to look meeting Lynch's family for the first time. Been weird, the last few days, what would push Lynch's buttons. Little choked up at his mom's place when he'd opened the medicine cabinet, his leg barking at him, looking for the Tylenol, and had seen his mom's old brush, the one with the Abalone inlay in the back, the one his dad had brought home from the Pacific after Korea. Liz rushing in like this, making the effort, that had him tearing up, too.

Liz walked straight to him, hugged him, held him. "I'm sorry I'm so late, I came as soon as I could."

"It's OK," he said. "Lot of people aren't coming at all. I didn't expect you to drive all the way back up for this."

Liz pulled back, still holding Lynch's hand, as he introduced her to his sister. "Liz, this is my sister, Collie, and her husband Brad." They all shook, the usual nice-to-meet-yous and I'm-so-sorrys. Lynch pulled his nephew up, Tommy sort of hanging back. "And this is my nephew, Tommy."

"Tom," the boy said, correcting Lynch, putting his hand out, and Lynch realized the boy was what, thirteen now, as tall as his mother, all that time gone.

Liz shook his hand.

"You're really a reporter?" Tom asked.

Liz nodded. "I work for the *Tribune*."

"I like to write," Tom said. "But my teachers say there may not even be newspapers in a few years."

"Not like there are now, probably," Liz said. "Most of it will be online. But we'll always need writers. Maybe you'd like to come down to the newsroom sometime? See how it works?"

Tom smiled at her. "That would be cool."

Tommy retreated back to the wall, trying to find a space to ride out the wake, Lynch realizing there wasn't another kid in the room, not one. Tommy caught Lynch's eye for a second, raised his eyebrows a little, stuck his thumb up, and Lynch realized again that his nephew was thirteen, and that, even not taking any time to pull herself together, Liz was pretty damn hot. Lynch gave his nephew a quick thumbs up back.

Liz leaned over and whispered in his ear. "I'll pretend I didn't see that."

"What are you gonna do?" Lynch said "Kid's a teenager, hormones."

Starshak, Bernstein, McCord, and Cunningham had staked out a corner. Lynch went back to join them.

"Thanks for coming guys, means a lot. I know the word's gone out." He turned to Cunningham. "You especially, Darius. We got no history."

Cunningham shook Lynch's hand. "Fuck that shit."

"I'm not here for you, Lynch," said Bernstein. "Just trying to get some intel on this whole Catholic thing so I can report back to the international Jewish conspiracy." That got a laugh.

"I just thought there'd be booze," said Starshak. "Irish wake and no booze?"

McCord pulled a leather-wrapped flask from his pocket and handed it to Starshak. "Of course there's booze."

Starshak looked Lynch straight in the eye, serious suddenly. "I'm taking names, Lynch. You find out which side people are on, you mark that down."

"Amen to that, brother," said Cunningham.

Lynch sitting with his sister, maybe an hour left.

"Lot of cheeseheads here," he said. "Lot of people made the drive down."

"Don't be too impressed. Half of them probably report to me at work, just racking up brownie points."

Lynch smiled. "Save your hard-ass act, Collie. I think they actually like you."

Collie shrugged. "Tom's in love with your girlfriend, by the way. Just thought you should know you have a rival."

Lynch had seen Liz sitting with his nephew for quite a while.

"Yeah, well, you know what? I'm in love with her, too. Tell the kid to back off. Remind him I got a gun."

She laughed. "John Lynch in love. My, my. It was nice of Father Hughes to come. He's the one saying the funeral?"

"Yeah." Father Hughes was talking to a few of his mom's old neighbors, up by the casket.

"Kind of sad, Mom dies, and you have to recruit a priest from one of your cases."

"Yeah," said Lynch.

"We should have him say a rosary," Collie said.

Lynch turned and looked at her. "Really? You even remember how?"

She shrugged. "It's like falling off a bike, I guess. I'll go talk to him."

Collie went up and talked to the priest, and he made the

announcement, the staff from the funeral home walking around, handing out plastic rosaries. Lynch passed Bernstein on his way up to join his sister at the kneeler in front of the casket.

"Get ready to take notes, Slo-mo. Here's the shit you came to see."

CHAPTER 51 – CHICAGO

An hour later, everything over, Lynch and Johnson were in the hallway by the front door.

"Listen, John, I'd come over but I still owe the *Trib* a thousand words on this pension mess and I'm running on about two hours sleep," Johnson said.

"It's OK," Lynch said. "I'm kinda washed out myself. We gotta talk though. A lot's changed. A lot's changed since yesterday."

"I thought so. Last night, Hurley's acting like he's got a man crush on you, then I get down to the capital and Harrigan's giving me a hard time about an interview, telling me I need to be careful about my friends, telling me I keep swapping spit with John Lynch, I'm going to find a lot of doors that won't open for me. I guess you can be bad for a girl's career."

Harrigan was the speaker of the Illinois house, the top Democratic gun down in Springfield.

Lynch nodded, thought for a minute about how and what to tell Johnson. Not a trust thing anymore. He knew he could trust her. Just this whole thing had spun off into an entire new universe for him. A universe where it didn't matter where you were, who you were, what you'd done, there were guys with guns ready to take you off the board just for a little edge. The old school part of him was saying you don't throw your woman in the deep end of that pool. But he knew that

302

wasn't his call. Johnson was a big girl. And this was her game, too. Maybe the biggest story out of this town since, well, ever. She got to decide what pools to jump into all on her own. And he needed the press on this, needed to get some pressure on the other team.

"The Harrigan thing, here's the deal. We're off the case," Lynch said. "The whole Chicago PD. Feds have bogarted it, which means Clarke is calling the tune, because there's no way Hurley shows his ass to the Feds on his own."

"Clarke as in President of the United States Clarke?"

Lynch nodded. "And the Feds have got the whole thing hermetically sealed. Got it in cover-up mode. Listen, I got a whole mess of new shit the last couple days, got to catch you up. Not tonight, though. I still got some dots to connect. But breakfast?"

Johnson nodded. "Sounds like you might be good for a girl's career after all."

"I don't get you killed, yeah," Lynch said.

A commotion came from down at the far end of the hall, somebody staggering out from the viewing room, knocking over one of the floral displays, lurching across the hallway into the men's room. Rusty.

He'd kept to his corner all night. Collie'd gone over on her way out with the family, said her goodbyes. She was headed back up to Milwaukee. Holy Thursday tomorrow, so they couldn't have the funeral until Monday. Catholic rules.

Rusty'd had a bottle of Jameson's and a few glasses out on the table next to his chair all night, the ring kissers taking a slug here and there, but Rusty working his way through most of it, and he'd been pretty well lit when he came in.

One of the guys from the funeral home pushed in to the men's room behind Rusty, some noises coming out, not happy noises. The guy came out, walked down the hall.

"Detective," he said, "we may need some help with your

uncle. He's a little, eh, distraught."

"OK," Lynch said. He hugged Johnson. She pulled back, put a hand to his face for a long moment, something passing between them, something he didn't have words for, didn't need words for.

"Breakfast," she said.

Lynch nodded.

Rusty was sitting on the floor of the men's room when Lynch walked in, pants half open, a puddle of urine under his legs. He looked up, his eyes red, his face washed in tears.

"Pissed myself," he said.

Rusty was shrunken, hollowed out, shattered.

Lynch squatted down, got the old man under the arms, pulled him to his feet. Rusty fumbled his pants closed, leaned back against the wall, panting from the small effort, tried to hold Lynch's eyes, white hair hanging sweaty and stringy over his fleshy face, the huge head shaking back and forth.

"I didn't know," he said. "Not then. Didn't know nothin'. Not for a long time. And I never did know nothin' for sure. I didn't know."

Part of Lynch wanted to bury a fist in the old man's gut. Part of him wanted to hug him. Lynch reached up and took Rusty's chin, steadied his face, looked into his eyes.

"You didn't want to know, Rusty."

The old man came apart, falling forward, Lynch holding him up while Rusty wept into his shoulder.

"Pissed myself," Rusty muttered. "Your mother's wake and I pissed myself."

A kaleidoscope of emotions swirling in Lynch's head, Lynch not knowing which of them to seize on, which of them to feel. Rusty didn't know up front. Lynch was sure of that. Probably didn't even have a clue for a while. And he'd made a promise to Lynch's dad the day Declan Lynch put on the uniform. Said he'd watch out for the family, it ever came to that. He'd kept that promise, the promise maybe being the reason that, once Rusty knew there might be something, that maybe his masters had had a hand in his brother's death, that promise being the reason he never looked, never pushed it. Rusty maybe thinking there was the truth, and then there was his brother's family, and there was no way to serve both of them.

Now Lynch didn't know either. Didn't know what to say, what to think, what to feel. But he knew what his father would do.

"You're still family, Rusty," Lynch said, turning the old man toward the door, getting an arm around him. "Let's get you home."

CHAPTER 52 – CHICAGO

Next morning, Cunningham stepped out his door, saw a FedEx guy with a huge box on a dolly in the front foyer.

"Hey, good timing," the guy said. "I was just getting ready to leave. Tried the buzzer, wasn't getting anybody. Looking for Jackson? Paperwork says unit one, so I'm guessing that's you?"

"I'm unit one, but I'm not Jackson. He's on four."

"Always some damn thing," the FedEx man said, pointing his little hand-held scanner at Cunningham and pulling the trigger. The darts were similar to a Taser, but stronger. Cunningham hit the floor in a heap, twitching. The FedEx man laid the large container flat on the floor, squatted down, opened the lid and flipped Cunningham inside. Then he pulled a small syringe out of the end of his clipboard, injected Cunningham with the sedative, and buckled the cuffs attached inside the box around Cunningham's wrists and ankles. He clamped the top of the box shut, tipped the box up on the dolly, and walked it out the door and into his truck.

CHAPTER 53 – CHICAGO

Holy Thursday, early morning.

Lynch saw Johnson drinking coffee in a booth by the window when he got to the McDonald's on Western just north of Pratt. Her condo was on Lunt, just a bit east. Lynch picked the McDonald's. It was close to her place and it was public. His phone beeped. He checked it. Text from Paddy Wang. Wang wanted a sit down. He forwarded it to Ferguson along with a time.

"You're running late, Lynch," Johnson said as he walked up. "I'm the one working on no sleep here."

"Bus was slow." Lynch was carrying a nylon messenger bag over his shoulder.

Johnson paused a count. "Bus?"

"Hard to follow a guy on a bus."

"Things that bad?"

"Probably worse," Lynch said. "C'mon, let's take a walk. Little park near here. It's kind of nice."

"Let me guess. It's hard to follow somebody in a park, too."

Lynch smiled. But he also nodded. They grabbed some crap at the counter, walked up to Indian Boundary Park.

"What kind of name is Indian Boundary for a park?" Johnson asked.

"This was the line between the US and Pottawatomie land, some treaty after the War of 1812."

"How long did that last?"

"I dunno. Week and a half maybe. I only know about it because they've got a historical marker up by the corner there. Had to check out a body next to it once, back when I was in uniform. Just some drunk, passed out one night, middle of January. Froze to death." Lynch shrugged the bag off his shoulder held it out to Johnson. "This is for you."

Lynch ran down what he knew. The Hurley murder-suicide back in 1971, his father's murder, the Fishers, father and son, Clarke's involvement, Ferguson, Chen, how they needed the press to push in this, needed her to push it, all of it.

"Jesus," Johnson said. "My god, your father?" She stopped, turned to face him.

Lynch just nodded.

"And you never knew?"

"Still don't know, not for sure. Not everything."

Johnson started to say something, but Lynch held a hand up, cut her off.

"Listen, part of me didn't want to give you this. Didn't want you in this. These people, they've got no boundaries. Nobody's off limits. Nobody. But it's a big story, important story, and that's what you do. So it has to be your call. Somebody's gotta do it, but nothing says that has to be you. I don't want it to be you. But that has to be your call."

She stopped, turned to face him.

"You know I'm going to run with it. I have to."

"I know."

Another pause, then walking in silence again, Johnson talking first.

"This going to be a problem for us?" she asked.

Lynch shook his head. "You grew up with cops, you knew the risks, hell, you've seen me get shot. You're still here. What am I supposed to do? Tell you to stay home and bake cookies? You love somebody, nobody says you get a free ride, that you're gonna like everything. Can you do me a favor though?"

"What?"

"Don't get greedy, try for some kind of exclusive on this. Spread it around a little. Make sure your editor's up to speed, maybe loop somebody in on the TV side. You start poking and these guys think they can stuff the genie back in the bottle with one bullet, they're gonna take the shot. You get enough people involved, then they'll know it's too late for that."

Johnson nodded.

"Too much for me to handle alone anyway. I don't have DC contacts, I'll need the help. And trust me, I'm all about not getting shot."

They passed the small zoo at the back of the park, most of the cages empty now, budget cuts. A lone goat looked up for a moment, went back to picking at the long grass that grew up along the edge of the fence.

Johnson nudged the bag that hung from her shoulder now. "What's all this got to do with the killings now?"

"This Zeke Fisher? His kid went into the spook business, but he's gone off the deep end. He's on some kind of redemption mission."

"Killing people's children? Grandchildren? What kind of sense does that make?"

"Guy's a nutjob. Only one it has to make sense to is him."

Quiet again for a minute.

"The children he wants to kill. You could be one of them," she said.

Lynch nodded. "Good thing I haven't been to confession in thirty years."

Johnson smiled. "I tell you what, big boy, you promise to stay out of the confessional until this is over, I'll make sure you've got something really juicy to confess." She reached down, squeezed his ass.

Lynch smiled. "Deal."

Johnson took his hand and they walked quietly for a while, both with the sense that this could be their last good moment.

"*Après cela, le déluge*," Johnson said.

Lynch let out a short laugh. "The reporting is one thing, Johnson. But you start in with the French and I'm dumping you."

They both laughed, more than they should have, stopped at the corner at the northwest edge of the park. Lynch looked at his watch.

"Need to catch your bus?" Johnson asked.

Lynch shook his head as a black sedan pulled up. "I got a ride."

"Your new friends?"

He nodded.

"Where are you headed?"

"Going to see Paddy Wang," Lynch said. "He says he wants to talk."

Johnson looked at the car, looked back at Lynch.

"The only way these people know how to solve things is to kill people, you know that, right?" she said.

Lynch nodded.

"Please tell me you're not OK with that."

Lynch shook his head. "No, I'm not."

"What are you going to do about that?"

"I wish I knew," Lynch said.

CHAPTER 54 – CHICAGO

Lynch and Paddy Wang, alone in Wang's office.

"Young Lynch, in current circumstances, you are likely suspicious of all motives, but I mean this sincerely. Ever since the unfortunate passing of your father, I have had a kind interest in you."

"That's great, Paddy. You help Hurley and his punks kill my old man, or help cover it up, or at least know about it and say nothing, and you tell me what a kind interest you have in me. I'm all choked up."

"I understand your anger, young Lynch."

"Keep up that condescending bullshit, and I'm coming across this desk. You've got no fucking idea about my anger."

"At losing a parent unfairly? My parents were killed by the Maoists. I was, well, present for that. Whether you choose to believe it or not, I had no prior knowledge of your father's death, and saw no benefit to anyone – most particularly to you or your sister or your mother – of exposing what I knew later."

"And I have no way of knowing if that's true or just more of your crap."

"As with all our demons. They drive each of us in all we do, and yet have no currency outside our own souls."

"Look, Paddy, you got down here for some reason. Can we just get to it?"

Wang just looked at Lynch for a moment, his eyes hooded.

"Have you ever heard the theory that a man is great in proportion to those who take an interest in him?" Wang asked.

"No."

"By that measure, young Lynch, you have always been a great man. The Hurleys, of course, have an interest. Your uncle has an interest. I, too, have an interest. And now I hear that the President of the United States has an interest."

"It's an interesting world."

"I have always found it so. But perhaps a different world than you imagine."

"More than is dreamt of in my philosophy?"

Wang chuckled. "Ah, young Lynch. I truly do wish you would visit more often. Yes, yes. Far more."

"Paddy, you got a point to get to here? Every time I talk with you, I feel like I'm going to end up farting smoke for a week."

"I'm afraid that my Eastern proclivity for circuitousness and your Western preference for straight lines will always leave us at odds. Very well, to the point. You believe that you are a champion in a great contest between good and evil and that, as a result of your current actions, power will be shaken to its foundations, yes?"

"I think your proclivities run more to hyperbole, Paddy. I believe some assholes got away with murder a long time ago. I believe some other assholes capitalized on it. I believe a lot of other assholes sat by and did nothing."

"And so you will drag these scurrilous cowards into the light of day so that they may reap that which they have sown."

"I'll chase it down and see how it plays out. I know you're trying to protect them, Paddy – Hurley, Clarke, all of them. You can't. And if I can prove you're in it, then I'm taking you down, too."

Wang sat back, nodding. "Finally, we come to the crux of the matter. You never have understood, young Lynch. You still don't."

"So enlighten me."

"Do you really think that the Hurleys of the world matter? Or the Clarkes?"

"Do I think that one of the most powerful political families in the country matters? Do I think that the President of the United States matters? I'm leaning toward yes."

"Power matters, young Lynch. And it has a public and a private face. These men are merely its skin – skin that changes with each election or the fall of each dynasty. The Roosevelts, the Kennedys, all so many shed skins."

"And you're the snake?"

Wang snorted a short laugh. "Always these scandals. The private face of power decides, young Lynch – decides direction, decides policy, decides strategy. But there must be a public face to translate that vision into useful social action – into law, into commerce, into treaties. And so we find the public faces, and we cultivate them, and we allow them their vainglorious belief in the infinity of their own power. But the public face is always flesh, and the ways of the flesh are always its downfall. And so the face is changed. And so the public face may be changing again. The private face of power does not care and does not involve itself. But the public face cares greatly. The greater the threat, the harder the public face will fight. Do not misunderstand, Lynch. The power of the public face is no threat to the private face – it is venal, banal, grubbing power – but it is still very dangerous."

"You called me down here to warn me? I'm touched."

Wang shook his head. "Surely you did not need me to advise you of your current danger."

"So what do you want?"

"What is your marvelous American saying? I have no dog in this fight? That is all I wanted you to know. Should the Hurleys or the president fall, the private face of power will adjust. Sometimes such tumult presents opportunities for change that are less incremental than those mandated by more tranquil times. We shall watch, and we shall await the outcome. That is all I wanted you to know."

"So you don't have my back, but you're not gonna put a knife in it, either?"

"To paraphrase. Although, in my passion for fairness, I would like to help your new friends with their shopping."

"Help what new friends with what shopping?"

"Feigned ignorance is trying. Ferguson and Chen. They are used to operating with the equipment and material afforded the minions of power's public face. They now will need to find new sources. Please give them this." Wang slid a small card with a phone number on it across the table.

"You're on our side?"

"I am on the same side I am always on, young Lynch. The winning side. Whichever side that proves to be. Whoever wins, however, I prefer that they be in my debt."

CHAPTER 55 – CHICAGO

Weaver hung up the phone. Hastings Clarke, calling from the private residence. Clarke was coming apart. Somebody, probably Lynch, had spilled to the press. Not all of it, but enough. Lynch's squeeze, that blond from the *Tribune*, she'd started in hard that morning, and it was pretty clear somebody'd given her a big leg up. Then a guy at CNN she'd played ball with before chimed in. That was enough to churn the water. Now the whole DC press corps was scrambling, knew the Big Story Train was leaving the station, everybody looking for their own angle, trying to grab a seat before the thing got too far down the tracks. There were enough people pulling on the ends of the right strings. Give them enough time, and the whole thing would unravel.

Which meant two things. This shot at Fisher tomorrow, he damn well had to make that work because another day or so was all the time he had. And he had to get an alternative story out there, something for the press pukes who hadn't bought into what Johnson was selling, or who were too slow to grab a good chunk of it. Give that crowd something to push, have them start calling bullshit on Johnson's stuff, get everybody fighting over which one was the right narrative. Turn the whole thing from a potential PR nightmare for Clarke into a he-said, she-said hair-pulling contest.

He had Cunningham on ice, drugged up and ready to play

patsy just as soon as Weaver had a dead Fisher to swap him out for. With Clarke's clout backing him up, he had a whole passel of counterintel gurus ginning up a back story. Paravola and his cronies had hacked into the right databases and planted the right seeds. Skeff Young was laying some breadcrumbs in front of some FBI contacts. The feebs in DC would feed that shit back to the taskforce guys in Chicago, the taskforce guys would leak it, and that would chase the press right into the net of bullshit that Paravola and company were laying out for them. Which would make the whole story their idea. Cunningham would be all teed up.

All Weaver needed was Fisher off the board and a dead Cunningham lying next to Fisher's rifle. And he was twenty-four hours from pulling that off.

CHAPTER 56 – CHICAGO

Lynch, Chen, and Ferguson were in the basement of Lynch's mother's house, their new base of operations. Not enough room at Lynch's place. Also, Ferguson didn't like the idea of being four floors up. Pointed out that, if Weaver ran them down, they'd want more than one way out.

Lynch had passed Wang's card to Ferguson, and he and Chen had disappeared for a few hours. Now Chen was unpacking their toys. It looked to Lynch like she might be smiling.

"Four MP5s – two vanilla, two suppressed, all with folding stocks and laser sights," Chen said.

"You'll love these," said Ferguson, tossing one of the submachine guns to Lynch. "Light, relatively concealable, great cyclic rate of fire, magazines swap easy. Really nice room broom."

"Gee, you shouldn't have," said Lynch.

"For Ferguson, we have Parker Hale Model 85. 12x Leupold scope, reportedly tricked out in all those special ways you like by an ex-SAS master armorer," said Chen.

Ferguson snatched the rifle off the table and worked the bolt. "Ah, come to papa, baby."

Chen digging back into her toy chest. "Several Glocks for you gentlemen. A nice, efficient .32 for me. Sufficient ammunition for all. Flash bangs, night vision goggles, NOMEX suits, web gear, comm units, a couple of Claymores–"

317

"Claymores?" said Lynch. "You mean antipersonnel mines?"

"Front toward enemy," said Ferguson. "A nice-shaped wad of C4, a few hundred ball bearings. Pop the trigger and you can even up some bad odds in a big hurry."

"And we are going to use those where exactly?"

"Better to have them and not need them than need them and not have them," said Ferguson.

"By which logic we should have a fighter jet and an A-bomb."

"I am rated on the F-16," said Chen. "But I don't think even your Mr Wang has one of those in inventory."

"I wouldn't count on that," said Lynch, thinking to himself that he really needed a way to pull the plug on this which didn't end up with everybody dead.

CHAPTER 57 - CHICAGO

Weaver had seven shooters left after the Palmer House debacle, still should be enough. Had some new tech, too, that was going to help.

With Clarke backing his play, Weaver was able to shake a couple of radar-assisted anti-sniper units out of the DoD, new prototypes, next generation stuff a couple notches up the technical ladder from the Boomerang acoustic system the troops were using now, the one that triangulated sound waves to ID the point of origin for sniper fire. Boomerangs weren't going to help much with Fisher. He was a tricky bastard. That back-from-the-window shit he'd been using muddied up the sound, and that would cause some trouble with an acoustic unit, that and he'd used a suppressor downstate. Boomerangs would only give him a general direction.

The new system added 3D laser radar to the mix – actually picked up the flight of the bullet, traced it back to the point of origin. With these puppies, as soon as Fisher took his shot, Weaver's boys could put enough firepower on target to puree the son of a bitch. Scoop up Fisher, drop the black guy's corpse in his place. The only problem was the units were new, prototypes on their way to Afghanistan for field-testing. He only had two to play with, so he had to make sure he had them in the right locations.

That solved one problem. The other problem was this.

They were out of time. This thing had to go down tomorrow. Suppose this Manning chick's been behaving herself, doesn't feel the need to go to confession? Wouldn't matter to Fisher. Fisher would wait. Weaver couldn't. As of thirty minutes ago, though, Weaver was pretty sure he had that problem licked, too.

He flipped open the dossier from Langley, one of their few female paramilitary types, some hard-ass named Pat Brown. Manning was thirty-two, Brown was thirty-three. Manning was five-six, one hundred and twenty-two pounds. Brown was the same height, six pounds heavier, but it was all muscle, so she actually looked a shade smaller. Manning was kind of a dirty blonde, Brown's hair was almost black, but they could fix that. But the face was the real home run. Not identical twin material, but close, and the bone structure was perfect. Give the hair-and-makeup guys an hour, no way you'd be able to tell them apart, not through a 12x scope, not at seven hundred meters.

So he'd have a team grab Manning tonight. This Manning, though, she was one of the lectors at the parish. Good chance Fisher's done his recon, knew her voice. So they'd get Manning to record a confession. Snyder'd done background, had all the lingo for that down. Take the priest down in the morning, swap one of their guys in, have him do confessions. Have to get him a script. Have Brown lip-synch her way through whatever they get out of Manning for Fisher's camera. Plus, a fake priest would give Weaver a back-up gun in the church, just in case.

Everything was falling into place. Even God was on his side. Weather was turning. Temperatures in the low forties tomorrow, pretty good wind coming in off the lake. So he could stuff Brown in one of Manning's coats, put a hat on her, scarf, pretty much eliminate the possibility of anything that would tip off Fisher, queer the ID. With the coat on, Brown could even wear a vest. Not that a vest was likely to stop a rifle round, but the story Weaver had fed Brown was that they had Fisher's hide scoped. Just need her to show herself so he'd step up to the window and they could take their shot. Who knows? Might work out that way. She might come out of this alive.

If it didn't? Well, it's not like Brown would be coming back at him over it.

CHAPTER 58 – CHICAGO

Lynch left the house to pick up some pizza, flicked on the radio to WBBM to get the news just as a reporter started recapping a church sniper taskforce news conference.

"A taskforce spokesperson revealed today that an arrest is imminent in the Confessional Killings. Members of the taskforce have developed evidence linking the shootings of Helen Marslovak and Thomas Riordan to the police shootings of four black activists in 1971. The activists were part of a group called the AMN Commando, an offshoot of the Chicago Black Panthers that was formed after Black Panther leader Fred Hampton was killed in a police raid. Marslovak and Riordan are both related to persons tied to that raid. The taskforce believes that the current shootings are in revenge for the raid and is close to naming a suspect."

They were teeing someone up to take the fall, which must mean they were ready to make their move. It was all going down tomorrow.

Lynch's cell phone rang. Caller ID said Starshak.

"Hey, Captain."

"Lynch, you heard from Cunningham at all?"

"Not since the wake."

"Something stinks. Couple of feebs from the taskforce were just in my office, had some OPS puke with them. They tell me they need to talk to him. They tell me he's gone missing. And when I start asking questions, they pretty much tell me to go fuck myself. Then I hear this news conference crap. I think they're looking to pin the church shootings on him."

"You call his place?"

"Yeah. Answering machine."

"Check with his CO?"

"He didn't show today. OPS has been over there too, talking to everybody."

"He got any family?"

"Ex-wife. Called her. She's freaked. Feds have been to her place with a warrant, tossed it pretty good."

"Son of a bitch."

"Hearing some other shit too, Lynch. Shit about Johnson and questions she shouldn't know enough to be asking. You keeping your nose out of this? It's getting ugly."

"Don't ask questions you don't want an answer to, Captain." Lynch paused a moment. He'd been pulling at this thing ever since he teamed up with Ferguson, looking for a way to end it that didn't wind up with another batch of body bags. Whatever that was going to be, he was going to need help he could trust.

"But Cap, keep your phone on, OK?"

Back at his mother's house, Lynch updated Ferguson and Chen on the call from Starshak.

"Admirable," said Chen.

"I was thinking evil," Lynch said.

"I do not concern myself with ethical distinctions. I was commenting on the plan. Clearly, they also have identified Manning as the next target. They have kidnapped Cunningham and are holding him until Fisher takes the shot. They will take Fisher out, kill Cunningham, plant his body, and in doing so, given your association with him in recent weeks, discredit what you have given to the press."

"So Cunningham's dead?"

"Not yet," said Ferguson. "Too hard to disguise a time of death these days, and they'll want all the forensics to match up. Short-acting sedatives, stuff that passes out of the bloodstream quick. They'll take Cunningham off his meds in the morning, keep him in soft restraints, walk him right into the scene, and kill him there. Probably already be a fair amount of Fisher's blood splattered around, so Fisher will go down as one of their boys, probably Cunningham's last victim. That'll tie everything in nice and tight."

"But what about the press? They're already on this," said Lynch.

"Contradictory evidence is already being planted, I assure you," said Chen. "I assume you are being painted as a patsy. The story will be that Cunningham used his connection to you to plant this fairytale about your father and the Hurley murder, and that you, in your grief, failed to analyze the data objectively. Instead, you inadvertently provided Cunningham with information that helped him in his quest. They will recognize your previous heroism, talk of you in sad, glowing terms, order a psych evaluation, and then retire you due to mental health issues. Just another crackpot with a conspiracy theory. Your suicide will follow in short order. Whether and how long Ms Johnson lives will depend on which story she chooses to pursue."

"And you know all this how?"

"It's what I would do."

Lynch looked at Chen. No expression.

"You saying we're screwed?" Lynch asked.

"Not if we screw them first," Ferguson said.

CHAPTER 59 – CHICAGO

Weaver stood at the end of the table, leaning on his hands, staring down at the big aerial photo of St Mary's and environs. Damn, he missed Fergie. Weaver'd never been a long-gun guy, didn't know the sniper mindset. Fergie would look at this mess and see something. Also he wished he knew where the bastard was. Fergie and Chen on the loose, maybe on the other team, that was not a problem he needed. No time for that now, though. Things worked out tomorrow, then he'd run their asses down.

"You got anything, Uri?"

"When I take a long shot, it's usually across a lot of sand. Give me a target in a city, and I'll take an alley and a knife every time. But a few things. He likes to stretch it out, right? Every time so far, he's been a lot farther from the target than he had to be. And every time, he's hit them as soon as they are out of the building?"

Weaver nodded. "I don't know if he's showing off or if it's part of this religious crap, but he has been pushing the envelope. And he's been taking them fast."

"This Manning, she lives at the other end of this block," Uri running his finger up the photo, "up the street from the church. So he has to be expecting her to exit the front of the church and walk north up Sheridan?"

"Makes sense."

"First we set a limit. That first one in Wisconsin? You sure about that?"

"Chen's sure, which is pretty much like God being sure, at least about ballistics."

"Better than nine hundred meters through a twenty-plus crosswind with a weapon most people can't hit shit with beyond five hundred meters. OK, so figure he's going to be out at least five hundred and at most a thousand. Push it to eleven hundred just to be safe." Uri measured out a piece of string, pinned one end to the front of the church, and drew two circles on the map, one at five hundred meters, the other at one thousand one hundred meters. "He's going to be between the first and second circle."

Uri pointing at the photo again. "We have this building right across the street, what's that, three or four stories? Blocks any kind of shot due from due east. But tweak the line just a shade north, and you got this cluster here." Uri tapped a couple of high rises on the west side of Lake Shore Drive. "If he gets on the roof there, maybe an upper west-facing floor, it looks like he'd have a line. You're getting close to one thousand meters out there, though." The Israeli stuck a pin in the map, marking the location. "So that's one spot to watch, it is pretty much the only good option from the east."

· Uri looked at the map for another minute.

"The front door is on the east side of the church, so anything west is out. He'd have to wait for her to walk to the end of the building before he had a shot. That leaves obliques to the north and south, up and down Sheridan. The church is almost built right out to the sidewalk. If anybody coming out takes one step down, then they have to turn either south or north. Manning lives north. He likes to take them through the heart, and that's going to be a lot easier if the target is facing him. So that gives you these couple of blocks here." The Israeli ran his finger between the circles where they crossed Sheridan.

"Same thing with the south, just to be safe. From the south, he'd have to shoot her in the back, though. That would mean he would be in this area here."

Uri took a yardstick, penciled lines to the buildings that had line of sight to the church door and that were in the right range bracket. Looked up when he was done.

"Twenty-two possible buildings. Hard to say how many windows exactly."

Too many, thought Weaver, but no need to let the troops see him sweat.

"OK," Weaver said, "so where do we put our guys?"

"We need a line to him. Either we put shooters in the church, or we get teams spread out up and down the west side of Sheridan. Put the radar units in the first hides on either side of the church, network everybody in so we all get the data as soon as he takes the shot. How many long guns have we got?"

"Seven, but only five that have done the deed for real."

Uri went back to work with his string. When he was done, he'd marked five buildings with blue Xs, with two of the Xs circled. "Put your top five in these, with the radar units in the two spots I've circled. You'll have at least one top shooter with a line to any position he can take, usually you'll have two shooters, sometimes three. Put your two virgins here." He tapped a building just northwest of the high rises out at the thousand-yard mark. "If he shoots from out there, they'll only have two buildings to watch. They can pre-sight nearly every window, and the roofline. They'll have a narrow range to watch and they'll be inside two hundred meters. Even a virgin can't miss from two hundred meters."

Weaver nodded. "OK. Tomorrow, you place the teams."

Uri left the room to talk with the troops. Weaver worked on his other problem, where to keep Cunningham on game day, where to park the van. That would be his command post. Looked at the map. One of the buildings Uri had circled was

Manning's place. Less than a block to the church, private parking in the back that let out into the alley, so out of public view, a straight shot up or down Sheridan to most of the spots they'd ID'd as possible hides for Fisher. A thousand yards might be a long shot, but it wasn't much of a drive.

Manning's place was perfect.

CHAPTER 60 – CHICAGO

Lynch pushed out the door of the Walgreens and headed back to the house. Had enough small arms to overthrow a banana republic, but they were out of toothpaste. Needed to think anyway, so he walked up to the drugstore on Cicero. Halfway back across the parking lot, a fit looking guy in his sixties, buzzed gray head, walked up next to him.

"You Lynch?"

Lynch didn't say anything, just nudged his jacket open, switched the bag to his left hand, got ready.

The older guy gave him a little smile, held his hands away from his body. "Little nervous, huh? Don't blame you. I'm a friend of Cunningham's, from the old days. We need to talk. So how about I give you a lift back to your mom's place?"

"How do you know about my mom's place?"

The older guy shrugged. "Had to find you, it's public record, no real stretch."

Lynch looked at the guy for a minute, liked the vibe he got, but pulled out his 9mm anyway. "OK. You drive. You don't mind if I just hold on to this, do you?"

"Suit yourself."

Lynch followed the guy to the far end of the parking lot. The guy got into a tan Corolla, Virginia plates. Lynch jumped in.

"Sorry for the cloak and dagger shit, jumping you in the parking lot like that," the guy said. "Brian Jenks, late of the

USMC, currently an advisor to various folks on sniper and counter-sniper ops. I was Cunningham's CO for twelve years."

Lynch shifted in his seat, got his back to the passenger door so he could hold the gun on Jenks from across his body.

"You're the guy who told him about the Dragon?"

"Fisher? Yeah, few days ago. Then yesterday, I get these Fed types all over me, all over a mess of guys. Questions about Cunningham. Any Muslim sympathies, something about him being Nation of Islam, even hinting at some Al-Qaeda crap. Guy's a Baptist. Always has been. But they are tarring his ass with a big brush, and that pissed me off."

"It'd piss me off, too," Lynch said. "Not enough to drive half way across the country, though."

"It wasn't just the Cunningham shit. I've been working with some propeller-heads for damn near a year on some new counter-sniper tech. Real advanced shit. Combines audio and radar input to exactly – and I mean to the inch – pinpoint the source of gunfire. I've got two prototypes ready to ship out to Afghanistan for testing. We get these tweaked and in production, we're gonna save a lot of Marines. Army pukes, too, I guess. Then I get the call from Cunningham. I start hearing noises in the shooter community, somebody way up the food chain snatching up every trigger jockey he can get his mitts on. Then these Feds start nosing around. And now my prototypes get hijacked by some three-letter types – CIA, NSA, who the fuck knows. National security is all the explanation I get. I figure those units are headed here."

"And you've come to babysit them?"

"I've come to see what the hell is going on. This ain't the way this sort of thing is done. It's gotten way too high-profile." Jenks turned, looked at Lynch. "You've heard of black ops?"

"Been getting an education the last few days."

"This Fisher guy, from what I hear, he was with a group that's so black it would make the inside of your asshole look well-lit. These guys just do not like attention. Now they got FBI guys working on their frame job, they got three-letter pukes putting their heads up to hijack hardware. The game just ain't played that way. Somebody is both real fucking desperate and real fucking powerful."

Lynch decided that, if the guy wanted to kill him, he could have just popped him in the parking lot instead of saying hello. That, and what he'd said so far matched up with what Lynch had heard from Cunningham. And it wasn't a bad time to make a new friend. Lynch put his gun away.

"The powerful part?" Lynch asked. "Let me run a name past you, you tell me if it fits. Hastings Clarke."

"Jesus Christ."

"Yeah, OK, Jesus has more clout, but Clarke is up there."

"He's in this?"

Lynch nodded. "Long story, but this all goes back to a local clusterfuck in 1971. It's how Clarke got his start, got his Senate seat."

Jenks was quiet for a while, then "You still in this? What I hear on the news, they've handed the whole deal to the Feds, lotta noise about how maybe they can't trust Chicago PD on this thing."

"I'm not on the books, but I'm still in it."

"You got any assets?"

Lynch thinking for a moment, then deciding what the fuck, his neck couldn't be out any further.

"Couple people that used to work with this Fisher. They've been on this for a while now, trying to take Fisher out on the QT. You happen to hear about a big firefight downstate, a week or so back?"

"Anybody gets popped with a long gun, I take an interest. I saw that, I thought it smelled funny."

"That was Fisher setting up his old team to buy himself some breathing room. Head of that group is this guy Weaver."

"Tech Weaver? I know him. Nasty son of a bitch."

"One of his guys, Ferguson, was on-site for the shootout. Didn't like the way it played out. He ratted out Weaver who, I guess, was getting a little far outside the lines even for this sort of thing. Weaver got canned, and this Ferguson got put in charge. Ferguson's walking back to his hotel here two days ago, and four Israelis tried to punch his ticket."

"Sounds like Weaver got his job back."

"And I bet I know from whom."

"So you're with this Ferguson?"

"Yeah, him and some chick named Chen."

"Little Chinese sociopath?"

"That's her. You know her too?"

"Scares the shit out of me. OK, here's how I can help. Bag in the back, it's got a radar detector in it. We're working on this radar thing, and I figure if we've got one, then somebody we don't like is going to have one someday. So I do a little tinkering on my own, completely off the books at this point, and gin this puppy up. They get my units in place and turn them on, this is gonna tell you where they're at. Also, got one of the old audio-only Boomerang units. Won't give us the detail the new ones do, but when somebody starts shooting, it will get us close, ten meters or so, depending. And it's passive – no radar, so there's no way to track it."

"That's helpful."

"And in the trunk, I've got my rifle. You're gonna need all the guns you can get."

CHAPTER 61 – CHICAGO

Back at the house, Lynch made the introductions. Now Lynch, Ferguson, Chen, and Jenks sat around the dining room table looking at the same map Weaver's team had been looking at, coming to most of the same conclusions. Decided the best place to be was on top of the taller building directly across from the church. Gave them a shot at any place Weaver's people might set up on the west side of Sheridan.

"We're going to be out-gunned," said Ferguson. "Once the shit starts flying we got zero time for confusion. So here is how we designate locations. Church is zero. South is negative, north is positive. First building south is negative one, second is negative two, etcetera. Floor, if you have it, is the second digit. East side of Sheridan starts with E, west side with W. So if you see something three doors north on the second floor on the west side, it's west postive thirty-two, if it's south, then west negative thirty-two. Got it?"

Everybody nodded.

"So study the damn map. Get every location down cold."

More nods.

"Now," Ferguson said, "timing. How long is it going to take you to spot those radar units, Jenks?"

"Once they turn them on, less than a minute."

"They likely to have them on ahead of time? Give us a chance to get sighted in early?"

Jenks shook his head. "These are prototypes. Run off a battery. And one of the bugs we're trying to work out is the system has a tendency to lock up if you leave it running too long. They got the same intel we do. You gotta figure they'll have eyes in the church. I figure they'll spool em up once Manning gets in the confessional."

"Should give you enough time," Ferguson said. "So, once Fisher takes his shot, first thing we do is take out the radar units. You sure they gotta be outside?"

"Have to be. Just be sure to hit the damn thing. We're gonna bump up the processor in the production models to get better speed, but right now, you got like half a second after you shoot before it spits out your location. If we take a shot at these and miss, all we'll be doing is painting a big bull's eye on our asses."

"You hit yours, I'll hit mine," Ferguson said. "Figure there's gonna be at least one shooter with each of the units, so we take them next. Your acoustic unit's gonna give us a fix on Fisher?"

"Gonna get us real close. It will spit out a solution to my handheld."

Ferguson stopped a minute, thinking. "Weaver's gonna have an entry team ready to roll on Fisher's location. Van, panel truck, something like that. They'll have to pack Cunningham in – you figure one of our body boxes, Chen?"

"Most likely," said Chen.

"Body box?" asked Lynch.

"Covert restraint device," said Chen. "It looks like a standard shipping container. Inside, it has restraint attachments and a short-term oxygen supply. It's soundproof."

"Chen'll know what to look for. They'll have to have it on a dolly, so that's one guy with his hands busy. Figure two, maybe three more. Flag's up at this point. Whatever they do to Fisher after he fires, it's not going to be quiet. They'll be going in fast and hard."

"You and Jenks take the stationary positions. Take out the radar units, take out Fisher if Weaver's people don't. Lynch and I will stay mobile. When they move with Cunningham, we'll deal with them," said Chen.

The group was silent for a minute. "Best we can do," said Ferguson. "Gonna be a close thing."

Everybody was in bed, Lynch in his old room. Same room he'd been in when he heard his mother screaming at the news of his father's death. These shooters Weaver'd had trucked in that Ferguson kept talking about taking out. How much did they actually know? Probably thought this was a legit deal. Probably thought they were on the right side. At least some of them. And what about Manning? Just let her walk into a bullet? Fisher remembered his mother's scream, the sound of it, like her soul ripping. Wondered what kids would be listening to what mothers tomorrow, learning that someone was never coming home? Been wondering that the last couple of days, asking himself how to stop it.

Lynch picked up his cell, called Wang.

"Pacific Rim Services," answered a flat, accentless voice.

"I need to talk to Paddy Wang."

"I'm afraid you must have the wrong number, sir."

"No, I don't. Get Wang. Tell him it's the private face of power."

Some dead air on the other end, then Wang.

"Young Lynch," he said. "Calling about tomorrow, no doubt."

Forty-five minutes later, Lynch was standing in the same office on the fifth floor of City Hall where Hastings Clarke had stood thirty-seven years earlier. And David Hurley III was looking out the same window his grandfather had.

"Grandpa hated that statue," said Hurley.

"The Picasso?" Lynch said.

"Yeah. Called it the flying monkey, and a few other things. But my dad loved it, so I'm told."

"Had to be hard not knowing him."

"Let's cut the shit, Lynch. My dad was a faggot. Only reason I'm even alive was he needed a beard and he could act straight enough to get her pregnant. And your dad found out. Now they're both dead and here we are, better than forty years down the road, still trying to clean up the mess."

"So let's do that."

"What I hear, it is all cleaned up, or close to it. What I hear, I don't gotta worry. I got friends. What I hear, you've been losing yours."

"You know what your friends are doing?"

"Don't wanna know."

"Sure you do. That's why you're talking to me, that and when Paddy Wang talks, your lips move. Your friends kidnapped a cop and are going to kill him and frame him for murder. Your friends are planning to sacrifice an innocent woman tomorrow just to help clean up your mess. Your friends think they're the smartest guys in the room, that this is all gonna break your way. But here I am, twelve hours before game time, and I'm telling you isn't. Your friends are going to be dead or up to their eyeballs in indictments by the end of the week. All this shit from 1971, it's coming out. You can't stop it. Your press guy is already getting the calls, and you're sitting up here with your head up your ass. Your buddy the president is a dead man walking. I know it. More importantly, Wang knows it. Hell, Clarke probably even knows it. We are less than twenty-four hours from the biggest political scandal in this country's history. You can be on one side of it or the other. We both know what you are, Hurley. You're a cowardly piece of chicken shit like your grandfather. You're always going to be that. But right now, you've got a chance to decide what you're gonna look like, and that's what you really care about."

DAN O'SHEA 337

Hurley stood with his back to Lynch still looking out the window. Lynch expected a reaction, he got nothing.

"And what do you care about, Lynch?" Hurley asked.

"I care about ending this without being an accessory to murder."

Still Hurley didn't move. For a long time he didn't speak.

"Tell me what you need," Hurley said finally.

CHAPTER 62 – CHICAGO

Weaver sat at the table in the breakfast nook at the back of Manning's first-floor condo with the three guys he'd picked for the entry team. Out the window, he could see the white cargo van. Cunningham was locked in the body box in the back, ready to go. Weaver didn't know how far he could trust the shooters he'd shaken out of the president. He had the Israelis, a bunch of CIA paras, couple of contract guys. When they got their radar read, they'd shoot up Fisher's hide. That'd feel like a straight-up job to most of these guys. But they had no idea how far out in the breeze the president had hung their asses, and Weaver did. If things got hinky, they'd have to blast their way out – and that would mean shooting cops, civilians, whoever got in the way. And the loaners, they weren't going to play for those stakes.

But the entry team was his – long-time InterGov, and all of them with more than enough blood on their hands to know where they stood if things went south. When Fisher took his shot, Weaver was going with the entry team, to be with them personally to handle the dirty work with Cunningham. Besides, he wanted to see that fucking Fisher dead himself. So he was keeping these boys with him. If things got dirty, these boys would get dirty with it.

It had gone harder than they figured, getting the confession out of Manning, but they had it. He hadn't iced her yet, had her drugged up, on the bed in the room toward the front. Too late to dispose of her now and still have time to clean up the mess. They'd pack her out after, take care of it then. If it came to it, they could use her as a hostage.

Brown walked back into the kitchen.

"You got the player?" Weaver asked.

She pulled the small digital device from her pocket and waved it at him. Weaver looked her over one last time. She was dressed in Manning's clothes, hair matched perfectly. With the make-up, she was almost a dead ringer.

"You ready?"

Brown nodded. "Let's rock and roll."

Weaver clicked on his comm unit. "Brown is rolling. Ping me as soon as she's in the church and we'll fire up the radars."

Through his scope, Ishmael Fisher watched Andrea Manning leave her condo and walk toward the church. It was almost over now. They were near, he had seen signs, but it didn't matter. He was not where they would expect him to be. He would get his shot. After was after.

He felt an intense love for Manning as he watched her walk toward the church, grateful that he would be the instrument that would deliver her to paradise. His right hand worked the beads of his rosary. The Joyful Mysteries.

Cunningham lay in the body box working his left wrist. Most of the last two days were a blur at best. But the drugs had worn off that morning, and they hadn't shot him up again. Came to strapped to a bed in his shorts, leather cuffs lined with wool on his wrists and ankles. Somebody didn't want to leave marks. Four guys had come down shortly after, carrying some camo gear.

"Time to get dressed, big boy." It was the FedEx guy.

They only loosened one cuff at a time, slipping his arms and legs into the fatigues, rolling him around on the bed. Worst thing about it was that they'd done it before, they had a process. Cunningham tried to fight, but it was no good. They pulled his boots on him one at a time. They unfastened the wrist cuffs from the bed, clipped them together. Did the same with the leg cuffs. Someone came in with a dolly, a big packing box on it, the thing FedEx guy had had in the lobby of his place. They set that down on the floor and flipped up the lid. It was foam lined, with clips for the restraints attached to the sides.

"Time for a little ride." FedEx guy again.

They lifted him by his arms and legs, set him into the box, then clipped the restraints to the sides. When they snapped the lid shut, Cunningham knew they hadn't spotted their mistake. While they were dressing him, he'd bent the fingers on his left hand and grabbed the sleeve of the fatigue shirt, pulling the fabric up over his wrist. The fabric was fairly thick. It was trapped between the wool lining of the cuff and his wrist. Not much, but probably enough. Cunningham kept working the wrist, feeling a little more give each time.

Ferguson and Jenks were under the big AC unit on the roof of the building across from St Mary's, covered by a tarp, their rifles barely protruding.

"Here she comes," said Ferguson, watching Manning leave her building. Manning walked into the church. A couple of minutes later, Jenks's radar detector started to peep. He looked at the screen, moving it back and forth slowly. First reading was south. He got the line, put his eye to the scope, and looked at the building. The box was on the third floor, balcony on the right, sliding door cracked open, vertical blinds almost closed. Shooter.

"West negative thirty-three," Jenks muttered into his comm unit. He swung the detector back north, repeated the process. Window box. Slight shadow two windows over. Shooter number two. "West sixty-one."

"You sure?" Ferguson asked. "Doesn't make sense."

"West sixty-one," Jenks repeated.

Chen popped up in their earpieces.

"Where the hell is Lynch?" she said.

Lynch sat in the back pew of the church, watching the door. Manning came in. He got up, walked toward her, but she took a hard left into the first confessional. Lynch moved to stand between the confessional and the door to the church. He'd have to catch her on the way out.

Lynch waited, that weird feeling where you lose concept of time. Over the comm unit he heard Jenks give the radar locations. West sixty-on? What the hell? That was Manning's place.

Then Manning stepped out of the confessional.

Captain Starshak sat in the back of one of the SWAT vans lined up two blocks west, still not believing that all the shit Lynch had told him over the past ten hours was actually going down. Lynch had gone over maps with Starshak, explained the location codes, given him the comm frequencies that Ferguson would be using. Starshak had briefed the leads in all the other units. Now they were listening in, waiting for Ferguson to name the locations, ready to roll. Only thing Lynch hadn't said was where Ferguson and this Jenks guy would be. Said he didn't know. Starshak had let that go. Knew the line Lynch was walking. Hell, if he were in Lynch's shoes, he'd be walking it himself. Things worked out right, it wouldn't matter. Things worked out wrong, well, it wouldn't much matter then, either.

The SWAT guys weren't thrilled with Starshak being CO, but Starshak had been SWAT before, and with what Lynch had on the mayor, Lynch was calling the shots. The circle of people Lynch trusted was closing in, and he wasn't going to have anybody outside of it in charge of anything.

The SWAT guy in the front passenger seat said, "Roger that," and then turned back to Starshak. "Manning just left her building."

Then the radio tuned to Ferguson's frequency went live. "West negative thirty-three." A pause. "And west sixty-one."

Starshak keyed the command channel.

"Go, go, go!"

As the van lurched forward, Starshak ran his finger along the map, counting down the buildings. West sixty-one was Manning's place. What the fuck?

Starshak keyed his mic. "We're taking west sixty-one."

Fisher watched Manning on his monitor and listened to her confession. The priest ordered no penance. Fisher cursed the priest's weakness as he set the monitor and his rosary down and brought the stock of the rifle up to his cheek, his eye behind the scope, the doors of the church as clear as heaven.

Lynch watched as Manning walked toward him.

"Ms Manning, my name is John Lynch. I am a detective with—"

The eyepatch killed Lynch's peripheral vision. He barely saw the kick coming. Manning's left foot flashed up toward the right side of his head. He only managed to turn with the kick a fraction before the boot hit his head and he hit the floor, his vision narrowed to a small tunnel, his ears ringing. Manning was rushing past him to the doors of the church. The doors were pushing open. Lynch was just up to his hands and knees when he saw her stagger and drop to the ground, the door closing behind her.

Ferguson and Jenks didn't have time to think about west sixty-one. They saw the church doors open, saw Manning drop, heard the report to the north. Close. Real close. Both fired at the radar units.

Weaver heard three things almost at once. A rifle shot from right outside the front of the condo, the radar box being hit by a bullet, and a loud screech of tires. He snatched his M4 off the table and ran up the hall to the front window. Cops in raid gear were piling out of a big Chicago PD truck. Fuck this, Weaver thought. The president was on his own. Gotta slow things down just a tad, get to the van, get out of Dodge, live off the money in the Caymans.

Weaver fired a long burst from the hip through the front window and into the line of cops running from the truck. Aiming low, going for legs. Didn't need to kill anybody. And they'd be armored up anyway. A few of them dropped. That ought to keep them away from the door for a few seconds. Then Weaver put a three-round burst into Uri, who was crouched at the window looking back at him. He didn't need any of the lend-lease guys Clarke had dug up swapping stories for plea deals.

"Fire up the van," he yelled to the entry team as he sprinted for the back door, swapping out his magazine on the run.

Starshak was first out of the truck, bolting toward Manning's condo. He was closing on the door, the two guys with the ram behind him, when he heard shots from somewhere south and a bullet slammed into the small box sitting in the planter hanging from Manning's window. Must be the guys Lynch had told him about taking out the radar units. Then a burst of automatic fire came from inside, shattering the glass. A couple of the guys behind Starshak went down, and he and the ram team broke left, flattening against the building. He heard another short burst inside the condo.

Further back, two of the assault team returned fire, chewing up the window the shots had come from.

"Let's move," shouted Starshak, and the ram team went around him and hit the door.

Starshak and the ram team went through the door first, the rest of the team streaming in. One dead to his left, by the window. The team spread out through the condo, Starshak hearing "clear, clear, clear," as they checked the rooms.

"Got one in here, Captain."

He walked into the bedroom to the right off the hallway, saw one of his guys checking the pulse of the girl duct-taped on the bed. Manning. But Manning was at the church. What the fuck?

"She OK?" Starshak asked.

"She's out, but her pulse is good."

Someone yelled from the back. "Got a white van headed south down the alley."

Ferguson was about to fire on the shooter in Manning's window when the police truck squealed around the corner and slammed to a stop. Fucking Lynch had gone Boy Scout on them, still trying to color inside the lines. Manning was still dead, though.

"Lynch, you asshole – you didn't even save the girl," Ferguson shouted into the comm. Only one thing left to do. He turned to Jenks.

"Your audio unit – you get a read on Fisher?"

"Ground level, straight across from Manning's place. Got to be the red pickup with the white cap."

Ferguson swung his rifle right, lined up the truck, and started putting rounds through the roof and truck cap as quickly as he could. Jenks did the same, both spacing their rounds so that nobody in the truck could avoid being hit at least two or three times.

"Got him or we didn't," said Ferguson. "Time to go."

The two men dropped their rifles on the tarp, walked to the ropes at the east end of the roof, clipped on, zipped to the ground, and trotted down the alley heading east.

Fisher lay prone on the street beneath the bed of the pickup, listening to the rounds ripping through the cap on the truck and thudding into the bags of sand he had set across the bed. Methodical fire, rounds walking down and across the truck bed. Then the firing stopped.

He looked up toward the church. He saw Detective Lynch stumble from the church porch, dive off the porch, and then start toward the truck. Behind Lynch, a young priest walked through the door. Not one of the priests Fisher had seen during his recon. The priest pulled a hand gun from the slit in his cassock and began to raise the weapon toward Lynch.

No time. Fisher snapped the Dragunov into position and fired.

Lynch got to his feet and staggered to the church doors, leaning on them and pushing them open, his head still fuzzy. Manning was flat on her back, arms splayed, the entrance wound center chest, just like Marslovak and Riordan. The top of her coat was open. It looked like she had a vest on under it. What the hell?

Up the street, he saw the first of the SWAT units squeal around the corner and angle in toward the curb in front of Manning's place, the assault team scrambling out. He heard shots coming from inside the building.

He heard Ferguson in his comm. "Lynch, you asshole – you didn't even save the girl." Then he heard rifle fire from Ferguson's position. Lynch hit the cement on the church porch and rolled off the south edge, thinking Ferguson was after him, but he heard no rounds hitting. He looked up. More fire from Ferguson's position. Ferguson and Jenks were shooting up the red pickup parked across the street from Manning's condo.

Had to be Fisher's hide. Lynch got to his feet, stumbled down Sheridan, and then he heard another rifle shot, saw a muzzle flash underneath the truck, felt the round zip past him, left of his head, heard a shot immediately behind him, pistol, felt a tug and a burning on his left arm, heard a grunt. Lynch span around. The young priest who had been hearing confessions was sprawled in the street, a big chunk of his head gone, a Glock on the asphalt near his right hand.

Lynch dove to his right, rolling behind a parked car. He didn't know if Fisher was trying to kill him or save him, but if it was the former, he wouldn't miss twice. He looked at his arm. A chunk was missing along the side of his left triceps. He remembered the pistol on the pavement next to the dead priest's hand. Fisher's shot had gone past his head, so Fisher hadn't shot him in the arm. That meant the priest had. Which meant Fisher had saved his life.

Cunningham was soaked in sweat, but he'd freed his left hand. He reached across his chest, rotating his trunk as far as he could, and unbuckled the cuff on his right wrist. No way to get to his ankles in the box.

He unclipped the leather wrist cuffs from the sides of the box. Heavy bastards, big buckles. He looped one cuff through the other, and buckled them tight. He held the cuffs in one hand, snapped his wrist a little. All together, maybe two feet long, good heft, decent leverage. He fiddled with them a bit so that the heavy buckles were right where he wanted them.

Motherfuckers would have to open the damn box eventually.

Weaver held on to the door grip as the van spun out of the spot behind Manning's condo and south down the alley toward the church. Never set up a mission without a back door. Weaver had four rental cars in the basement garage of a building three blocks east.

The three guys in the van were all long-time InterGov pros. They knew the drill. At this point, it was get away or get dead.

Just as the van neared the end of the alley, a PD truck pulled into the alley from the south, blocking their exit.

The InterGov driver swung the van hard left into the parking lot on the north side of the church, barreled through the church lot out on to Sheridan on a diagonal, clipping the front end of a car as it made the turn east.

A Chicago squad car shot out an alley on their left, trying to cut them off. Weaver's driver swerved to give Weaver an angle. Weaver already had the M4 out the window. No aiming for legs now. He put most of a clip through the windshield of the squad as the van shot past it, two wheels up on the curb, pedestrians diving out of the way. The cop car swerved, slowed, bounced up the curb and crunched into the brick three-flat across the street.

Weaver couldn't believe it, but they just might get clear. One more block. He could hear sirens, but nothing in sight. He hit the button on the door opener and the van shot down the drive into the garage, pulling up next to the rentals. Weaver put the door down behind them.

Weaver turned to the guys in the back. "Do me a favor. Open the box and shoot the cop. We won't be needing him."

Cunningham heard the first latch on the box flip up. Box would open from his left. He tightened his right fist around the linked cuffs and tensed his torso. As the lid swung up, Cunningham jackknifed up with it, his right arm already swinging the linked cuffs even as he spotted the target. One of the guys who had dressed him.

The cuffs caught the guy right across the eyes, the heavy buckle ripping into one of them, blood spurting. The man's head snapped back against the side window of the van, and his hands flew to his eyes, the automatic he had been holding clattering to the floor of the van next to the body box.

Cunningham was already twisted toward the gun. He reached down, snapped it up off the floor, and swung it back around just as the man on the other side of the box tried to push the lid back down on him. Cunningham squeezed off a round, not aiming, just looking for an edge, the noise in the van deafening. The man behind the box ducked down, losing his leverage on the lid. Cunningham reached up over the lid and shot down at the man twice – hitting him first in the shoulder, then in the head – and the man flopped dead to the floor.

Cunningham felt the man he had whipped with the cuffs grabbing him now, an arm locking around his neck. He could see the older guy in the passenger seat trying to get a M4 turned around on him, but the muzzle caught in the shoulder belt. Cunningham shot him through the back of the neck and kept the pistol tracking left toward the driver, who had his pistol out and was swinging it toward Cunningham. They fired simultaneously, Cunningham's round hitting the driver high in the center chest, knocking him back, just as Cunningham felt his right hand jerked away, the pistol knocked loose by the force of a round hitting the edge of the barrel. The pistol bounced off the lid of the box to the floor to Cunningham's right. He tried to bend, to reach for it, but the man behind him held him back.

The man he had whipped with the cuffs tightened his right forearm against Cunningham's throat, had his left hand locked on his right wrist for leverage. With his feet still strapped in the box, Cunningham couldn't use his legs to move. He jerked his head to the side, trying for a head butt, just catching the edge of the man's chin. Gave him a feel for where the guy's face was at least. Cunningham grabbed the man's forearm with his left hand, levered around it, swinging with his right. The blow caught the man on the side of the head, but there wasn't enough to it. Cunningham couldn't get his legs into anything, the arm across his throat closing tighter, tighter, Cunningham beginning to feel the panic as his body ran out of oxygen. He reached back again, fingers extended, felt the other man's face slick with blood streaming from the ruined left eye. Cunningham's fingers found the right eye. Cunningham dug in, his middle finger digging in, finding the corner of the eye socket, pushing, pushing, and suddenly something giving, the man screaming now, but still holding on, still the crushing pressure on Cunningham's throat. Cunningham dug harder into the eye socket, felt the finger sliding in, curled it toward him and pulled, some resistance, then it giving, something ripping loose.

The man broke his grip and slumped back against the window, both hands pressed to his face, something between a sob and a scream coming through his hands. Cunningham shook the ruined eyeball from his fist, grabbed the hair on either side of the man's head and rammed the head against the side window three times. Four. Five. The man went quiet, his hands falling away from his face, one ruined eye and one empty, bloody socket staring at Cunningham. Then the man slumped sideways to the floor, unconscious.

Cunningham sat up and undid the buckles holding his ankles. He rolled over the side of the box onto the blinded man, rolled him onto his stomach, jerked his arms behind him. Cunningham grabbed the leather cuffs off the floor of the van, buckled them around the man's wrists. He made a quick check on the other three, but they were all dead.

Cunningham was just stepping from the van when the door to the garage went up and two squad cars sped down the ramp. They fanned out right and left of the van, braking, two cops in each unit, all four men jumping out, crouching down behind the squad car doors, guns extended.

"Freeze and show us your hands," one shouted.

Cunningham wasn't sure what had gone on, but based on the wild-ass ride over and then faint sound of gunfire he'd been able to hear while he was still inside the box, he figured it was a hairball. No point doing anything right now other than assuming the position. He held out his hands, turned to the van, and leaned against the side.

"Got four in the van," he said. "Three dead, one cuffed. My name's Cunningham. I'm a cop."

"We'll see," said one of the cops, walking up behind him. "Just give me one hand, nice and easy."

Cunningham let the cop take his wrist, but he was getting a little tired of being cuffed.

Lynch rolled past the car and then started running north up the sidewalk toward the pickup, crouching to keep behind the line of cars. When he could see the side of the truck two cars up, he slowed, his gun extended.

An arm reached out from under the truck, holding a rifle by the top of the barrel. It dropped the rifle in the gutter next to the curb.

"Chicago police!" Lynch shouted. "Slide out from under the truck. Slowly. Head and arms first." Lynch looked across the street. No more firing from the Manning condo. No more firing from Ferguson's position. No more firing that Lynch could hear anywhere.

Lynch saw a man's head and arms extend from under the truck, the man easily sliding out, rising to his feet. He was Lynch's age, shorter, maybe five-eight, compact, his face placid.

"Show me your hands," Lynch said.

The man raised his hands, locked them behind his head.

"My work is finished, Detective Lynch. I am at your mercy. And I am sure there is much you want to know."

Lynch heard a thud. Fisher staggered and groaned. Two more thuds milliseconds apart, and Fisher dropped to the ground.

Lynch squatted, spun, looking for a shooter, seeing nobody. The shots had to have come from across the street, from near Manning's condo, but he couldn't see anyone. He hadn't heard the shots, just the sounds of the rounds hitting Fisher's body. He turned back to Fisher. Blood was spreading all along Fisher's right side and sputtered from his lips as he muttered something. Lynch leaned down to hear. The Act of Contrition.

"...for having offended thee, and I regret all my sins–" Fisher's head fell to the side, his eyes open, no more blood bubbling from his mouth.

Chen was standing next to the car when Ferguson and Jenks got there.

"Let's go," she said.

"Not sure we got Fisher," said Ferguson.

"I got him," said Chen.

"That's swell," said Jenks. "Now let's get the hell out of here."

Lynch was sitting on the curb next to one of the ambulances that were parked in front of Manning's condo, arm bandaged, drugs kicking in, adrenaline wearing off. Crashing. Crime scene guys all over the place – Fisher's truck, Manning's place, down by the church. The fake Manning and the fake priest were under tarps down that way. The press were three deep behind the barricades at either end of the block, the commissioner and a crowd of department brass hanging out in the middle of the street where they knew the TV cameras could pick them up.

Cunningham walked up and sat down on the curb next to Lynch. "Get shot again? What's that, twice this week?"

"Yeah. How you doing? You really rip some guy's eye out?"

"Fuckers tase me, drug me, lock me in a damn box, and sit around talking about how they're gonna waste me and frame me for all this shit. He's lucky all I got a hold of was his eyeball."

Starshak walked over, still in his raid gear.

"How you doing, Lynch?"

Lynch shrugged. "Alive. Way this thing's gone, that seems pretty good."

"How about you, Cunningham?" Starshak asked.

"Oh, I'm just dandy. Just fucking dandy."

"Went about the way you figured, Lynch," Starshak said. "Most of these guys, once we showed up, they sat it out. Had their orders, and I guess shooting it out with the cops wasn't one of them. Got six in custody, nobody's saying nothin' to nobody. Hear there have already been some interesting calls from DC. Even some guy from the Israeli consulate wanting to take a look at the stiff in Manning's window."

"How'd our side make out?"

"That Weaver puke did most of the damage. Hit a couple of the guys on my stick on their way up to the door. Nothing serious. Leg wounds. He shot low. Either he was trying to do us a favor or he was trying to miss the body armor. Take your pick. He shot up a squad car couple blocks out, driver took one through the chest. They say he'll pull through. We got lucky."

"I heard Manning's OK?"

"Had her trussed up in her bedroom."

"So who was in the church?"

"Decoy I guess. Never did find Ferguson, or any of the rest of your buddies."

"I'm OK with that." Lynch nodded across the street at the tarp over the body by the pick-up truck. "So that's Fisher?"

Starshak shrugged. "May never know for sure. Whoever it is saved your ass, taking the priest out – or the fake priest, I should say. Real priest is up in the rectory, neck's broke. If it's Fisher, he took three transverse through the right chest. Looks like small caliber."

Lynch nodded. Chen. "Whole damn thing is just weird."

An EMT walked up, leaned over. "We're ready to transport you, detective."

Lynch nodded.

"I'll stop by later, I ever get out of here," Starshak said.

"I'll be fine," Lynch said. "Probably sleep for a week or so."

"Don't sleep too late. OPS wants everybody downtown in the morning."

"They may have to subpoena me to get my ass out of bed."

Cunningham got up, stretched. "You guys do me a favor. Next time you want somebody to eyeball something for you, call somebody else."

CHAPTER 63 – WASHINGTON, DC

President Hastings Clarke sat behind the desk in the Oval Office. It was late. He'd come down from the residence after watching the television coverage of the events in Chicago. No mention of him yet, but the inquiries to his press people had increased exponentially from the already fevered pace of the past day. Tomorrow. He'd already been warned. His name would be in it tomorrow.

He ran his hand over the surface of the desk – a gift to the United States from the Queen of England, constructed from the planks of the HMS *Resolute*. The *Resolute* was a British ship on an Arctic research mission that got trapped in the ice. The ship was freed by an American whaler and returned to Great Britain. Queen Victoria ordered the desk made in thanks.

Clarke loved the desk. He loved the Oval Office. He loved being president. No more sucking up to the Rileys of the world. He had his own Rileys now. Weaver, for example. But his Riley had failed him.

Clarke opened the desk and took out the one reminder he had from his days with David Hurley. Hurley's Walther PPK.

The Walther had been the key piece of evidence in the case against those AMN Commando patsies back in '71. After the investigation, Hurley asked for the gun. He looked at it now, sitting on the desk. He'd never really understood why he wanted it then or why he'd kept it all these years. He didn't even believe Americans should own handguns. Until this moment, he didn't believe that violence solved anything.

But it was going to solve this.

The President of the United States raised the pistol to his head. Easier on the knees this way, he thought to himself, and fired.

CHAPTER 64 – CHICAGO

Four days later, the day after his mom's funeral, Lynch stood in his dress blues on the side of a temporary stage on the plaza off Washington Street across from City Hall, just outside the shadow of the Picasso. Blue skies, light breeze, temperature in the seventies.

There'd been press conferences a couple times a day as details broke. Too much press to keep things indoors. Trucks from all the networks, all the Chicago stations, dozens of affiliates from major markets nationwide had lined the streets all around City Hall ever since the story broke.

Damage control was in full spin. The official story? The president had tabbed Weaver, a rogue agent upset at his demotion, to prevent the president's dark secret from destroying his re-election chances. Today, Hurley and his Chicago crew wanted the big local climax – the DA giving an update on the legal situation, the commissioner outlining the successful undercover operation led by Lynch in cooperation with national intelligence liaisons. Then it was Hurley's turn. He was going to give a speech and give Lynch a medal, the Chicago crowd hoping that, after today, the press would go home, that it would be a Washington story.

Hurley walked to the podium and paused a long moment.

"I stand before you today both proud and ashamed. Proud of our police and our city for the profound courage

356

and determination with which they have confronted and overcome remarkable odds and intense opposition to bring this dark chapter in our city's – in our nation's – history to light and, finally, to a close. And ashamed, for the first time in my life, of my family. I never knew my father. He died before I was born. Murdered, I had always been told, by agents of intolerance. By people who would not abide his attempts to heal the racial divide in our country. And now I learn that he himself killed to hide the secret of his own sexuality, to hide it from the intense bigotry that my own grandfather – the man who raised me, who raised so much of this city, a man I loved and still love today – did far too much to engender. And we have all learned how those secrets kill, not just thirty years ago but still today. These secrets, these bigotries, kill not just in this recent outbreak of violence but every day – when a child's dream is deferred, when a community's soul is torn, when any person cannot become who they ought to be because of who someone else sees them to be. When any child feels that his or her dream, however large or small, may be beyond their grasp because of the color of their skin, or the nature of their faith, or, yes, because of their sexuality. These secrets still kill. Lives and dreams."

Hurley paused, looking out over the crowd. Lynch couldn't believe it, but the son of a bitch actually had tears rolling down his cheeks.

"In the coming weeks, my administration will be announcing a series of initiatives to help ensure that every dream is nurtured, every child valued, every secret hatred rooted out. But this is not the day for that. Today, I want to recognize another Chicagoan who had to grow up without his father because of my own family's failings. A man whose personal integrity and courage, I must admit even in the face of the initial reflexive resistance of my administration, is responsible for exposing this last evil. I am proud to bestow the Chicago

Police Department's highest honor on Detective John Lynch."

Lynch walked up to the podium, let the commissioner drape the medal over his head. He took a quick look at Johnson. She was sitting in the middle of the front row with the network guys, the national guys out of New York and DC. She was a front-row property now. He raised an eyebrow, asking, and she gave him a quick nod. Everything was set to go.

Two hours later, Lynch was back in his jeans and a sweater, backing the TR6 out. On the radio, it started.

"The *Chicago Tribune* will report in its morning edition that Mayor David Hurley III is implicated in the ongoing cover up involving the recent Confessional Killings and the shootout on the north side four days ago that left seven dead. The *Tribune* reports the mayor's involvement is proven in part by a recording captured by Chicago Detective John Lynch, and has released the following excerpt–" The radio started playing part of the conversation between Lynch and Hurley that Lynch had taped in Hurley's office the night before the shootout.

Lynch had heard enough. Johnson was holding up her end. He switched over to FM, the classic rock station, right into the middle of "Born to be Wild". Laughed a little at that.

Cubs home opener today. Usually that meant forty-five degrees and rain, but today the weather was a postulate for the existence of a benevolent God. Johnson's bosses at the *Tribune* had given her two tickets to the corporate field boxes, first row behind the Cubs' on-deck circle. But Johnson was flying back to New York for another TV thing, so Lynch had a ticket to burn.

He pulled out his cell, called Dickey Regan.

"Still owe you lunch, Dickey. How about a dog and a beer?"

"Dog and a beer? You cheap bastard. Jesus, I would have dropped trou for you, you told me you were gonna serve up the president and the mayor."

"Nobody wants to look at your pasty white ass, Dickey."

"Sure. Johnson's off to do the New York circuit again. I gotta dust my Pulitzer just to keep my self-esteem up."

"Listen, the dog and the beer? That's in the *Trib*'s field boxes for the opener. You can even wear your *Sun-Times* cap, stick it in their eye."

Regan laughed. "OK, Lynch. Give me twenty to put my 'Hurley-gets-his' column to bed, then pick me up out front."

Lynch hung up, dropped the cell on the seat, decided to take a spin around Grant Park while he waited for Regan, wondering would Hurley slip out of this somehow. What he had on tape, it would muddy him up, but it might not take him down. Lynch decided it didn't matter.

Done his part, done his best.

CHAPTER 65 - SAN FRANCISCO

Ferguson sat in the new InterGov offices, watching CNN. Of course, Ferguson wasn't Ferguson anymore, and InterGov wasn't InterGov.

Nice day in San Francisco, nice view of the Bay from the Embarcadero Center. Emerging Market Investments was the name on the door. That had been the transition plan for a while - get out of the government contracting business. Too many ties someone might run down. Take their seed money, move it into the private equity/hedge fund space. More than enough inside knowledge to make most of the right calls. With a focus on business opportunities in the Middle East, China, India, the Pacific Rim, even Africa, they had built-in cover, could get teams wherever they needed them. And everybody on board was going to get filthy stinking rich.

Ferguson needed to get some people into a couple of places right now. Big spike in traffic on a lot of the nets the various three-letter pukes were monitoring, the Al-Qaeda types thinking this was their big chance to kick the Great Satan while he was down. Really, that just meant they were sticking their heads up out of their rat holes for a change. Target-rich environment. Ferguson had to go. Had a flight down to San Diego to brief a SEAL team on a little exercise in Malaysia.

Ferguson was about to click off the TV when the Hurley story broke. Son of a bitch. The Boy Scout had not only saved the girl, he'd gotten Hurley, too, or dinged him good at least. Ferguson smiled. His boy Lynch had game - even made that punk Hurley hang a medal on him before Lynch stuck the knife in. He clicked off the set, grabbed his go bag by the door, stuck his head into the next office.

"Wheels up in twenty, Chen."

The small Chinese sociopath just nodded.

ACKNOWLEDGMENTS

To my parents, the late Tom and Debbie O'Shea, who always supported my dreams, and Dad especially, for raising me in a house full of books where reading was cool.

To my family. For my ex-wife Meg, we might not be together now, but we were when I wrote this, and it didn't make things any easier when I would run off to play with my imaginary friends. For my daughter, Shannon, a fine writer herself and often my first reader. This book is better for her insights. And for my sons, Danny and Nick, who make every day happier than it should be.

To the teachers who first made me respect language and its rules – Dorothy Weiss and Sr Mary Loretta at Holy Angels School and Fr Peter Enderlin at Marmion Academy. And the others who then made me love it – Jim Boushay at Marmion and the Stockings, David and Marion at Beloit College. And finally Tom McBride, also at Beloit, who put a boot up my ass because love is hard and you have to put the work in.

To my agent, Stacia Decker, for taking a shot on a guy who didn't know nothing about nothing and making this work. The lady makes dreams come true for a living.

To my editor at Exhibit A, Emlyn Rees, and his Limey compatriots. Their help and faith has been nearly enough to overcome my genetic antipathy toward the English. (He's Welsh, and therefore claims exemption, but he should know better than to expect that degree of geopolitical awareness from a bloody Yank.)

To the writers I am fortunate to call my friends for their support and, occasionally, their booze. Kevin Fenton, John Hornor Jacobs, Joelle Charbonneau, Chuck Wendig, Chris F Holm (and the lovely Kat), Lou Berney, Hilary Davidson, Scott Phillips, Frank Bill, Matt McBride, Kent Gowran, Jay Stringer, Steena Holmes, Thea Harrison and so many others. For a lot that spends so much time thinking of ways to kill people, they really aren't that bad.

When did you last google yourself?

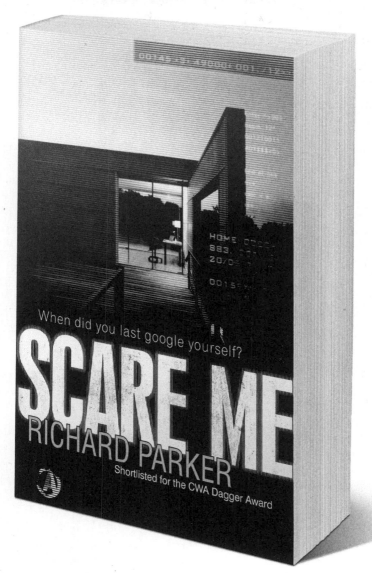

It's time to finish
what he started.

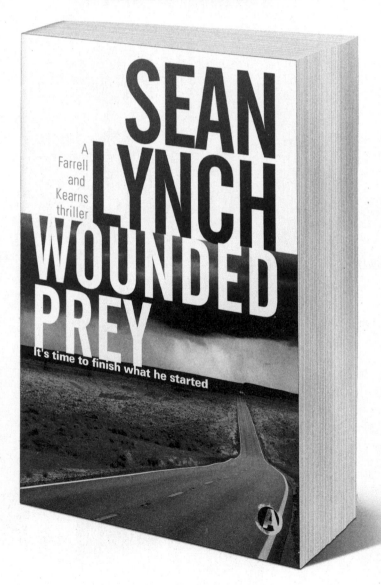

A Farrell and Kearns thriller

SEAN LYNCH

WOUNDED PREY

It's time to finish what he started

It's where *Apocalypse Now* meets *The Beach*

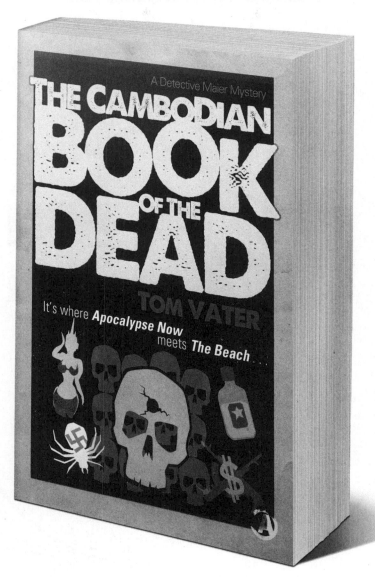